THE GREAT COLLAPSE

THE GREAT COLLAPSE

SURVIVORS OF THE PULSE

JEFF W. HORTON

TATE PUBLISHING & Enterprises

Published by Tate Publishing & Enterprises, LLC
127 E. Trade Center Terrace | Mustang, Oklahoma 73064 USA
1.888.361.9473 | www.tatepublishing.com

Tate Publishing is committed to excellence in the publishing industry. The company reflects the philosophy established by the founders, based on Psalm 68:11,
"The Lord gave the word and great was the company of those who published it."

Book design copyright © 2010 by Tate Publishing, LLC. All rights reserved.
Cover design by Kellie Southerland
Interior design by Bekah Garibay

Published in the United States of America

ISBN: 978-1-61663-844-3
1. Fiction / Christian / Futuristic   2. Fiction / Christian / General
10.08.05

DEDICATION

For my Lord and my family, my wife Donna, and my precious children Rachel, Hannah, and Will, and for my son David, whose tireless effort and support throughout this project made all of the difference in the world.

" ... as for me and my house, we will serve the Lord."

AUTHOR'S NOTE

For all but a tiny fragment of human history, civilizations around the world prospered and advanced technologically *without* electricity. People learned how to understand and overcome the many challenges of everyday life through the knowledge and experience gained over thousands of years. Whether using salt to preserve food in ancient Mesopotamia, precision engineering to build the pyramids in Egypt, or aqueducts to transport water over vast distances in Rome, the ancient peoples learned how to overcome and shape their environment. They discovered ways to prevail over the many obstacles that confronted them, and perhaps most importantly, they passed along the knowledge they gained to their descendants, with each subsequent generation building upon the technology handed down to it by their forefathers.

They developed simple yet pragmatic approaches for dealing with the complex challenges of their day. For example, in order for urban centers to flourish, people built cities near lakes, rivers, and streams for easy access to water, a necessity for human life. In order to endure the punishing summer heat and humidity, homes and other structures were often built with extra–high ceilings to allow heat to rise, which in turn, enabled the air closer to the ground where people live to stay cooler.

Civilizations of the past frequently relied on animals such as horses, donkeys, or oxen to travel on land, and built ships for navigating the great oceans. Possessing an effective means of transportation enabled trade, allowed ancient people to travel vast distances, and provided a means for ancient armies to attack distant lands.

In 1879, however, Thomas Edison changed everything when he invented the light bulb and later formed the Edison Power Company, and the world has never been the same since. Today, the human race uses electricity to power almost every aspect of the modern world. Food is grown and harvested on large tracts of land using massive machinery before being processed, shipped, and stored using electricity. Water and sewage are recycled, purified, and provided to homes everywhere using electric pumps and meters, as well as many other electronic devices that measure and regulate chemicals. Very few people in the modern world use horses, oxen, or sailing ships to move people and goods around, relying instead on cars, planes, and other means that again, depend on electricity. Clearly, our entire civilization has been built upon and continues to rely very heavily upon electricity; and has for several generations now. Consequently, the knowledge and means of how to deal with many of these challenges without the benefit of modern technology, has been lost and forgotten over time, as the dependency on modern electric power grids across the globe has increased dramatically.

So imagine, for a moment, what would happen if modern technology all over the planet, in every home, business, government, and military facility, suddenly and completely vanished. What would happen if all electricity, everywhere, were gone in an instant, as if turned off by a switch?

What would *you* do if you woke up in the morning, and discovered that your world was gone?

PROLOGUE

It is the third decade of the 21st century, and man has achieved by far the most technologically advanced civilization in human history. Countries have launched satellites outside of the solar system, have established the first permanent base on the moon, and have even sent people to Mars.

It is the period of humanity's greatest technological achievements, a time commonly referred to, as "the Golden Age." Indeed, man *has* mastered the modern world through his technology. From almost any perspective, it truly is a *Golden Age*.

Very few scientists and politicians however, have considered the significant downside of this complete and irreversible dependence that humanity now has on technology, or its inherent weakness.

During the waning years of the Golden Age, the United States Congress commissioned a study of the impact of an electromagnetic pulse attack against the United States' critical infrastructures and the aftermath of such an attack. Included in the report was an assessment of how deeply electronic components had become imbedded in the country's critical infrastructures ranging from aqueducts to power plants.

Scientists studied the likely aftermath of an EMP attack against the United States, and its impact on society. What they found terrified them...

CHAPTER 1

Deep into that darkness peering, long I stood there,
wondering, fearing, doubting, dreaming dreams no
mortal ever dared to dream before.

Edgar Allen Poe, "The Raven"

A magnificent, brightly colored flash of light exploded silently
and without warning in the night, quite unlike anything he had
ever seen before. The explosion of light gave birth to something
new in the heavens. The strange and new phenomenon con-
sisted of many colors including green, yellow, purple, and blue.
It moved through the night sky, traveling in a *wave*. As he gazed
upon the strange dance of lights in the heavens, the spectacle
reminded him of something he had seen somewhere before. As
he continued watching the inspiring evening performance, it
finally came to him, the *aurora borealis*. He had come across a
science program on television as he had been flipping channels
one evening a year or so earlier. The narrator explained that the

spectacular display is created when a coronal mass, or solar flare, from the sun collides with the earth's magnetic field. He had no idea what the light show was that now danced across the heavens, but one thing he knew for certain, it was definitely *not* the aurora borealis; *this* was *something else, something new, something different.* While pondering the brilliant display of lights in the night sky, he felt his heart stop in his chest and the blood freeze in his veins as he looked down from the sky for a moment to find only blackness. The streetlights, the neon signs, the lights in buildings and homes all over the city had suddenly and inexplicably, *vanished.* As he pondered what he had seen, he heard a deep voice like the voice on the waters say to him, "Behold and remember all that you have seen."

Then, there was a brilliant flash of white light, and he found himself walking the streets of a great city. Everywhere he turned, he witnessed horrific scenes. People of all ages roamed the crowded streets, begging for food and water. Fights, even murders were commonplace as competition over food, water, and supplies, grew increasingly fierce. Again, he heard the voice say, "Behold and remember."

As he wandered around the city, he found doctors working feverishly to save as many people as they could, while trying to determine who among the sick and the walking wounded were most likely to survive. James White began to sob as he witnessed the death, starvation, and disease. Again, he heard the voice say, "Behold and remember."

Everywhere he looked; all signs of technology had disappeared. There were no artificial lights shining in the night. Instead, he saw only candles, oil lamps, and torches, providing light in the darkness. Again he heard the voice say, "Behold and remember."

There was another intense flash of light, and he found himself standing at the edge of the city, where he watched as people fled the metropolitan area in massive numbers, heading for the countryside in search of food and water.

A few minutes later the scene transitioned once more, and he found himself in a jungle, surrounded by ancient ruins. He soon realized however that he was not in a jungle at all, but *still* at the edge of the same great city, only at some point in the distant future. Nature had taken back much of the city, with trees breaking through concrete and grass growing through the sidewalks. The landscape had changed significantly and there were no people anywhere in sight. Then without warning, it was night once more as darkness flooded the landscape, and he found himself looking up at the night sky. His eyes fixated on the strange ribbon of light, which *now* looked very different. It was dimmer, weaker, and nearly impossible to see anymore. He continued watching as it started to flicker and fade, before disappearing altogether. Once more he heard the voice say, "Behold and remember."

When he finally awoke, he opened his eyes to find himself once more in his bed at home, drenched in sweat. He sat up and saw that much to his great relief; he still had lights and electricity in the house. He climbed out of his bed, walked into the kitchen, and poured himself a cup of coffee. The coffeemaker was set to start brewing automatically, and he could tell based on the fresh aroma of the coffee grounds that still hung in the air, that it must be close to seven o'clock. As he sat down at the table and sipped on the hot coffee, he found himself deeply disturbed as he reflected on the dreadful events in the dream. He would have dismissed it as nothing more than the consequence of his over–indulgence in some pizza the night before, were it not for *that voice*. He knew, somehow, he knew, that the voice in the dream belonged to God. The dream had not been a dream at all but instead a vision, he was sure of it, but what had been the message? There was the strange display of lights in the sky, followed by lights going out across the city. Then there was the chaos, the *suffering*. As he finished his first cup of coffee for the day, James White decided that the dream had generated more questions than answers. All he could do was be patient, until God gave him another piece to the puzzle.

CHAPTER 2

The large group of men and women wearing fatigues gathered around the grassy area in a large circle. Two men were moving around inside the crowd; one man held a large knife called a KA-BAR, while the other was unarmed. The unarmed man, the leader of the group, addressed the gathering.

"Remember, the most important thing to keep in mind when you face an armed opponent is to keep your eye on the weapon. The enemy can lie to you with his eyes, easily leading you to believe that he will attack with a slash to the neck, while he is actually planning a thrust to the torso. Always keep in mind that it is the knife, not his eyes that will kill you." The man attacked with a thrust to the torso. Colonel Conrad Simmons easily evaded the attack, stepping to the outside of the weapon, blocking the man's attacking arm as he did so. He followed the defense with a strike to the attacking man's groin, followed with a second attack to his throat. He finished by grabbing the attacking arm and sweeping the leg, causing the attacking man's legs to fly straight up into the air, landing him on his back. The man landed so hard that he had the air knocked out of him.

"Are you okay Frank?" he asked. The man held up his index finger and nodded.

"Give me just a second," he said weakly as he struggled to regain his composure.

"So, Colonel, you're saying that we should focus more on the weapon, and not on the attacker's eyes?" asked one of the few female Rangers in the group.

Conrad took his eyes off his friend, who was still struggling to catch his breath, long enough to face the Ranger that had asked him the question. He liked Sara Collins because she was one of the fittest Rangers in the group, and the most intense when it came to hand–to–hand–combat. Women rarely lasted long as Rangers without a healthy amount of combat training. They knew, as Conrad did, that their lives and the lives of their fellow soldiers would depend on it.

"Correct, Collins. However, don't misunderstand me; you have to learn to study the eyes as well. As the old saying goes, 'The eyes are the window to the soul.' In close hand–to–hand combat, you *must* learn to read your enemy. What is his state-of–mind? Is he scared or fearless? If you work at it hard enough, you can learn to read an attack even before it comes."

Conrad paused to help his friend up from the ground.

"Are you sure you're okay Frank?" he asked again.

"Oh yeah, I just had the wind knocked out of me for a moment, that's all."

Conrad continued in his instruction, as he placed the knife back into its sheath.

"Another important point to remember is this: you must never allow an enemy to get too close to you, because if he does, he will win. Remember, this is combat to the death, so if you lose, you *really* lose."

"Can you please explain what you mean, Colonel?" someone asked.

"Sure. Take, for example, Major Martin here. This time, I will be the attacker and Frank will be the defender. If I were a step or two away from him, he would easily be able to defend my attack. Observe." He grabbed his KA-BAR and nodded to Frank just before launching an incredibly fast thrust to Frank's torso. Frank defended easily and counterattacked.

"You see, given enough distance, an experienced fighter can often defend even a fast attack. However, watch what happens when I get closer in. This time, I will even tell him where I am going to attack." He moved closer to Frank this time and Frank grimaced, knowing what was coming next. "All right, Frank, you know the drill. Get ready, because I'm coming in with an attack to your solar plexus." Frank nodded in response.

Conrad held the sheathed KA-BAR in his front hand, standing close enough so that he could easily reach out and touch his friend. He then attacked with a thrust to the gut. Frank reacted, but by the time he moved to block, the knife had already struck his body. After waiting a few seconds, Conrad attacked again, but this time with a slash to the neck, with the same result. By the time Frank reacted, the attack was over, and he was left with a red slash across his neck at the carotid artery. It would have been a fatal wound without the sheath.

"You see," Conrad said to the group, "we are all human beings, and as such, we all have the same limitations. It takes about one–tenth of a second for me to reach Major Martin here with my KA-BAR. However, it takes about two–tenths of a second for him to react. His eyes see the attack coming, and signals are sent from the eyes to the brain. The brain perceives that there is an attack coming, and signals to the legs and to the arms to move to counter the attack. This process is what we collectively refer to as a 'reaction–window'—the time it takes to react to an outside stimulus, like an attack. If you allow an attacker inside your reaction–window in a combat situation, you're as good as dead."

One of the other Army Ranger students raised her hand. "Colonel?"

"Yes, Corporal?"

"What can we do if we find ourselves in a close–quarter fighting situation, with an attacker inside *our* reaction–window?"

"Simple," he answered. You remember that it cuts both ways. He, or she, is also a human being, and as such, they have the same limitations as you do."

"You mean that I should be the first to launch the attack, because I would be inside of *their* reaction–window?"

"Exactly," he replied. Conrad looked up at the sun before checking his watch. It was late in the afternoon, and they had been drilling all day. Ranger School was intense, and every one of his students was in top physical condition. However, even Rangers had to eat. "Okay, listen up. We will re–convene right back here at zero–six–hundred hours tomorrow morning. We will begin by reviewing how to defend the KA-BAR, followed by learning close–in defense of firearms, both rifles as well as small arms. Class dismissed."

The group disbanded, many of them talking with each other about everything they had seen. Conrad enjoyed teaching new Rangers. They were always full of energy, eager to learn, and anxious to fight. *Anxious to fight.* He knew that it would take their first tour to cure them of their desire to see combat. They were young, just as he had been when he first went to Ranger School, and he had been no different.

Sergeant Sara Collins walked over to him as she was leaving. Although she was an attractive woman, Conrad had learned long ago to never compromise his position by getting personally involved with recruits. It risked their lives and the lives of their fellow rangers.

"Colonel, I just wanted to say that this is everything I could have expected when I came to Ranger School. Thank you for everything, sir."

"You're quite welcome, Sergeant. That's why I'm here; to teach you everything I know that can keep you alive on the battlefield."

"Yes, sir." As she walked away, Conrad found himself unable to avoid taking a second look.

"Better secure those eyes of yours, Colonel." Frank laughed as he walked up behind his friend and patted him on the shoulder.

"Copy that," he answered, laughing as the two walked back toward the barracks.

"We have a pretty good group this time, don't you think, Conrad?"

"Yeah, I believe this group is one of the best I can ever recall having. They are attentive, inquisitive, and quick."

"Are you going to miss it?"

"What, teaching at Ranger School? You bet I am. I will get back down here as soon as I can. It's not that I don't appreciate the privilege of working in Washington, I do."

"But you would rather be here, where you feel like you can make more of a difference."

"Exactly. This is one place where I can use what I know to help some of these young men and women stay alive once they're deployed."

"You've got a big heart, sir. You care as much about your fellow Rangers as anyone that I've ever known. Well, look at it this way, at Ft. Myer, you'll be close to the Pentagon, where you might be able to make an even *bigger* difference, possibly even making decisions that will keep some of these soldiers from having to deploy in the first place."

"Maybe," answered Conrad as they walked into the barracks to drop off their things before making their way to the officer's mess. "But I would rather be somewhere that I *know* that I can make a difference."

"So when do we leave?" asked Frank.

"Next week. Oh, I forgot to mention something to you. I have a friend that lives just outside of Baltimore. He was one of my teachers when I lived near there five years ago. I spoke with him last week to let him know that I was coming back into the area. He has offered to continue my training in Kenjutsu, sword fighting."

"That's awesome, Conrad. Do you think there is any chance that he might be willing to take on any new students? I have always wanted to learn how to use a sword, not that I ever expect to need one mind you."

"Well I don't know, Frank, but I can certainly ask. I know that he has tremendous respect for the Army Rangers, so I expect he will at least be willing to meet with you. But keep in mind, Frank, that he is an old–fashioned, traditional, martial arts master."

"Great, thanks, Conrad. I can't wait to meet him."

CHAPTER 3

"Will you please stop fidgeting?" the man asked him, as Scott continued nervously pacing the hallway outside of the Pentagon conference room. He looked at the other man with irritation. The presentation was as thorough and complete as he could possibly make it, given the minimal amount of time that he had been given to prepare it. His new boss had given him only two days to pull together the presentation *and* all of the supporting material necessary to pitch the project to the military. *How could he possibly stop fidgeting?*

The project had been Scott's since well before his recent promotion. Initially started strictly as an R&D effort, it had garnered an increasing level of attention as more people learned about its potential, and about what it could do. The interest started building inside his own department first, then in others, before rising up the food chain to the executive leadership team of his company. Finally, news of the project and its potential application on the battlefield made its way into the corridors of the Pentagon. The interest at the Pentagon had intensified as confrontations with several rogue states with nuclear capabilities continued to escalate. A weapon like the one he and his team had developed might offer the President a third option when diplomacy failed, and an alternative to the unthinkable; a devastating and horrendous nuclear war. The increased attention had come with a hefty measure of stress. *What if my presentation is a dud and they end up passing on the project?* Scott was determined not to let that happen.

"Scott, *please* sit down." Scott looked at his boss, gritted his teeth, and let out a heavy sigh before sitting back down in his chair.

"How long are they going to keep us waiting?" he asked.

"I guess as long as it takes. What's gotten into you anyway?"

"Sorry, Mark. I guess I just have a lot on my mind today. I've been working on this project for several years. Now, we finally have a chance to make a real impact, perhaps even render nuclear weapons obsolete.

"Slow down now, Scott. They haven't even given a green light for the project yet."

"I know, I know. Still, once we have found a way to control the reaction, the applications are endless."

The door opened and a woman wearing an Air Force uniform emerged from the conference room. "Please come in," she said. "General Miller is ready for you now."

"Thank you," they both answered, carrying their briefcases into the meeting.

They entered a large conference room that looked more like a small auditorium, because of its size, than a meeting room. The room had obviously been designed for hosting larger meetings, just like the one they were attending. As they followed the Air Force representative to a table on the stage at the front of the room, they could see that there was more than just Air Force representation in attendance. While the room was filled with service members from the Air Force, there were also representatives from each of the other armed forces as well, along with a number of men and women dressed in business suits and ties. As Scott and Mark walked in and sat down, they glanced at the nametags on the suits, taking notice that there was representation by the NSA, the CIA, and the DHS as well.

After a couple of minutes, General Miller walked up and stood at the podium.

"Okay, I would like to ask that everyone please be seated." The crowd quieted as they took their seats. "You should have all been briefed by now about the purpose of this meeting today. We are here to discuss the proposal from Logan Aerospace to develop a brand new type of weapon, a weapon based on the technology they have been researching for the past few years. Without any further delay, I would like to introduce Scott McBride, from Logan Aerospace Engineering." The audience clapped politely as Scott rose and walked over to the podium to address the group.

General Miller shook his hand and stepped aside. Butterflies filled Scott's stomach as he looked out at a packed auditorium. "Ladies and gentlemen, I would like to introduce you to a revolutionary new technology that has been under development at Logan Aerospace for the past several years. Although we still have a way to go toward finalizing the application of the technology into a weapon that we can completely control, we are well on our way." He paused to gauge the atmosphere in the room. It appeared to Scott that he had everyone's full and undivided attention. "Ladies and gentlemen," he continued, "I would like to introduce to you our proposal, the development of a device that we affectionately refer to, as the 'Pulse'…"

Two hours later, as he pulled out of the Pentagon parking lot, Scott checked the time. It was already five–o'clock, and he still had an important stop to make.

He felt on top of the world. After years of waiting, the moment had finally arrived. He had no doubts whatsoever about wanting her to become his wife. The truth was, he adored her, and he had from the moment they had first met. His greatest fear was that she would say no. Despite his hesitation and his fears, he knew that it was finally the perfect time to propose.

Thanks to his work on the project, Logan Aerospace had promoted him only a few months earlier to a senior position with the company. The new position required significantly less travel, allowing him to spend more time at home, where he could finally get married, settle down, and raise a family. *Of course, it didn't hurt that the promotion came with a significant salary increase.* It seemed that finally, things were going his way.

The promotion had also enabled him to purchase a new car, a next–generation automobile with new cutting–edge technology, powered by the newer and much more efficient model of hydrogen fuel cells. The price of gasoline had skyrocketed over the past ten years as the world's crude oil supply began to dwindle. Before getting the new car, Scott had no choice but drive to a neighboring city just to find a station that even sold gasoline. Many such stations had closed up in recent years or converted to hydrogen fuel cell stations, as it became public knowledge that the Congress was on the verge of passing a bill banning the sale of gasoline. The new vehicle also had the latest version of the experimental Automated Navigation System, or ANS software, which he suspected would one day prove very useful given the number of late nights he had been working in his new position. With the latest ANS, he hoped he would eventually be able to nap on the way home, confident that the car would know the fastest, safest, route back to his apartment.

By far the greatest advantage of the new position, however, was that by reducing his travel, he was finally comfortable with asking Susan to marry him. Though they had discussed marriage many times in the past, Scott had not been comfortable asking her to commit to him until he was able to spend more time at home.

As he neared the restaurant, he looked at his watch and saw that he would be cutting it rather close. He was supposed to meet her at six o'clock for dinner; it was already five–fifty–five. *Just my luck. I will probably be late for the wedding too!* He pulled in at five–fifty–eight and breathed a deep sigh of relief. He placed the ring in his pocket, jumped out of the car, and raced inside the restaurant, pausing only to speak with the maitre'd for a few moments. As he spoke with the man, he noticed Susan sitting at a small table in the middle of the restaurant. As he was watching her, she looked in his direction and saw them talking. The maitre'd looked down at his watch, smiled, and then nodded. When they had finished talking, Scott made his way over to where she sat waiting. She stood up and kissed him as he arrived at the table.

"Scott, what was that all about?" she asked him.

"What was what all about?" he responded, feigning ignorance in regards to the specific meaning of her question.

"I saw you talking with someone up front. Was that a waiter? Do you know him?"

"Oh, him! No, not really. Well, sort of. He's the maitre'd."

"Okay. Do you normally stop and talk with the maître'd?"

"No, of course not." he replied, smiling as he did so. "So what do you think?" he asked, changing the subject as he gestured throughout the inside of the restaurant.

"Oh, it's very nice Scott. *It is also very expensive,*" she added in a whisper. "Just take a look at the menu!"

About that time, the waiter showed up at the table. He took a few moments to introduce himself, and after sharing the house specialties with them, he passed out the menus and took their beverage orders.

"Are you sure you can afford this?"

"Sure,—no problem at all!"

"Okay, Scott, what's going on, what's the big secret?"

"Well, since you asked, I was promoted to a new position at Logan a few months ago," Scott said. Susan noticed that he was grinning. She wondered what he was planning.

"A few months ago? Why didn't you tell me?" she asked.

"I was keeping it a surprise. Anyway, the position came with a *significant* salary increase. I'll have greater responsibility, and I will continue working on some of the same projects I have been working on, and best of all, I won't be traveling as much, at least not for a while."

"Wow that *is* great news, honey. Congratulations!" she exclaimed, wrapping her arms around his neck.

The waiter brought out the drinks and the appetizer. As the two enjoyed their crab cakes, Scott swallowed hard and cleared his throat as he prepared to speak. His tone and demeanor suddenly took such a serious turn that Susan became alarmed.

"You know how much I care for you, don't you, Susan?" Susan's countenance fell and her face took on a look of fear with a flash of anger.

"Scott McBride, what's going on here, are you breaking up with me? That's not what this is all about is it?" she asked, with fire in her eyes.

"No, honey. No, of course not, calm down." He grabbed her hands and continued. "I have always felt guilty that I haven't had the courage to take the next step with our relationship. I just never felt prepared, until now, that is." Scott looked over at the maitre'd and nodded. The maitre'd nodded back in response as he motioned to someone else at the restaurant.

"Susan, you must know I adore you, that I love you more than life itself."

Two men with violins walked over to their table and began playing. She looked at Scott, then at the men with the violins, and started to smile.

"I know it's clichéd, but you see, Susan, I wanted everything to be perfect." Susan put both hands over her mouth. Tears began welling up in her eyes. Scott stood up and walked around to where she was sitting, dropped to one knee, presented the ring to her, and asked, "Susan, love of my life, will you please marry me?" Tears now flowed freely down her cheeks.

"I can't tell for sure whether those are tears of happiness. Is that a yes?" She grabbed Scott, wrapped her arms around his neck again, and kissed him.

"Scott, you can be so ridiculous some times!"

"Susan?"

"Yes, yes, yes! I *will* marry you!"

Other patrons in the restaurant smiled and clapped their approval. Susan and Scott looked around the restaurant and then at each other, finally kissing and embracing once more before settling down to finish their meal.

CHAPTER 4

تنأ ىلع مالس ، تاايحت (*asalaam ʿa laykum*)
"Greetings, peace be upon you."
مالسلاو تنأ ىلع أيض (*wa ʿa laykum asalaam*)
"And peace be upon you, as well."

The two men greeted one another in the doorway of the older man's home. The younger man was barely in his thirties while the other was well into his sixties. Both had dark skin with dark black hair and beards, a common characteristic of someone from the Middle East. The older man had tough, wrinkled, leathery–looking skin, the result of many years under the hot desert sun.

Omar noticed that his young friend looked nervous, constantly looking around outside as if fearful that he was being watched, or *followed*.

"Hassan, my friend. Please, come into my home and sit with me."

"Thank you, Father. It is so good to see you. It has been far too long."

"And I am glad to see you as well my young friend. Can I fix you some tea?" Omar asked him, switching to English, with a nearly perfect American accent.

"Yes, Father, thank you," answered Hassan, also in English. His accent was at least as good, if not better then Omar's was.

Omar walked into the kitchen and poured them both some tea. He handed Hassan his tea and sugar on a small dish.

"So tell me," said Omar, still in English. "What news do you bring me this evening, Hassan?" The two walked back into the living room and sat down on the sofa.

"From what I have been told, they have been making great progress, Father. They have been able to obtain all of the information that they need to take the next step. They are making the final preparations even now. From what they tell me, whatever this thing is, it is said to be the perfect weapon, guaranteed to prove to the world that even the 'Great Satan' is not beyond our reach. When we have stabbed them in their heart, they will learn that that they too, can be beaten down by the servants of Allah and defeated. They tell me that it will take the Americans many years to recover from even this small strike. By then, the implementation of the Supreme Leader's plan will be complete, and we will deal with them easily. The Americans will know that they will never be able to threaten our people anymore."

"You put great faith in technology, Hassan. I think too much maybe. Perhaps we should put more faith in Allah. Ah, but what can we do? These are desperate times, my friend, and we are desperate men. What are the estimations in terms of the potential casualties?"

"They do not know Father, but they think it will be minimal. It should affect only the city that we attack, though there will certainly be some loss of life."

"Such loss of innocent life is unacceptable. I doubt that this is what Allah would truly have us do. It seems I no longer hear his voice, Hassan. I wonder whether we have fallen in with evil men, instead of with the servants of Allah. How many times have evil men perpetrated evil deeds in the name of religion? If only I had known the truth about my friend, Aref, that he was planning a terrorist attack against the Americans when they killed him, *before* I joined this group, I would never have approached them about joining. I could have spared us both this decision. I just do not know, my friend," he said, his voice trailing off.

"You know that they will never let us leave now. The moment that they brought us inside the group, our fate was sealed. They will surely kill us both, along with our families, if we try and leave now!"

"I know that, Hassan. I know." Omar grimaced as he said it. He knew that Hassan had only joined the terrorists because he had, during the days following the death of his friend, Aref. "How soon before they can locate the weapon? Will they have time to test it before they attack?"

"I do not know. They told me only that we must be ready, *and* that we will be leaving very soon. They also told me to make certain that we pack spare bags so that we can leave on short notice."

"What about passports and papers?" asked Omar.

"They said that they would have everything ready when they pick us up."

"May Allah have mercy on both of us my young friend, and forgive us for what we are about to do."

"Yes, Father, may Allah have mercy."

A loud knock on the door startled the two men.

"Are you expecting someone, Father?" asked Hassan.

"No, I am not." Omar walked over and opened the door. A middle–aged man with a smile and an arrogant sneer stood at the door. Omar noticed that there were streaks of red on his white shirt. He wasn't certain, but it looked like blood.

"*Asalaam 'a laykum,* Omar."

"*Wa 'a laykum asalaam,* Abdul."

"May I come in?" Omar realized that he had been distracted by the red streaks on the man's clothing and had left him standing in the doorway.

"Yes. Yes, of course, please come in."

Omar watched the man as he closed the door. He disliked the man that he knew only as "Abdul." The man was the sort that acted pleasant enough, but Omar sensed that under the surface he was a vile, angry man.

"Ah, Hassan, you are here as well! Allah has certainly smiled on me today!" he said, shaking the younger Hassan's hand with one hand while placing the other on his shoulder. It was a gesture of superiority that humiliated Hassan, and caused a look of anger to flash across Omar's face. Omar came back in and offered Abdul some tea, and a place to sit down.

"So what can we do for you this evening, Abdul? What brings you to my home? Is it time for us to leave, already?" Abdul looked steadily at Omar for several moments, as if he was searching for something.

"No, not yet, but soon, very soon."

Omar smiled at Abdul while saying nothing else, politely trying to suggest to Abdul that his arrival was an interruption. Omar wanted to ask him to leave, but he knew all too well how temperamental and dangerous the man was.

"No, I am here now on a different matter. One of the members of our little group, Farrokh, I believe you know him well Omar, tried to leave us without permission a few weeks ago. We finally caught up with him in Tehran this morning. While we were questioning him, his wife somehow managed to escape unnoticed, though we thought she was already dead. We are going around to everyone's homes where she might go for help, looking for her."

"But has she done anything wrong, anything deserving of death?" asked Hassan. Omar braced for what he knew was coming.

"Yes! She married an infidel husband, a traitor to the cause!" Abdul answered, his eyes bulging and the veins in his neck standing out. "You know the penalty for those that choose to betray our cause!" Hassan stared back at the man helplessly. Omar looked down at the floor so as not to inflame the situation anymore. After a few moments, Abdul regained his composure. "The truth, my friends, is that Farrokh betrayed us," he said with a sneer. "He brought an American spy into our cause, and then helped him escape once he learned of our plans to attack America. Upon learning that the American spy had been killed by one of his own countrymen before he had a chance to report on our plans, Farrokh, *and* his wife, planned to leave us and defect to the Americans with the details of our plan. That is why we must find her, for the sake of our country." The man began looking around the house. .

"May I have a look around your home, Omar?"

"Of course, help yourself," Omar said, waving his hand towards the inside of his home.

Abdul opened the door and two men dressed in civilian clothes, but with a strong military bearing and firearms strapped to their belts, came inside. They proceeded past the three men and searched diligently throughout the small house. A few moments later, they returned and stood before Abdul.

"Nothing. No one else is in the house." One of them said to Abdul.

"Okay, proceed to the next address, I will be there shortly."

"Yes, sir," the man answered.

Abdul rose and started to leave, before stopping to face Omar and Abdul.

"As I said, we will be ready for you soon gentlemen, please be ready to go."

"Yes, of course," Omar answered.

Abdul started out the door before turning once more to the pair.

"By the way, notify me immediately if you see Farrokh's wife."

"Of course," answered Omar, as Abdul turned and walked out the door.

No sooner had the door closed than Hassan raced across the room to where Omar stood next to the door. Omar gave Hassan a stern look and raised his finger to his lips. He looked outside the window, before opening the door. Abdul and his men were gone. Omar closed the door.

"Father, we cannot turn Farrokh's wife over to him!"

"No, of course not. However, you must be very careful what you say, Hassan! Abdul is a very dangerous and powerful man. You must think of your family!"

"Yes, Father, you are right, of course."

Once again, the two men were disturbed by a knock at the door. Omar opened the door, expecting to find Abdul.

"Did you forget something...?" Omar gasped as a woman, who had once been very beautiful, stood there for a moment unsteadily.

"They killed him, Omar, they killed Farrokh," she said weakly. "Please help me..."

She then collapsed in a bruised and battered heap at his feet. Omar looked around outside and after determining it was safe, he looked back at Hassan.

"Quickly Hassan, help me bring her inside." Hassan rushed over and helped Omar lift her up off the floor. They gently carried her to the back of Omar's home, laying her on his bed. Omar could tell that she had been badly beaten and probably tortured as well.

"Who is she?" asked Hassan.

Omar said nothing for several moments as he placed his two fingers on her neck.

"Her name is Farrah, she is Farrokh's wife."

"Is she still alive?"

"Yes, but her pulse is very weak. We need to get her some medical attention immediately."

The men were interrupted by yet another knock on the door. Omar sighed, left Hassan in the room with Farrah, and closed the door. The knocking grew louder until finally he made it in the living room and opened the door. He swallowed hard when he saw it was Abdul.

"Forgive me for disturbing you yet again, Omar, but there was one other thing I needed to tell you. I wanted to let you know that since Farrokh is no longer with us, I will need you and your young friend to help with transporting the device once the American traitor we have hired has it in his possession. I will give you his contact information once we are ready for you to leave. Is that clear?"

"Yes, absolutely," said Omar. He was doing everything he could to convey that everything was normal. He was worried that the young woman would not live long without medical attention. Omar noticed that something had distracted Abdul, who was now staring past him. Omar turned and saw Hassan standing there, frozen with a look of fear mixed with anger at the sight of Abdul.

"Is everything okay here?" Abdul asked, clearly starting to grow suspicious.

"Yes, yes, of course. Everything is fine," said Omar. "So, was there anything else that you wanted to tell me?" Omar looked back and saw that Hassan had recovered and was now sitting down on the sofa. Abdul looked around inside once more, before finally turning and walking back to the door.

"Just be ready. We will come for you in the next few days."
" We will be ready," answered Omar, as Abdul walked out the door.

Once more Omar waited until it was clear.

"Quickly Hassan, we must get her out of here and to a doctor, immediately."

Hassan looked at Omar. Tears began to stream down his cheek.

"Is she … ?"

"Yes, Father. She is dead."

CHAPTER 5

Dr. John Abbott was enjoying a quiet and peaceful dinner at home with his wife for the first time in recent memory. He had spent many late nights at work as of late, meeting and working with engineers from the International Space Station Team. He had hardly even seen his wife over the past several weeks, much less had an opportunity to share a meal. He wondered how long the moment would last.

His wife, Beth, had prepared a wonderful meal for them. The table was adorned with an immaculate seven–course meal, including salads, French onion soup, prime rib, and baked potatoes. She had even set a bottle of white wine on the table. She had been working on the meal all afternoon and made it a point to let him know it as soon as he had walked through the doorway. She wanted to ensure that her husband would stay and *finish* his meal this time.

"Honey, I don't know how this will taste, but it looks and smells absolutely delicious."

"Well you had better stick around long enough that you can tell me how delicious it *tastes* as well once we are done tonight, Mr. Abbott," she told him with a smile on her face. "So, tell me John, what have you been so busy with these last few weeks? You have been gone every morning before I wake up, and you get home well after I have already gone to bed."

"I know, Beth, and I am sorry, really. We have been researching and discussing the increased solar activity recently."

"Really, is it that important? Is it anything that we should be worried about?"

"Well, we really don't know for sure, at least not yet. We are very concerned though. There is a potential for serious disruptions in communications however, maybe even worse," he said.

"What is the concern all about? Are they afraid it may interfere with cell phones, satellite communications, that sort of thing?"

"One of the things we are concerned about is the impact on the space station and the space telescope. We are concerned that if the mass corona ejection is large enough, it could have the potential to destroy electronics onboard both."

"Really? That certainly does sound serious. What about the electronics here on earth, will they be affected as well?"

"Again, we don't know yet; it is largely dependent on how powerful the ejection turns out to be. It could amount to nothing, but we cannot afford to take any chances."

"But what can you do about it? Can you move the Hubble or the space station?"

"No, at least not in time to avoid the flare. What we can do is attempt to position them in such a manner that the impact is minimized." Her husband picked up a dinner roll from off of his plate and turned it around in his hand. "Take this roll for example. If the top part of the roll is the hardened sunshield, we turn the top of the roll to face the oncoming flare."

"Will that be enough to protect against the flare?"

"Well, it depends on the size of the flare. Anyway, we are concerned, so we have been discussing various approaches on dealing with it. We have to take the threat seriously." John lowered his head for a few moments, lost in deep thought."

"Are you okay, John?" his wife asked him, troubled by the concern she saw on her husbands face. He looked exhausted and she was concerned about the toll that the long nights were taking on his health,

"Beth, I have been watching this solar activity increase exponentially over the last several months. We may be facing the most powerful solar weather that we have seen for at least a hundred years."

"Shouldn't you warn someone about this increased activity, someone in the government?"

"We already have, honey. They are hesitant to bring anything to the public yet. They fear that there will be panic and frankly, we were unable to provide enough convincing evidence to support our concerns."

The couple sat down and got to work on the elaborate meal. Just as they were getting to the prime rib, the phone rang. Beth looked at John and said; "Now don't you answer that phone, I spent all day working on this meal, and besides that, I haven't seen you for weeks!"

"Honey, you know what I just told you. This is just too big to ignore! I'm sorry." Beth just sighed and shrugged her shoulders.

"Hello? Good evening, Marcus, what's going on? Oh no, how long?...Have you told everyone yet?...Have they taken steps? Oh no...Well, we always knew this was a possibility. Maybe we should—no, you're right. What time do you project it will strike and where? Have you warned the President's office yet? Okay, Marcus, thank you for calling me with this information. We'll do damage control in the morning. Okay, please let me know if anything changes. Sure, you too, good night."

When he hung up the phone, he plumped back down into his chair and let out a deep and heavy sigh. "John? John what is it, what did they tell you?"

"That was Marcus Brown. He told me that they just found evidence that the sun is about to produce a massive coronal mass ejection."

"Is it heading here?"

"It's impossible to know for certain until the ejection occurs, but depending on timing and location yes, they believe it will come our way."

"Where is it expected to strike?

"It looks right now like it will strike somewhere in the northern hemisphere. It's too early to tell for certain, but early projections have it striking the United States, possibly somewhere on the east coast, most likely somewhere in the Washington, DC area."

"Oh my, *we* are in the Washington, DC area," she replied.

"I know. There is not much that we can do now, honey, except to sit and wait."

"When is it expected to strike?"

"Marcus told me that it is projected to strike the earth in thirty–six hours."

CHAPTER 6

Bubba Jones let out a low growl. He was getting irritated with the short man in front of him. He kept stopping every few steps and Bubba wanted to get on inside of the bus so he could sit down and get comfortable for the long ride. After a few more steps, the small man stopped again; only this time, Bubba did not. He intentionally bumped into the man, knocking him down to the ground. While Bubba was a big man at six foot–five and weighing in around three–hundred pounds, the man in front of Bubba was a small man, Bubba guessed he was only around five–eight and probably weighed no more than one–hundred and seventy–five pounds.

The guard came over to investigate the commotion. "Okay now, ladies, knock it off now, or you two will spend your first month in the hole after we get to the prison. Do you understand me?" The two men gave weak nods to the guard and continued walking. The prisoners all climbed onboard the bus and sat down.

Bubba sat down in the seat next to the smaller man. He turned and looked at the man.

"You just wait, little man. I am going to break you in half the first chance I get." The smaller man seemed to be quite unaffected by the big man's threats, which caught Bubba quite by surprise. Normally when he threatened someone, he would see his or her eyes open wide in fear because of his enormous size. Bubba chuckled to himself. He liked to call them "fish eyes," because of the way people's eyes often betray their fear by opening wide, in a manner that resembled those of a fish. Bubba studied the man for a moment, frustrated that he was not acting at all the way he had expected.

He turned to the man and said, "Aren't you scared, little man?" The man slowly turned toward Bubba, stared directly at him, and let just the hint of a smile appear on his face. "'You win battles by knowing the enemy's timing, and using a timing which the enemy does not expect.' Miyamoto Mushashi—*The Book of Five Rings*." Then, he turned back facing forward, never saying anything else to Bubba.

"Hey, I asked you a question, you little punk!" Bubba reached over the man with the intent of wrapping the chain around the man's neck. Reacting with lightning speed, the smaller man's elbow came up from around his stomach and raced toward Bubba's head. The edge of his hand then struck Bubba's throat right at the larynx, crushing his windpipe. It took a couple of seconds for Bubba to realize what had just happened, when he tried to take his next breath and found that he could not. Bubba tried yelling for help, but the only thing that came out was a slight gurgling sound.

Of all of the prisoners that were sitting around the two men, only two of them had seen what had taken place. They were so surprised that they sat for a full minute simply staring at the two men, looking back and forth at the two. The guards glanced back in their direction and looking at Bubba simply assumed that he had already fallen asleep. The smaller man simply sat staring out of the window, acting as if nothing had happened.

"Hey, mister!" One of the two men that had seen the very brief altercation hollered across the aisle to where they were sitting. "Hey, mister! Who are you, and how in the world did you do that? Bubba is as big as a house and as mean as a junkyard dog." The smaller man continued looking out of the window, ignoring the other man's question. The man asked him again, "Mister, come on tell me, who the heck are you?"

"The name is Masters, Vic Masters."

"Awesome. I'm Joey, Joey Garfola. Vic, huh? That's cool, man. Hey listen, that was some next–level stuff that you did there man. I mean, that was *really* cool! So where did you learn how to do that?"

"I used to teach '*that*,'" said Masters,

"Wow, you mean, you were a martial arts instructor?"

"Yes. No. I was an Army Ranger. I taught hand–to–hand combat."

"Really! Man that is really cool. Have you killed with your bare hands before?" asked Garfola.

"Yeah, a few times. One of those times put me here with you."

"What happened?"

"A man said something that I didn't like," said Masters.

"What did you do?"

"I broke his neck."

"Awesome."

Masters turned and looked at Garfola. He was a younger man, probably in his early twenties. He then shook his head and turned back toward the window.

"I'm here because—."

"I don't care why you are here. Leave me alone."

Garfola stopped talking to the man and started talking with the inmates next to him on the bus about what had happened. As word began to spread, more and more of the inmates started talking. It was an unusual event among inmates. Certainly, inmates kill each other all the time in prison. What was different this time was the fact that Masters had used his bare hands, the fact that Bubba had been killed so quickly and so quietly, and the fact that the only ones that even knew that Bubba was dead were the ones that had seen what had happened. The only reason that *they* had even seen anything was that they happened to be looking in that direction when it happened.

The man continued staring out the window. However, this time he wore a small smile as he listened carefully to everything that the other inmates were saying. This was exactly what he had hoped for when he decided to talk with Garfola. He expected that the young convict would spread the word about what he had seen. He started laughing quietly as it occurred to him that he had not even gotten off the bus yet, and he already had a reputation that he would carry with him into prison.

As he sat looking out of the window, watching the familiar surroundings of the city, the tall buildings, the bridges, and the throng of busy people, give way to the rural surroundings of pastures, livestock, and granaries, a famous line from *Paradise Lost* crossed his mind.

"The mind is its own place, and in itself Can make a heav'n of hell, a hell of heav'n."

Vic Masters decided that maybe prison wasn't going to be so bad after all.

CHAPTER 7

He tried rubbing his numb hands together in an effort to generate a little heat. It was freezing cold outside, and James White feared that he had not packed warmly enough for the conference. He had forgotten how cold it could get in Washington in the winter months. The temperature was well below freezing as he stood on the mall waiting for the sun to rise over the Capitol Building. He had always admired the architecture of many of the buildings in Washington, DC, but the Capitol Building always seemed to stand head–and–shoulders above the rest. It was one of the oldest buildings in the Washington, DC area, its capstone having been laid by the great George Washington himself.

He turned around briefly to take in a very picturesque view of the Washington Memorial as the first rays of sunlight peaked around the capital building. The monument rose to the sky like an ancient Egyptian monument, looking to distant points of light in the night sky. The monument—completed in 1885, to honor General George Washington's contribution to victory in the Revolutionary War—rose behind him with the lingering backdrop of the darkness of night.

James White enjoyed visiting Washington, DC and did so as often as he was able. Something about being in the capital always gave him goose bumps. The ideals upon which the country of the United States was founded had always moved him, the dreams of a government that was able to lead only with the consent of the governed, and a government of the people and by the people. It stirred something deep inside him. He wondered whether it was a common thirst for righteousness, justice, and freedom, which caused so many to leave their native countries and travel across the vast oceans for a chance to live in America.

As the darkness began to give way to the light of the rising sun, he turned back just in time to see the sunrise over the Capitol. He felt a sudden rush of pride at being an American. *Wow,* he thought to himself, *I do love being an American. There is just something about being here in Washington, DC, the history, the capitol of the good old USA!* Dr. James White glanced down at his watch to check on the time. It was 7:11 am, just enough time to grab some breakfast and a cup of coffee before the conference started.

It was a Monday morning, the beginning of a typical workweek for most people around the world. Nevertheless, James White knew that this was not going to be another typical week for him. In fact, he was genuinely excited that it would not be. As a retired pastor and as sitting president of the International Baptist Convention, he kept quite busy year round. He normally could not afford to take time out of his schedule to attend a conference, especially one that would take him as far as Washington, DC. However, James White felt—no, he *knew* that this conference was going to be worth the trip.

He walked to his car and drove back to the hotel where he was staying, since it was also hosting the conference. He parked and made his way to the restaurant. After ordering some break-fast, he sat down to enjoy a refreshing cup of coffee, even as he reflected on the ramifications of the coming week. While he waited for his food to arrive, he pulled out the printed invitation that he had received several months earlier asking him to attend the conference. The letter read:

Dr. James White
President, International Baptist Convention
125 Divinity Drive
Seattle, WA 98101

Dr. White,
You are cordially invited to attend The First Annual Reconciliatory Conference of Theologians and Scientists. The conference is scheduled to begin December 5, at 8:00 am in Washington, D.C. and is scheduled to end on December 9, at 4:00 pm.

This conference will be the first one of its kind ever held in recorded history. The intent of this confer-ence is to discover how two groups of human beings, theologians with their faith in God, and scientists with their faith in science, can come together to find the common ground necessary to form a united front capable of addressing the historic and challenging problems of our time.

We hope that we will be able to bridge the gulf that divides us. We hope to end the bickering between the religious and the quantitative, to find and chart the proper course that will enable us to learn from one another and to respect one another's beliefs and points–of–view, enabling us to work together to end some of the world's most pressing issues.

We hope that you will make every effort to attend this exciting event and that you will bring with you a spirit of cooperation and understanding. Additional information regarding the event has been included along with this invitation.

Our very best regards,
The Unity

The Unity—what a novel concept, he thought to himself. *Scientists and Theologians meeting together to find reconciliation and common ground. What I would give for the Church to have such a spirit of unity and understanding!*

"Good Morning, Dr. White, is it?" A tall, slim, middle–aged man had appeared at the edge of his table. He must have approached while he was deep in thought.

"How—."

"I saw your name tag Dr. White. My name is Bjorn Yvornsky, *Doctor* Bjorn Yvornsky. May I join you?"

"Of course, Dr. Yvornsky, please sit," James White told him, eager to learn more about the other attendees at the conference.

It seemed that opportunities like this were just what he needed. He laid the invitation down on the table so he could focus on the younger man now seated across from him.

"Thank you. So, Dr. White, what are you a doctor of?"

"Theology. What about you?" James noticed that the younger man twitched slightly when he said "theology." He wondered whether something had happened to turn Bjorn Yvornsky against religion.

"Computer Science. So, what do you do, Dr. White?"

"I am a retired pastor. Soon after I retired however, I found myself a bit restless so I did some part–time work with the International Baptist Convention that ended up becoming not so part–time. What about you, Dr. Yvornsky?"

Yvornsky, fiddled with his coffee cup before answering. "Oh, I get to design, build, and play with supercomputers for a living. It's not a bad way to make a living now, let me tell you. Sometimes, I have such a hard time believing that they actually pay me to do this that I have to pinch myself just to make sure I'm awake!"

James White took a sip of his coffee and assessed his newfound acquaintance. Bjorn Yvornsky was what he expected a super nerd to look like. He was casually dressed in blue jeans, sandals, and a worn–out casual sport jacket. He had long, premature gray hair with some brown still mixed in that he wore in a long ponytail.

"So, Dr. Yvornsky, after I received and read the invitation, I found myself quite curious about our hosts. I guess they call themselves 'The Unity.' Do you know anything about them?"

"Yes, I do. I know Dr. Norman Weller, the founder, who also heads the Department of History and Philosophy at Washington State University. He and I go back, way back, to our time as students together at MIT. What would you like to know about them?"

"Well, I did a little research online after reading the invitation, and I saw Dr. Weller's name listed. Apparently, he and a friend of his, Dr. Joseph Clark, a conservative pastor and professor at Divinity University, shared some ideas over email and over a number of dinners about the need for more civility between the two disciplines, science, and theology. Like so many of us, they had grown weary of the constant, back–and–forth bickering in the public forums, the constant barbs and insults around why the other is wrong and how ignorant the others are for their beliefs. Did I miss anything?"

"No, that's about it. Actually, Joe, Norm, and I all attended MIT together for a while. Even back then, Norm and Joe used to go back and forth all the time discussing science and theology. You know how it is in college, students staying up late, engaged in deep philosophical discussions, solving all of the world's problems, etc."

"Yes, I do, indeed. We used to burn the midnight oil many nights when I attended Dallas Theological Seminary. We would often discuss our own solutions to the many ills that trouble mankind. Then we would scratch our heads trying to figure out why the early church fathers had been unable to solve the problems without our help!" The two men laughed.

"Anyway, Joe eventually left MIT to pursue a divinity degree and we all went our separate ways, but the two of them stayed in touch, by phone and snail mail at first, then later by email. Even though they often disagreed, they developed a deep and honest rapport, and a respect for each other's viewpoint. They discovered that there was surprisingly quite a bit that they could learn from one another and that perhaps, if given the chance, these two groups as a whole might come to the same conclusion. They formed The Unity with the intent of bringing these two groups together for a meaningful and ongoing dialogue. I, for one, believe it is quite noble of them to at least attempt to reconcile these two groups of people after so many years of animosity and mistrust, even if it turns out that they are not successful."

"I have to agree," said James White. "As someone once said, 'Blessed are the peacemakers ...' The two groups have been at each other's throats for so long, it would certainly be wonderful if The Unity could at least get some dialogue started. It certainly seems to me that there is no reason that we cannot work together on important social and scientific issues, without sacrificing the integrity of our beliefs to compromise."

"I am so glad to hear you say that, Dr. White. It gives me great hope for this week's conference!" Someone had come up behind James White long enough to overhear part of their conversation. He turned to see who it was.

"Dr. White, may I introduce—."

"Dr. Weller," James finished for Yvornsky. "Yes, I recognized your face from my research."

"Well, I am flattered, Dr. White. Thank you so much for coming."

"It is my great pleasure. I must say that I have been looking forward to this conference ever since I received your invitation."

"Thank you, as have I. I must tell you that I have heard some very good things about you as well, Dr. White."

"Really?"

"Indeed. From what I have heard, you have worked tirelessly to bring competing factions together within the church. It seems you have been quite successful in your efforts as a peacemaker, working with congregations that are about to split, helping them to reconcile and remain whole."

"Thank you, Dr. Weller. You are too kind."

"You're welcome. Now, gentlemen, if you would please join us, I believe we are about ready to get started."

The three men walked together into the conference room, with Norman walking on up to the podium to the applause of many in the audience.

CHAPTER 8

A red Honda carrying two men pulled up to the curb and stopped in front of an attractive, yet somewhat ordinary–looking, home. Frank opened the door and climbed out of the car, studying the home and the property on which it sat. It was a two–story home with a taller than normal privacy fence surrounding a large yard. With a closer inspection, the more careful observer might discover that the fence around the yard was not made of the store–bought privacy fencing sold in sections at some of the larger retail hardware stores. Instead, the fence was made from a softer wood found mostly in Pacific Rim countries. Each picket had been carefully placed close together it ensured that there were no gaps large enough for curious eyes to peer through. The privacy fence had been placed twenty feet inside of the property line. Along the outer–edge of the yard was a small chain–link fence that made uninvited access to the property even more difficult. He concluded that the man that had built the home definitely valued his privacy.

"Here we are, Frank. Remember, Master Takata is a *very* traditional instructor, so please do not be offended if he will not accept you. He teaches only a handful of people anymore."

"Yes, yes, I know, Conrad. You mentioned it already, *several* times."

"Sorry."

The two men walked up to the door, and Conrad rang the bell. After a minute, an elderly, oriental man opened the door.

"Good evening, Master Takata. How are you doing today, sir?

"I am fine, Conrad. How have you been?

"Fine, sir. Thank you. I would like to introduce the old friend that I mentioned to you last week, Frank Martin."

"Hello, Frank. It is nice to meet you."

"It is nice to meet you as well, sir."

"Please, come in, both of you." Takata escorted the two men through a courtyard and into a small building. Frank thought that it looked like a traditional Japanese dojo. The room contained a heavy bag hanging from a stand, stalks of straw tied into bundles, and several wooden swords. At the front of the room was a picture of an elderly Japanese man whom Frank concluded was Takata's master, and a stand made for holding swords. In it were two swords. Frank had been reading up on Kenjutsu in anticipation of the meeting, so he recognized them. The first, a long sword called a *katana,* measured thirty to forty inches long. The short sword, called a *wakizashi,* measured between twelve to twenty–four inches long. They were polished and looked razor sharp as well.

"Thank you so much for considering taking me on as a student. I am honored and very, very grateful."

"You are most welcome, Frank. Well, let us see here then. Tell me about yourself. Are you a black belt in Tae Kwon Do, like Conrad?"

"Yes, sir, I am. I have trained in Tae Kwon Do for many years."

"So why are you interested in learning Kenjutsu, and why should I accept you as a student?" Frank could see that the old master was studying him, assessing his aptitude as well as his attitude.

"I want to learn the *old* ways, sir, the discipline, to learn the skills and the ways of ancient sword fighting."

"But why? Do you desire to learn it for self–defense? You might look a little odd walking through the local mall with a sword on your side, don't you think?" Frank thought that he detected the hint of a smile on the master's face.

"Yes, sir, I most certainly would. In all seriousness, sir, I no longer care for tournaments, or for fast food martial art. I desire to learn *true* martial art, the ancient ways. I value what you have to teach, sir. I would like to learn the art of Kenjutsu. To be honest, sir, I cannot explain it, but I feel like I must be here, that I am *meant* to be here."

"We shall see about that, Mr. Martin, we shall see. There will be no tournaments here. There will be no fans, no trophies, and most certainly no applause. If I do select you as a student, I will tell you what you find here. You will find much sweat, Frank, and you will find pain. You will find repetition, repeating every movement until you practice them in your dreams. You will learn detail, excruciating detail. You will find humiliation. You will train until you learn all I have to teach you. If you become my student, you will have to do everything that I instruct you to do. Would you still like to do this?"

Frank looked at Conrad, who just shrugged his shoulders, and then back at Takata.

"I will train as hard or harder than any student you have ever had, Master Takata. I promise you." At this, the old master raised his eyebrows and looked at Conrad, who then shrugged his shoulders once more.

"Will he finish what he starts, Conrad?"

"Master Takata, if Frank says he will do something, he will do it. In the many years that I have known him, I have never known him to start something and not finish it. Nor have I ever seen him not deliver on a promise. He is as hardworking a man as I have ever met."

Takata nodded, answering with nothing but, "Hmmm."

"Master Takata, if you choose to take me as your student, I will not disappoint you."

"Conrad speaks highly of you, Frank Martin. Honestly, I am interested in finding out what you can do. Please, wait just a moment."

The master stepped out of the building and returned a short while later. He handed a black uniform to Frank.

"Frank Martin, I accept you as a student."

"Thank you, Master Takata. I am deeply honored."

"Now, honor me by stepping into that room over there, change into your uniform, and join us for some training. We will start with some Jujitsu training. I hope that you are used to sore muscles."

After changing into his uniform, Frank joined Master Takata and Conrad for warm–up exercises, followed by some Jujitsu throws and breaks that Frank had never seen before. As promised, the training *was* quite intense; they spent several hours going through various joint locks, throws, and breaks before finally stopping to take a break. While Conrad and Frank rested, Master Takata left the training hall for a few minutes before returning with several poles of thick bamboo and a base that held the bamboo poles. He took a bamboo pole, inserted it into the base, and pointed to Frank.

"Frank, do you see that sword over there? It is an old training sword, but it is razor sharp. I want you to take that sword, and cut this bamboo stalk."

"Yes, sir," he answered, a bit unsure of himself.

Frank picked up the sword, unsure even how to hold the sword correctly. He grasped it with both hands, and with a downward slicing motion, cutting diagonally from top to bottom. He cut the bamboo pole in half with a single slice. Master Takata's eyebrows rose once more. He looked at Conrad.

"Conrad. You told me this man had never trained with the sword before. Explain yourself!"

"Master Takata, I—."

"Master Takata, I swear to you that I have never used a sword before. It was just beginner's luck."

The old man looked at both of them, and then suddenly his face broke into a large grin as he looked at both of them and started laughing. Then, as suddenly and quickly as the grin appeared, it then disappeared, replaced this time with a stern and focused appearance. He replaced the pole that Frank had cut in two, walked over to where Frank had laid the sword, and walked back over to the stalk. Then, as he let out a loud yell, he began cutting the stalk, beginning at the top. Within the space of three seconds, he had cut the stalk into ten small pieces.

Conrad and Frank just looked at the pieces of bamboo lying on the floor, looked back at each other, and then back at Master Takata.

"Now then," the old master said, "let us begin."

CHAPTER 9

Scott looked over the report for the tenth time. He knew that he was about to be bombarded with questions this time so he wanted to make certain that he had everything in order regarding his facts about the upcoming test. It appeared, at face value, that the test was successful, and that they had a working experimental prototype. If it worked as expected, they had revolutionized the battlefield. He decided to pick up the phone and call for help.

"Ali, would you please give me a hand here? Something in the report does not look quite right."

Ali, whose full name was Mohammed Ali Abachmed, was an Iranian–American that had been in the United States for over twenty years. He had worked his way up the ladder at Logan Aerospace Engineering from a part–time technician to a senior systems engineer. Ali got up from behind his desk and walked into Scott's office.

"What is it, Scott? Is something wrong?"

"It's these numbers. The yield should be much lower than what is reflected in the report. Are you certain that the numbers are accurate?"

"As far as I know they are. Let me see. Hmmm ... I believe I see what is bothering you. The yield will be much, much lower given the safety measures that we plan to add into the device," Ali answered.

"But the numbers already include the safety measures; they were implemented before the test was run." Scott responded.

"Oh, that's not good."

"What's not good?" Mark Hinshaw, the program manager and Scott's boss, had walked in unexpectedly. Ali excused himself and left the office.

Scott paused for a few moments, trying to decide whether to say something.

"Mark, do you mind if I ask you a question?"

"Sure Scott, no problem. What's on your mind?"

"Do you think maybe we are opening Pandora's Box with this device? Think about it—what would happen if it fell into the wrong hands? Maybe we are playing with fire here."

Mark walked in, closed the door, and sat down in the small armchair in Scott's office.

"Listen, Scott, I understand your concern, I do. I have asked myself that same question a hundred times."

"And what did you come up with?"

"Well, the way I see it this is not up to me. If the President of the United States or the military decided that they need this weapon on the battlefield then they need to have it. It could save many lives in the end. Either way, it's not our call."

"But *we* created this device Mark. If something happens, do we not have responsibility for creating it? Remember what Robert Oppenheimer said, 'I have become the destroyer of worlds.'"

"Scott..."

"All right, all right. I am just...concerned. The test results just came in. Even with the safety measures we implemented, the yield is still much too great. Mark, we just don't seem to be able to control this thing, no matter what we do. If we activate this weapon outside the lab, the result could be something much more powerful and catastrophic than we originally anticipated. Think of the consequences."

"Have you said anything to Ali about your concerns yet?" he asked. Scott shook his head.

"He knows something is going on, he just doesn't know *what*. He hasn't seen all of the data that I have yet. I was going to talk to him about it later today."

"Please don't say anything to him about it, at least not yet."

"Really, but why not? Don't you think he should know?"

"Just don't say anything to Ali, or to anyone else, at least not yet, okay? You can both keep working on the problem, Scott. You have one week. Between you and Ali, I have all of the faith in the world that you can work this thing out and find a solution. Scott started to say something, but Mark stopped him.

"Listen, Scott, I really *do* understand. I don't know what good or ill may come from this device. The fact is, however, that this technology has been around since Oppenheimer and the Manhattan Project. If we don't find a way to somehow exploit and control it, someone else will, perhaps sooner than later. According to our intelligence, several nations are already working feverishly to develop a similar device for themselves, and that some have been working on it for decades. Of course, it goes without saying that not all of these nations are friendly to the United States. We have to get everyone focused back onto getting this device ready as quickly as possible. Besides," he said casually, "we need it ready for the demonstration next week. There will be a representative from the Joint Chiefs here to witness the field test."

"Excuse me; did you say a demonstration, a field test? Next week? Mark, we are not ready! There are so many variables that we have not even accounted for, much less addressed. The device is still just too experimental, and it is *extremely* unstable. I just told you that we haven't been able to find a way to control the reaction!"

"Nevertheless, they want to see it next week. They want to know where all of their hard–earned American tax dollars have been going. Think about it Scott, there are just so many hot spots in the world right now. The Joint Chiefs say that they desperately need tools like this at their disposal. If we can pull this off, think what it could mean!"

Scott just kept shaking his head. "We have to tell them, Mark. We have to explain to them that no matter how badly they feel they need this, it's simply not ready."

Mark threw up his hands.

"I tell you what; let's get busy getting this thing ready for transport. You can continue working on controlling the reaction after it's on site." Mark Hinshaw leaned over and looked earnestly at Scott. "You have to find a way to get this thing working. You have to find a way to control this thing, Scott."

"And if we are unable to solve the problem before the scheduled test?"

Mark let out a heavy sigh, rubbing the top of his head with his hand. "Then I will tell them—*we* will tell them, together.

We'll just postpone the test until you can figure this thing out." Scott knew that Mark was a man of his word. If he told Scott that he would postpone, he could count on it. He let out his own heavy sigh of relief. He suddenly realized that his heart had been racing.

"Thank you."

"Yeah, yeah, whatever. Now just get that thing ready to move by tomorrow morning, and Scott?"

"Yes?"

"Please figure this thing out, will you?" Scott just smiled as Mark just shook his head and grimaced. They both knew well enough what the reaction of the Joint Chiefs would be if they had to cancel the test.

Scott got to work right away. It took only a couple of hours to get the weapon ready to move. He had worked quickly, because he wanted to leave plenty of time to work through some of the equations. Perhaps he could make a breakthrough while he still had it in the lab. He was close; he knew he could find a way; he just needed more time. It was already dark out, but he would work through the night if necessary. He was deeply engrossed in various formulas and calculations when there was an unexpected knock at the door of his office. The interruption broke his concentration. He looked up to find a man standing outside of his office. He was carrying a briefcase full of papers with him.

"Good evening, Mr. McBride. How are you doing tonight?"

"I'm doing fine, I guess, Stewart. What are you doing here at this time of night?"

"I have here some papers for you to sign, authorizing the transfer of the device to the test site."

"What? Already? We were not supposed to be transferring the device until tomorrow!"

"Sorry, Scott. I guess they moved up the timetable. They want the device in New Mexico by Friday morning. If you can please sign the paperwork, I have a security crew waiting to escort us all the way."

"This is highly irregular. I need to speak with Ross first."

"I believe Ross is out for the rest of the week. It appears there was some kind of family emergency. I heard his wife was in a car accident and was severely injured."

"Oh, no." He didn't really know Ian Ross, Mark's boss, very well. He had not even known that Ian was still married for that matter. The timing of the accident certainly couldn't have been much worse. "Very well, Stewart. Now I'm counting on you to make absolutely certain that nothing happens to that device between here and New Mexico, understand? If that thing falls into the wrong hands…"

"I understand, Scott. Don't worry; we will take good care of it." Scott signed the paperwork and handed it back to Stewart, who looked it over and nodded his head. "I'll see you at the test site on Friday, Scott."

"Okay, see you there."

Stewart walked out of the room and to the elevator, sweating profusely. *Had Scott noticed it?* When the elevator finally reached the sub–basement, he exited the elevator, where he was approached by a security detail. Stewart noticed that each man wore a firearm on his side. The two guards even had automatic weapons. He tried his best not to draw attention to himself by staring at them.

"Good evening, sir. Identification please." Stewart presented his ID and was escorted over to the retina scanner. He looked into the scanner and the computer responded, "Identity confirmed: Stewart Reginald Smith."

The bars retracted and Stewart proceeded to the next and final security barrier, the palm scanner. "Identity Confirmed, Stewart Reginald Smith." He walked into the room and proceeded directly to the lab tech in charge. "Good evening, Harry."

"Stewart, what can I do for you?"

"I am here to take this device to New Mexico for testing."

"I was told that it wasn't supposed to happen until sometime tomorrow morning."

"That's true. It was originally scheduled for tomorrow morning, but I guess they moved things up."

"I am going to have to check with Scott on this."

"No need, Harry. I have his signature right here. However, feel free to call him if you would like. He was still upstairs just a few minutes ago." The man looked at the paperwork.

"No, that is Scott's signature all right. Okay, I will have my crew bring the device around to the dock for you to take possession. Will you need an escort?"

"No, I brought plenty of security with me."

"Okay. Give me a few minutes, and we will meet you there."

"Excellent. I will be waiting."

Smith left the lab and took the elevator back up to ground level. After exiting the building, he walked over to a non–descript eighteen–wheeler that had pulled up front. Smith walked over to the driver, who appeared nervous and frightened. He was sitting next to another man that appeared more composed but still very edgy. He decided that he should try to calm them.

"Okay, settle down now, you two. Everything is going as planned. We just need to move this thing over to the docks. By the time we get the truck into position, they should already have the device at the loading dock." He looked at the two men, evaluating them. They both looked like they were about to explode.

He had complained about having two strangers working with him, but his employer had insisted that some of his own men accompany him. Smith evaluated the situation and decided that he needed to remind them of what was at stake.

"Listen very carefully to me now, both of you! If you both don't calm down and get yourselves under control, and I mean right this second, they are going to become very suspicious. If they become the least little bit suspicious, they will begin to dig just a little deeper, and if they dig a little deeper, they *will* find out the truth. I promise you this: if they find out the truth, they will throw all of us into a deep, dark place for so long that even our families will forget we ever existed. If we fail to deliver this device, what do you think the folks we work for are going to do? Don't you realize that they will assume that we backed out or worse yet, never intended to go through with the deal? What do you think will happen? I'll tell you what will happen. They will murder our families—our wives, and our children." He looked at them once more and determined that he had gotten their attention. "Besides, everything is fine. Our job is simple. All we have to do is load up the device, deliver it across the border, and our friends will take care of the rest, okay?" The two men nodded. Everyone understood what was at stake. It was too late to turn back and they were out of options. Deliver the device or prepare themselves for their own deaths and the deaths of their families.

The crew secured the device inside the trailer and Smith closed the door. Just as they prepared to leave the dock, Mark Hinshaw appeared. Smith felt his stomach tighten and his heart race.

"Good evening, Stewart."

"Good evening, Mark."

"What's going on? Scott McBride called me and told me that you are moving the device tonight?" Smith handed the paperwork to Hinshaw.

"That's right."

"He also told me that you said that Ian's wife was in a car accident?"

"Yes, I did. She's been in the hospital for the past few days."

Mark looked at Stewart in an odd sort of way. Smith scanned the dock area, trying to find an escape route in case he needed to make a quick getaway. If something happened, the two Iranians in the cab would be on their own.

"Well, it sure is odd that Ian didn't say anything about that this morning, though he did seem a bit preoccupied."

"I was told that the prognosis is good. Would you like to contact General Miller just to get a confirmation on the shipment?" It was a complete and desperate bluff. If Mark Hinshaw called his bluff, he was going to jail. Hinshaw stood there for several moments, deliberating the pros and cons of trying to reach Ian or General Miller.

"No, that's all right," he answered, glancing over the paperwork once more. I'll see you in New Mexico."

"See you there."

As they pulled away from the dock and made for the highway, all three men let out a collective sigh of relief. Smith reached into his pocket and retrieved his cell phone. His hands were shaking as he struggled to make a call and while he waited for someone to answer. After a number of rings, a woman finally answered on the other end.

"Hello?"

"I need to speak to Abdul ... Yes I'll wait ... Yes, it's me. We have it. We're on our way to the rendezvous site. We should be there in eighteen hours. We will be changing trucks a couple of times along the way, just in case. Yes, we can handle it, we brought along some equipment that will help.... Okay."

As he ended the call, he sat quietly pondering whether the extraordinarily large sum of money they had given him and the even larger sum they were *going* to give him would be worth the cost. Stewart Smith was now a traitor to his country. If he were ever caught, he would be tried, convicted, and thrown into a maximum-security prison, most likely never to be heard from again. If they *did* make it, he knew he would probably never see the United States again.

As he ended the call with Stewart Smith, Abdul excitedly placed another call.

"*Asalaam 'a laykum.* You can tell our government that we will have the device to them by this time tomorrow. Tell them to be prepared to meet us at the airport the moment we arrive, that there is no time to waste. The Americans will act immediately once they discover that the device is missing. Will they be ready to launch on schedule? Excellent—praise Allah! We will have our vengeance upon the Great Satan. Nothing will stand in our way!

As he hung up the phone, Abdul smiled. *By this time tomorrow,* he thought, *the Americans will suffer, as we have suffered. Praise Allah!*

CHAPTER 10

He took a sip of coffee as he opened the door. Sunlight filled the office as he walked inside, revealing a large envelope lying unopened on top of his desk. It looked like another report. *When it rains, it pours.* He knew that the report must contain something of importance for it to be placed in such a prominent place on his desk. Normally, such reports simply found their way to his assistant and into his inbox. Only the most important ones were placed on his desk. He had instituted the policy the very day he moved into the office following President Michael's inaugural address. He took another sip of his coffee as he sat down and looked at the envelope. A sticky note was stuck to the front of the envelope. The note read, "I thought this might come in useful, given what happened with Project Blackout–Hank."

After five years as the president's Chief of Staff, it seemed to Rob Thornton that he would have gotten used to all of the secrecy and project codenames. *These spooks and soldiers, how they enjoy playing their games.* However, Hank Miller, General Hank

Miller, had passed along this particular report to him, and Rob knew that any report that the five–star general felt was important enough to have delivered in such a fashion, would be something that he would have to attend to immediately, doubly so if it had anything to do with Project Blackout. Of course, it had to have been *Project Blackout* that was stolen. How could they have allowed such a powerful weapon to be taken from a top–secret facility, right out from under their very noses?

What had happened to the country that the government had allowed security to lapse so much that something known to be so dangerous could be stolen so easily? Rob Thornton already knew the reasons for the lapse in security; he just hated to admit it. *Politics.* The politics of the previous administration and the previous Congress, both of which had been swept out of office when the tide of public opinion turned against them after the last election, were to blame. The previous Congress and administration, in their zeal and false sense of superiority and elite ideology, had blamed America for all of the world's evils, vowing to peel away the layers of secrecy that had been put in place to protect the United States, and the rest of the world. They had repealed laws, held hearings, and threatened and intimidated the intelligence community to the point that security had taken a distant second place when it came to political correctness. *Idiots.*

He opened the folder and pulled out the report. It was entitled: "The New and Deadly Threat Posed by New Advanced Electromagnetic Pulse Weaponry, and the Potential Impact to the United States of America."

Thornton skipped the first couple of pages until he got to the section entitled, "Introduction."

Consider for a moment, a world without electricity.

In April 2008, a report commissioned by the government of the United States of America was finally completed. The report was entitled, "Report of the Commission to Assess the Threat to the United States from Electromagnetic Pulse (EMP) Attack." The report highlighted the extreme risk associated with an electromagnetic pulse resulting from a high–altitude explosion of a nuclear warhead high over the continental United States. The report goes on to detail the vast and extremely deep reliance that our society has on a complex and vast networking of systems, based on electrical and electronic components that serve to support our way of life.

When considering the greatest impact of an EMP attack, the first component that is likely to come to mind is the electrical power grid, used to carry power into homes and businesses across the United States. However, the grid itself is only a single component in a chain of the many components of technology that we depend upon twenty–four hours a day, three hundred and sixty–five days a year just to survive. Dramatically affected would be a myriad of other critical functions that affect our everyday life, including food distribution and storage, water treatment facilities, transportation, communications, not to mention the government, jobs, and education.

If electricity were to disappear around the world, virtually no aspect of our lives would be left untouched; our lives would change dramatically. Unless electricity returned soon after, the result would be nothing short of catastrophic for humanity. Without electricity, there would be no water coming into our homes from water–treatment plants. For those without wells, there would be no water to drink, to bathe with, or for our sewage systems. Without electricity to power the refrigerators and freezers that grocery stores and restaurants use to preserve meat, vegetables, milk, juices, and other perishables fresh, they would all soon spoil. With no electricity and with no way to keep food fresh, the stores and restaurants would soon close, and people would have nothing to eat.

Without electricity, there would be no communications between governments or between people, resulting in the failure or collapse of civil society. The total collapse of civil society and the increasingly scarce resources would create an unprecedented level of competition for the food, water, and supplies that we all need to survive.

The sudden and total collapse of civilization would likely result in vast migrations of people out of the heavily populated urban metropolitan areas, and into the more rural areas in search of food and water. Moreover, adults, concerned with finding and cultivating necessities such as food and water, would have no time for educating their children, resulting in a skyrocketing illiteracy rate within only a few generations.

Those living in such a world would be forced to discover, or in some cases re–discover, methods and technologies for interacting with the world in a pre–industrial manner that had taken ten–thousand years of time in a linear progression to develop. Raised in a post–industrial world where such knowledge had faded away completely over the past one–hundred and fifty years, most people would have little idea of where to begin in their struggle to survive.

There was another time long ago when much of the human race was forced to learn new ways to survive after the world fell apart around them. Technologies were lost, governments collapsed, and society came unraveled for hundreds of years following the collapse of the ancient Roman Empire, the hub of civilization at the time. That period, a time when much of the knowledge that existed in that ancient world was lost, has been commonly referred to as the Dark Ages.

Included with this report is an excerpt from the report issued in April 2008, by the EMP Commission, sponsored by the United States Congress.

[See Attached]

Thornton thumbed through the document until he reached the following section.

The physical and social fabric of the United States is sustained by a system of systems, a complex and dynamic network of interlocking and interdependent infrastructures ("critical national infrastructures") whose harmonious functioning enables the myriad actions, transactions, and information flow that under gird the orderly conduct of civil society in this country. The vulnerability of these infrastructures to threats—deliberate, accidental, and acts of nature—is the focus of greatly heightened concern in the current era, a process accelerated by the events of 9/11 and recent hurricanes, including Katrina and Rita.

This report presents the results of the Commission's assessment of the effects of a high altitude electromagnetic pulse (EMP) attack on our critical national infrastructures and provides recommendations for their mitigation. The assessment is informed by analytic and test activities executed under Commission sponsorship, which are discussed in this volume. An earlier executive report, Report of the Commission to Assess the Threat to the United States from Electromagnetic Pulse (EMP), Volume 1: Executive Report (2004), provided an overview of the subject.

The electromagnetic pulse generated by a high altitude nuclear explosion is one of a small number of threats that can hold our society at risk of catastrophic consequences. The increasingly pervasive use of electronics of all forms represents the greatest source of vulnerability to attack by EMP. Electronics are used to control, communicate, compute, store, manage, and implement nearly every aspect of United States (US) civilian systems. When a nuclear explosion occurs at high altitude, the EMP signal it produces will cover the wide geographic region within the line of sight of the detonation. This broad band, high amplitude EMP, when coupled into sensitive electronics, has the capability to produce widespread and long lasting disruption and damage to the critical infrastructures that underpin the fabric of US society.

Because of the ubiquitous dependence of US, society on the electrical power system, its vulnerability to an EMP attack, coupled with the EMP's particular damage mechanisms, creates the possibility of long–term, catastrophic consequences. The implicit invitation to take advantage of this vulnerability, when coupled with increasing proliferation of nuclear weapons and their delivery systems, is a serious concern. A single EMP attack may seriously degrade or shut down a large part of the electric power grid in the geographic area of EMP exposure effectively instantaneously. There is also a possibility of functional collapse of grids beyond the exposed area, as electrical effects propagate from one region to another. The time required for full recovery of service would depend on both the disruption and damage to the electrical power infrastructure and to other national infrastructures. Larger affected areas and stronger EMP field strengths will prolong the time to recover. Some critical electrical power infrastructure components are no longer manufactured in the United States, and their acquisition ordinarily requires up to a year of lead–time in routine circumstances. Damage to or loss of these components could leave significant parts of the electrical infrastructure out of service for periods measured in months to a year or more. There is a point in time at which the shortage or exhaustion of sustaining backup systems, including emergency power supplies, batteries, standby fuel supplies, communications, and manpower resources that can be mobilized, coordinated, and dispatched, together will lead to a continuing degradation of critical infrastructures for a prolonged period of time.

Electrical power is necessary to support other critical infrastructures, including supply and distribution of water, food, fuel, communications, transport, financial transactions, emergency services, government services, and all other infrastructures supporting the national economy and welfare. Should significant parts of the electrical power infrastructure be lost for any substantial period of time, the Commission believes that the consequences are likely to be catastrophic, and many people may ultimately die for lack of the basic elements necessary to sustain life in dense urban and suburban communities. In fact, the Commission is deeply concerned that such impacts are likely in the event of an EMP attack unless practical steps are taken to provide protection for critical elements of the electric system and for rapid restoration of electric power, particularly to essential services. The recovery plans for the individual infrastructures currently in place essentially assume, at worst, limited upsets to the other infrastructures that are important to their operation. Such plans may be of little or no value in the wake of an EMP attack because of its long-duration effects on all infrastructures that rely on electricity or electronics...

The Commission's view is that the federal government does not today have sufficiently robust capabilities for reliably assessing and managing EMP threats...

Thornton dropped the report on his desk. When they had first learned that Project Blackout had been stolen, they had primarily discussed its potential threat as a weapon used on a battlefield. Based on the report he had been reading, the weapon's potential for devastation might actually be much greater than any of them had considered. It could not only cripple the United States, it could destroy it.

Is that what Hank had been concerned about?

If Hank Miller was concerned about this threat, and it certainly appeared that he was, he knew that the president would want to be notified immediately. Thornton grabbed the report and left to find General Miller. He wanted to try to find out who or what was behind the theft before taking the information to the President. He would talk with every security agency if he had to, the NSA, the CIA, the FBI, the military, everyone. He needed answers, and fast. As far as they knew, an enemy could be planning an imminent, pre–emptive attack against the United States. They could be on a verge of a war.

They would find out who stole the weapon, and soon, *they had to*. After some deliberation, he decided that he could not wait; he had to tell the president immediately about what was happening. It was a conversation he was not looking forward to having.

CHAPTER 11

Amir Nouri sat back down in the large, comfortable office chair as he hung up the phone and breathed a long sigh of relief. He had spent the entire evening in his office, waiting to hear the outcome. It had been an extremely risky proposition for him from the very beginning; and he had taken considerable risk in undertaking the mission. Had the mission failed, it could have easily proven disastrous not just for him, but for his entire country as well. After all, he had just committed an act or war against the most powerful nation on the planet. Poking a stick at a caged lion was one thing, letting the lion out of the cage was an entirely different matter altogether.

Amir let out a heavy sigh and shook his head. It was a miracle that they had successfully stolen the device from the Americans. The mission had experienced numerous brushes with failure since the very beginning. The plot had nearly been exposed early on after an American spy, who had successfully infiltrated the top–secret IRGC (Pasdaran) covert operations group, had learned about the plans to steal the weapon. Only his unexpected murder by one of his own American Army Rangers over some lewd advances and comments directed at the Ranger's wife, had spared the plot from discovery. Fortunately, the spy had died before sharing the information about the plot with anyone. The American spy's libido and foul mouth had prevented the mission's ultimate failure, sparing Amir and the rest of the group from execution at the hands of the Supreme Leader.

A large smile then slowly crept over his face as he began to relish the moment. Despite the many setbacks, his people *had not failed;* they had in fact succeeded in stealing a most powerful weapon, right out from under the noses of the American military. It was a great victory for him no matter the outcome of future events. He slid down into the large chair until it seemed as if it would swallow him. At six–foot–two, he was a big man for an Iranian. Although gray hair had appeared long ago, at fifty–five, he was still considered very young for someone in his position.

Nouri paused to reflect on the curious series of events that had brought him to this point. He had experienced no small amount of consternation when the Supreme Leader unexpectedly paid him a surprise visit the year before. It was in fact almost completely unheard of that the supreme leader would visit any government official so far beneath him. He met only with the country's top leadership. On the rare occasions that the Supreme Leader had made such unexpected visits, it had invariably spelled trouble for the man that received him.

When he suddenly showed up that hot summer's day at his office, he brought a sobering message. He had chosen Nouri to undertake a great mission; he was to find a way to strike at the heart of the United States of America. He offered no explicit instructions regarding how he should do it, preferring to leave it to his discretion, only that he expected results. There had been a sense of urgency in his voice as he stressed that he had come to deliver the message himself to ensure that nothing was lost along the way. Nouri was to find a way to punish America; he wanted the Great Satan humiliated or better yet, destroyed. They had to pay a price for attacking and blaspheming the Supreme Leader, calling him a petty dictator, and for their transgressions against the Iranian Republic, and against Islam all over the world. Nouri was given exactly one year, no more, to accomplish the objective or his life would be forfeit. As the head of the General Ministry of Defense and Armed Forces Logistics, it would be his responsibility to execute the attack against the evil forces of American imperialism.

It had been only by sheer coincidence that the means and opportunity to meet the Supreme Leader's demands had fallen squarely into his hands. By a strange twist of fate, one of Nouri's assistants had a relative in America, a relative that had been working on some type of top-secret military weapon. It was not so unusual for such information to find its way to Nouri's ears, especially given his position within the government. When his assistant had first mentioned something about the weapon, Nouri had laughed it off, assuming it just an idle tale. However, with the one-year deadline rapidly approaching, Nouri was grasping at straws. He had started asking for more specifics about the cousin and what it was that he was working on for the Americans. After speaking with some of the top government research scientists that dealt with electromagnetic theory, Nouri gradually had became convinced that the cousin's stories were indeed true. He spent weeks searching for the leverage against the cousin that he would need to make it happen, but he was eventually rewarded for his efforts. He had permitted his assistant's brother, Abdul, to handle the theft of the weapon. The brother's terrorist connections had often proven useful to Nouri.

Now, at last, everything was finally coming together. From the moment his assistant had first made him aware of the top–secret experiment that the Americans had been working on, he knew such a weapon could be the means to achieve the end that he had been instructed to accomplish. They would not only humiliate the American dogs, they would crush them.

Now that he had received word that the device was in transit, he needed to confirm that the rocket was ready for launch. He had already notified the other world governments that they planned to launch a "communications" satellite into space. They would launch the "satellite" the moment the device arrived at the launch site. They would have to activate the device immediately once it was in position, as the Americans would surely retaliate as soon as they linked the theft of the device to his government. Nouri knew that there would unquestionably be a military response. While their allies in the Russian government had been able to keep the Americans at arms length for decades, it was doubtful that an American response to such a hostile action on their part would be anything they could help with. They would be on their own this time.

Nouri contacted the man he had placed in charge of the launch site to ensure that they were ready. "General Sadr, I need to know the exact status of the launch.... Excellent, I expect the package to be here within the next two hours. Be prepared to get it onboard and ready as soon as you receive it. You will have no more than one hour to install the weapon, understand? We will have only a one–hour window before we must launch. Do you understand? ... excellent. I know, and I understand the challenges, General. You must however understand how critical it is that we move with all expediency. If we are not successful in achieving our objective, we can expect a swift and determined retaliation by the Americans. We have no choice now but to proceed according to plan for the glory of Allah, and for our Supreme Leader. We have already crossed beyond the point of no return. We execute our plan and crush the Great Satan, or we perish, there is no other option. Very good then, General, I will make certain that our man is onsite in time to ensure the package is installed correctly. May Allah be praised! Goodbye."

Amir paused for a few moments before calling for his "expert" on the device. A young man walked into his office a few minutes later.

"Hello, Ali. I trust that you have been enjoying your stay in your beautiful native country."

"Is my family safe?" he asked.

"Yes, of course your family is safe, at least for the moment. Unfortunately, however, I cannot tell you for how long this will remain so. The Americans will soon learn of what has happened to their precious weapon. They will martial their full resources and launch an attack against our noble republic. I recommend that if you ever want to see your family alive again, you should work quickly to install the device as soon as it arrives at the launch site. You must work as quickly and accurately as possible to prepare it. We must not miss our launch window, if we are going to activate it as it passes over America. Remember Ali, the life, or death, of your wife, your children, your family, and the rest of your countrymen, now rests solely in your hands, not mine. Look at the bright side my friend, if you are successful, you will be celebrated as a national hero among our people for many generations to come, the man that brought down the Great Satan! May Allah be praised!"

"May Allah be praised," Ali offered weakly. Nouri pressed a button and several Revolutionary Guards came into the office. "Escort our friend here to the launch site. Let nothing deter you. Do you understand?"

"Yes, sir," they answered.

"Now go, Ali. May Allah be with you."

As he watched them leave his office, Nouri was confident that he could now depend on Ali to install the EMP device. After all, he had just given him plenty of motivation, which happened to also be the truth. He just hoped that it would be enough.

His phone rang.

"Really, that is excellent news my friend! Please get it to the launch vehicle immediately. A technician of mine named Ali will be arriving to install the device any minute now. Please ensure that the device is onboard when he arrives and that he has everything he needs. Keep a close eye on our friend while he does his work, just in case..."

Nouri felt his stomach tighten He wondered if this was how Khrushchev felt during the Cuban Missile Crisis. The launch of this EMP weapon was going to change everything. He and his people would be victorious over the Great Satan, or they would end up as radioactive ash after the Americans went nuclear. Either way, it appeared that the protracted struggle with the West was about to end. The great Persian Empire was about to rise again, or fall forever.

Sometime later, the phone rang again.

"Hello? Yes, sir. All is going as planned. I am having the device installed now even as we speak. The rocket is ready for launch immediately after the installation is complete. Yes, sir. May Allah be praised!"

A minute later, the phone rang yet once more.

"Very well, I understand. Are you certain that the installation has been done *exactly* as I instructed, in accordance with all of the instructions that I provided? Very well then. You do understand that we will not get another opportunity to strike at the Americans? Very well then, you have a go, you are cleared to launch. May Allah be with us."

Nouri walked over to the cabinet and took out a glass and a bottle. It was his favorite brand of whiskey. The irony was not lost on him that his favorite brand came from the very same country that he was now preparing to destroy. To him, the whole business with the Americans was regrettable. Like many in his country, he *liked* the Americans. He was a victim of his times and of his leaders. He would do what he had to, what was required of him, and accept whatever came from it. Perhaps, one day, his people would make peace with America and end the many years of hostility with the West.

He looked out of his window and watched as the rocket lifted off and then raced toward the sky. With a successful launch, the weapon was now on its way to its rendezvous with destiny. According to General Sadr, they would have to wait approximately four hours before the satellite would be in position. Nouri hoped that the diplomats would be able to buy him the time he needed. Once the Americans learned that the device was missing, they would be devoting all of their resources to finding it, and there could be little doubt that Iran would be on the Americans' short list of suspects. Furthermore, they would certainly be watching the launch closely as they always did to assess any threat, it would only be a matter of time before the

CIA or NSA put the pieces together, linking the missing EMP weapon with the Iranian satellite launch, with the Americans showing up at their doorstep soon after. In addition to a retaliatory strike, the Americans would certainly attempt to destroy the device in space before it was ever in position to fire. There were many risks with an effort like this, but the payoff, if they were successful, was just too enormous to pass up. There was a knock on the door. It was his assistant, Habib.

"Sir?"

"Yes, Habib, what is it?"

"We have been contacted by the American State Department. They are demanding we return their EMP device to them, immediately, or they will consider it an act of war and act accordingly." Nouri considered the news for a few moments.

"Well then, that is good news isn't it? It sounds like the Americans suspect we have something to do with the missing device, but they do not yet have enough evidence to act. What has our response been?"

"The standard denial, sir. The minister of foreign affairs has told the Americans that we have no knowledge of any stolen EMP device. In fact, he asked why the Americans would create such a device to begin with."

Nouri stroked his moustache, as he was prone to do when he pondering weighty matters.

"Good, good. This will not last long, but it should buy us some time. What of any American military movement?"

"They are in the process of moving aircraft carriers into the Persian Gulf. There has been increased chatter among the members of NATO. It sounds like the Americans are moving their military into position to attack us."

"We must act quickly, Habib. Contact the president and the Supreme Leader. Let me know when you have them on the phone. We must receive authorization to act the moment we are in position."

"Yes, Sir."

CHAPTER 12

John Abbott arrived at the NASA Headquarters in Washington, DC just as Smith, and the others were taking possession of the device. He was nervous about the phone call he had received a couple of hours earlier. When he got to his office, Marcus Brown met him at the door.

"Hi, John. I'm sorry to bother you at home."

"No problem, Marcus. You did the right thing. We need to get on top of this right away. Have you contacted the NOAA's space weather prediction center yet?"

"I have. They had already seen it and are preparing to generate a warning."

"We need to warn the president."

"I have already started working on pulling together some of the data for the briefing."

"Good. I will call his chief of staff to give him a heads–up. How soon can you have the briefing ready?"

"About thirty minutes."

"Excellent. Did you call Nancy?"

"I did. She is already here."

"Good. We need her to go ahead and run this up the flagpole for everyone now. DHS, DOI, DOD, they all need to know that this is coming."

"But, John, what if it turns out to be a false alarm?"

"It isn't. I have been watching the activity for a while now. I predicted something like this was going to happen. Do you have the data?"

"Sure. Here you go."

John took several minutes to review the data, nodding his head as he read the data. "This is bad, Marcus. This looks like it will be the worst Coronal Mass Ejection ever recorded, or even heard of for that matter. Are you certain about this data?"

"I am. I checked it three times before I even called you," said Marcus.

"This will *definitely* be big enough to affect the power grid, it could cause interruptions coast–to–coast. We better make sure someone notifies them immediately."

"They are on the list, John."

"What about the International Space Station?" John asked.

"Fortunately the crew was due to return tomorrow anyway so they should be back on the ground by the time the storm hits," answered Marcus.

"Well, at least there is *some* good news to be had."

Marcus left the office as John looked up the number to the president's chief of staff and placed the call. This was definitely one call he was not looking forward to make. Rob Thornton was a jerk to deal with on a good day, but with news like this, he predicted the conversation would be something less then enjoyable. His secretary answered the phone.

"Chief of staff's office."

"Good evening, Harriett. It's John Abbott with NASA. I need to speak with Rob immediately. Can you call him for me please?"

"May I ask what the call is in regards to, Dr. Abbott?"

"It's a national emergency," said John.

"I will call him immediately. Your callback number please?"

"Sure. He can reach me at 555–1122."

"I will ask him to call you right away," she said.

"Thank you." The phone clicked in his ear.

As he hung up, Nancy Lee appeared in the doorway. "John, I just wanted to let you know that I have contacted everyone on the list to make them aware of the situation, and I have forwarded the brief to them."

"Great, Nancy, thanks. Would you tell Marcus I would like to see him again, please?"

"You bet."

A couple of minutes later, Marcus appeared.

"Yeah, John?"

"Any estimation of the amount of damage we can expect to see to the grid, Marcus?"

"Not yet. I expect this storm will be powerful enough to knock out most of the grid for up to a week or so. It's hard to say for sure however."

"What about the military?" John asked.

"We should probably recommend grounding all non–essential aircraft during the storm," said Marcus. Only..."

"Only what?" John asked.

"Well, I have a friend over at the DOD, and he told me something earlier today about some kind of a flare up in tensions with the Iranians."

"Oh no."

"Yeah, that's what I said. You know how it goes, timing is everything," said Marcus.

"Sounds like I might as well go ahead and call home and let the wife know it's going to be another late night."

"I'll wager that Beth will be happy about that."

John just grimaced and nodded his head. "Ecstatic."

CHAPTER 13

President Michaels lay down on the sofa, hoping to get just a few moments of rest. After yet another exhausting day filled with constant briefings, rushing from meeting to meeting, and dealing with constant flare–ups all over the world, he had finally found a precious fifteen minutes alone before his next meeting. It was on days like this that John Michaels questioned what had ever possessed him to seek the office of the presidency. The occasional spells of regret rarely persisted for very long how-ever, because despite the occasional moments of doubt, John Michaels enjoyed his role as president, he *relished* it. Like so many others that had attained great power, he enjoyed the pres-tige, power, and control that his office afforded him over oth-ers. As he reflected on this sad state of affairs, he felt the pangs of regret once more as he recalled how, during the course of his studies at Harvard, he had written a paper on the found-ing fathers. During the course of his research for the paper, he had been surprised to learn the degree of personal sacrifice that so many had endured for the sake of freedom. To the founding fathers, it was not about power and control over others, it was about freedom *from* the power and control *by* others. According to what he had learned, the first president, General George Washington, had only, with great reluctance, accepted the office of the presidency and did so only for the sake of a fledgling country which was only in it's infancy.

Perhaps the founding fathers had been more noble and just, both in their motives and in their intentions, but then they did not have to contend with twenty-four hour news programs, with billion-dollar organizations, and with individuals that expected some kind of return on their investment once the election had been won. No, he had long ago concluded that it was his job just to hold things together, to keep things from falling apart. He would be content if he were able to do that until his term was over.

Michaels yawned as he began drifting off to sleep. It would be good to catch a quick nap before his meeting with the joint chiefs. He closed his eyes, and soon he was fast asleep. He was jolted awake by a knock on the door.

"Yes, come in," he said, rubbing his eyes and shaking himself awake. Rob Thornton opened the door and walked into the Oval Office.

"Am I disturbing you, sir?"

"No Rob, not at all. What can I do for you?"

"Mr. President, we have a situation that I felt required your immediate attention."

"Wait just a moment, Rob. Please take a seat." The president looked at his watch. He must have slept longer than he thought. He was late for his meeting with the joint chiefs. He pressed a button on his phone. "Susan?"

"Yes, Mr. President?"

"Please let the joint chiefs know I will be a few minutes late for our briefing."

"Yes, Mr. President," she answered.

"What is it Rob?"

"I am sorry to disturb you sir; especially since we are already running behind schedule. It's important, sir, and it really can't wait. I felt that we need to discuss this before meeting with the joint chiefs."

"Well get on with it, Rob. What is it that is so important? Does it have anything to do with the solar flare? By the way, have all of the utility companies been alerted so they can take steps to mitigate the impact of the flare?" the president asked.

"Yes sir, Mr. President," answered Thornton.

"What about the military?"

"Yes, sir, Mr. President."

"Have we alerted our allies and NATO?" the president inquired.

"Yes, sir," Thornton answered.

"Have we done everything that we can possibly do to prepare for it, Rob?"

"I believe we have, sir." Thornton replied.

"When is it due to strike the earth?"

"ETA is about thirty minutes, sir," Thornton answered, after glancing at his watch.

"All right then, I guess all we can do now is wait to see what happens. I'm sorry, Rob. You said there was another important matter you wanted to discuss?"

"Yes, Mr. President, it concerns the Iranians."

"Not the Iranians, again! I'm sick and tired of hearing about the flipping Iranians! We should have taken them out fifty years ago when they took those hostages. What is it this time?"

"We think that it was the Iranians that took the missing EMP device, Project Blackout, which vanished from the lab recently."

"Oh, *now that's great, just great.* Do we have any idea what their intentions are?"

"No, sir. You know how the Iranians are—they are as unpredictable as ever."

"Is it possible that they simply intend to use it as leverage, to try and persuade us to lift sanctions?"

"Well, Mr. President, that certainly is a possibility. There are many in the CIA and the NSA, however, that are firmly convinced that their intentions are much more bold and aggressive than that. They believe that it is highly unlikely that even the Iranians would be foolish enough to hijack one of our most advanced weapons without expecting repercussions."

"Then what are you saying, Rob? Are you saying that the CIA thinks Iran will attack us with our own weapon?"

"Yes, sir, I am. We can probably conclude that with something this big, it is likely something that they intend to use against us, and soon."

Michaels stood up and walked over to the window. "Now why would they be stupid enough to do that? Don't the Iranians know that we will use overwhelming force, even nuclear weapons, if they attack us directly?"

"Well, let's think about that for a moment sir. If they were able to launch a successful attack with the EMP weapon, they could conceivably knock out our communications systems and cripple our ability to coordinate a successful counter–attack."

"That still doesn't make any sense. It would take more than one weapon to cripple us to the point that we can't handle a country the size of Iran."

"The CIA doubts that the Iranians would attempt something like this on their own, Mr. President. Intelligence points to them getting support, *substantial* support."

"Who would dare help them launch an attack against us, the Russians? The Chinese?"

"They believe North Korea; possibly even China, Mr. President."

"Terrific. This just gets better and better, Rob. North Korea *and* China." At this, Michaels began pacing the Oval Office. "Any idea how and when they will attack?"

"We believe it's *imminent,* sir. Do you remember someone mentioning that the Iranians launched a satellite into space earlier today?"

"Yes, I remember there was something about a communications satellite being launched in one of the briefs this morning."

"Yes, sir, that was the briefing from the NSA. They now believe that the so–called "communications satellite" may have contained something other than just communications equipment, Mr. President."

"But the EMP device was only just reported missing yesterday!"

"That is correct, sir. However, the device was *stolen* two days earlier. Apparently, the Iranians have been planning this operation for quite some time."

"Well then we will have to take that satellite out immediately just to be on the safe side. Better to risk a confrontation with the Iranians over taking out their bird than to be caught with our pants down. I will give the order during the meeting with the joint chiefs."

"There may be no time to wait, sir. The Iranian satellite will be over the United States in a matter of minutes. We *might* have as much as thirty minutes, sir, but no more, depending on whether they are attacking a specific city or trying to take out the entire grid. The Iranians obviously fear retaliation and a pre-emptive strike Mr. President, so they are likely to strike at us at the first opportunity they have. However, it will take us at least that long to prepare our satellite killers to take out their bird."

"Let's go, Rob."

The two men walked briskly down to the meeting room where the joint chiefs were waiting. Everyone stood up when the president walked in.

"Please be seated. Ladies and gentlemen, I'll get right to the point. I've just learned that the Iranian satellite that was launched earlier today might be carrying our missing experimental EMP weapon onboard, and that we have less than thirty minutes until they are in position to attack. Is the aircraft carrier USS George Walker Bush still in the Persian Gulf?"

"Yes, sir, it is."

"Very good. I want you to raise the readiness level to DEF-CON 2."

"Yes sir, Mr. President."

"Rob, I want you to contact the Iranians. Tell them that if they launch or attempt to launch an attack against us with the EMP weapon, it will be considered as an act of war, and we will be forced to *immediately* retaliate with any and *all* means at our disposal. Tell them that we'll turn their country into a parking lot."

"Yes, Mr. President."

"And Rob?"

"Yes, Mr. President?"

"I want you to convey that same message to the Chinese and the North Koreans. If they are involved in this, the same goes for them. Make it clear that we are quite serious. Also—I want you to notify our NATO friends and make them aware of the situation."

"Yes, Mr. President," Rob Thornton said before leaving the room. President Michaels continued, "General Miller?"

"Yes, Mr. President?"

"What are our options for taking out that satellite?"

"We can shoot it down with our ground–based or satellite-based laser system, Mr. President, or we could try shooting it down with a missile," answered Miller.

"Which will take the least amount of time?" asked Michaels.

"The ground–based laser would be the fastest way, Mr. President."

"Make it happen, General—now. We need to take it out before their satellite passes overhead and they activate the EMP."

"I understand. I will give the order right away, sir." the general replied.

"Thank you."

General Miller left the table and walked over to a far corner of the room where several phones were located. He picked up the phone and started making calls. He returned to the table after a few minutes.

"Mr. President, I have given the order. They will fire the laser as soon as they are ready. Their bird should be in position within a few minutes."

"Thank you, General Miller."

"Mr. President. There is something I feel I need to share with you about that EMP device."

"Go on, General."

"The Iranians may not know that the EMP device is still experimental, something we were still developing. There is something else, sir, something very important that they *definitely* did not know; something that none of us were aware of, something that was not included in any of the reports that had been forwarded to us from Logan. The device is extremely powerful *and* is *highly* unstable. After the Iranians stole the device, Scott McBride, the project manager for Project Blackout, called and told me that this is a new and extremely powerful experimental prototype. It still wasn't even considered a viable weapon yet because they had been unsuccessful in finding a way to control the blast."

"Get to it, General—what is your point?"

"Sir, if the Iranians try and activate this device, it may well impact a much larger area then they think it will. Mr. President, it is possible, remotely possible perhaps but still possible, that the *entire planet* could be impacted if that device is activated at just the right altitude."

"And how high is the orbit of their satellite, General?"

"It's at just the right altitude, Mr. President."

"Great."

Just as President John Michaels finished saying "great" to General Miller, there was a brilliant flash of light outside, followed by a crackling sound. Two seconds later the White House went dark.

CHAPTER 14

Vic Masters squinted as he awoke to find he was staring into the morning sun. He turned his head away and when he tried to open his eyes again, he found everything was blurry. He tried to move and felt a sharp pain in his side. He cursed as he realized that he must have broken some ribs. Slowly, his awareness came into focus as he emerged from the fog of unconsciousness. He tried to piece together what had happened. They had been driving along the highway when the driver had suddenly lost control of the bus. When they came to a sharp curve, he had been unable to follow the curve and after leaving the road, the bus had run over an embankment before finally coming to a stop on its side in a ditch.

Masters noticed that the chain that had bound him had snapped sometime during the crash. After looking around, he found the driver still unconscious, bleeding on the ground not far from the bus, next to where the armed guards lay sprawled out on the ground in like fashion. After considering what action to take next, he decided that he would take some of the weapons and the keys from the guards and make a run for it. He made his way to the front of the bus and found that the guards were unconscious but not dead. He searched for the keys and found them clipped to the belt of one of the guards. After relieving the guards of the two .45 caliber semi–automatics handguns and one of their shotguns, he looked at the two guards and weighed whether he should kill them or let them live. After some deliberation, he grabbed the gun by the barrel and smacked them both on the back of the head with the butt of the firearm. *Now at least I don't have to worry about a couple of cowboy guards breathing down my neck anytime soon,* he thought, as he walked away from the wreck. Masters looked around, trying to get his bearings on where they were. Judging by the surroundings and a single road sign, it looked like they had been about halfway between the jail and the prison when the wreck had occurred. That meant that they were pretty much in the middle of nowhere, which troubled him. It was always easier to lose oneself in a big city than it was out in the countryside. Strangers stood out like sore thumbs in rural communities, whereas anonymity is commonplace in the larger, metropolitan areas, where someone that does not want to be found can easily blend in.

The prison bus had wrecked on a smaller state road and not on a federal highway, where traffic was typically much heavier. He had not seen any cars, trucks, or any other traffic on the road since the bus, which even for a state road seemed a bit odd, but he attributed it to being in redneck country. He decided to follow the road a bit in hopes that it would lead him to a nearby town. After walking along the road for another hour, he came along another wreck and two cars stopped in the middle of the road. He was mildly curious why there were no police or ambulances onsite yet as it looked like someone had been injured.

As he continued walking down the road to the next town, he continued to find more and more abandoned cars along the highway. When he finally found one that he liked particularly well, he decided to see if he could drive instead of walking, figuring he might have less chance of being picked up by federal marshals or the state police. After several failed attempts at hot–wiring the car, he eventually abandoned the effort and pushed on. Frustrated that the risk with the attempted car theft had accomplished nothing, he picked up the pace and moved a little faster down the road. He decided that it would be safer to stay just off the main road. In the first populated area that he came across, he saw a number of large gatherings of people outside. It looked as if entire neighborhoods were just standing outside of their homes talking. While he was curious as to what had brought so many people out of their homes in such large numbers, he was beginning to find it difficult to stay out of sight, not to mention the fact that he was still wearing his prison uniform. *Why didn't I think about taking the guard's clothes?* Just then, he saw a home that had clothes hanging on a clothesline in the backyard to dry, and decided to take a quick look for something else to wear. As he approached the house, he noticed some men's clothing hanging on the line. Judging by their appearance, the clothes would be a little big on him, but he was not in any position to go buy a tailor–made outfit, at least not yet. He quickly took the clothes off the line and made his way into some nearby woods.

He changed out of his prison uniform and into the stolen clothes before continuing on his way. Based on the growing number of residential neighborhoods he was passing, he estimated that he would be coming across a town soon. The borrowed clothing would enable him to move around more freely now, even in a busy town, but he needed a plan regarding how he would proceed once he found the right one. He figured he would probably just steal some money and then buy himself a bus ticket to the nearest big city. Perhaps then, he would have a better chance at blending in and going unnoticed by the authorities.

With the day already well spent, it looked to Masters as if the sun would soon set. If he did not make it to a town soon, he would try to find a place to stay for the night. While he had spent many nights sleeping under the stars, it was getting cold, and he was not properly equipped for camping. The last thing he needed was to get sick.

Finally, after another hour of walking, he came to a sign that said, "Brighton: One Mile." It would be over the next hill. He was looking forward to getting some rest before moving on. He had been walking for most of the day and he was exhausted. What he saw as he approached the small town however stunned him. The town appeared to be the size of a typical, Midwestern small town, with many of the characteristics of small towns scattered across the American landscape. There were a few tall buildings, mostly clustered around the middle of the downtown area. There was also a large water tower and an ancient railroad track that ran along the eastern part of town. The most unusual feature in this particular small town however, what stood out the most to Masters as he stood under the night sky transfixed, watching the town from the top of the hill, was the large passenger plane that had crashed in the middle of the downtown area, and the inferno that had nearly consumed the entire town. Even more surprising yet to Masters was what he didn't see, something was missing from the scene that he could not explain. There were no firefighters, no ambulances, and no media. There were only a small handful of people hopelessly throwing bucket-fuls of water on a raging inferno.

Masters finally asked himself the question that had been nagging at the back of his mind for most of the day. *What in the world is going on?*

CHAPTER 15

"History...and the future...." Dr. Norman Weller began, "that is what we are here to discuss; that is what has brought us together today. We have come together to build a bridge, a bridge over troubled water, a bridge that can reach across the great divide that has separated the two worlds of science and theology since the Middle Ages. As everyone here knows so very well, the common belief, held for centuries, is that the barriers that stand between us are insurmountable, that our two worldviews are simply incompatible.

Our critics sit idly on the sidelines complaining while doing nothing to help, watching as humanity races headlong toward self–annihilation, victims of our own phenomenally successful technological achievements. These useless spectators do nothing themselves, except scoff at us for simply suggesting that perhaps, just maybe, the world's greatest minds should engage in a productive and civil discourse on finding ways to address the many problems that plague our post–modern world. They laugh when we propose looking for common threads, and finding common platforms, and when we emphasize the common stake that we all share for addressing the many dangers that threaten our society, our culture, our civilization. These critics ridicule and belittle us as we search out ways to find consensus on a course of action that can keep us from destroying ourselves, because make no mistake about it, when technology and the lust for power races ahead of morality and wisdom, destruction awaits for all.

Now, it is true that our mission runs counter to the prevalent belief that our differing points of view will cause us to fail. Most people continue to believe that the underlying hostility and distrust between science and theology have run so deep for so long that cooperation is out of the question and that we cannot possibly succeed. However, it is my unwavering belief that we have no choice *but to succeed,* that failure is not an option! I believe, I know, that in order for humanity to survive, we must shatter this ancient myth once and for all, that we must confront our differences and overcome them!" The crowd rose to their feet as the auditorium erupted in a roar of applause.

James White looked around as many in the audience rose to their feet, clapping their hands fervently in affirmation of the message they had just heard. He looked to the right of the stage and then to the left, admiring the large screens that hung at either end of the stage. A close–up of Norman Weller's smiling face adorned each screen, as his eyes wandered across the audience. James White quickly decided that Weller was nothing, if not a charismatic speaker, albeit with a bit of a flair for the dramatic.

"My friends," continued Weller, "please consider the following: global warming, the proliferation of nuclear weapons, the spread of chemical and biological terrorism, the moral and ethical considerations involving abortion, genetics, and the troubling aspects of human cloning. I am mindful of the considerable perspective I gained in college as I studied Dr. Frank Drake, and his now famous Drake Equation, which attempts to calculate the probable number of communicating civilizations in existence throughout the galaxy. As I am sure many of you know, the final component of Frank Drake's equation fL, is the fraction of the planet's life during which the communicating civilization survives. Put another way, 'f' represents the number of civilizations that survive the dangers that accompany the development of powerful, advanced technology, long enough that they are able to reach out and communicate to other civilizations across the cosmos. Drake assumed that most civilizations would end up destroying themselves with their own technology. I suppose his reasoning was that most civilizations tend to develop powerful technologies faster than they can mature as a species, invariably leading them to destroy themselves with those very same technologies. Without a corresponding growth in the development of spirituality and peace, of civics and morality, of freedom and liberty, of maturity, of respect for the weak as well as the powerful, how can any civilization survive?"

James noticed that Weller paused for a moment to let the last thought sink in to his audience.

"That is why I believe that we should, that we *must*, find ways to work together so that we can help guide *our* world on a path to develop our civilization in a balanced and comprehensive manner. That is why we formed The Unity, an organization with a vital mission, to bring together the best and the brightest of the world's foremost theologians and scientists." Another roar of applause circulated throughout the auditorium. He paused long enough to soak in the generous amount of enthusiasm and excitement in the room. It was easy to see that everyone in the room felt that they were part of something special. Weller continued.

"Just take a look around the room, my esteemed colleagues, take a look at the great minds, from some of the most prestigious institutions on our wonderful, beautiful planet. Representing the Church, we have men like Dr. James White, president of the conservative International Baptist Convention, as well as Monsignor Fennini, representing the Holy See on behalf of the Roman Catholic Church. Each of these men holds doctorates in theology *and* ministry, and if that was not enough, each holds a PhD in philosophy as well.

Representing the scientific community, we have again some of the best and brightest scientific minds, men such as Dr. Bjorn Yvornsky, the world's foremost computer scientist, currently blazing a new trail as a pioneer in grid computer design, as well as Dr. Henry Miller, the world's foremost climatologist and leading expert on global warming.

Let there be no doubt that the mere presence of such a diverse group of brilliant and educated men attests to their great wisdom, to their recognition of the danger our world is currently in, and to their determination like so many of us here, to do something about it and act!"

James White reflected that, while a bit theatrical, Weller's words and mannerisms reflected a sincerity and forthrightness that he found very refreshing. As he joined in the applause, he realized that indeed, such a diverse group of men and women *could* change the world, or at least have a significant role to play in such a change. In a brief flash of recognition, his thoughts turned back to the most unusual dream he had experienced just before making the trip to Washington. He once again found himself wondering for a moment whether the dream and the conference were somehow related.

As fate would have it, just as this thought crossed his mind he noticed a young man trying to get Weller's attention from the side of the stage. In response, Weller motioned to the young man to come forward to speak with him. After a few moments, Weller nodded his head as the young man left, and motioned to someone at the back of the room.

"Ladies and gentlemen, I apologize, but we have something of a breaking and somewhat serious situation developing, that I feel we should take a look at for just a few moments, before continuing with the conference. With your indulgence…"

Weller gave a nod to the man who in turn motioned to someone in the back of the room. The large screens that had been displaying Weller's on the two screens suddenly switched to a television news broadcast. Headlines splashed across the screen read, "New Crisis in the Persian Gulf."

"We have several new reports coming in now. We do not yet have all of the details, but it appears that the United States has been steadily moving forces into the Persian Gulf area and the South China Sea for several days. Just moments ago, President Michaels ordered the extraordinary and nearly unprecedented step of raising military readiness to DEFCON 2. According to sources within the administration, the Iranians may have stolen an extremely dangerous, top secret, experimental weapon from the US Government, causing the flurry of recent activity in and around the Persian Gulf. Our sources tell us that the Iranians, possibly with the support of the North Koreans and perhaps even the Chinese, may be planning an imminent attack against the United States using that very same weapon. I—wait just a moment please."

The journalist was handed a piece of paper that he quickly scanned. "I have just learned that there have been rumors that the stolen device could be a highly experimental Electromagnetic Pulse, or EMP, weapon of some sort. Obviously, the president must be very concerned about this development since he has ordered several carrier strike groups to the Persian Gulf. We have also been told that if true, such a weapon might be used to ..." *Click.*

In an instant, the room was plunged into complete darkness as the screens went blank and the room went black.

As he struggled to find his way in the darkness, James White thought about the dream, and found that he had a sinking feeling in his gut.

CHAPTER 16

"Thank you, Master Takata." Conrad said as he looked down and bowed to the aged oriental martial art's master. "We need to return to the base now, since Frank and I both are on duty this evening. I hope that your power comes back on soon."

"Thank you, Conrad," Takata answered, smiling as he pointed to the lamps. "It has been a long time since I trained students by lanterns; it brings back many warm memories. It is a different experience, is it not?"

"Indeed it is sir," Conrad answered.

"Thank you, Master Takata," Frank said as he also looked down and bowed to Takata.

"You are also welcome, Frank. You have made remarkable progress over the past year. You and Conrad are among the best students I have ever trained. I am honored to have you both as my pupils."

"The honor is all ours, sir. Take care," said Conrad. Frank and Conrad left the compound and climbed into the Honda.

"That's odd," remarked Conrad.

"What is it, Conrad?"

"I'm not sure." He pushed the button to start the car but nothing happened. "It looks like it won't start."

"Maybe we should call the base to let them know we will be running behind." Frank pulled out his cell phone to make the call.

"Well, now, what are the odds of that happening?" Frank asked. "My cell phone is dead!"

"Let's see if we can use Master Takata's phone," said Conrad. The two men climbed back out of the car and went back inside the compound. After a few moments, the elderly instructor appeared at the door.

"Is something wrong?"

"Yes, Master Takata. My car will not start. May we please use your phone?"

"Of course, please come in." They walked into the house and Takata led them to the phone.

"Thank you, sir." Takata smiled and nodded his head. Conrad picked up the phone and began to dial. After a few moments, he added, "Master Takata, *your* phone is dead, too!"

"Strange, that has never happened before. I have a cell phone back in my bedroom. Give me a moment and you can use it to call your base."

"Thank you, sir."

After several minutes, he returned with the phone. "I cannot explain this. The phone should be fully charged, but now it is not working."

"That is strange," Conrad mused, puzzled by the strange coincidences.

"What is the likelihood that the car, the land line, which still receives power from the phone company, *and* both cell phones just happen to all be dead, all at the same time?" he asked.

"I would say that the odds of them being unrelated are astronomical," Frank answered. "Still, we can't know for certain."

Takata reached walked over to a drawer and removed a set of keys. Here, try my car. You can take it to the base and see about getting some assistance with your car."

"Thank you, Master Takata. I am extremely grateful, sir. We will have your car back within two hours—I promise."

"You are most welcome, Conrad."

The two left and walked over to their instructor's car. After climbing in, Conrad inserted the key into the ignition and said, "Okay, here we go!" He turned the key and nothing happened.

"Wow. That is really strange." The two sat in the car for a minute or two before Frank spoke first.

"Wait, I have an idea." The pair walked back over to the door of their instructor's home. The old master returned once more to the door.

"*My* car would not start either?" he asked, raising his eyebrows.

The pair shook their heads in unison.

"That is very strange indeed."

"Master Takata, do you have any battery powered radios?" The man thought for a moment.

"Yes, I believe I do. Wait just a moment." He walked into the living room and returned with a small portable radio in his hand. "Here, try this. I replaced the batteries the day before yesterday," he said to Frank as he handed him the radio. Frank turned the dial to turn on the radio and once again, nothing happened. "What do you think is happening, Conrad?" asked Takata.

"I don't know for certain, sir, but I do have an idea. It is a bit far–fetched, but it is something we studied in War College."

"What are you thinking, Conrad?" asked Frank, who by now wore a puzzled expression with a furrowed brow.

"We were studying various ways of knocking out an enemy's communications infrastructure. The theory was that if you interrupted their command and control infrastructure, you could eliminate the enemy's chain of command, making it much easier to penetrate the enemy's defenses."

"What are you talking about, Frank? What does *that* have to do with the cars not working?"

"It's called Electromagnetic Pulse or EMP for short."

"You believe that some enemy has launched a military attack against the United States?" asked Takata.

"I believe it is a *distinct* possibility, sir. A nuclear bomb detonated high enough in the atmosphere could affect a very large area, perhaps whole sections of the country. It would be an effective strategy against a much stronger enemy," said Conrad.

"We have to get back to the base, Conrad," said Frank. "If that is the case, we may well be at war."

"But how will you get back to your base? It is an hour's drive from here, well over sixty miles. You cannot walk that far without provisions; it would take you several days to make such a journey on foot."

"What about you, Master Takata? Do you have provisions enough to last you?"

"My wife and I have a large garden," he said pointing behind his house. "We already grow most of what we eat."

"What about water? If there has been an EMP attack, the water supply is at risk as well."

"We have a well from which we draw our water." He thought for another moment before asking, "Will the government not rebuild the damaged infrastructure?"

"Oh, yes sir, they are probably working to repair the damage even as we speak. However, we have never experienced anything quite like this before, so we are quite unprepared for such an attack."

"I understand. Come with me. You will need provisions if you are determined to go. My wife has canned some of our fruits and vegetables. You can take some of them as well as water. You are welcome to stay here with me, should you choose to do so either now or later. We have plenty for you both. You will always be welcome."

"Thank you, sir," they both answered, almost in unison.

"Ms. Takata and I will gather your supplies. Please, sit while you wait."

The two men bowed deeply and respectfully to their elderly teacher. The man had not only opened his home but his heart to them as well. They could not help but be greatly moved by his generosity.

Conrad and Frank sat and talked for a long while about what the ramifications of such an attack might be and how the military might respond. There was no way for them to tell how widespread the power outages were, or how deeply affected the military, specifically, and the country, in general, might be.

It was well over an hour before the man and his wife had gathered enough supplies for the two men to take with them on their journey. When he came out, he had several containers of water as well as sacks full of food including fruits, vegetables, and even some canned meat.

"Remember," Takata said to them as they set out on their journey, "you are welcome to return to stay with me, should you choose to do so. My home is always open to you *and* to your families."

The two men bid farewell to their teacher and began walking in the direction of the base, wondering the entire time what they would find once they arrived.

CHAPTER 17

It was an incredibly beautiful day; the sun hovered like a bright golden globe in front of a brilliant blue background peppered with snow white clouds. He was young again, sitting outside of his old home, sipping on a cold drink, while his beautiful young wife massaged his shoulders. There was a cool breeze blowing that made him feel so alive. Listening to his children laughing and playing in the yard, he wondered how life could possibly be any better.

He was soundly asleep when the knock came on his door. It was a gentle knock at first, growing steadily louder and louder.

"All right, all right, I'm coming, I'm coming!" Eventually the agitated old man climbed very reluctantly out of his comfortable bed, leaving behind the beautiful dream, the memories from better times long ago. He climbed out of his bed and walked over to the door.

"Who is it?"

"Please open the door, Father—it is me, Hassan!"

Omar opened the door and invited his young friend in.

"What is wrong, Hassan? What are you doing here so early? Is everything okay?"

"No, Father, something is dreadfully wrong. Have you not noticed it? People are talking about it all over the city!"

"What are you talking about, Hassan? I was asleep."

"The power is out all over the city, Father. It is as if the device that we stole from the Americans has been used against *us*. Nothing that uses electricity is working now, anywhere. The power went out sometime last night."

"But, Hassan, I was told just yesterday that they had launched the weapon into space, so that they could activate it over the United States. If that is the case, how could the weapon possibly have been used against us?"

"Perhaps it was Allah's will, his decree that the evil we sought to unleash against the Americans has come down upon our own heads!"

"Now calm down, Hassan—peace. We will find out what is happening. I have friends in the government. I will go and see them later, see if I can find out what they know."

"What are we going to do, Father? This is all *our* doing."

"Peace, Hassan, peace. Everything will be fine."

"But how can we survive without electricity?"

"Our people have done so for thousands of years. Besides, I am sure the government will have the power restored very soon."

"I hope that is so, Father."

As he continued consoling his friend, Omar contemplated what it all meant.It was late in the afternoon when Omar finally arrived outside of the Ministry of Defense. It had taken much longer to make the journey on foot. He had tried starting his car, but found it just as his young friend had said. It appeared that, indeed, all modern technology in his country had failed overnight. If that were the case, it would have a profound impact on their country. It was one thing for the electricity to be out temporarily, it was something altogether different, however, when even battery-powered technology failed. His people had not experienced life in the heat of Persia without the benefit of electricity for a hundred years. How would they react when they learned what had happened?

As he walked up the stairs leading to the entrance, Omar wondered whether his old friend would even remember him, much less see him, after so long. It had been many years since they served together in the Republican Guard. It was possible he would no longer remember their friendship. Still, they had been such close friends at one time, staring death in the face many times over and living to tell the tale. His friendship with Amir notwithstanding, he and Hassan had been instrumental in the capturing of the American EMP Weapon, surely that would count for something. He stopped and sat down on a bench outside of the entrance to the Ministry of Defense to catch his breath. As he rested, he contemplated his role in stealing the EMP weapon. Would he be able to live with himself after learning the truth? His old friend would see him; he would have to.

As the burning in his lungs eased and he felt strength returning to his weary legs, Omar rose and passed through the double doors at the front entrance to the MOD. The first thing that struck him was how warm it was inside the building. Because of the low ceilings and the modern materials of which it was constructed, it was clear to him that the building had been built with modern air conditioning in mind. Without the higher ceilings traditionally used for thousands of years, that allowed the heat to rise, it trapped it instead closer to the floor. The heat was almost unbearable. There was a guard sitting at the front desk, with many others scattered throughout, all of them were soaked in sweat. Omar had never seen so many people clustered around the lobby area of the Defense Ministry before.

He approached the front desk, where the guard was busily engaged in a conversation with a man in front of him. After a few minutes, the man left, and Omar stepped up to address the guard.

"The Defense Ministry is closed today. Come back tomorrow."

"I was hoping to talk to my old friend, Amir Nouri, for just a few minutes."

"Minister Nouri? What is your name sir?"

"Omar Obassi."

"Wait here." The man disappeared for a few minutes and then returned."

"Mr. Obassi, Minister Nouri said that he will see you. He requested that you wait a few minutes—he will send someone to get you. Please, be seated here in the waiting area."

"Thank you."

Omar walked over and sat down, thankful for the additional rest as he anxiously awaited a meeting with his old friend. Despite the many people gathered inside the first floor of the ministry, an eerie silence persisted throughout the building, much as he had witnessed on his long walk over to the Ministry building. The result was a somewhat surreal atmosphere, almost as if a collective shock had descended on the city.

As he waited, he reflected on how much the world had changed during his lifetime, in contrast to the thousands of years that preceded the twenty–first century. His ancestors had lived much the same way for thousands of years. Only over the past century had their lifestyles changed so dramatically, with much of it occurring during his lifetime. It was ironic that they, just like the West, had become increasingly dependent on technology. Iran and the West seemed to have more in common than either cared to admit.

For a short while at least, they would have to learn to live in a modern world without modern conveniences. He supposed that given time, they would find a way to restore electricity, but how many of his people would die until that time came? How would his people endure the intense heat of the summers without air conditioning? What would they eat when the food in their refrigerators as well as at the grocery stores and markets went bad? How would they get to work? Where would they work? He wondered how the Americans had been able to turn the tables and use the weapon against his people.

"Mr. Obassi, Minister Nouri will see you now." A young man had come to escort him to see his old friend. The young man was dressed in formal business clothing and was paying a heavy price. He sweat profusely as they climbed the three flights of stairs to the fourth floor where the minister's office was located. The stairwells were substantially warmer then the rest of the building. *Comfortable living*. They had become so dependant on modern conveniences. It was becoming more and more obvious to Omar just how deceptively elegant and effective this EMP weapon was. It gave an army the ability to win a war without shedding a drop of blood.

Finally, they arrived at the minister's office, where his friend worked. The young man knocked on the door. Amir Nouri looked up from the paperwork he had been reading and smiled as he saw his old friend standing in the doorway.

"Mr. Obassi."

"Thank you, Hamid."

Amir Nouri stood up and walked over to his old friend, embracing him for a long moment before stepping back to address him.

"Omar Obassi, it is so good to see you once again, my old, dear friend! How long has it been? "

"I'm not sure really, twenty–five, maybe thirty years?" asked Omar.

"Those were good times, my friend, and I remember them fondly—well, most of them," said Nouri.

"As do I. There are a few I try to forget as well, such as the time we were escorting the president and—."

"Please, I have tried very hard to forget that!" The two men laughed as Nouri motioned for his friend to take a seat. It was very warm in his office, but it was much more comfortable than the walk had been in the stairwell.

"So what brings you to see me, my old friend, after such a very long time?" asked Nouri.

The mood assumed a more serious tone as Omar struggled to find the right words.

"Amir, I don't know whether you are aware of this or not, but I was recently part of an operation that *acquired* something from the Americans, something that could be used against them. You know of what I speak?"

Nouri raised his eyebrows in a manner that suggested a bit of surprise. "Omar, Omar. I am the Minister of Defense. Do you really believe that an operation of that magnitude would be something that I was not aware of? I must confess however, my old friend, that I was not aware that *you* were involved. We opted to call upon the skills of outside agencies that could not be directly tied to us should something go wrong. I would never have permitted you to be involved, had I known—it was much too dangerous for you, my old friend."

"It's not like we never faced such danger in the past?"

"This is true, Omar, but you and I, well, we are not as young as we used to be."

"This is true." Omar paused for a moment and noticed that his friend was becoming slightly agitated; perhaps Omar's surprise visit had taken him away from dealing with the crisis. "Amir, it seems like the entire city lost electricity last night. Is it somehow related to the device we took from America? If so, why have *we* lost power, and not the Americans?"

This time, it was Nouri that paused, reflecting on his friend's question and then how best to answer. He seemed troubled and resistant to answering the question at all. Finally, he let out a heavy sigh and said, "Listen, Omar. What I am about to tell you is above top secret. You and I worked very closely together, and unless you have changed more than I could imagine, which I doubt you have, you will understand the reason for secrets and the potential damage that can be caused when secrets are shared. Promise me, old friend, that what I am about to tell you will stay between us?"

"You have my word, Amir."

"That is good enough for me. Some time ago, I was appointed to lead a mission by our Supreme Leader, a mission to find a way to strike a heavy blow at the Americans. Through some contacts, I learned that the Americans were working on developing a top secret device, an EMP weapon more powerful than any in existence before it. I made our Supreme Leader aware of the device and asked for his permission to steal the device and to use their own weapon against them. He agreed, so we launched the mission that unfortunately you were caught up in."

"Has the weapon been activated and used against the Americans yet?"

"Well that's just it. We launched a satellite with the weapon aboard yesterday. We activated the device last night as soon as it was in position over the United States. Only a few moments after we launched the device the power went out *here* instead."

"Then you mean something went wrong and the weapon was used against us instead? Perhaps the Americans somehow took control of the device at the last minute?"

"I do not believe that to be the case. We had a year to plan this operation and made certain that such an occurrence would not be possible. We implanted a safeguard to ensure that the device would self–destruct before being turned against us."

"Well what happened then?"

"Omar, I believe that the device may have been much more powerful than we ever imagined. As incredible as it might sound, I believe that the device knocked out power all over the planet."

"What, that is impossible! Why would the Americans create a device that would inflict as much damage on their own country as it would on ours? That seems extremely unlikely."

"The device was experimental, perhaps even more experimental than we realized. It must be the reason that the Americans have not already deployed it. They must have had difficulty finding a way to control it. Too bad, the advantages to having such a weapon would be substantial indeed."

"May Allah help us. How long before the power is restored? Do you expect an immediate counter–attack by the Americans once they recover?"

There was another long pause as his old acquaintance struggled once more to answer.

"There is another problem my old friend. When our electrical grid went out last night, we immediately switched our communications to new equipment running on a battery backup system, but it didn't work. In fact, nothing works. It doesn't make any sense; anything not connected to the grid at the time of the attack should still work!"

Nouri threw his hands up in the air in exasperation. As he did so, he got up from his desk and walked over to the nearby window in hopes of catching a breeze. He looked down at the road in front of the ministry building. He noticed a large group of men crossing the road on their way to the ministry building. They were heavily armed and moving quickly. Suddenly, a look of horror emerged on his face.

"Amir, my friend, what is wrong?"

"The Supreme Leader is here. He's come—for me."

CHAPTER 18

Susan awoke to find that the power was still out. She pulled the blankets back over her head in a futile attempt to go back to sleep. Finally, she gave up and pulled the covers off her. She reluctantly climbed out of bed, grumbling and complaining to herself as she did so. Having grown up in Virginia, she had grown accustomed to the occasional power outages in the wintertime, when the ice would build up on the power lines. There was no ice or rain now however; in fact, there was not even a cloud in the sky. Perhaps a car wreck had knocked out the power in her neighborhood. Still, it was unusual for the power to be out for so long with no word from the power company. She had burned candles again for light the night before and done the best she could to stay warm. She checked the phone to see if it was working yet, only to find that it was still dead. She had gone two days without power or a phone. She was also beginning to wonder where her husband was when she needed him the most.

Susan walked into the kitchen looking for something to eat. She was hungry, despite the queasy feeling in the pit of her stomach. She opened the cupboard only to find a dwindling supply of dry goods and can food. She had attempted to go shopping the day before, only to find that the car would not start either. She wondered what else could possibly go wrong.

Susan opened the door just as she felt another wave of nausea come over her. She quickly closed the door and made a run for the bathroom. *At least the water still works.* She flushed the toilet and brushed her teeth. The nausea was getting worse. She could not be certain, since she had missed her doctor's appointment, but she estimated that she must be near the end of her first trimester, which meant she was approximately three months pregnant, assuming of course, that the home pregnancy test was accurate. She had always heard other women talk about morning sickness, but in her estimation, the reports had been substantially *underrated.* Soon the nausea passed, and she made her way back toward the kitchen.

After having more dry cereal for breakfast, she walked back into the bathroom and started the shower. She liked the water nice and hot and hoped that she still had enough hot water in the water heater for one more bath. What she found when she walked through the bathroom door hit her like a blow to the gut. The water was on but barely dripping out of the showerhead. She shook her head, supposing that she had simply turned the water off when she left to grab the towel. Walking back over to the shower she tried turning the water back on only to find that she had never turned it off. Puzzled, she walked over to the sink and tried the water there. Water came out in a stream before slowing to a trickle and finally stopping altogether. She had lost water as well as electricity. *Terrific,* she thought as she stormed out of the bathroom.

What else can go wrong?

She reluctantly dressed without a shower, bemoaning the missed opportunity for a warm, caressing shower first thing in the morning. Without even thinking, she automatically walked over to the kitchen counter to start the morning coffee brewing before catching herself. *Oh yeah, I can't make coffee without electricity, great.*

Exasperated, aggravated, and feeling a bit dirty and unkempt, she walked out of her apartment and made for the elevator. She pressed the button several times before finally realizing the futility of the action. After throwing her arms up in the air and screaming in frustration, she reluctantly made for the stairwell. She walked down the stairs, muttering under her breath. She had decided that she would just walk down to the small grocery store down the road to try to pick up some supplies. Just as she made it to the floor below, she discovered that she was not alone. A tall and slender elderly man, with curly gray hair and spectacles, met her at the stairs. She was relieved to find that it was only her neighbor, Dick.

"Hi, Susan. How are you?"

"Hello, Dick. I'm fine. I—well, no, actually I'm pretty miserable to be honest with you. I'm three months pregnant, nauseous, the power is out, the shower is out, my cell phone doesn't work, and my husband is missing in action." She looked at her friend, realizing that she had been venting on him. "I'm sorry, Dick, I've just had a rough morning; that's all. So what in the world do you think is going on?"

"I don't know, Susan," he said. "I've never seen anything like this before."

"Is your power out too?" she asked.

"Yes, it is," he said. "It has been for days."

"What about your water?"

"Yes," he answered, looking down at the floor. "As a matter of fact, it is. That just went out this morning."

"Same here. Is your phone out too?" she asked.

"Our phone is out as well. It's very strange, really. In fact, we can't get anything to work, even flashlights with batteries."

"Dick, what could possibly cause everything to go out all at once like this? It just doesn't make any sense!" Dick just shrugged his shoulders.

"I wish I knew, Susan. What does Scott think about all of this?" he asked.

Susan bit her lip. Dick knew it was a nervous habit. She only did it when she was very upset. He could now see that Susan was distraught. He walked over next to her and put his arm around her.

"Are you okay?" he asked.

"I haven't seen or talked with Scott for two days now," she said, "and I haven't heard anything from anyone else either for that matter. I was off work Friday, and today's Sunday, so I haven't left my apartment all weekend."

"Susan, why don't you come over and stay with us for a few hours. You need to get out of that apartment for a while."

Susan nodded at the older man and accompanied him into his apartment. He had retired the year before, so she had seen more of him and his wife, Eleanor, recently than she had the entire time since she had known them.

Dick's wife, Eleanor, walked into the living room, unaware that she had company. She was preparing to ask her husband a question when she noticed Susan sitting in a chair in the living room.

A petite, older woman with a kind and caring face, Eleanor was at least a foot shorter than Dick. In addition to the height difference, Eleanor had an air about her that made her seem considerably more prim and proper than her husband. Dick, who was scholarly in appearance as well as behavior, was akin to the quintessential professor. When she had first met them, Susan thought the two appeared to be quite the odd couple. However, after spending some time with the two of them together, she learned that though quite different on the outside, the two were a perfect match on the inside, complimenting each other perfectly, something like bread and wine, bacon and eggs, or peanut butter and jelly.

"Susan, how are you, dear? Look at you, just aglow with motherhood!" Even though she was worried and upset, Susan managed a weak smile.

"Hello, Eleanor," she said warmly, embracing the older woman with the warmth and sincerity that one often sees between a mother and a daughter.

"Are you doing okay, dear? Where's Scott?"

Susan's warm smile faded, replaced by a sad expression mixed with concern and fear. "I haven't seen *or spoken with* him for two days now, Eleanor. He keeps a small bag in the car because he sometimes sleeps over when working very late on projects, but he usually calls me. Since the phones are down, I haven't heard anything from him since he left for work last week. I'm afraid that something terrible has happened, Eleanor. I need to know that my husband is okay!"

Finally, the dam broke and the flood came as Susan unexpectedly burst into tears. Dick offered her a handkerchief, as Eleanor rushed over to sit down beside Susan, placing her arm around the distraught young woman.

"Now, now, dear, take it easy. Everything is going to be okay. I'm sure that Scott is just fine. He's probably worrying about you right now just like you are worrying about him." It was quite awhile before Susan's tears finally began to ease. Dick walked over to a cabinet and took out a bottle of Jack Daniels. He brought it over and offered to pour some for Susan, who simply shook her head and pointed at her abdomen. After a few minutes, Susan regained her composure.

"I'm sorry. I guess I just feel so lost and scared. Why has everything stopped working? Nothing works, not even the water!" said Susan.

"I know, dear, I know," said Eleanor.

"I guess it's a bad time to be so hormonal, sorry," Susan said with a smile.

"Peculiar, isn't it?" asked Dick, staring out a window.

"What, Dick, the water going out?" asked Susan.

"No. How everything stopped working several days ago," he said.

"Yes, so?" asked Eleanor.

"Well, we practically live in Washington, DC, the capital of the United States; yet we have seen no National Guard, no troops, and no planes. The crews with the power company should have had plenty of time to start restoring power, yet we have seen no one. Why is that? Why aren't things working now? And why haven't we heard anything? Where is everyone?"

CHAPTER 19

There was chaos throughout the White House. The lights were out, but Michaels was still able to see, at least a little. The sun had not yet set, so a small amount of daylight was still able to filter in through the windows.

For the first five minutes following the electromagnetic pulse attack, it seemed as if the world had turned upside down, as everyone tried to figure out where everyone should be, how he or she would get there, and what each should be doing. To Michaels, in the surreal minutes following the attack, it predictably seemed that the only ones that knew what to do at that moment were the Secret Service Agents that rushed into the Oval Office guns drawn, surrounding the President of the United States, prepared to die, if necessary, for the leader of the free world.

For the first time in over two hundred years, it was dark inside the White House. It had taken a few minutes, but Michaels had calmed himself and decided that it was time to lead once more.

"Can someone please find out what happened to the emergency power? In the meantime, Agent Brody, please bring me some candles."

"Yes, Mr. President." Agent Brody returned a few minutes later with a pair of candles sitting in very old candlesticks, and a lighter. "I found these downstairs, sir."

"Thank you, Agent Brody." Michaels looked at the pair of candlesticks as he lit the candles. Light filled the room, as the president admired the artisanship of the candlesticks. "I bet these candlesticks have not been used in over a hundred years," he remarked as others began to filter into the oval office. He smiled as he considered the history, considered the famous men, and women, that might have used the candlesticks before him, perhaps Teddy Roosevelt, Abraham Lincoln, perhaps even John Adams or George Washington, though he doubted they were quite that old.

"Mr. President?"

He looked up and saw Rob Thornton sitting across the desk. He raised his eyebrows and nodded in the direction of the growing assembly that had been gathering in the Oval Office. Michaels understood his intention; he could see the panic and concern in the eyes of everyone in the crowd.

"Okay, let's try and get some perspective. Rob, what's your assessment?"

"Well, it appears to be painfully obvious that the Iranians were able to activate the weapon before we were able to destroy it."

President Michaels looked around the room, peering into the darker areas in the office, looking for someone in the crowd.

"Is General Miller in here?"

"Hold on, Mr. President," said someone in the crowd. "I believe he is in the next room."

A few moments later, several people came in. "Mr. President, you wanted to see me, sir?"

"Yes, General. I would like your thoughts, your assessment on our situation."

"Well, Mr. President, we were obviously too late to stop the Iranians from activating the weapon. However, to be quite honest, I am a bit confused about a number of things."

"About what exactly, General? The EMP knocked out our electrical grid and all communications. Isn't that what it was designed for, knocking out all enemy power and communications?"

"Yes, sir that *is* exactly what it was designed to do."

"What is your assessment of our military situation? Will they attack us now or will they wait?"

"Sir, we don't have a lot of intelligence regarding this attack. To be perfectly honest, Mr. President, they caught us with our proverbial pants down. They were somehow able to keep this from us. We have virtually no information."

"Well, what would you do, General Miller, were the situation reversed?"

"Sir, if I were going to declare war against the most powerful military on the face of the planet, I would want to level the playing field by taking full advantage of our situation. With power out and communications down, I would have already launched by now. However, it has already been several hours now and nothing. Of course, it could be that the device really *did* affect the entire planet, and if that *is* the case, the *enemy's* power and communication systems have been affected as well. Then, there is also the other thing..."

"What *other thing?*" The general held up a satellite radio and laid it on the table.

"This radio doesn't work, sir."

"Of course it doesn't work, it was knocked out by the Pulse," interjected Rob Thornton.

"Normally you would be correct, Mr. Thornton. However, this phone was specifically designed to withstand an EMP blast, as long as it was not turned on at the time of the attack, and it was most definitely not active when we were hit. I turned it on sometime after the attack to contact NORAD."

"And what happened then?" asked President Michaels.

"Well, sir, it came on for a moment, cracked, and fizzled, and then it died. I can't get it to do anything now, Mr. President, but I should be able to."

"Maybe it's just malfunctioning. Agent Harris?"

"Yes, Mr. President?"

"Doesn't the White House have any kind of a backup emergency power system? I mean, this is the *White House* after all, is it not?"

"Yes, sir, there is an emergency power backup system sir. However, we experienced the same problem as General Miller. The backup system started to come on just after the power went out. However, it cracked and fizzled before shutting down. The system is fried, Mr. President. It's dead."

"I don't understand how this is possible. General Miller, this was your project. Can you please explain to me what is happening?"

"I'm sorry, Mr. President. I cannot. We knew that our enemy would likely have some sort of backup systems that would come on after we hit them, so we always planned to follow the initial EMP attack with a second blast to knock out the backup systems that came online immediately after the primary systems failed. While most systems would have a backup system, few have tertiary systems, usually because it was deemed unnecessary and prohibitively expensive to do so."

"So that is the explanation, then. Perhaps they attacked *us* a second time, knocking out *our* backup system, and also your radio, General Miller."

"I don't think that's it, Mr. President." It was Rob Thornton, who was standing by the window. It had grown dark outside and Thornton was looking up into the darkness.

"What are you talking about, Rob? What is it?"

"You might want to come have a look at this, Mr. President." President Michaels walked over to the window and looked for the object of Rob Thornton's interest. Thornton pointed up to the sky. President Michaels looked up and gasped. In the sky was something as beautiful as it was inexplicable. A wavy ribbon of light that looked like colored lightning flowing in waves, illuminated the sky, like some uncanny fireworks display during an electrical storm.

"What in the name of God is that?" he asked?

"Well, sir, I am just not sure exactly what it is," Thornton said.

"General!" the president exclaimed, motioning for the general to join him and Thornton by the window.

"What is that, General? Was that caused by the EMP device?" The general looked up at the dazzling lightshow against the black velvet of the moonless night sky.

"I cannot explain what that is, Mr. President. If that *is* the result of the weapon's activation, there was no mention of anything like it in any of the reports given to me. I have no idea what that thing is, sir."

The president stared at the ribbon for quite some time before he turned and looked at Rob Thornton. "Rob?"

"Yes, Mr. President?"

"When the attack came, wasn't it about the same time as the solar flare was supposed to strike?" Thornton thought about it for a moment.

"Yes, sir, I believe it was. I believe it was exactly the same time, sir"

"General?"

"Yes, Mr. President, I see where you are going. I would have to check with the scientist that designed and tested the device, but it certainly is possible that what we see in the sky could be the result of some sort of interaction between the flare and the EMP."

"Could that explain why the electronics fizzled, about the backup system, and the phone?" Michaels asked.

"Perhaps, Mr. President. If what we are looking at has something to do with some sort of interaction between the flare and the attack, it could have been trapped in the earth's magnetic field. The result of such an interaction could be what we are looking at, something similar to the aurora borealis. I suppose that it is also possible that a lingering EMP–solar–flare effect would be able to prevent any electronics that were inactive at the time of the blast from coming online."

"Oh, no, no, no, no. That is not good." President Michaels looked at his old friend Rob Thornton and noticed a look of fear that he had never before seen on his face.

"Rob?"

"Mr. President, don't you see? Don't you understand what the ramifications are if General Miller is correct?"

"What about it? We can re–build, we can—."

"No, Mr. President, that's just it. If he's correct, we cannot *rebuild.*"

"I don't understand."

General Miller rubbed his chin for a moment before offering an explanation.

"Mr. President, let's just say for a moment that the attack *did* coincide with that monstrous solar flare. Let's also assume that the interaction between the two produced the "Effect" we see in the sky. Let's further assume that the Effect has the same characteristics as an EMP blast, except that it didn't dissipate immediately after the blast."

"That's a lot of assumptions, General."

"Yes, sir, it certainly is. However, it fits the facts. Please don't get me wrong, Mr. President. I hope to God Almighty that I *am* wrong. However, if I'm not, it means—." President Michaels finished his sentence for him.

"It means that there is no rebuilding until what you called the 'Effect' is gone."

"That's right, Mr. President," the general confirmed.

"Any idea how long this thing might last?" As President Michaels looked around the room, one by one everyone shook their heads, shrugged their shoulders, or simply stared into space with blank looks on their faces.

"General?"

"I have no idea, Mr. President."

"Rob?" Thornton shook his head.

"Well then get me someone that can answer that question!"

"Mr. President?" It was Agent Brody.

"Yes, Agent Brody?"

"All communications are out, sir. Anything and everything with electronics are out. That means the subway, all automobiles, airplanes, almost everything sir."

"Well I don't care if you have to take a bicycle or walk, get me someone, ASAP!"

Agent Brody cast a confused glance in the direction of General Miller and Rob Thornton, looking for something, a suggestion, some direction, something. Rob Thornton finally came to his rescue.

"Mr. President, perhaps we *can* reach someone. With all communications down, I don't know how we can track down the lead scientist working on the EMP device. However, we might be able to find Dr. John Abbott, from NASA, the expert on the solar flare. He was supposed to be in at the Capitol today meeting behind closed doors with members of Congress. I believe he was meeting with members of a subcommittee on the anticipated aftereffects of the flare."

Michaels turned back toward Agent Brody.

"Go find him," he said to the disconcerted agent. "Bring him here as quickly as possible."

"Yes, sir, I will do my best."

Michaels looked at the young agent, and thinking he had been a bit hard on the young man added, "And Agent Brody?" The man stopped and turned around to face the president. "Thank you."

Agent Brody nodded at the president and left the room.

"Okay, is there anyone else that can help us, anyone at all?" There was silence as everyone strained at possibilities.

General Miller spoke up, "Mr. President, I can walk over to the Pentagon after this meeting, see if anyone is still there that can help us out."

"Thank you, General. That sounds like a good idea. Anyone else?"

Rob Thornton cleared his throat and said, "Mr. President, this may be a long shot. There was supposed to be a gathering of some of the world's top scientists and theologians at a conference here in the DC area this week. It seems like they were meeting at a hotel not too far from here. Perhaps someone should get over to that hotel, see if any of the scientists there can help us."

"That sounds like a good idea, Rob. I would also like to talk with some of the theologians—get their take on this thing as well. I'd like to know how they think people will react."

"Very good, Mr. President. I will also leave after this meeting, and if I find anyone, I will do my best to bring them back with me."

"Thank you, Rob. We may be grasping at straws here, but that's just where we find ourselves now, isn't it?"

"Yes, sir."

Michaels walked back over to his desk and sat down. He pondered the situation for several minutes, taking time to digest everything he had taken in. After a while, he let out a heavy sigh and said, "Okay, ladies and gentlemen, we need to determine where to go next. I want ideas, and I want them fast. I need to understand what we can expect to happen should Rob and General Miler turn out to be right about that thing. We could end up finding ourselves without electricity for an extended period. Someone please bring in some more chairs so that everyone can gather in here."

A Secret Service agent took one of the candlesticks and a number of people left the room looking for chairs. Those remaining in the room gathered what chairs they could find and sat down in the Oval Office. After a few minutes, the rest filtered back in.

"Okay, so I know most of you here, but there are a few I do not know. Please briefly introduce yourselves and tell us what you do. Starting from my left."

"Emily Swanson, State Department."

"Agent Harris, Secret Service."

"John Malcolm, Secretary of Homeland Security."

"Joe Gibbs, White House Press Secretary."

"Karen Johnson, US Senator from North Carolina."

They continued going around the room until everyone had introduced themselves. President Michaels sat back and after a moment's pause, sat up straight. Clasping his hands, he rested them on the desk.

"Ladies and gentlemen, this is an event that is unprecedented in human history. You have all heard what Rob Thornton and General Miller had to say, what is your take on the situation?" Everyone sat silently as Michaels looked around the room. Finally, Michaels turned to John Malcolm. "John, what do you think? What can we expect?"

John Malcolm squirmed a bit in his chair before responding. Having been appointed by Michaels only six months earlier and confirmed by the Senate only the month before, Michaels suspected he felt woefully unprepared for such an unprecedented event.

"Mr. President, I don't—"

"Listen John," Michaels interrupted him, "I know that you weren't looking to become the next Secretary of Homeland Security. Nevertheless, I chose you, because frankly, you were the best–qualified individual that I could find for the job. Please, just tell me what you think."

"Well, Mr. President, I am afraid that the situation is quite grave."

"Explain."

"Well, sir, the real problem goes well beyond the loss of electricity and communications. Humanity lived on the earth for thousands of years without the use of electricity and yet prospered. The situation is a bit complex, Mr. President, but please let me try to explain. First, our society has become *completely* dependent on electricity; it permeates almost every aspect of our lives. We use it to communicate, to light our homes and businesses, for transportation, for keeping our homes cool in the summer, warm in the winter, for preserving our food, for moving goods and services, and for our military. Our entire infrastructure, including the electrical grid, our water supply, our health care, and our entertainment—virtually every aspect of our lives is touched in some way by electricity. In fact, our entire global society depends on electricity just to function, especially our government."

"So what is your point, John?" the president asked.

"Mr. President, if you wanted to order the military to launch an attack right now, right this minute, how would you give the order?"

President Michaels thought about the question for some time before answering.

"Well, normally I would just pick up the phone. Now, I have no idea."

"Exactly. You cannot use a cell phone or a desk phone. You cannot have someone drive over or fly you to the base to carry the order in person. Moreover, even if you were somehow able to get the message to them, how would they launch the attack? Today's military has been completely paralyzed, incapable of launching any kind of attack short of a local ground assault."

"General Miller?"

"I agree, sir, he's correct. Without electricity, there is no command and control system, no transportation of people or equipment, and no long–range weapons for that matter."

"Please, John, go on."

"Now let me ask you another question Mr. President. Do you believe that there are a lot of scared people throughout the United States this evening?"

"Yes, of course, I am certain there are."

"So how will you explain to them what has happened? How will you comfort them, Mr. President? How will you communicate your plan to them for handling this crisis? Will you send men on foot, or horseback perhaps, to send messages out to people all across the country? How will you instruct them how to find food and water? How will you tell them, especially those in crowded, urban areas, what they need to do to stay cool, to stay warm, and to simply survive?"

"Not to mention the government itself, Mr. President," added Rob Thornton. "The United States is a now a very large country. Without electricity, there will be no way for federal, state, and local governments to communicate with the citizenry. With no electricity, there will be no way to coordinate aid, no way to coordinate activity of any kind outside of smaller municipalities."

"So what exactly do you recommend we do about this situation gentlemen?" he asked.

Rob Thornton and John Malcolm looked at one another for a long while until finally, John Malcolm answered.

"Mr. President, there are two things that I recommend doing at this point sir. The first is trying to do what little we can before our society completely unravels. For example, we can distribute what supplies, medicine, etc. that we can here in Washington, DC."

"And the second?" asked Michaels.

"Do what we can to prepare for the time when the Effect finally dissipates," Rob Thornton answered for him. Malcolm nodded in affirmation that he had answered correctly.

Michaels grimaced after hearing from the two men. He looked back at General Miller.

"General, do you have any additional comments?"

"Only this, Mr. President. Tell me sir, what do you think the chances are that one of the most powerful weapons ever invented just happens to be stolen, launched into space, and activated at exactly the same time that a monstrous solar flare, that happens to occur only once every thousand years, arrives at the Earth?"

"What are you trying to say, General? That this was planned?"

"Only that if it *was* planned, it was planned and executed by the hand of God, Mr. President."

President Michaels pushed away from his desk, stood up, and walked over to the window. He looked up and stared at the beautiful but troublesome colored ribbon in the sky. He stared at it for some time before letting out another heavy sigh.

"Hand of God," he muttered quietly to himself as he continued staring at what General Miller had called, "the Effect." "The Hand of God," he quietly repeated as he walked back over to his desk and prepared for a very, very, long evening.

CHAPTER 20

Masters belched loudly as he finished the beer. All around him lay empty beer cans, sandwich wrappers, and chips strewn across the floor. It had been his first meal since he had boarded the bus the day before, and he was feeling much better now that his stomach was full.

He decided to push on after watching the futile effort by a handful of townspeople to put out the raging inferno caused by the crashed plane. He had come across a number of stores like the one he was in, with no lights or traffic of any kind anywhere around. Why were so many stores vacant and where were the people? It was just another in a long line of unanswered questions.

He had always enjoyed having a beer with a sandwich, especially when it was free of charge. "How nice of them to provide this 'banquet' just for my benefit," he muttered quietly to himself as he peered out of the window. He wanted to check the perimeter just as a precautionary measure, though he doubted anyone would be coming around. It was already late, and the power was out to boot. He walked back over to where he had been sitting and sat back down.

His mind wandered as he relaxed for a bit. The plane, the power, and the cars. Something strange was definitely going on and had been ever since he had walked away from the bus. He decided that he would have to try to find out what was happening in the morning. It wasn't that Vic Masters was afraid, nor was he concerned, nor did he really care. The fact of the matter was that Vic Masters was simply curious. He was also an opportunist; he liked to know what was going on in the event there might be something in it for him. He was beginning to think that whatever was going on, whatever was happening, it was big, and if it was going to keep him from being locked up, it was all that much better.

A yawn crept up from nowhere. Masters looked around one last time before concluding that it was a safe place for him to get some sleep. He spread out a blanket he had found in the back office and drifted off to sleep.

"Hey, mister, I said get up!" Masters woke up to a sharp, piercing pain on his left side. He struggled to see the man while shielding his eyes from the brilliant light of the morning sun. The man kicked at Masters again, but this time, Masters rolled away while reaching under his belt. He pulled out the .45 caliber semi–automatic he had taken from the guard and shot the man in his right knee. Pulling the weapon and firing at his assailant was a reflex, as natural as driving a car. It took considerable self–discipline however not to kill the man, but he had already decided that he needed information, and this was as good a time as any. *Besides,* he thought to himself, *there would always be time to kill him afterward.*

The man dropped to the floor hollering and screaming, holding his knee in the air. When Masters walked over with the weapon pointing at the man's head, the man stopped screaming as soon as the severity and immediacy of his situation became clearer.

"Don't kill me, mister—please don't kill me!" Masters studied the man for several moments. He looked to Masters to be some kind of a local, most likely either a farmer or perhaps even the store's owner.

"I'll think about it. You know, you really should find out who someone is before you commence to kicking him in the ribs. You're just lucky that I only shot your knee off. Some men would have put the bullet between your eyes instead." Masters walked away from the man and walked over to the window. It appeared the coast was clear. He had just turned around when the man abruptly started cursing.

"You piece of garbage, you shot off my knee. I ought to—." The man stopped when the bullet bounced off of the floor no more than a couple of inches from his head.

"Now, now, friend, the way you are carrying on someone might think that maybe you weren't my friend anymore. I certainly hope that doesn't happen, because then I would have to kill you. Only my friends can call me names, and even then, only once, twice at the most.

"I—I—I'm sorry, mister. I meant no disrespect!"

"What is your name?"

"My name is Bill Miller. I—*Oww!*" Masters placed his foot on Bill Miller's bleeding knee.

"Okay, Bill, now that we are on a first name basis, I have a few questions I would like for you to answer."

"Okay, okay—just stop it, will you?" Masters took the pressure off but kept his foot on Miller's knee.

"Why are you here?" he asked. "Are you the owner?"

"No, man. I was looking to get something to eat and drink, and I saw you lying there.

"So why did you kick me then?" he asked.

"Because, I wanted it all for myself. I mean, who knows how long this thing will last?"

"How long *what* will last?" asked Masters.

"What are you talking abo—aagghhh!" Masters was applying steady pressure to Miller's knee again.

"Now, I'm the one that gets to ask the questions, understand?" Miller looked up at him from the ground and noticed the slight grin on his face. He could tell Masters was enjoying it.

"Sure, whatever you say—just *please* stop!" he cried out, as Masters twisted his foot on the man's knee before removing the pressure.

"Now answer the question. How long *what* will last?"

"The power's out everywhere, and not just in the houses. It's out in the cars, radios, everything. Where have you been the last few days, man?"

"I've been out for a walk. Now tell me more."

"Well several days ago, the power went out. That would not have been so strange, but the cars stopped working too. Even radios, toys, anything running on electricity, even on batteries, it all stopped working at the same time. The same day that strange looking lightning appeared in the sky."

"Strange looking lightning?"

"Yeah, you haven't seen it? It first appeared a couple of days ago. It was pretty cloudy this past week, so you probably couldn't see it. I saw it again last night for a bit though."

"Interesting. Tell me more."

"Well, no one knows what's going on. Everyone's running around trying to figure out what to do. Me, I decided I was going somewhere where I could find food and water."

"Water?"

"Yeah. The water went out yesterday afternoon. I knew as soon as that happened that it was time to visit the store."

"Hmmm." Masters left Miller and walked back to the window. Bill Miller looked at his knee and tried to stop the blood flow. He hobbled over to the counter and tore a piece of cloth in two. Masters stood watching as Miller prepared to wrap the cloth around his leg in a tourniquet.

"Hold on, let me have a look at that." Miller sat down, looking fearfully at Masters, certain that he was going to finish what he had started. He noticed that Masters had tucked his gun back into his belt. He thought for a brief moment that he could take him, but then that moment passed. He had seen how Masters moved, more like a big cat than a man, and he felt certain that he was overmatched. He decided to wait and find out what he was up to, no matter what that might entail. Masters knelt down and studied the wound for a moment.

"It looks like the bullet passed through the muscle. I guess you're lucky that I'm such a marksman. You will be able to walk again; you just need to stop the bleeding." Miller prepared to tie the tourniquet one more time until Masters, who was walking away said, "And oh, one more thing, if you really want to lose your leg, I would be happy to cut it off for you, though it would certainly make a mess. If you tie that tourniquet the way you were just about to, forget everything I just said. Within minutes, your tissue and then your muscle will begin to die below the tourniquet. Eventually, your leg, foot, all of it will die, before eventually falling off of the bone altogether."

"But you said—."

"I said to stop the bleeding, you idiot, not cutoff the blood flow to your leg. You'll be no good to me if you can't walk."

"What do you mean *no good to you?*"

Masters turned, grinning again, this time, in a way that made Miller's skin crawl.

"Why, my good friend, Bill, weren't you wondering why I let you live? Did you *really* think I would allow your pathetic attack on me go unpunished? No, no, no, my good friend Bill. I believe that you may yet prove useful to me."

"What do you mean? What are you going to do?"

"I'm not sure yet, but I'm working on it. Say, my good friend Bill, do you happen to know anyone else, others like you, of *like* character, friends of yours maybe? Perhaps they might be interested."

"Interested in what?" replied Miller, who was fumbling with some Tylenol; he picked up off the shelf, hoping that it would help ease his suffering a bit.

Masters walked over and smacked the Tylenol out of his hands just as he swallowed down a couple with a soft drink.

"Interested in living, you fool! Can't you see what is going on? Nothing electrical is working, nothing! I thought things were odd several days ago, but now it is all starting to make sense. The bus I was in that wrecked, no cars on the road, the plane that fell from the sky, the people gathering outside, wondering what was going on, it all makes sense. Now, I know of something that can destroy electronics, but not like this, no not quite like this. This is something new, something different, and unless I miss my guess, something that might be around for a while. Have you noticed that there are no National Guard, no military, no airplanes, no helicopters, and no cars? Whatever is happening, I bet it is like this across the entire country, or else we would have seen *some sort* of government intervention by now. No, this is big, really, big. I'd bet my life on it." Looking at Miller he added, "and yours too!" Masters started laughing as Miller hesitantly and nervously joined in. Bill Miller wasn't sure he followed everything that the man had just said to him, but it sounded like he had a plan, and as far as he was concerned, that was a whole heck of a lot more than anyone else had over the past week.

"Maybe we were attacked. Maybe we are even at war with someone!" replied Miller.

Masters looked at him for a few moments. "It's possible, but I doubt it, for the same reasons I just mentioned. You are certainly correct, however, that it certainly is a possibility. It would explain a few things. We will have to consider that possibility on the way."

"On the way to where?" asked Miller.

"On the way to where we are going, my friend. We're heading east. Why don't you and I see about trying to find ourselves some horses? Do you know where we can find any?"

Bill Miller nodded his head. He wasn't sure exactly what the man was planning, but he decided it sounded good to him. At least he might be able to survive whatever was happening, if he stayed with someone like him.

"Good man," replied Masters. Then, extending his hand out, he said, "Bill Miller, my name is Vic Masters."

As the two men left the store, Vic Masters' head filled with the endless possibilities that the future now held for him. Things were different now, the world had changed as order faded away giving place to chaos. He recalled something Byron had once said, "Every day confirms my opinion on the superiority of a vicious life – and if Virtue is not its own reward I don't know any other stipend annexed to it." Men like *him*, were going to be in charge now, hardened men who were ruthless, vicious, and determined, and if he had anything to say about it, Vic Masters would be on top.

"Look!" Bill Miller exclaimed, pointing to several buildings that had caught on fire and were now engulfed in a raging inferno. He turned and looked at Masters.

"The whole world's been going to Hell ever since the power went out Vic."

Masters just smiled and laughed.

"Well, like the devil said after he was cast into Hell by God in Milton's Paradise Lost, 'It's better to rule in Hell than to serve in Heaven.'"

First, however, he had business to take care of back east.

CHAPTER 21

The four men had surrounded the woman. Clearly, they were serious and quite prepared to back up their threats with action. The woman clung to the bag as if her life depended on it. She was pleading with them as tears flowed down her flushed crimson cheeks.

"Please, I'm begging you, don't take my food and water; my son and my daughter, they need water. They need nourishment. They haven't eaten in days, and our water ran out yesterday. My babies will die if I don't take this to them!"

James, who had happened upon the scene quite unexpectedly while taking in some fresh air, heard the older man, who looked to be in his fifties, say to her, "We already told you, lady—with the power and the water out, *everyone's* starving *and* everyone's dying of thirst, it's every man, woman, and child for themselves." The man started advancing on the woman, who had been backing away from him. She turned and prepared to sprint away with whatever was in the bag. She was stopped abruptly, however, when she ran into a much larger man, who had been standing quietly behind her the entire time.

"Sorry, lady." The big man reached down and took hold of the bag. Despite her best efforts, he was much too strong for her. The sight was more than James could stand.

He had to do something, but if he wasn't careful, someone would get hurt. People were getting more and more desperate. His heart began racing as he pointed at the big man.

"Now see here, what is going on?" he asked.

"Stay out of it, mister," answered the older man. "It's none of your business."

"It most certainly *is* my business. Now, you hand that back to her, or I'll—!" The blow knocked him to the ground. The older man had sucker punched him and the four took off. As he struggled to stand back up, he looked around, and just as it had been for days, there were no police, or any authority of any kind in sight.

The woman sat crying, tears now flowing freely, until her sobbing became overwhelming.

"Now, now, my dear," started James, still reeling from the blow with the taste of fresh blood flowing from his lip. "What's the cause of all of this distress?" The woman's sobbing slowed as she stopped for a moment to look at the man.

"You tried to help me, thank you," she said as the uncontrollable sobbing was gradually replaced with anger and fear. "How could they do that? How could four grown men take food and life–giving water from the mouths of children? What's happening—the world's gone mad!" With the outburst of emotion, she once more broke into tears.

James White felt his heart aching for the woman, and her children.

"Here, now, why don't you come back with me to the hotel, perhaps we can find something for you, and your children there?"

"Do you have electricity, or water? Please tell me you do!"

"No, I'm afraid our power is out also, as is the water."

"Then how—"

"It's a hotel, remember? They have lots of bottled water, and a little bit of food that hasn't spoiled yet. At least we should have a little that we can give to you." For the first time, her countenance changed, her face brightened, and the trace of a smile appeared. James noticed what a beautiful smile it was. As the two started walking back toward the hotel, a fight broke out across the street, James watched for a moment, trying to see if he could discern the cause of the altercation, but it was impossible. The two men, both in their twenties, threw blows and kicked at one another, before winding up in a wrestling match on the ground.

"Do you have any idea what happened to the power and the water?" she asked. "And why isn't anyone doing anything about it?" the woman asked in desperation.

"I don't know the answers, but they are fair questions. We, a group of us, were in town for a conference when the power went out. We probably would have gone home by now if—"

"If you could find a car that you could start, or a taxi that was driving by, or even a plane or helicopter in the sky!" The woman buried her head in her hands and started sobbing again. "What am I going to do for my babies? There's no water, nothing to eat, and I have no idea how long this is going to last!"

"Listen, I don't mean to sound like a preacher, but there *is* someone that understands, someone that cares, and someone that is still in control, even when we are not."

"You mean God? Where is God when my babies cry to me because they are thirsty, cry to me because they are hungry, cry to me, and beg me for something to eat, or they cry because they are scared?" James paused for a few moments before answering her.

"I guess I can only say that I imagine that Jesus asked those same questions while he was hungry, thirsty, suffering, and dying while nailed to the cross. I don't have all of the answers my dear, but God certainly does, if you only ask him." The woman looked at him with an expression that seemed to strike an even balance between anger, hope, and curiosity.

"Listen," he continued, "I believe that some difficult times lie ahead, for all of us. Perhaps we could all benefit from some more faith, and perhaps hope, hmm? Please, allow me to introduce myself. My name is James White, Dr. James White."

"Elizabeth, Elizabeth Moya. Are you a doctor?"

"Oh, no, Doctor of Theology."

"You mean that you're a pastor?"

"Quite right, well, at least I *used* to be a pastor. I am currently president of the International Baptist Convention, or at least I was. I don't know anymore." As the two continued walking toward the hotel, James looked up at the sky. It was getting colder and threatening to rain, maybe even snow. "We should hurry—it looks like it's about to rain. The hotel is just down the road a bit, just another block or two."

"Why were you here in Washington?" she asked as they made their way down the street toward the hotel.

"I was invited here for a conference. The goal was to break down some of the barriers that have separated science and religion, to find and foster the development of points of mutual respect and cooperation between our respective groups."

"How did it go?"

"Well, it seemed to be going well. We were really just getting started when the power went out. Soon after, our discussion turned toward the sudden power outage and the possible—err, ramifications of the event,"

"What do you mean? Do you have any idea what is going on, and why our government isn't doing anything about it?"

"Well, the short answer is no, we don't really know what happened. However, there have been several theories put forth by our group about what *might* explain what happened." They stopped in front of a large, older hotel, located near the Mall. "We're here. This is the place."

James opened and held the door for her, and the two walked inside. Elizabeth looked around and noticed that it appeared to be only a few people around, none of whom seemed to work for the hotel.

"Where is all of the hotel staff?"

"Oh, they all left a couple of days after the power went out. The hotel manager was here until earlier this week checking up on us, and the hotel. We're pretty much all on our own now."

They walked further into the hotel until they arrived at a large conference room, named the Washington Ballroom. A number of people had gathered inside, an assorted group from what Elizabeth was able to tell, most were men but a few women were there as well. She saw several priests and cardinals and a number of protestant pastors in the group. She assumed most of the rest were scientists.

"Hello everyone. This is Elizabeth, Elizabeth Moya. She and her children have no more food or water. I offered her some of ours."

One of the men stood up and walked toward James. "What? What are you talking about? We don't have enough food for ourselves, much less anyone else! You can't be giving what little food we have away! Are you out of your mind?"

"Someone stole what little she had to feed her two children," said James White. "Would you condemn her two innocent little children to death?"

"We don't know how long we can live on what we have as it is!" the man replied.

"Then it won't make much difference if we give some of it to Elizabeth and her two children, isn't that right, Carl?" someone asked from behind them. Norman Weller walked into the room. "My apologies, Ms. Moya. As you know, things have been a bit tense as of late."

"It is *I* who am sorry. I did not intend to cause you any trouble, or take your food. I was attacked, my food and water taken, my children are dying of thirst, and hunger." She fell to her knees, sobbing. "Please, I'm begging you, please, let me keep just enough food and water for my children." The man that had voiced the objection stood and watched the woman beg for the lives of her children. As she fell at Carl's feet, burying her face in his feet while clinging to his ankles, tears suddenly appeared in the man's eyes and began streaming down his cheeks.

"What has happened to me? Have I become some sort of *animal?* I feel like some kind of monster!" He walked over to a table and returned with a box full of food and water. He sat the box down and walked over to where Elizabeth was kneeling. Looking down at her he said, "Here is some food and water for you and your little ones. Please forgive me, my dear woman." Elizabeth stood up, looked at the box, and hugged the man tightly. "Thank you, thank you so much!"

As she was preparing to leave, James walked over to her and motioned for her to sit. "Please, wait just a moment. Some of us here, have come to believe that what we have been experiencing could last for quite some time. I recommend that you take your children and get away from the city as quickly as you can, at least until this is all over. Outside of the city, you should be able to find a river, a stream, or some other source of water. Even then, I would suggest trying to push on to the mountains, where you might find relative safety. Do you have someone, anyone, a husband, brother, boyfriend, perhaps?"

"No, my husband died last year, and I am originally from Los Angeles.

"Do you have a firearm? Hopefully, you won't need one, but we expect things will get worse before they get better." She shook her head.

James looked around the room, and then, looking at Elizabeth, he asked, "If there is anyone that would like to leave and do the same, perhaps Ms. Moya would like some company?" She looked at him and after thinking for a moment, she nodded. "Well, anyone interested in making for the mountains, along with Ms. Moya?"

One man stood up, "I would be. I'm ready to get out of here, and the mountains sound as good a place to go as any."

Another man and his wife answered, "We'll go too." After several others decided to go along as well, the group decided to spend the remainder of the day gathering their belongings. Meanwhile, a couple of men offered to go with Elizabeth to her apartment to collect her two children and some of her belongings. Soon after they left, James spoke to everyone he could find and called a meeting. They met in the large ballroom after dinner, the same room where they had originally gathered when the conference had first started several weeks earlier. They lit candles and a number of kerosene lamps that had been found throughout the hotel. The light filled the ballroom.

"Okay, so it looks as if the time has come for us to discuss what has happened. I would like to have an open discussion about our situation. I know that most of us flew in here from all over the country for the conference, so we don't have family and friends close by. It has been over three weeks now, and the power has not returned. I don't know about the rest of you, but I have yet to see a car, a plane, or even a motorcycle in operation. I also haven't heard any radios, television, anything, not even anything running on batteries. Now I know that a number of you have family in other parts of the country and that you are determined to try to get home by whatever means necessary, and I can certainly understand that.

However, if you plan to stay for a while, it is my view that since we have some of the greatest minds in the world here in this ballroom tonight, we should see if we can figure out what has happened, and whether there is anything we can do to help. Therefore, I would like to get your assessments of our situation. At this point, I would like to open up the floor to discussion. Any thoughts?"

"Dr. White, my name is Dr. Henry Williams, and I have something to say. I chair the department of electrical engineering at NCU. Based on my observations, I have concluded that, without a doubt, what we have experienced is the result of some type of electromagnetic pulse. It is the only explanation that accounts for the widespread simultaneous failure of electronics."

A woman in the back of the gathering stood up to speak. "I have a question for everyone. If the loss of electricity that we have been experiencing *is* the result of an EMP blast, then why haven't we heard anything from the government, especially the military? Don't they have equipment that is supposedly immune to an EMP attack, as long as they are not active when the attack occurs?"

An older man stood up. "That's right. My name is Major Henry Jefferson, USAF–retired. I worked with avionics while in the Air Force for thirty years, and I know for a certainty that we had a significant number of such systems and equipment. I agree with the woman that just asked the question. Many of the systems and equipment in the military built during the Cold War *were* shielded from the effects of an EMP blast, as long as the equipment was not active at the time of the blast. We should have seen at least *some* military activity by now. I cannot explain why we have not."

Norman Weller motioned that he would like to say something. "Okay, then we all agree that an EMP blast would account for what we have been experiencing. However, we cannot explain the fact that it has been three weeks now and we have yet to see any outward signs of recovery from the blast. Does anyone have any explanation for this?" Silence fell across the ballroom for several minutes as everyone struggled to find an answer.

"Okay, let's try another approach then," said James White. "Does anyone have any information on anything unusual or different that might be distantly related to what we are seeing— anything, no matter how far–fetched, even if at first it seems to be unrelated?" Once more silence fell across the auditorium. Finally, someone in the middle of the assembly rose to speak.

"I may know of something that might be useful for this discussion. My name is Monsignor Fennini." Monsignor Fennini stood up to address the crowd. "I arrived in Washington a couple of days before the conference was scheduled to begin. I wanted to be well rested for the conference after the long flight from

Rome. Anyway, the day I arrived I began following a story that I found on the news. It seems there has been a violent solar storm raging over the last few weeks, creating massive solar flares, and sending them in all directions. While none of them had yet been directed towards the earth, a number of scientists feared it was only a matter of time until one did. It sounded like scientists were expecting problems with communications and equipment in many parts of the world. Now, I don't remember them mentioning anything as bad as what we are experiencing, but since you asked about anything unusual, I just thought I should mention it."

"Okay, thank you, Monsignor Fennini," responded James White. That sounds like valuable information. Certainly, a massive solar flare could explain communication disruptions and perhaps could cause at least some of the problems we are seeing. Okay, any thoughts or comments?"

Major Henry Jefferson rose again. "I do not believe that a solar flare, even a big one, could explain the extent of the outages we are seeing. I can't even get a flashlight to work! No, only an EMP would explain what I have witnessed."

Norman Weller stood up. "Major, you said yourself that you could not explain why we haven't seen any military or government activity, not even here, in Washington, DC! An EMP blast alone does not appear to account for the facts."

"That is correct, my esteemed colleagues." A man stood to be recognized. "However, has anyone considered the alternative?" Everyone turned their attention to the tall man in the front of the ballroom. Bjorn Yvornsky continued, "That is, what might happen if an extremely powerful EMP were to strike *at exactly the same time* as a massive solar flare?"

Another woman rose to speak. "My name is Dr. Emily Masterson, and I work, or at least I did work, at ISM electronics as a research scientist. I specialized in satellite components, and in particular, how solar flares affect complex communications, and how they can interact with the Earth's magnetic field. One of the subjects of my research was the *aurora borealis*. Speaking of which, has anyone noticed the unusual ribbons of light that have been visible in the night sky ever since this all started?"

"I did notice those strange lights, but to be honest, with everything going on lately, I hadn't given it much thought. Do you think it could have been caused by the solar flares?" asked James White.

"Yes, it certainly is possible," she responded. "I propose that not only is this new aurora borealis the result of the solar flare, but that it could be the cause of our current dilemma. If it is … oh no—." Emily Masterson buried her head in her hands.

"What is it?" asked James White, "what's wrong?"

"It means trouble," answered Yvornsky. "It means that there must have been some sort of freak interaction between the EMP and the solar flare. It appears that the outcome of this interaction has not only resulted in the destruction of electronics, most likely on a global scale; it seems that it has also somehow become trapped, caught up in the Earth's magnetic field."

"Is that even possible, Dr. Masterson?"

Emily Masterson considered it for several minutes, scribbling various formulas and diagrams on a piece of paper. Finally, she looked up and said, "It is not only possible, I would say that it is extremely likely. It fits, it lines up with everything we have seen, the sustained loss of electronics, the aurora borealis effect, all of it."

James White cleared his throat, afraid of the answer to the question he was about to pose to Emily Masterson. "Dr. Masterson, tell me something. Can you tell us how long this aurora borealis "effect" might last, and what impact it will have?"

"That is precisely the right question to ask, Dr. White, but I doubt that you will like the answer."

"Try me, please."

"Well, it is difficult to say. The good news is that I doubt that it will be permanent."

"And the bad news?"

"It could last for quite a while, perhaps for many years."

"For how many years?" someone asked.

Silence fell across the room like a blanket smothering out a flame. No one spoke after that for a long time.

CHAPTER 22

As he walked, he gradually began to perceive that the world was changing around him, though to be certain the rate of change was not constant. It all seemed quite surreal to him, the changes were gradual, yet so very rapid at the same time. Sometimes these changes were easy to detect, while at other times, they were barely perceptible. It was the strange, uncharacteristic absence of noise, the lack of activity, and the dark traffic lights. It was the empty skies above that normally stayed so busy with planes full of foreign dignitaries, big shot Washington lobbyist insiders, and just plain ordinary people.

They had lost power at the building where he worked. After waiting for days before finding that all transportation was down as well, most of those with homes in the area had decided to leave the office building in hopes of making it back to their families. While he knew that it would take a while to reach *his* home on foot, Scott had expected to make it back to his home long before now. The journey was taking him much longer than what he had counted on. It had been slow going even from the beginning. He had grossly underestimated how much water he would need, and he had been able to carry only so much with him anyway. There had been very little food, so he had been weak from hunger almost from the start. While still in the city, he had tried several times to procure something to eat. On the few occasions where he actually found food, he had been threatened and almost killed when someone else got to it first. He soon realized that his best bet was going to be to find something along the way, perhaps as he left the city. The constant stops to scavenge for food and water had further conspired to delay his getting home.

The sun was already high in the sky now and the heat cut through the bitter cold, showering Scott with a welcome, embracing warmth. He looked down and stared at his watch, thankful that at least this one, small bit of technology still worked. He thought it ironic that the watch that he had inherited from his grandfather, an ancient relic of a forgotten past, was the only piece of technology that he had seen working for weeks. He looked at the time and saw that it was almost noon. He had been walking all morning and was getting tired, as well as hungry, so it was no surprise when his stomach let out a long and painful growl. It was so loud that a few weeks earlier he would have been quite embarrassed. As had been the case for several days, he had gone yet another morning without finding food. He would need to find something to eat soon, or he would become too weak to continue.

At least the weather had held up. It had been getting colder, particularly during the night. He had been able to find shelter, and on a couple of nights, he had even been able to start a small fire to stay warm. He was grateful that at least he had packed some comfortable clothes when he had left the house several weeks earlier. He sometimes stayed overnight at the office when he knew that he was going to be working late, so he made it a habit to keep several changes of clothes in the trunk of his car. He also liked to pack a heavy coat and some layered clothing during the winter months, just in case his car was to break down on a drive back to his apartment during the early morning hours. Fortunately, he had packed a heavy coat and a pair of running shoes the last time he left the house. Scott was sure that the shoes had surely made his long walk much easier, though the growing tallies of blisters on his feet were beginning to make that harder and harder to believe.

He had been creeping closer and closer to the edge of the city and he was looking forward to getting out. Making his way through the city over the past week, he had seen more atrocities than he had seen during his entire life. He had seen men and women attacking each other, even children, for food and water, for supplies, even for just a warm place to sleep.

Walking along the road, he came across a car, a Crown Victoria, still sitting in the middle of the road ahead where it had met its unexpected end. He had walked past hundreds, perhaps even thousands of cars over the recent weeks, and there was nothing unusual about this one. He decided to look inside anyway just in case, hoping that getting closer to the outskirts of DC might increase his odds of finding abandoned supplies of food or water. Something caught the sun and reflected a blinding light into Scott's eyes for a moment. He covered his eyes to block the rays of the sun and peered back inside the vehicle. Scott's heart raced as his eyes found two bottled waters thrown carelessly in the floorboard of the car. He tried the door but found it still locked. He looked around for a moment before shattering the glass with his elbow. He reached in, unlocked the door, and opened it. After retrieving the waters, he placed one inside a hidden pocked inside of his coat and twisted the top off the other. He decided that once he had found Susan, he would stock up on all of the bottled water he could find. He drank slowly and took only a little. The clear liquid, that had once been no more than a walk to the kitchen away, had suddenly quite literally become more valuable than all of the gold in Fort Knox. He continued scouring the car for food or more water, but came up empty. He counted himself fortunate just to have happened upon what he had found. The next step would be to find food.

He walked for several more miles, passing more vehicles but with no additional success. His heart raced as he began to panic. *What if he was unable to find food?* Surely, others had been trying to leave the city just as he was. What if something had happened to Susan? *Susan.* He was feeling guilty over the way he had left his wife alone in Virginia while he stayed overnight at the office—what had he been thinking?

Looking ahead, Scott saw something in the distance. He could not be certain but the size and the shape was about right. He picked up the pace a bit, as hope of finding something to eat filled him with a second wind. As he drew nearer, he found that his hope was well founded. It *was* a small convenience store. Now that he was getting closer, however, reality set in. Since the front door was ajar, it was evident that he had not been the first to find this particular convenient store. He walked over to the doorway and peered inside the store. His heart sank when it became obvious that the store had already been picked clean. The soft drinks, water, bread, chips, everything was gone. He went inside anyway, hoping to find something, anything that might have been missed. He looked into the coolers, looking for something, perhaps a fruit drink, but all was gone, only cartons of warm milk, that had spoiled weeks earlier, remained.

On a whim, he knelt down close to the ground hoping to find something, and was rewarded for the effort. Several packs of candy bars and a pack of chips lay underneath a long over-hanging shelf, just enough to hide their presence from the previous visitors.

Scott decided to eat the chips and one of the candy bars, saving the rest for the next morning. He knew the nourishment would give him the energy he needed to push on for the remainder of the day. First, however, he decided to sit down and rest a while, wearied from the constant walking and desperate for a moment's rest. Within a few brief minutes, he was sound asleep.

Scott awoke when he heard the door creek open. He lay motionless as he slowly began to recall where he was and what he had found. He hoped that if he were quiet enough, perhaps the visitor would turn around and leave. However, like Scott, the visitor was desperate enough that he started walking around the barren store, looking for scraps of food. The footsteps moved away from Scott before turning and moving toward him. Finally, fearing he was about to be discovered, he slowly grabbed the chips and stood up, trying to stay low to avoid detection. Despite his best effort however, the sound of the chips and the candy bars in his pocket betrayed his presence. The stranger looked directly at Scott and started walking toward him.

"Hey, you, stop! You give that food to me, and give it to me now! If you don't, I'll *kill you* where you stand!" Scott stopped in his tracks, paralyzed with fear. As the man drew closer, carrying a pocketknife with the blade opened, Scott was able to see that the man appeared to be the most unlikely sort of attacker. He was an old man, wearing a business suit that looked rather worn. Scott surmised by his appearance that the man could have been a lawyer, a lobbyist, perhaps even a congressional representative. Only a few weeks earlier, that man would likely have been relaxing in a hot tub, perhaps playing a round of golf at an expensive club, not threatening a man's life for a candy bar in Washington, DC.

Scott backed up and made a run for the door. The older man, weak from hunger and from dehydration, never stood a chance. Scott was at the door before his would–be attacker even realized what was happening. Looking back at the poor man and feeling compassion for him, Scott reached into the pocket where he had shoved the candy bars. Once he was outside of the door, he took one out and laid it at the doorstep, along with the extra bottled water he had placed inside his coat. "Here mister, you can have these."

The gesture stopped the old man's threatening forward movement in his tracks. He looked down at the water and candy bar and then at Scott, who was already well outside of the door and beyond the man's threats. Tears filled the man's eyes as he tried to talk.

"I'm very sorry I threatened you. I'm just *so* hungry, *so* thirsty, and so *very* tired." He tucked the knife away in his pocket and reached down for the candy bar and the water. He drank half of his water before ripping open the candy bar and shoving it into his mouth. Now that he was in the light, Scott could see that he was very frail looking and gaunt. He could not help but speculate how much longer the poor man would live.

"Listen, I have to get home and find my wife. I hope you make it okay."

Scott had started walking away when the man yelled after him, "God bless you, young man—God bless you!"

Scott walked by more cars sitting in the middle of side streets, thoroughfares, and highways, as he made his way out of the DC suburbs. They sat motionless, as if frozen in a moment of time. He found his mind beginning to wander aimlessly as he tried to get in a few more miles before nightfall. It would be getting colder soon, *much* colder. He knew that he would have to find shelter, and fast. He was haunted by the fear that he would be forced to sleep outside, exposed and unprotected from the elements, not to mention from other desperate people that would kill him for what little he had.

He thought of some of the disturbing sights that he had witnessed as of late. Just a few nights earlier, Scott had come across a man that had been badly beaten and left for dead, lying along the side of the road. Scott had stopped to try to aid the man but soon realized there was little he could do to help him. It looked like he had several broken ribs and based on the blood he was coughing up; there was a considerable amount of internal bleeding.

Scott had also become aware of a growing number of people braving the colder weather in search of food and water, something that had been as accessible as a short walk to the kitchen sink only a few weeks earlier. A disturbing trend that he had noticed over the course of the last several days was a growing number of people that seemed to be coughing and sneezing, obviously sick with bad colds, the flu, or even pneumonia. He speculated that more and more people, ill prepared for the cold, had ventured out in search of food, water, and supplies. This, in turn, weakened their immune systems, making them more susceptible to disease. If something did not change soon, he surmised that it was only a matter of time before a major flu pandemic would strike, killing scores of people. Without medical intervention, such a plague would be able to burn through entire populations like raging wildfires. It was a grim picture that Scott could only hope and pray would never come true.

Still, not everything Scott had observed as he traveled to get back to his wife, had been negative. A young man carrying nothing but bottled water had given the precious bottle to an old woman that was obviously dying from dehydration. Scott had seen men huddled around a fire they had built inside a trashcan, offering a jacket to a freezing child. Then there was the man that had risked his life to help a woman, attacked by a group of men when she tried to bring some food and water home to her children.

It seemed to Scott that sometimes, difficult circumstances *can* bring out the best of humanity, the part that is noble, selfless, and compassionate, *or*, it can bring out the worst. Scott pressed on. Now well into the suburbs, he knew that he was getting closer to home. It was only a matter of another couple of days before he made it home, if he could only keep it together until then.

He walked on well past nightfall. He was drawing near to Sterling, not too far from home, when he paused to catch his breath. While he was resting, he looked down the road, and what he saw caused him to stop in his tracks and made his heart sink. Just up ahead was a group of men, staring straight at Scott while talking amongst themselves. Looking at them, he knew that he was too exhausted to outrun them or try to fight them. He would have to hope for the best and pray that he survived the night. As he got closer, one of the men, a big man, walked toward Scott. His heart began racing as he tripped and stumbled over something in the road. The big man began moving quickly toward Scott, catching Scott just as he nearly collapsed on the cold asphalt.

"Welcome, brother. How would you like a hot meal and a safe place to sleep for the evening?" Scott looked at him with a strange look of astonishment, before cracking a big smile that reached from ear to ear.

"Friend, have I died?" The big man laughed as he grabbed him around his waist and helped him walk toward a church building.

"Brother, I certainly hope that when you die and go to heaven, that what you find there is a lot better looking than my ugly face. The man helped him inside to the church's fellowship hall, where Scott sat down in a chair at the table. The man brought him a glass of water and some bread. Scott looked at the water and then back at the man.

"Don't worry, friend, we have a well outside where we get our water. Several of the families that come here have gardens; a few even have farms not too far from here. Being Christian brothers and sisters, they have been sharing food and drink with us, and have allowed us so to share it as we minister to folks just like you, folks that have been struggling as they try to leave the metro area."

A woman came in carrying a large bowl of hot vegetable soup and some more bread.

"Thanks, Wendy," the man said.

"Have there been a lot of folks passing through here like me?" Scott asked.

"You might be surprised by how many we've had come through here over the last several weeks. By the way, the name's Hank," the big man said as he extended his hand toward Scott.

"I'm Scott; Hank, it's nice to meet you." Scott tried some of the soup, drank most of the water, and added, "I take that back—it's *extremely* nice to meet you, Hank!" said Scott.

"When you're done eating, we have some beds setup in another section of the fellowship hall."

"How about a hot shower?" asked Scott raising his eyebrows, hoping for the best, but expecting the worst.

"No, Scott, we all wish that we had hot showers, believe me. The good news is that there is a river not more than a mile or so from here."

"Thanks, Hank, but I *really* have to get home. I *will* take you up on the offer for that bed once I finish this soup. I am exhausted."

"I understand, Scott. Well, enjoy your soup. I'll show you to your bed whenever you're ready."

CHAPTER 23

Conrad was awakened by the sound of a door slamming shut in the barracks and a rush of cold air. Ironically, he was glad that it was winter and not summer. If there was any one thing that the base still had in abundance, it was blankets, good, old, warm, wool blankets. One thing it did not have any longer however, was air conditioning. The heat in the barracks would be unbearable come mid–summer.

He looked around the room, taking note that it looked like more grunts had left in the early morning hours, at least half of the men and women who had been there yesterday were gone, most likely hoping to get an early start. It had been the same way every day since he and Frank had arrived back at the base a week earlier. In the beginning, most of the men and women on the base had stayed on despite the loss of electricity, heat, and even water. They were soldiers, trained to endure the worst of circumstances. Conrad and Frank, like all Army Rangers, had been through survival training. Most of the men and women on the base however were not Rangers but part of one of the many support organizations stationed to support the brass in Washington, D.C. Some of them would be able to survive if the situation remained as it had been for the past month, but he suspected that many, perhaps most even, would not.

The morale on the base had been steadily declining. The military structure that had so heavily depended on the chain–of–command and effective communication up and down the line to function successfully was largely gone. There had not been much of either over the past week, and Conrad could see the discipline slowly beginning to break down. The base commander, General Montgomery, had left with an escort to walk over to the Pentagon several days earlier to see what he could learn and to get his orders. The commanding officer he had left in charge, Colonel Adams, came across as largely unprepared and uncertain as to how to deal with the circumstances he was facing. Adams had come out of West Point to a number of comfortable commands, mostly in support positions in the Pentagon. He had never been on the front lines or come under enemy fire before, he had never seen combat, and he had never confronted anything even remotely similar to what he was facing now. Conrad knew that in all fairness however, even the most seasoned veteran officers were scratching their heads trying to figure out how to handle the current crisis.

Once the initial shock of the EMP attack had worn off, the thoughts of almost every man and woman on the base had instinctively turned to their family and friends. It was one thing for a soldier to risk death fighting the enemy knowing that their loved ones were safe at home; it was something quite different when their families, their spouse and children, were at great risk of serious injury, starvation, or even death. He wondered how long the discipline would hold.

Since he was an orphan as a child, Conrad had no family to return home to see. The Army had been his only family since high school. Many however, like Frank, had a wife and children at home that needed protection, and food. Frank had already shared some of *his* fears with Conrad just the night before. He did not know whether his wife and children were able to stay warm, whether there was food to eat, or even whether they were still alive. Since he could not reach them by phone, Frank had confided to Conrad that he almost felt compelled to go A.W.O.L. just to check on his family.

Conrad grabbed his toothbrush, bottled water, and razor and walked into the bathroom. He would walk down to the cold river later if he wanted to get a bath and wash his clothes. He had suggested to his commanding officer that they dig some wells so they could have fresh water on the base, but Adams had shot down the suggestion, citing some obscure regulation and upholding the appearance of the base.

The entire company was unexpectedly called to muster by General Montgomery just as Conrad finished brushing his teeth. There had been no muster for the past week, so it took him by surprise. Conrad hustled outside and gathered with the others.

"All right, you grunts, listen up," This is General of the Army, Howard K. Manning."

General Manning walked up to what remained of the assembled company. On his face was an odd mixture of confidence, compassion, and stone–cold determination. Conrad had never met or served directly under General Manning before, but his record and his credentials were impeccable. He had a reputation for his honesty and bluntness with the men that served under him. Conrad hoped that he would have some answers for them.

"At ease." The company relaxed slightly as they prepared to listen to what Manning had to say. For one brief, final, shining moment, the company once more seemed like a cohesive military unit.

"To begin with, I'm sorry that you were kept in the dark for so long as to what has taken place. The sad truth is that many Americans will never have access to the information that I'm about to share with you now. As you might imagine, over at the Pentagon, we've been piecing together the events that led to this tragedy. *I* know the details only because I happened to be with the president the day when the attack came. The Iranian government stole a top secret, experimental weapon from us just days before the attack, and successfully activated it just minutes before we would have destroyed it. This experimental device was an electromagnetic pulse—or EMP—weapon, designed to disable or destroy all enemy electronic communications just before a major offensive. However, the weapon was still highly experimental, and it was much more powerful than anyone anticipated. While we cannot be certain, we have formed a theory. We believe that the EMP weapon was activated by the Iranians at exactly the same time as an extraordinarily powerful solar flare struck the earth." The general, an experienced leader and speaker, paused to give everything he had been saying a chance to sink in. After a few moments, he grimaced and continued, "Unfortunately, there was some kind of an interaction between the flare and the EMP blast. Listen people, I am not going to sugarcoat this thing. We believe that the entire country, the entire world for that matter, has been impacted by this event. All electronics across the globe were instantly fried when this EMP thing was set–off, and the worst part of this mess is that this *thing,* this EMP *"Effect,"* continues frying any electronics that we turn on. The bottom line is that there will be no more electricity, no more electronics of any kind for a very, very long time."

One of the soldiers hollered out, "For how long sir, does anyone know how long this will last?"

"That is a very good question, soldier. Unfortunately, however, there is just no way for anyone to know for sure, because nothing like this has ever happened before. They believe that eventually this thing will just fade away on its own. From what they told the president, it could be a hundred years or more before that happens."

Another soldier asked, "What are we supposed to do now, sir?"

General Manning looked over the faces of the men and women standing before him. He pondered the question, staring at the ground and pacing for several minutes, before finally answering the soldier.

"Well, young lady, *that* is the million–dollar question. The president has requested that we do everything possible to try to preserve order in the capital for as long as we can. The president is a realist though, he understands the situation, and he knows that our chances of preserving our way of life for very long are slim at best. With no electricity, there is no heat to keep people warm. There are no grocery stores where they can buy bread. There is no more water when they turn on the faucets in their kitchens. Society will start falling apart very soon now.

As to the Army and the United States' Government, with all electronics down, there is no way for us to communicate with our military units, to the people, or with the state and local governments across our great country. Honestly, we don't know what is going to happen."

The general looked once more at the faces of the men and women. He could see that fear and despair had set in.

"Now, you just listen to me," he began. "We had an army long before we had electricity, we had a *government* long before we had electricity, and by the grace of God Almighty, we *will* get through this. But first, we need to do what we can to help the people inside of Washington get out of the metro area, so that we can at least give them a *chance* for survival."

Conrad decided to speak up, "General Manning, sir, you're saying that the impact was global, so does that mean that any follow–up attack that the Iranians may have been planning will never happen now?"

"That's correct, Colonel. We believe that the Iranians acted recklessly and impulsively, with no idea whatsoever, how wide-spread the damage would be or how long it would last. The only way they can attack us now is with a very long march or with wooden ships."

"Thank you, sir."

"Now, first things first. I want to say that the president has authorized honorable discharges for those of you that need to attend to your families. He asks that those of you that *are* able to please stay just a short while longer, just a couple of days, in order to help your fellow grunts dig some wells, procure rations, and get mobilized.

The general looked over the company one final time. Most of them were well–trained, highly experienced soldiers, so he was optimistic that the majority of them had a very good chance of making it to their destinations. He worried however for those with the more ambitious goal of crossing the country to get back to their loved ones, though he would never presume to try to talk them out of making the attempt.

"God bless all of you *brave* men and women. For those of you that are leaving and to those that choose to stay, I say, God bless you, and to you all, I say, thank you so very much for your service."

The General saluted the men, turned, and walked back toward the Pentagon.

CHAPTER 24

It was warmer outside than it had been all week. Susan reclined on her sofa, wondering what was going to happen to her, to the baby, and to Scott. It had been several weeks since the power went out and Scott had still not come home. As the weeks passed, she had become increasingly concerned that something had happened to him, there was simply no other explanation. Scott would have already been home unless something had happened; nothing could have kept him away for so long otherwise. It was time for her to prepare herself for the very real possibility that he *never would* come home. She was on her own now. She knew that somehow, she was going to have to reach deep down inside herself, to find the kind of strength that she was going to need for the months and years that lay ahead. Susan was beginning to feel panic set in, but she fought it. She knew that she had to steady herself somehow, because she had to do everything that she could to survive, for the baby's sake, if not for her own.

There would be plenty of time to mourn and cry over Scott later, once she and the baby were safe.

Life was becoming increasingly difficult for her and for the other tenants that remained in the apartment building where she lived. When the water had stopped working several weeks earlier, a number of men in the building got together and with no word from anyone regarding what had happened; they took it upon themselves to erect some temporary outhouses behind the building. Pleased with the results of the outhouses, they decided to also try to dig a well using shovels that a few of the residents had kept around to tend their small flowerbeds. Unfortunately, for all concerned, the efforts with the well were not as successful as the effort with the outhouses had been. After digging no more than seven or eight feet, they hit some hard clay and broke both of the shovels. Disheartened by the disappointing loss of the shovels, they had no choice but to give up the digging.

Hearing noises coming from outside, Susan got up from the sofa and looked out her window only to find more families leaving the building. Judging by their dress and the packs on their backs, it looked as if they were leaving for good. More and more residents had decided to abandon any hope of waiting out the current crisis. Some left to try to find family members, some left to try to find supplies, but all left to find food and water. She could hardly blame them.

There had been a nagging thought that had been eating away at her, gnawing at the back of her mind for the past several days. Soon, it would be time for her to leave as well. She had tried not to think about it, she couldn't think about it, but it was becoming increasingly difficult for her to drive the thought out of her mind. Despite all of her resolve to be strong, a small part of her believed that Scott was still alive. Leaving their apartment now would mean abandoning Scott, and any hope of ever seeing him again.

She walked into the kitchen and decided to take her mind off leaving by taking yet another inventory of food and water. She had spent the last several days tightly rationing the water, opting to drink what fruit juices and soft drinks they still had scattered around the apartment. She was growing increasingly tired as the days went on. She knew that the longer she waited to leave, the more difficult it was going to become.

After finishing her inventory, she walked back into the living room and lay back down on the sofa. Susan was just about to drift off to sleep when there was an unexpected knock at the door. Her heart raced as she struggled to temper her excitement with reality. She simply could not afford to continue getting her hopes up only to have them dashed. She opened the door to find Eleanor with several large, empty bowls in her hand.

"Here my dear, take these, quickly and place them outside on your patio. I suggest you empty them regularly into a larger pitcher, anything you have that will hold water."

"What's going on, Eleanor? What's this all about?"

"Why, it's raining, my dear! For the first time since the world turned upside down, *it is raining!* That means fresh water to drink, at last. Dick has been placing several large containers outside already, and we are working on finding a way to keep it fresh. It seems like we bought some chlorine pills when we did our disaster planning years ago. Anyway, get those containers outside as soon as you can. You will need all of the fresh water that you can carry."

"What do you mean?"

"Honey, we have to get out of the city as soon as possible, all of us. It's our only chance of survival. The city is dying. We need water and food, and we will find neither in the city if we wait much longer. Now, please hurry, dear—get those containers outside as soon as you can, we'll talk some more later."

Susan nodded and closed the door. She hurried over to the patio and opened the door. The rain was coming down in buckets. She cursed and muttered under her breath, wondering how much fresh water she had missed collecting and how she could have gone on without noticing the life–preserving water coming down outside. After setting the buckets out on the patio, she waited to be certain that the buckets were positioned to collect the maximum amount of water. After watching for a moment, she had an idea.

She ran back inside and began rummaging through a box. She was ecstatic when she finally came across the vinyl tablecloth. She then ran over to a drawer and searched through it before taking out a roll of duck tape. She ran out to the patio and began taping the tablecloth to the top of her patio deck. After a few minutes of experimentation, she had it positioned in such a manner that the bucket began to fill quickly. She ran back into the kitchen and started searching for more containers. She finally found some large punch bowls and set them on the patio. She was relieved but surprised to find that the first bucket had already filled with water. She quickly replaced it with one of the bowls. She then reached under the sink and pulled out several pitchers. She began transferring water from the bucket to the pitchers, all the while keeping an eye on the punch bowl as it too was beginning to fill.

She had never been so excited to see rain before nor had she been so thankful. She had grown concerned as the supply of water bottles and can drinks had begun to dwindle. Had Scott been there, they would have run out of food and drink some time ago. As much as she hated to admit it, Eleanor was right; they had to get out of the city and get close to a river or stream, maybe in the mountains, where they might also be able to grow vegetables and hunt for game. She laughed to herself as she recalled how she had ridiculed rural living for so long, and now here she was, trying her best to leave the city for the country.

As she watched the rain falling outside, once more her thoughts turned to her husband. Where was he? Was he still alive after all this time? Was he hurt? She knew that it was natural to assume the worst, even during the best of times, but these were not the best of times. This was something that no one in the history of the world had ever experienced. A noise startled her, waking her from her daydreaming, as she realized that the punch bowl was full of water. She grabbed the second bowl and proceeded to transfer water from the bowl into pitchers.

Susan looked at the amount of water that she had collected so far and determined that she already had enough water to last for a week or two. The rain had fallen heavy and hard, so she felt reasonably confident that the water would be pure enough for her to drink, since the pollutants in the air would have been washed out soon after the rain first started. It was important that she take extraordinary measures for the sake of her baby. She felt sad, as she tried to imagine what kind of world her child would grow up in, and the difficulties that lay ahead for him or her, if the situation didn't improve soon.

Her sadness soon turned to anger however, as she considered what Dick had said. Someone, or something, had stolen her world away, kept her husband from her, and taken away the relative safety and comfort of the world that she had known. It had been allowed to happen, maybe even caused to happen, perhaps even by her own government. Where were the politicians, the military, and the government? She lived no more than an hour's drive from the Capitol of the United States. Why had they been left to die of starvation and dehydration?

Watching the bowls fill on the patio, Susan struggled to recall some of the food and water safety measures that she had learned as a nurse with the Red Cross several years earlier. It had been someone else's responsibility to handle the food and water safety for the people in the small town, after the hurricane had wrecked havoc on the burgeoning coastline. She had been a nurse and was part of the group that cared for those injured by the natural disaster, so her attention had been focused on the injured and dying at the time. Nevertheless, she had attended a one-day food-and-water safety-training course before she had left for the site, where an expert taught her how to handle and treat water after a disaster. She remembered something about chlorine tablets, and salt, and boiling water.

The second punch bowl began overflowing. Susan replaced the bowl with the bucket, walked back over to the sofa and tried to relax a little. As she had done for weeks, she kept panic at arm's length through her determination to be strong for her baby and to survive no matter what she had to face, no matter what she had to endure. Reclining on the sofa on that rainy day in December, Susan McBride decided that she was going to re-invent herself. The old, fragile Susan McBride was no more. In her place was a strong and resourceful woman, determined to face the brave new world on her own, or die trying.

It was time for her and the others to plan, to prepare for their journey into the wild, leaving the city and their memories of the former life behind. Perhaps things would change; perhaps the world would begin to heal and recover from the devastating attack. If that happened, they could always return and play their part in the recovery. If it did not, they would be ready. Her mind began to fill with ideas, with possibilities, and with some of the tasks that would need to be completed if they were to survive. First, they would need to determine where they were going. They could leave for the mountains, perhaps the other side of the mountains, or maybe somewhere in the Midwest, or the south. They would need maps, supplies, and camping equipment. They would travel lightly while bringing as many supplies as possible. But where would they get everything they needed, and how would they carry it? She decided that she was finally ready to talk over arrangements with Dick and Eleanor. She walked toward the door, with pencil and paper in hand, ready to make preparations that would help ensure her baby's best chance of survival.

She was halfway out the door before she stopped cold in her tracks.

"Hello, Susan." Before she was able to reply, everything suddenly went black, and she collapsed in the man's arms.

CHAPTER 25

Judging from the aroma coming from the steaming cup of coffee, he anticipated that it was going to be the best cup he had ever had in his entire life. There was enough bottled water stored in the White House kitchen that he could afford to use some to brew coffee for those that wanted it. The fire they had started in the ancient fireplace had made a convenient spot to heat the water for the coffee.

"We need clear heads so that we can develop a plan of action that can chart a course for our country through this crisis," he said. It was a brave front, a charade, a lie, whatever they wanted to call it. He knew that there was little that he could do now; the window for preventing this had come and gone with the attack.

One momentary lapse in security at a high–tech lab, one theft by an enemy spy, one reckless action by a hostile state, one push of a button, and the Pulse had ushered in the complete collapse of civilization, ending the Golden Age of wondrous and amazing technology. One day, man could fly to the moon, the next he could not even drive to the next town.

A person does not rise to the position of President of the United States without being a bit of a fighter. By the time an election is over, there are plenty of wounds to lick, many of them made by knives in the back, left there by those you trusted the most. No, Michaels had always been a scrapper, never one to back down from a fight. He was one of the rare few that truly craved challenges, especially no–win scenarios, just so he could find new and ingenious ways to overcome them. However, the current crisis was beginning to shape–up like one that was beyond even his considerable abilities.

It was still early morning, so they had not yet gathered again in the Oval Office, but at least he now had everyone that they had been able to round up on short notice there with him in the White House. Rob had returned late the night before with some of the scientists and theologians from the hotel, General Miller had returned with some military contractors from the Pentagon about the same time, and Agent Brody had that morning returned with the NASA scientist that was supposed to be an expert with solar flares.

All of the experts gradually began assembling in the West Wing of the White House. Rob was coordinating the event, getting together stencils, pads, markers, slide rules; anything he could find that might help them find a solution to the crisis. He knew it was a long shot, but they had to try. Everything depended on it. If they were unable to find a way to fix things, then they would come up with a plan to do whatever they could to safeguard the precious knowledge acquired over ten millennia. They would have to find a way to preserve at least some measure of civilization, to hold on to whatever they could for the day that would eventually come, the day when civilization, and hope, would return to the world.

"Mr. President, we have everyone assembled and ready in the Situation Room, sir."

"Did they all get breakfast, and coffee?"

"They did, sir. That is one reason we are running behind; some of them had not eaten a meal like that since this all began."

"I'm not surprised, Rob. I imagine that the same could be said for just about every man, woman, and child on the planet about now." Michaels frowned and furrowed his brow. Rob Thornton looked at the man he had called friend for over twenty–five years. "Mr. President, John," he said, "how are *you* holding up? I know this must be an extraordinary burden for you to be carrying now. You had nothing to do with the onset of this crisis yet you shoulder a heavy burden, perhaps the heaviest of any man that has ever held the office."

John Michaels looked at his friend, smiled, and looked down at the floor, fighting the flood of emotion that suddenly overwhelmed him.

"I guess I'm doing about as well as can be expected, Rob. Knowing that so many people will not survive this crisis, Rob, well, it's almost more than I can bear."

John Michaels, a strong, proud man, looked out the window that overlooked the city, tears streaming down his face. "So many innocent men, women, and children out there are going to die, Rob, and there is nothing I can do to stop it! What did I ever do to deserve to be the president that presides over the…" Struggling to continue, he took a moment to try to compose himself before continuing. "What *evil* have I done that I must be the man that presides over the end of the world?"

Rob Thornton looked on his friend with the compassion that one feels for a family member dying slowly of cancer, watching them suffer in pain and agony. It pained him to see his friend like that.

"Maybe, just maybe, you are in this position because *you* are just the right man for the job, at just the right time, at just the right place."

"But what am I supposed to do, Rob? What is *anyone* supposed to do?"

"You are supposed to survive, Mr. President, and you are supposed to help as many others survive as you can. If there is nothing that can be done to fix this situation, to eliminate the Effect so we can re–build, we will have to make a determination about what we can do to make the best of things, to play the cards that we have been dealt."

President Michaels looked at his friend and managed a slight smile. He felt better having let some of the emotion out, much like valves release pressure to keep pipes from exploding, so too the momentary outburst of emotion relieved some of the pressure that had been building. He shook off the despair and worked to sturdy himself for the meeting that he was about to walk into.

"Please forgive me, Rob—I don't know what came over me."

"Mr. President, I was beginning to worry. I was afraid of what was going to happen to you if you *didn't* let off some steam. The burden you carry is more than any man should ever have to bear, even a president."

"Thank you, Rob." After several minutes, President Michaels let out a heavy sigh. Finally, he said, "All right, Rob, let's move to the Situation Room, then, shall we?"

Rob walked in first and announced the president. "Ladies and gentlemen, the President of the United States, John Michaels."

All rose as Michaels entered the room. He motioned to them and said, "Thank you, please be seated." As he surveyed the room, Michaels noticed that the room was filled with an odd assortment of people. There were longhaired men with ponytails that Michaels assumed were scientists. There were a number of clergy in attendance as well. From what he could tell, a variety of denominations were represented in the room. Some of the clergy were unmistakably Roman Catholic, some appeared to be Protestant, while still others were Eastern Orthodox. Of the men and women that remained, he assumed they could have been the contractors from the Pentagon, clergy, or scientists. Also in attendance were many of the same people that had gathered with President Michaels several days earlier. Regardless of their association, everyone had a very serious demeanor about them.

"Welcome to the White House, everyone, I am John Michaels. I have asked all of you here so that we might discuss our current situation, and to see what can be done to address it. Failing that, I would like at the very least to come away from this discussion with a plan for going forward, a plan for preserving what we can of our way of life. Now then, let's get started. I assume that everyone has been briefed?" Everyone in attendance nodded in affirmation.

"Very good. Let's have a quick round of introductions so that we can learn each other's names and backgrounds. As I said, I am John Michaels." He looked to his left at Rob, who then introduced himself as they started a round of introductions. Among the attendees were Dr. John Abbott from NASA, Cardinal Pierre Cousteau of the Roman Catholic Church, Dr. James White, President of the International Baptist Convention, computer scientist Dr. Bjorn Yvornsky, Dr. Mark Rainier with Logan Aerospace, the company that had developed the EMP weapon, and Chris Bollinger, with Martin Space Engineering, an advanced weapons consulting company. When the introductions were finally over, Michaels concluded that if *they* were unable to find a solution, then no one would. "Okay, I know that we have already had a number of conversations about this event. As you should all know by now, we were recently hit by an advanced weapon of our own design, a highly experimental EMP weapon, stolen by the Iranian government just days before the attack. By an extraordinary twist of fate, at the exact moment the Iranians activated our weapon, our planet was hit by the largest solar flare ever recorded. It is the consensus of our experts that—while it was the extraordinary power and instability of the EMP weapon that initially knocked *out* power, we believe all over the world—it was an interaction between the EMP and the solar flare that has caused this crisis to *perpetuate.* General Miller, do you have anything to add?"

"Yes, Mr. President, just a couple of things. First, we believe that as you said, sir, the interaction of the solar flare and the Pulse somehow acted in such a way as to trap an EMP Effect within the earth's magnetic field. We believe that is why we have the unusual light show every night after the sun goes down. Without the proper equipment for studying this Effect, we have no way of knowing for sure. Secondly, we believe, at least we hope, that eventually this aberration will begin to dissipate and fade away."

"Mr. President, my name is Dr. Mark Rainier, Logan Aerospace. As you may know, our company contracted with the government to build the EMP weapon. I was only involved on the periphery of that particular project, sir, but I might be able to shed some light on what's happened. The weapon, code–named Project Blackout, utilized a controversial method of exponentially increasing the kinetic energy used to build an electromagnetic field through electromagnetic induction. The weapon utilized a new technique for increasing the yield of a non–nuclear EMP device by drawing power directly from and interacting with the earth's magnetic field. The weapon was never put into production however, or even full–scale testing for that matter, out of fear that the EMP would create widespread outages across the entire planet, instead of only in the target area. This is exactly what we have witnessed in recent days. The EMP device, what we called, 'the Pulse,' was highly unstable. There was also some concern, given how it drew power from the earth's magnetic field, about what would happen if it were ever activated in the presence of a solar flare. Mr. President, I told them they should destroy this device and all documentation about it, but they were convinced that given time, they would eventually learn how to control the reaction. No one ever dreamed that it would be stolen and used against us."

"No, they never do, do they? We're not here to assign blame Dr. Rainier; the damage from the Pulse has already been done. Is there anything we can do about this Effect from the blast?"

"Honestly, sir, I just don't know. If I had some way of studying this phenomenon, maybe I could offer some possible solutions. However, sir, this thing exists in the higher atmosphere. Nothing short of an ICBM, and a few aircraft, are able to reach these altitudes, Mr. President. Moreover, even if we were able to reach it, sir, and we are not, we have no way of knowing what we could do to counteract it. We might as well be trying to reach the sun on wings of wax, sir."

"Thank you, Dr. Rainier. I wish you had better news for us."

"So do I. sir. Believe me—so do I."

"General Miller, do you have anything to add?"

"Not really, Mr. President. I agree with Dr. Rainier's assessment. If there *is* some way of stopping that thing, I am afraid that I have no idea what it is, sir."

"Does anyone have anything to offer, anything at all?" Michaels looked around the room, searching, hoping. Finally, he turned his attention to Bjorn Yvornsky, who was sitting near the back of the room.

"Dr. Yvornsky, do you have any suggestions? I understand that you were one of the best and brightest to ever graduate from MIT."

"Sorry Mr. President, my expertise is in computer science, specifically in AI, artificial intelligence."

"Even so, do you have any insights that you would like to share?"

"Well, sir, if you are asking if I have any suggestions about how we can take out this remnant from the Pulse, the electro–magnetic ribbon of energy you refer to as, 'the Effect,' no, sir, I do not. I am afraid that I can only concur with Dr. Rainier and General Miller. Given our level of technology without the benefit of electricity, we might as well be trying to split the atom with a knife."

"That's not very helpful, Dr. Yvornsky," the president said dryly.

"Well, with all due respect, sir, what did you expect me to say, that we can launch a bottle rocket into the sky and make that thing disappear? What were you people thinking, creating something like this to begin with? Did you ever stop and consider the fact that this thing could be used against us, or the impact it would have on a civilian population, especially our own? Do you have any idea how much of our civilian infrastructure depends on electricity, on electronic components of one kind or another?"

"Why don't you enlighten us, Doctor?" Michaels was now visibly angry.

"I'm sorry, Mr. President."

"No, please, Doctor, it's alright, that is after all why we are gathered here—to discuss this from all angles."

"Well sir, the electric grid is probably the most obvious casualty of the Pulse, because losing the grid will have a cascading effect, like knocking down dominos, one problem causes another which causes another, and so on. It is certainly the most vulnerable and losing it has the greatest impact. Consider for a moment that homes use electricity to power their refrigerators. Without power, there is no way to keep food cold and safe to eat. There is no way to keep homes cool in the summer and warm in the winter. Many of today's homes have no fireplaces, so the only way to heat is with electricity. Perhaps even more important than heat is water. Today's water utilities depend on electrical pumps, valves, and small computers called programmable logic controllers to control the flow of water to homes. There are virtually no areas in our lives that have not been touched, in some way or another, by electricity."

"But, Dr. Yvornsky, man did just fine for thousands of years without electricity," interjected Rob Thornton.

"Well, Mr. Thornton, that is certainly debatable, but I understand your point. You mean that since mankind did just fine without electricity for thousands of years, why can't he do it again?"

"Exactly."

"Well you are correct, Mr. Thornton. Humanity will be able to live without electricity. However, only after many millions of people die."

"What are you talking about?"

"Our society, our world, is addicted to technology. We have built our entire way of life around technology. We have become completely dependent on it. If you were to take that away gradually, people would adapt, our society would adapt. However, the Pulse has not taken them away gradually; it took them away, *all of them*, at once, in a blink of an eye. We have had no time to adapt. Our grocery stores are gone, our heat is gone, our transportation is gone, and our water is gone. What do you think people will do when they start dying of thirst while there is still water in the lakes, in the rivers, and in the ponds? I will tell you what they will do sir. In their desperation, they will drink the contaminated water, and they will become sick with Cholera, diphtheria, or some other disease. And what about competition?"

"What do you mean, Doctor?" asked Michaels.

"Well, sir, our modern cities utilize technology to support the burgeoning growth in populations. Our cities could never have grown to the size they have without electricity. Many cities pump water from distant rivers, lakes, etc., and recycle the water using electricity–based technologies to treat the water and pump it into people's homes. When was the last time you walked to the river for water, pumped it from a well, or walked out to the outhouse in the middle of the night? Resources will become scarcer as time goes on. People will begin turning on one another, just to survive. I'm telling you, sir, the death toll across the planet will be substantial, and many will die. It is the end of civilization as we know it."

President Michaels, who had been standing, listening intently to everything he said, fell back into his seat.

"It's a frightening future you have laid out for us, Dr. Yvornsky," Michaels said grimly.

He looked around the table, before focusing his attention on James White, who had been staring at the floor during the discussion.

"Dr. White, what do you think?" The pastor looked up at President Michaels.

"Mr. President, I know that you would probably like to know where God is during this crisis, why he is allowing this to happen, why he doesn't act. As a retired minister, I can only say this: God did not create the EMP weapon, *and* God did not activate it—people did that. I am only a simple man, Mr. President, a man that decided to serve others in the name of God, because I felt God's calling to minister to others. As a mere man, I cannot presume to know why God permits any disaster, be it natural or man–made, to occur. Perhaps he allowed it to happen because so many people have embraced technology and rejected him. After all, he has warned humanity time and time again that if we reject him he will also reject us. Honestly, Mr. President, I just don't know. I can only say that I know that during these difficult times, as with *all* difficult times, he is here with us." Michaels mulled over some of the lively discussion they had already had.

"Dr. White, would you agree with Dr. Yvornsky's somewhat bleak assessment of how people will behave as resources become scarcer?"

"Mr. President, have you ever read *Moby Dick?*"

"Yes, I have, but why? What does that have to do with anything?"

"Did you know that Herman Melville based Moby Dick on a true story?"

"No, what does that..."

"Please bear with me for a moment, sir. Melville based Moby Dick on the events around the Essex, a whaling ship that left Nantucket in 1819. On one hunting expedition, an unusually large sperm whale attacked the ship while the whaleboats were off hunting other whales in the pod. The larger whale destroyed the Essex. Now the crew of the Essex survived, for a time, in the whaleboats, until food ran out. In the end, they resorted to drawing straws and cannibalism to survive."

"I see," the president responded.

"I believe he is right in saying that difficult circumstances can bring out the worst in human nature," James White continued. "However, I would also add that difficult circumstances can bring out the best in people, as well. I have witnessed acts of brutality over the past month by people I thought incapable of such things, but I have also seen acts of kindness by people I imagined were incapable of ever caring for another human being. I believe one other thing as well, Mr. President, that there is always hope. We can rebuild civilization at some point, Mr. President, once this *thing* is gone, if we develop a plan. As Saint Francis of Assisi once said, 'Start by doing what's necessary; then do what's possible; and suddenly you are doing the impossible.'"

"Thank you, Dr. White," Michaels said thoughtfully. "Cardinal Cousteau, do you have anything that you would like to add on behalf of the Church at Rome?"

"Only that I would like to echo what Dr. White has said, that it is impossible for us to know the mind of God while we walk this earth. I know that the Holy Father has voiced concern on a number of occasions that something like this could happen.

Humanity as a whole *has* rejected the Lord in so many ways, choosing to put their faith in people and technology rather than in God, even while the faithful struggle to hold on. We must urge everyone to turn back to the Lord, for truly we are all in his hands."

"Thank you, Cardinal Cousteau that is very interesting. Does anyone else have anything that he or she would like to discuss before we take a short break? All right then, when we return, I would like to discuss plans for evacuating the Washington, DC area, as well as a proposal from General Miller to form a small company of men from Ft. Myer to escort some military families, as well as civilians, to government land west of the Washington, DC area. "

Michaels waited as people began filtering out of the room. When he saw General Miller walking past him towards the door, he walked up beside him and placed his hand on his shoulder.

"General?"

"Yes, Mr. President?"

"Can we talk for a moment, please?"

"Of course, sir, what can I do for you?" Michaels took the arm of the general and gently led him toward a window, away from the others that had been congregating near the center of the room. Michaels looked out the window and began rubbing his chin. General Miller knew President Michaels well enough to recognize that he was deeply troubled about something.

"It's going to get bad out there, isn't it General?" he asked, still stroking his chin.

"Yes, Mr. President, I'm afraid it's going to get *very* ugly out there sir."

"I've been thinking, General," Michaels started, "thinking that I need someone that I can count on to help some key people stay alive long enough to develop a plan, a plan for the future of mankind." Michaels turned away from the window and faced the general with a furrowed brow. I need one of the toughest, most dedicated men that you have, General, someone who is capable enough and dependable enough to entrust the continuity of our way of life."

The general stared back out the window again, allowing his eyes to survey the monuments, the Washington, D.C. downtown area, and then the Potomac River. He abruptly turned back and met the president's gaze.

"Sir, I believe I know of just the man, assuming I can still find him. He's not in the Air Force he's in the Army. I know him through a friend of mine who's a general in the Army."

Michaels face brightened for just a moment. It occurred to the general that it was the first time he had seen the president smile since the attack.

"Well get on it then General Miller, find me that man!"

"Consider it done, Mr. President."

CHAPTER 26

It was getting colder, and for the first time, it was beginning to look like snow. Soon they would have to find a place to rest the horses and wait out the approaching storm. He knew better than to be caught out in the open by a Midwestern snowstorm in the middle of winter. Besides, they had been riding for several days, and the men and the horses needed rest and food.

Masters looked around at the thirty or so men that now accompanied him. They were all well armed and eager to fight, ready to follow him wherever he led them. He knew where *he* was headed all right, but he was not eager to share the destination with his new friends. It might be a bit too dangerous for them, but he was determined to see it through.

There were farms all around him. As it was winter, he knew that most of the crops had come in months ago, so the farmers would have food. As he looked around, he noticed that the sun was sitting just above the horizon. He estimated that they had maybe an hour of sunlight left, maybe two. Ahead in the distance, he saw something reflected in the sun. He strained to make out what appeared to be a farm ahead. As they got closer however, he could see that it was not a farm, but a small town. As they continued riding, he could make out that there were a number of people standing in the streets, watching them draw closer. He also noticed that the townspeople appeared to be well armed; each was holding a rifle, shotgun, or a handgun. Masters chuckled to himself, as he looked the men over. From what he could tell, the townspeople were just farmers or simple towns-people—not exactly what he would consider warriors. Masters, however, *was* a warrior. He was a hardened, experienced soldier, who had seen many veteran soldiers like himself killed by civil-ians, just like the ones that stood before him. He would not let down his guard for a moment.

Masters motioned for everyone to stop as they approached the town. Some of the men came out to meet them halfway, pointing their weapons at Masters and his men as they did so. One of the men, the town's sheriff, came out to meet them. Since Masters was in the front, they approached him first.

"Who are you, and what do you want, mister?" he asked Masters, who just smiled.

"Why, my men and I are just tired, and we are looking for something to eat and some rest."

"Well we have no place for you here, mister. We have barely enough to take care of our own. You and your men had bet-ter be pushing on." Masters just looked at the man and smiled. Bill Miller, who was sitting on a horse just behind Masters, rec-ognized the smile and gripped his weapon, anticipating a fight with the armed townspeople.

"Now listen, Sheriff. We are tired and just want something to eat, that's all, and we will push on after the snowstorm has passed. We're not looking for any trouble. I suggest that you change your attitude and start showing a little more hospitality." He smiled again. "Either way, we *are* going to be here for a few days whether you like it or not."

The man walked over to Masters and pointed the shotgun at his head.

"Now, friend," said Masters, "didn't anyone ever teach you that you should never point a gun at someone unless you are going to shoot them?" Just as he completed the sentence, Masters leaned to his left and grabbed the barrel of the shotgun with his right hand. Just as he grabbed it, the shotgun went off, firing a shot beside Masters head. Moving so fast it was only a blur to those watching, with a yank on the barrel, he snatched the barrel out of the man's hands, turned it around, and before anyone even had a chance to react, he pulled the trigger. The blast from the shotgun struck the Sheriff in the shoulder, knocking him f to the ground. There was another momentary exchange of gunfire before two more of the townspeople fell.

Several of Masters' men were struck by shotgun blasts and knocked off their horses. The two groups exchanged gunfire for several minutes until several more townspeople were injured. Eventually, the last of the townspeople lost their taste for the fight. They started to lay down their weapons, and surrendered. Masters took aim with the shotgun and shot two more of the townspeople in their kneecaps.

"If any of you tries anything like this again, I promise you that I will kill the lot of you. Do you understand me? On the other hand, if you cooperate, stay out of our way, and do what we tell you, we will leave in a couple of days—once the storm has passed. I have no interest in killing any more of you, but as you can see, I certainly will if I have to. Does everyone understand me?" There was a moment of silence as no response came. He took aim at the several more of the townspeople, moving from person to person, with his index finger on the trigger.

One of the men answered, "We understand, mister—just *take it easy*." Masters just smiled and laid the shotgun across his lap.

"Now, then, that's better. Do you fine folks have a hotel here in err—what's the name of this town?"

"The name of the town is Providence, and yes, the hotel is about three blocks from here. Of course you know there is no power anywhere in town," one of the men answered.

"I understand. Now, we will need food, drink, and feed for our horses. You fine folks might also want to put up a couple of outhouses behind the hotel. In addition, we need a doctor for our injured men; afterward he can tend to your wounds. Do you understand my instructions?"

"We understand you, mister. We'll fetch a doctor and some shovels. The outhouses are a good idea." Masters began to ride on toward the hotel when the man said, "One more thing, and mister?" Masters stopped his horse and turned to face the man.

"Yes, what is it?" he asked.

"We've listened to *you*, now, you listen to *me*. We will provide you with food, shelter, and a place to weather the storm. But just so we're clear, and you should make no mistake about this, we will gladly die fighting if we must. We will kill you *and* your men if you push us too far. Do you understand that?" Masters looked hard at the man for several moments before smiling, and nodding at the man.

"I've got it. I'm glad we understand each other!" Masters rode on with a big smile on his face. He had underestimated the resolve of the people in the small town of Providence. It was obvious to Masters that the people would risk death standing up to invaders if necessary; he would have to remember that going forward. He admired the courage of the townspeople. Vic Masters was a killer, but he did appreciate and respect courage like what he had found in this town. He would honor his promise as long as they stayed out of his way, and he would push on with his men in a few days, once the storm had past. He had bigger fish to fry and was anxious to catch the biggest one.

As they rode on into town, Masters noticed a restaurant where some people were gathered. He was a bit surprised to find a restaurant open. It looked as if a number of the townspeople were at the restaurant, so Masters assumed that they must still have food and drink. He and his men stopped at the restaurant and tied up the horses outside. It was a bit odd pulling up to a restaurant on a horse instead of in his Porsche, but it was just a sign of the times.

When they walked inside of the restaurant, they noticed that most of the people inside were wearing firearms. Masters shook his head and wondered for a moment why he had chosen a town where everyone was armed. A woman walked over and met them as they walked in.

"What can we do for you?"

"We need something to eat and drink. What do you have?"

"Well, with the power out, all we have left are a few canned goods, some fruit, and some fresh vegetables. As far as beverages, we have boiled water with a pinch of salt added, as well as some warm bottles of beer still left."

"What about meat, do you have any kind of meat?"

"Well, it's been kind of hard since we currently have no way of keeping the meat fresh. We do have a few folks that know how to cure meat, but they are still getting things setup. We have been slaughtering a cow in the mid–morning hours once a week, and chickens twice a week. There is a chicken house outside of town and a large cattle ranch as well. Now in terms of payment, you realize that money has no value anymore, so you will need to have something to trade. What do you have?"

"Becky, can I have a word with you?" It was one of the men that had met them when they first arrived. After talking with the man for a few minutes, Becky walked back over and addressed Masters."

"Look, I understand your situation, mister. But we have to survive here too."

Masters looked at her for a moment and smiled. "We have a couple of extra horses that we won't need anymore, would that cover us for a couple of days?"

"That would be just fine. Thank you for your cooperation, mister."

"Think nothing of it. My men and I will be here for a few days. See to it that we all have enough to eat and drink while we are here," he said.

"Consider it done," she said.

The men sat down and clustered in the only part of the restaurant where there was still plenty of seating. After they had sat down and had been brought something to drink, a woman began bringing candles out and setting them on the tables. Masters looked out of the window and noticed that the sun was setting. The waitress had nearly finished lighting the candles when one of Masters men grabbed her and sat her on his lap.

"Hey *you*, leave her alone!" Becky walked over to Masters. "Are you going to do something about your man there, or do I have to?"

Masters looked over at him and said coldly, "There will be none of that, now—leave her alone. There will be plenty of time for fun later." The man had only recently joined up with Masters and his crew a few days earlier when they had passed through the last town. He looked over at Masters for a moment, and then proceeded to struggle with the woman. As soon as she had broken free from the man, Masters pulled out a 9MM Glock and shot him right between the eyes. Everyone in the room that had seen the move was shocked by the speed, the accuracy, and the smoothness in the execution of the shot. One woman whispered to the man sitting next to her that this was a man not to be trifled with.

"Would anyone else like to challenge my orders?" he asked, looking coldly over his men. Every man shook his head as he pointed to two of them. "Get him out of here. Take him and bury him after dinner somewhere outside of town. Is that clear?" The two men nodded. Masters looked at the woman and asked, "Are you okay, lady?"

"I—I'm fine. Thank you for helping me." Masters just nodded.

After checking on the other woman, Becky walked back over to Masters' table.

"Thanks mister."

Masters looked at her with a cold smile, similar to the one that he had given the man he had just killed.

"Don't get the wrong idea about me, lady. I'm not a nice man, and I never pretend to be. I have an understanding with some of the folks in your fine town here, and it suits me, for now, to honor that. As long as your people stay out of our way, we will stay out of theirs. However, if anyone crosses me, I absolutely *will not* hesitate to kill them." She looked at him with a puzzled look on her face.

"Okay," she said as she walked to the back of the restaurant to bring them something to eat.

The snow had already started to fall when Masters and his men made it to the hotel. They brought their horses into the parking deck to get them out of the bitter cold and snow. They tied the horses up to a rail and walked into the hotel, before walking up to the front desk where a man stood waiting. He had keys sitting out and waiting for the men.

"Here you are, sir. I was told that you and your men would be coming. The rooms do not have fireplaces in them but we have placed extra blankets in each room. You should not have any problem staying warm. They have been working on the out-houses outside the back of the hotel; they should be done in a few hours."

Masters took a key and started for the door. He turned and said, "It's been several weeks since I had a bath. Set us up some hot baths for in the morning, and I will make it with your while."

"I'll see what I can do, sir," he said.

As Masters and the others began walking up the stairs, the man knew he would not rest easy until Masters and his men were long gone.

CHAPTER 27

Susan awoke to find herself lying on the sofa with a man sitting in the chair across her. She sat up and scooted to the other end of the sofa, frightened to find a stranger in the apartment. The man looked unkempt, and he smelled awful.

"Susan, don't be afraid."

"I'm not afraid," Susan answered, not bothering to hide her contempt. "It was hot in here and the heat finally got to me. Who are you? What are you doing here? How do you know my name?"

"Susan, it's me!"

"Who?"

"It's me, Scott!"

"Scott? No, my husband, Scott, is dead."

"Susan!" She looked at the man. She had already convinced herself that Scott was dead and thought that she would never see him again. She calmed herself for a moment and studied the man before her. His hair was matted, his clothes worn out, and he wore a lumberjack's beard. Scott had always been clean–shaven and meticulous about grooming. She tried to see beyond the tattered clothing and the scruffy appearance.

That voice. "Scott?"

"It's me, honey. I'm home."

"Scott!"

She jumped off the sofa and into his arms, causing him and the chair to fall backward. They both landed on the floor. She lay on top of him for several moments, holding him tightly, afraid he might suddenly vanish like a mirage if she let go, even for a moment.

"Scott, is it really you?" She sat back up and looked at him intently.

"Yes, it *is* me. It took me a little longer than I figured to make it back home."

"Oh, Scott, I've missed you so much! I…" Susan, who had been smiling from ear to ear for the longest time, suddenly changed. Her smile changed to a grimace, her eyebrows sharpened, and her forehead wrinkled. All of her fear and anxiety over everything that had happened, all of her fears and doubts, her nightmares of Scott lying dead on the side of the road, her fears about having to raise the baby all alone in the middle of all of the chaos, everything began rushing to the surface all at once . She began beating him in the chest.

"You—you—how could you do this to me? Do you have any idea what I've been going through here, fighting every day just to stay alive, worried sick for our baby? Do you realize that the power has been out for almost a month now? The food is almost gone. It finally rained today, so I finally have some water. Where were you all of this time? Why did you always have to stay at the office, anyway, when you could have been here? I cannot believe you!" She jumped off Scott and dropped onto the sofa, weeping.

"I'm sorry, Susan. I can't imagine how hard it must have been for you, here all alone during all of this, this—" Scott abruptly stopped talking. "Um, Susan, did you say *baby?*"

Susan stopped crying and looked over at Scott, smiling. For the moment, at least, her anger had vanished.

She whispered, "I never told you, did I?"

This time Scott ran over to her side and embraced her, rocking her back and forth.

"A baby, *our* baby?"

"That's right. I never had the chance to tell you about it. I was supposed to be going to the doctor to be certain, but then, all of this—whatever *this* is—happened!"

"How far along are you?"

"I should be around four months, maybe five."

Scott sat back as the full weight of the news began to sink in.

"Oh Susan, that is wonderful news. But with everything that's been happening—"

"What? Like I haven't noticed? Like I never gave that a moment's consideration?" Angry Susan had returned.

"I'm sorry, honey, this is just, such a surprise," said Scott

"You're telling me!"

"Wow, a baby. That really is great news, honey. Listen, everything is going to be just fine—I promise." Scott and Susan said nothing for several minutes, just enjoying one another's company, until Susan interrupted the silence.

"Scott, I'm sorry for the way I behaved earlier. I guess the pregnancy was already wreaking havoc on my hormones, even *before* all of this happened. I've been so worried Scott, so afraid. What are we going to do, how are we going to survive? We don't have any idea what's happening, what's caused all of this ..." She paused when she noticed a familiar look on Scott's face, as if he was hiding something.

"Scott, you know something about what happened, don't you? Dick has some crazy idea about some sort of attack with an EMP weapon. I thought it was crazy, but *there is* definitely *something* wrong with the power grid."

Scott looked up at the ceiling and then around the apartment. Susan could tell by the wild look in his eyes and the tension that had appeared in his face that he was distraught. He was starting to scare her.

"Maybe, I'm not certain Susan, but I believe I have a pretty good idea what has happened. Let's just say that I think Dick is probably right." Scott started to tear up, before burying his face in his hands. "May God forgive me, Susan; I think that all of this may be because of *me!* I don't know how I can live with myself if it turns out to be true." Susan's initial curiosity changed to deep concern for her husband's welfare.

"Scott, what are you talking about, honey? How could any of this possibly be *your* fault?"

"Do you remember the project at work that I told you about, the one that I spent so much time working on recently, and the one that earned me that promotion, and has kept me in the office working late so many nights over the last several months?"

"You mean the one that you said was so secret that you could be arrested for treason, just for telling me about it?"

"Yes, that's the one. Well, I guess it doesn't matter anymore. The government commissioned a project and contracted with our company to deliver it. The project was the development of a new, highly experimental type of weapon, an electromagnetic pulse, or EMP device, that was *supposed* to *save lives,* to make nuclear weapons obsolete. Instead, it's done all of, *this!*"

"Oh no—Scott." Susan tried for a moment to imagine what it would be like to know that something she had created had caused so much suffering, and so much death. "Scott, my Scott...how do you know that it was the weapon *you* created that did all of this?"

"Because it was stolen just a few days before this all started. It was still highly experimental and extremely unstable. We were not even able to field test the weapon out of fear over what might happen. How can I live with myself, Susan? Look outside at what is happening, it's my fault, *all of it!*"

Susan held him close, just trying to console him. A wave of guilt came over her as she realized how selfish she had been; complaining about how much *she* had suffered while Scott had been carrying such a heavy burden of his own.

Scott continued, "You see, Susan, I believed that my work was so important! I wanted to develop a device that could instantly incapacitate an enemy's ability to wage war, a device that could end a war before it ever started! After years of research, I developed a highly advanced type of an EMP weapon that, when activated, would instantly disable electronics, the key to all communication systems, computers, missile guidance systems, and the like during a conflict. Once the conflict had ended, they could rebuild their electronics easily enough.

I thought that if only we could develop a weapon that could subdue an enemy, a rogue state, or even a terrorist organization, without the bloodshed and the devastation of conventional or nuclear warfare. Such a weapon would enable us to defeat a powerful enemy, even another nuclear power, without the use of a single nuclear weapon, or the risk of something as abominable as a nuclear war. I had only the best of intentions, Susan, I promise; I thought I was *saving* the world, not *destroying* it!" Susan held her husband tightly as she struggled to find the right words to comfort and console him. She knew that it was not his fault; she just needed to find a way to convince *him* of that fact.

"Scott, now you listen to me. What you did was to work on something that would offer the world a way to win wars without the death and destruction that have been a part of war for so very long. Whatever caused all of this; it was not caused by the device that you were working on. The device that you were working to create doesn't exist yet. The device that was stolen was something else. It was experimental and unstable—you said so yourself. This is *not* your fault, Scott. What you *were* doing was a noble and caring thing. You wanted to save lives, because you are a wonderful man. The people that stole the device, the ones that activated it, it was their fault, not yours, do you hear me?"

Scott seemed to be responding to her, she was looking for one more nugget of encouragement for Scott, and then it hit her.

"Scott, the device you were developing, it was designed to affect electronics that were on when it was activated, correct?

"Yes, that's right."

"Until they could be rebuilt or repaired?"

"Of course. It would only take out electronics that were not shielded against EMP and were active at the time. What are you getting at?"

"Well, if the device was designed to only knock out electronics that were active at the time, why hasn't the power been restored yet?"

Scott looked at Susan, looked around their apartment, and then looked back at Susan again.

"I don't know, I guess I would have expected it to have been restored by now. You're right, that is very odd now that you mention it. Something else must have happened. I've been so wrapped up in my guilt that it never occurred to me."

"Well then, there you go, problem solved."

Scott looked into his wife's eyes and said, "You know something? You are an incredible, wonderful, *amazing* wife, and I absolutely *adore* you!" He kissed her, placed a hand on either side of her face, and with a very serious look on his face, he gazed into her eyes and said, "Thank you, Susan; I needed to hear that. You really are incredible."

"Compliments will get you everywhere with me, as you know so well!" She leaned back and pushed him away. "Listen," she said, "we had a nice, heavy rainfall today. I was able to collect a good amount of water, which I have stored in some pitchers, and other containers in the kitchen. I will get a pot from your camping equipment that we can use in the fireplace so that we can heat up some water. Would you *please* see if you can clean up a little and please, *change* your clothes?"

Scott looked at his clothes, took a quick whiff, and laughing said to her, "Would you still love me if I said no?" She looked at him and cracked a big smile.

"Well, let's just not find out, okay?"

Susan took some of the water that she had collected and carried it into the living room where the fireplace was. Scott had already started a fire and the logs were red–hot by the time she arrived with the water. When the water had warmed enough, Scott took the water, along with a change of clothes, and went into the bathroom. It was cool in the room, but the warm water and the bar of soap did a world of good for him, causing him to feel refreshed and reinvigorated afterward. It was not quite as effective or as easy as a shower, but it was good enough that he felt like a new man afterward. When he had finished with his bath, he dressed and looked for his razor. While he worked diligently to remove the facial hair that had grown in over the past month, he found himself wondering how he was going to shave when his razor blades were dull. He supposed that he would have to start using a straight razor, or a knife, if he wanted to remain clean–shaven. It was just one of the many adjustments that they would have to make, as they adjusted to a world without electricity. *A world without electricity. Who would have thought only a month ago that there would soon be a world without electricity?*

He found himself questioning how his EMP device, or any device for that matter, could continue to fry electronics so long after the Pulse had been activated. There was something, gnawing at the back of his mind, something relevant, something that he had seen on the news and then dismissed out of hand, something important. He decided to focus on his shaving, thinking it would come back to him. He nicked himself with the razor and reached for the toothpaste. He was not accustomed to shaving by candlelight, and was surprised at how hard it was to see. He noticed that the candle was flickering and was burning rather low. They were going to have to find supplies, perhaps in the morning, when the sun came up. Then it hit him: *the sun.* He had watched the morning news the morning before the Pulse struck, as he was getting ready for work. NASA had warned the public that there was a lot of unusual solar activity anticipated that day. Scott knew that "unusual" for the government was often code for *dangerous.* They had warned that satellites, cell phones, possibly even the power grid could be impacted. He knew that they must have been anticipating a major coronal mass ejection for NASA to be warning of potential damage to the power grid. It certainly was *possible* that the flare and the pulse could have interacted in some way, resulting in their present dilemma.

"What are the odds of them *both* occurring at exactly the same time?" he asked himself aloud.

He finished shaving and opened the door, only to find his wife standing in the doorway.

She looked up at her husband's now smooth face and asked, "Tall, dark, and handsome, where have you been all of my life?"

"Careful now, ma'am, I am a happily married man."

Susan grinned from ear to ear and said, "That's okay. I won't tell if you don't." The two embraced for the first time in over a month. Suddenly all of the worries, fears, doubts, and anxieties seemed to melt before fading gently away into the *gentle*, blissful night.

CHAPTER 28

The drums were beating, as he raced to get away, and someone was chasing him, He wanted to get away from the city, to
escape the suffering, to get back home to his family. The drums,
they seemed to get louder and louder until finally, he sat up and
screamed, "Susan!" Scott awoke to find his wife still soundly
asleep next to him, despite the outburst. Someone was knocking
on the apartment door. Scott dressed and made his way to the
door. He opened it to find Dick standing in the doorway.

"Scott! Scott, oh, man, you're alive!" Dick grabbed Scott in
a bear hug that made Scott uncomfortable for a moment. Scott
could tell by the look of surprise on Dick's face that *everyone*
thought he was dead.

"Hello, Dick."

"When did you get back, Scott? Hold on for a minute." Dick
left and raced over to his apartment, emerging thirty seconds
later with his wife in tow.

"Scott, my dear, is it really you?"

"In the flesh, Eleanor. It really is good to see you both. There were times that I never thought I'd see any of you ever again."

"We are just so glad to see that you made it! We were all so worried that something terrible had happened to you. She never said anything, but I fear that your dear wife had given up all hope of ever seeing you again. It was so hard on her, the dear thing."

"I would have been back much sooner had I been able. The trip was considerably harder than I would have imagined."

"I bet it was," responded Dick, his face taking on a more serious look. "Most people in this country have not traveled without benefit of a car, or horse for that matter, for well over a hundred years."

"Scott, dear, we will leave and give you and Susan a chance to get moving this morning. We have some fresh coffee and some corned beef hash we have been saving, if you and Susan would like to join us for breakfast. It would also give us some time to discuss the future, to discuss preparations for the trip."

"What trip?" asked Scott.

"Oh my, I guess she hasn't had time to tell you yet. We were planning to leave the city, to head out toward the country; maybe even the mountains, where we can find food, and water, where we can grow vegetables and *survive*. We have to leave the metro area before things get any worse."

"I understand. That certainly sounds like the right thing to do, Eleanor. Susan is still sleeping at the moment. We will come after she wakes up and talk about it—is that okay?"

"That will be just fine, Scott, just fine. It is so good to see you again young man, for Susan's sake, as well as yours."

"It's good to see both of you too, Eleanor."

"We'll see you later, Scott."

"Sounds good, Dick. Thanks for checking on us."

Scott closed the door and sat down in the chair. *We were planning to leave the city.* He had not given a lot of thought as to what to do next. He considered the benefits of staying in the city versus getting outside of the city. There seemed to be pros and cons to doing both. If they stayed in the city, they had shelter and more access to stores, where they might find food and supplies. However, based on what he had already experienced on his journey home, he knew firsthand that they would not be the only ones rummaging in those stores for food and supplies. The competition for food and water in particular would be getting fiercer with each passing day. As he gave it more consideration, it became clearer to Scott that if they stayed in the city, they would likely die. Maybe not next week, or the week after, but eventually, there would be little or no food left in the city.

Scott walked back to the bathroom to clean up a little and then looked in on Susan. He found his wife still soundly asleep in bed. He decided to wait a while, wanting her to get all of the rest that she could. He poured himself some water and sat down. He had never tried drinking rainwater before, because he had never *had to* before. It tasted much better than he ever would have imagined. In fact, he thought it tasted better than the tap water he had been drinking for the last several years.

He looked around to see what they had left to eat and noticed that the food was almost gone. The discovery of the dwindling food supplies had instilled within him a real sense of urgency. Susan had really proven herself a real survivor. With everything that had been going on, she had the presence of mind to collect a quantity of water that he felt certain should be more than enough to last them the entire trip to—Scott suddenly realized that he had no idea where they were going. *What had Eleanor said? The country, maybe even the mountains?*

It seemed strange to him that he had not given any thought to the future while he was walking back from DC. The trip had been long and hard, and he had been woefully unprepared for the journey, but then, who *had* been prepared? He suspected that most people, like himself, had always expected that the power would come back, that cars would suddenly start working again. How could anyone have known?

Scott fought back the growing flood of fear and despair that threatened to overwhelm him. He had grown up in a relatively safe and secure environment in a happy home. Looking back on his past, he realized that he had really led a charmed life. Despite his comfortable upbringing however, he recognized how important it was not to allow despair a foothold in a survival situation. It was something that he suspected he would be reminding himself about repeatedly, perhaps for the rest of his life. The situation was dire to be sure, but no amount of despair would be of any help to them.

He found a pack of unopened crackers and a can of Spam that had fallen in the corner. He sat down at the kitchen table to his crackers and Spam as his thoughts turned back to the future. They would need to be extremely selective about what they took with them if they were going any appreciable distance, and he thought they would need to. They would need to hunt, grow crops, find and carry water, dig a well, and build a home.

"Good morning, sweetheart. Enjoying your Spam?" Susan wrapped her arms around him and squeezed him firmly from behind.

"How did you sleep, honey?" he asked.

"That is probably the best that I have slept in well over a month. Oh, I have missed you so much!" She bent over and gave her husband a kiss.

"Eleanor came by this morning. She invited us to join her and Dick for breakfast. They want to talk over plans for leaving." A concerned look came over Susan's face.

"Scott, I'm sorry, I should have told you last night. I—"

"No, no, it's okay honey. I had some time to think about it afterwards, and she's right, we have to leave, and soon."

"What makes you say that?"

"Our food is running low, and there's not likely going to be a grocery store where we can go to buy some more food. At first, I thought that we might be better off to just stay put right here where we are. However, I don't know that staying here is going to be safe or sustainable. As hard as it's going to be, I think we will be better off if we put some distance between the metro area and us. When you're ready, let's get on over there. I would like to get a plan together today and leave, maybe in another day or two. We have a lot of planning to do." Susan glanced at him with a look of astonishment on her face. He had never been the serious, take–charge kind of guy. She wasn't sure at first, but she smiled as she decided that she thought she might like it.

After she dressed and had something to eat, they walked over to Dick and Eleanor's apartment. Eleanor answered the door.

"Well, good morning, Susan—don't you look lovely this morning, and just glowing, look at you!" She glanced over at Scott and winked before facing Susan. "Happy to see your husband, I imagine, aren't you?" She smiled and held Susan's hands. "How are you this morning dear?"

"I am much better, now that *he's* home," she replied, smiling at Scott, her cheeks a little flushed. Eleanor turned back toward Scott.

"Scott, it's so good to see you again. When Dick told me that you were back, we were just so relieved. We offered up a prayer of thanksgiving to the Lord to thank him for your safe return. Can I offer you both some coffee? We brewed some over the fire just an hour ago." The two nodded in affirmation, as Eleanor continued. "It has taken a little experimentation, but I think I am getting the hang of it. I am old enough that I still remember my mother having one of the old kettles, the ones that used to sit on top of the stove. It's been so long though, and I was so young, I just couldn't remember how they used it!" She poured them some coffee and brought it to them in the living room.

Susan sipped her coffee and exclaimed, "Oh, this is good coffee! How did you do it? How did you make this, Eleanor?" Eleanor beamed in delight as she sat back down.

She replied with an impious smile, "Yes, it *is* good, isn't it? I remember my mother telling me that coffee was so much better the old–fashioned way. I just thought she was being nostalgic!"

After some more small talk, they finished their coffee, and the four were ready to get down to business.

Dick sat up straight, looked over at Scott, and asked, "So how is it out there Scott? I have walked around here a little, but you've walked all the way from the downtown DC." Scott looked a bit nervously at his wife, who had been waiting attentively for his response. She recognized the look of concern and shook her head.

"Now, listen here, mister. I've been in that apartment alone for over a month, not knowing whether you were dead or alive, figuring out how to get by without electricity, with little food, little water, and I'm still here." Looking down as she gently rubbed her belly she smiled and added, "and *still* pregnant!"

"Okay, okay. Well, it's a bit surreal to start off with. Most of the time it was quiet, at some times eerily so. I mean, I guess I got so used to the noise of the city. On the way here, though, there were no cars, nor busses, no trains, no planes—I think people are scared and are mostly staying inside, for now. I had an old man try to attack me with a pocketknife for a bag of potato chips. I don't think he was a bad man, just starving." Scott did not mention any of the dead he had also seen on the long walk home. "It would be wise to have some kind of weapons, just in case."

Eleanor looked at Dick. "Oh, dear." Dick pulled her close and tried to console her.

"We have had a number of discussions about where to go. I suggested going south, toward Richmond or possibly the Carolinas. What do you two think?" Scott and Susan looked at each other.

"We haven't really had a chance to talk about it," answered Susan. "What do you think, Scott?" Scott thought about it for a few moments.

"Dick, Eleanor, do you have a map that includes the surrounding states?"

"I believe I have one in a desk in our den, hold on a moment, and let me see if I can find it." He walked out of the living room and into the den. "Ah, here it is," he said triumphantly, handing the map to Scott. He spread the map out on the table in front of him so everyone could see it.

"Well, I guess we could so south, toward Richmond and North Carolina," he said. "Richmond would be a long trek, however, and North Carolina even more so. In addition, as for

Richmond and the Raleigh–Durham area, they are fairly heavily populated."

"And if we go north back toward DC, we are getting closer to the northeast. It's going to be *really* bad up there," added Susan.

Scott leaned over the map and pointed toward the ocean. "Well we can't go east to the ocean, so how about west?"

"Toward the mountains?" Dick nodded in approval.

"Yes, toward the mountains. Hold on, let's have a look at the map and see what we can find."

Scott studied the map carefully for some time, looking at cities, travel time, and perhaps most importantly, water.

"Okay. So here we are, in Leesburg. If we follow the river here, we can stay away from the larger cities. We don't want to go too far, the travel would be too hard, especially in the cold. Hmm. How about this?" he asked, pointing to a location on the map. The other three strained to make it out. Susan leaned over his shoulder.

"Harper's Ferry?" she asked?

"Yes, Harper's Ferry, well that general area anyway, there is a national park there, Harper's Ferry National Park, so there will not be as many people. It's a lot closer than some of the other places we could go. I'll tell you another reason why it's a good location. For one, since we will be following the river, we will have access to water the entire trip *and* after we arrive. We may need to boil it, but we can drink it nonetheless for as long as we have to, and we can bathe in it. If we have any salt, and better yet some chlorine tablets, that would be helpful. We will want to dig a good deep well once we get there, to give us a better chance of having access to water that is safe to drink. We may even be able to carry some water with us for the journey, though I wouldn't want to carry too much as there will be a lot of other things we will want to bring with us."

"Well, that makes sense, Scott. Where there is water, there will be game. Have you ever dressed a deer?" Dick asked with a sly smile.

"Um, no. I have never been hunting for that matter."

"Well, then, I will have to teach you young man. It has been a few years, but I enjoyed hunting when I was younger. I believe I still have my old hunting rifle."

"And *ammunition?*" Scott asked.

"And ammunition," he replied.

"We might also do some fishing. Look, I know it's not ideal, but at least if we follow the river, we won't get lost, and we should be able to make our way there in a week or two, if we keep up a good pace and keep moving," added Scott.

"It seems like I still have a tent tucked away somewhere from my old hunting days as well," Dick said enthusiastically. "I believe I may still have some camping equipment, though I gave a lot of it to my son several years ago."

"That's great, Dick. It certainly will come in handy. Thankfully, I believe we still have some of mine as well also, from when I used to go hiking, back before Susan and I were married. I bought a new, slightly larger tent just after we married, hoping that we would get to use it for weekend outings, but we never used it."

"Well, it sounds like we certainly will have a lot of opportunity to use it now!"

"Yeah, I guess we will."

"Winter is starting to set in. Won't the cold weather be a problem?" asked Eleanor.

"Yes, yes I believe it will, Eleanor. However, I bought quite a bit of thermal clothing over the years for when I went hiking during the colder months, I am sure I have a few pair I can give to you and Dick, if you'd like them. I believe I may also have an extra sleeping bag as well."

"Thank you Scott. We will have to go through all of our belongings to see what we still have. It's been so long since we did anything like this."

"I understand." Susan grabbed Scott's arm. "What is it, honey?"

"There is *no way* we are staying in tents all winter; we'll end up freezing to death. I *will not* take the chance with the baby, there has to be a better way."

"You know," started Dick. "I once helped a friend of mine with a log cabin he wanted to build at a lake in the mountains. I don't know if I remember all of the details, but maybe, once we have the food and water situation under control, we can work on getting a cabin put up, maybe even before it gets much colder. We are barely into winter, so we should be able to get something up before the worst of it gets here."

Eleanor got up and asked, "I need another cup of coffee. Would anyone else like one?"

"Yes, I'll take one, please," answered Scott. Susan gave him a gentle push. "Oh, and one for Susan also, thank you."

"You know," said Eleanor, "there is one thing that I am really going to like about living near a river."

"What's that dear?" asked Dick.

"The opportunity to wash some clothes. Our laundry has piled up over the last several weeks!" Dick smiled at his wife before turning back to Scott.

"You know, we really have to give some thought to what supplies we will need once we arrive," Dick said to Scott, rubbing his head as he tried to think ahead. "Simple things like tools, saws, etc. will be extremely important. I believe I *still* have some tools that might come in handy, stuck in one of our closets, including an old axe; I would like to take some of them as well. I didn't always live in an apartment you know!"

"Oh what I wouldn't give for a horse, or better yet, horses," said Susan. "We could get there by wagon."

"Well I will ask for one then; we all should," Eleanor remarked, bowing her head to pray.

They all breathed a collective sigh of relief. For the first time since disaster struck, they had a plan and for a moment, the future looked just a little bit brighter. There were still a lot of issues to address and still a lot of bridges to cross, and they all knew it. Not the least of which was going to be how to get all of the supplies they needed. They had the most important assets they would need however, they had faith, and they had hope.

CHAPTER 29

There was considerable activity all around the National Mall. Everywhere he looked, he saw men and women, young and old, of all races, creeds, and nationalities, of different beliefs and religions. He saw children running and playing, people laughing, and people crying.

They had divided the mall into two large sections to expedite the foot traffic. In the first section, several large tents were setup nearest the Washington Monument, where a number of military and civilian doctors were stationed, along with a number of nurses assisting them in examining patients, passing out antibiotics, and treating injuries.

At the second section, more large tents had been erected closer to the Capital Building, where they were distributing food, water, and supplies.

Armed soldiers patrolled the grounds on horseback as well as on foot, throughout the inner city area as well as the grounds of the mall.

For the first time since the Pulse, the world seemed almost normal, at least more than it had been since it all began. It was this very same illusion of normalcy however, that made it all seem so surreal. Though few spoke of it, everyone knew that *their* world would never be the same again. No matter how much they wanted their old world back, their old way of life, it was gone, perhaps forever.

The news had been spreading across the city for the past two days that there was some sort of large gathering on the National Mall. Soldiers had been walking the *streets* throughout the DC area as well, helping to spread the news, the best news most of them had heard for a long time, that there was food, water, supplies, even doctors at the Mall in DC. Just as important, there would be escorts for those wanting safe passage out of the DC area.

The president had ordered that government stores of food, water, clothing, and other supplies be distributed to citizens. To help ensure that there was no hoarding, the military personnel were using hand stamps that would wear off over the period of several weeks. There were military blankets, meals ready–to–eat (MREs), basic medical kits, and even a number of military tents being handed out as well.

Conrad tried his best to enjoy the temporary return to normalcy, regardless of how short–lived it might be. He found the familiar level of activity and excitement present on the mall, so similar to that which had been so commonplace in the days before the Pulse, very refreshing. It was an illusion and he understood that. Nevertheless, it was a break, a chance to catch his breath. He knew that the stark reality of their plight would come crashing down upon everyone again sooner rather than later, and he knew it better then most. In addition to spreading the word in regards to the gathering at the Mall, Conrad and the others from his unit had been escorting groups of civilians out of the city with supplies, for the past two days. Though it was hard to tell for sure, it seemed, at least to Conrad, that most of the residents in the capital had decided to stay, an extremely unwise decision in his opinion. There was little land available in the city where vegetables could be grown, there would be few game animals to hunt, and there would be plenty of competition for the scarce resources that did exist. With the Potomac River running through the middle of the metro area, water would not be as much of a problem, as long as people boiled it before drinking it. Still, it was going to get ugly, and he for one didn't want to hang around to see it.

Conrad weaved his way through the throngs of people and the portable toilets. He was about halfway to the Washington Monument when he saw them. The lines outside of the medical tents were nearly three times as long as the lines for food and water. Conrad wasn't why the lines for medical attention were so long, but he knew it couldn't be good. As he got closer, he noticed a station that seemed particularly busy. He slowed down his pace as he looked for someone in charge. He stopped near one of the larger tents, where he noticed a number of sick people inside, lying on cots. A woman in uniform emerged from the tent just a few seconds later. Conrad could not take his eyes off her. She was one of the most beautiful women he had ever laid eyes on, and judging by her uniform, she was a Navy Corpsman.

"You know what they say soldier," she told him. "If you take a picture, it will last longer." He blushed as she smiled and looked back toward where several doctors were standing."

"I'm sorry, ma'am, I..." She smiled at him warmly and noticed that he was still blushing.

"Or, forget about it, Colonel. I'm just happy to be admired at all these days."

"My name is Simmons. I thought I would see if I could help over here. I am not a doctor or a medic, but I did have some basic medical training in the Rangers."

"Hello, Colonel Simmons, my name is Rachel, Hospital Corpsman Second Class Rachel Bennett, it's nice to meet you *sir*. So you're a *Ranger?* Hmm, I've heard about you boys—well, how about that?" she said flirtatiously. She looked him over for several moments, trying to decide if she liked what she saw.

"You know what they say..." he started, smiling back. This time she was the one blushing. Not wanting to spoil the moment, he decided to change the subject. "So what's with the long lines? Is the flu going around?"

"The flu *is* going around, but I'm afraid that most of what we have been seeing is something far worse, Cholera."

"Cholera? I thought that was something that you see in third world countries, not here in the United States. Aren't people immunized against Cholera?"

"Well you and I were vaccinated, sure, since we are in the military. However, most of these civilians have not been. Cholera is a disease contracted by drinking from a contaminated water supply, which is exactly what these people have been doing. Most of them have been drinking from the Potomac. Think about it—they have been without running water for well over a month now. Even if they knew they might contract a disease, it's better than the alternative. Without water, we die in under a week regardless—better to take your chances." She stopped for a moment to look at him. "Listen, I'm sure that we both received a similar message, we are to remain here for a week, and then we are free to return to our base or—."

"Or we can leave, try to make it back to family, strike out on our own. It looks like everything is falling apart."

"Right. Well, Cholera can kill a lot, and I mean a lot, of people all across the country. People everywhere are going to get Cholera, or any one of hundreds of other diseases, especially in the cities where there are no wells, and they *are* going to die. It is going to be absolutely horrific. Hang on for just a second." She walked over to one of the doctors, also in a Navy Uniform. "Commander Wayne, sir, we are running out of beds in tent four, sir." The officer frowned.

"Very well. Go ahead and discharge those that are well enough to walk out. Give them a week's supply of antibiotics and send them on their way. Tell them we will be here for a few more days if they need to come back."

"Yes, sir." The pair walked back over toward the large tent.

"Do you have any family, Colonel?"

"No, not really. My wife died a few years ago, and I was an orphan as a child. I have some distant cousins, but none that I know very well. How about you?"

"No, not really. I'm sorry about your wife," she said.

"Thank you."

"I've never been married. I just never met the right man, I guess. My father died in Afghanistan when I was only a child. My mother died from cancer a few years ago."

"*I'm* very sorry to hear *that* Corpsman."

"Rachel."

"Excuse me?"

"Please, call me Rachel."

"All right, Rachel, only if you call me Conrad."

"Tell you what, Conrad, there are some more blankets in some boxes behind that tent," she said pointing to the tent next to the one she was working in, "would you mind bringing me a few more? I could also use some more water bottles—they are back there as well. Would you mind?"

"Not at all. I'll be right back."

Conrad walked around to the back of the huge tent. He felt giddy, like a schoolboy once more. There was something about her, her beauty, her mannerisms, the way she carried herself. Conrad felt an attraction to her that he could not explain. He did not know what it was about the Navy Corpsman that appealed to him so much, but he knew that he wanted to spend as much time with her as he possibly could. He had dated plenty of women before getting married, but he had never felt like that about *any* woman that he had just met, not even his wife. He had never felt this kind of connection before, almost like electricity. As he considered his intense feelings for the young beauty, it occurred to him that they would be leaving in only three days. *My timing always has been lousy.*

He found the blankets and decided to come back for the water. He walked back around and into the tent looking for Rachel. He entered the tent only to find a big man trying to drag her kicking and screaming, out through another entrance.

"Let *go of me!*" she screamed, her face flush with anger.

"Hey, you! I think you'd better let her go, and I mean now," Conrad said.

"Yeah? What do you think you're going to do about it, soldier boy?" The man pulled out a knife and held it to Rachel's throat. "You try anything and she's dead—do you understand me? Dead!" The man began edging closer to the door.

"Last chance!" Conrad yelled, with one hand behind his back.

"Bite me!" Conrad looked hard into Rachel's eyes trying to get her attention. He looked at her and nodded his head, once, twice, and on the third nod, Rachel drove her heel into her attacker's foot, elbowed the man in the gut, and jumped out of the way.

With a single blinding move, Conrad raised the Glock .45 caliber and squeezed off a few rounds just as it reached the correct height. The bullets struck the man in the middle of his torso. He dropped the knife and fell down dead on the spot. Rachel ran over to Conrad and wrapped her arms around him, squeezing him so tightly it nearly took his breath away.

"Hey, hey, it's going to be okay. That was a pretty nice move for a Navy Corpsman! Are you all right?" He placed his hand on the back of her head and held her close.

"Yes, I'm fine," she answered, sobbing quietly. After a minute, she pushed away from him and began wiping the tears away.

"Look at me; you would think I was just another helpless woman!"

"I know we just met, Rachel, but something tells me that you are anything but helpless."

She laughed, picked up some of the blankets, and began to distribute them to patients who had been shivering in the cool winter morning.

A couple of soldiers ran into the tent, weapons drawn.

"What happened here?" one of them asked.

Rachel pointed to the ground and said, "That man attacked me and held that knife to my throat. Colonel Simmons saved me, shooting the man after giving him several chances to let me go."

"Is that right, Colonel?"

"Yes it is."

"Well, okay then. Let's get that man out of here; we can bury him over by the trees." The two men picked up the dead man and carried him out of the tent."

Conrad picked up the rest of the blankets and began walking behind Rachel, giving him an excuse for staying close.

"So, Rachel, what do you do for fun when you're not being kidnapped by strange men?" he asked, trying to bring a little levity to the situation.

Rachel offered no reply. He could tell she was still pretty shook up. He was about to say something else when she spoke up.

"What do you think is going to happen to the world, Conrad? It seems more and more like everything is falling apart."

"Well, I don't know. I guess that eventually, things will stabilize, come into balance with the new reality."

"You mean that we will all be living back in the Stone Age."

"More like the Middle Ages, I'd say."

"Do you really think it will be that bad?" She finished passing out the blankets to several of the civilians in tent number four. "Sir, ma'am, you can both leave now. Here is a week's supply of antibiotics, and here are some chlorine tablets as well. Please try and boil any water you drink—use the chorine tablets only as a last resort." They walked back outside the tent as the civilians left for parts unknown.

"Well, it's hard to say, Rachel, but yes, I think it will be. People have firearms, for now. Without plants turning out more ammunition, however, they amount to nothing more than metal." They walked out of the tent and back to the water. Conrad carried the bottles of water. She stopped him for a moment.

"What are you going to do, Conrad? Where will you go? You've got no family to go back to. Will you stay here?"

"No. A number of us were talking about heading west out of the metro area, maybe to the mountains. I wanted to swing north first, by Baltimore, to pick up a dear friend of mine and his wife first."

"What will you do?

"Well, our commander said we could take some horses, some tents, and some equipment. I want to try to hold on to a small bit of civilization while getting back to some of the old ways. I think things are going to get a lot worse—and soon. I hope I'm wrong. I really do." They passed out the remaining bottled waters throughout the tent and walked back out.

"I don't know what I'm going to do, Conrad. Several of the doctors I work with have told me they are going to stay here. They believe that this will all be over soon. I thought so as well up until the last week or so. Things *aren't* getting better, they are only getting worse. Do you think anyone knows how long this will last?"

"We were told that they don't know, and that comes straight from the joint chiefs. They said it could be a hundred years, maybe less, maybe more."

Rachel gasped. "A hundred years?" Conrad just nodded.

Listen, Rachel, the group of people I mentioned—well, there's a group of Rangers, some other Special Forces guys, and some regular military, too. We've been talking about setting up a camp, probably a couple of days or so from here, on foot. We've talked about setting up a compound, developing a farm, digging wells, etc. We would build walls to protect our families, and try to hold onto a bit of civilization. Would you like to come with us? You have no one either, do you?"

"No, I don't, not really. That's very kind of you, Conrad. I *am* afraid of staying here. When are you leaving?"

"We were going to leave as soon as we are done here, about three or four days I guess. We have been helping mostly with the escorts out of Washington. I am supposed to help here until then, if that's okay with you." She looked at him and smiled affectionately.

"Well, I don't know. I suppose I should keep you close, so I can *protect* you." She smiled, and after a few moments, she asked him, "Can I think about it?"

"Of course. But, Rachel?"

"Yes, Conrad?"

"I hope you will say yes, I ... "

Conrad was cut short when a pair of Army soldiers in dress uniforms approached the pair. Whatever they wanted, Conrad could tell it looked like a very official visit. The soldiers saluted as they approached Conrad.

"Excuse me sir, are you Colonel Conrad Simmons?"

"Yes, I'm Simmons."

"Would you please come with us, sir?"

"Why, where do you want to take me? I was preparing to leave shortly to head west. General Manning said ... "

"We're sorry about the interruption, Colonel, but the president would like to speak with you as soon as possible." *The president.*

Conrad looked at Rachel, wanting to say something but at a loss for words. He didn't want to leave without ever seeing her again. Fortunately, Rachel must have seen the look of desperation he wore on his face.

"Don't worry Colonel; I'll still be here when you're done, *I promise.*" She took out a slip of paper, scribbled on it, and passed the paper to Conrad. "Just in case I'm not though, here's where you can find me." She smiled at him afterward with a look that let Conrad know in no uncertain terms that she was interested.

"I'll be back for you Rachel, I promise," he said, before turning and walking briskly with the two soldiers toward the White House.

CHAPTER 30

Most remaining members of the Unity were present in the hotel lobby when their absent members returned with a military escort. They were a bit shocked to see a team of horses on the sidewalk, pulling a wagon with supplies. It had been some time since any of them had seen a live horse, but given the circumstances, they thought little of it. It was what they saw next that *really* surprised them.

The group watched on in amazement as the soldiers brought in more and more food, water, blankets, supplies, and even weapons into the hotel where they had been staying. The last soldier carried in two large boxes of C–rations and field lanterns before walking back outside, where he joined another soldier standing guard in front of the door.

"What are they doing?" asked one of the scientists in the group.

"President Michaels has requested they stand guard for a few days, in case anyone watching them carry in the supplies gets any ideas," answered James White.

"And after that?"

"Well, after that, they leave," he said.

"Where are they going?"

"They are going back to be with their families, some might stay in Washington, DC. I don't know. They are going to try to survive, like the rest of us."

"What are *we* supposed to do after that? How will we protect ourselves after they leave?"

"I supposed that's what the weapons are for that they are giving us."

Monsignor Fennini walked into the room. "Dr. White, I thought that was you. Please, tell us what you and the others learned from the president."

"Well, I suppose the biggest piece of news is that we were right. It *was* an EMP blast that caused us to lose power; we were attacked by the Iranians. Apparently, the Iranians stole the highly experimental EMP device, from *us*. Moreover, it affected the entire planet, which means that no help is coming from inside or outside of the United States."

"I wish I could say that we were wrong." Emily Masterson had come in unawares while the soldiers had been unloading the wagon.

"Apparently, the attack by the Iranians couldn't have been timed to be worse, for *all* involved," James continued.

"Because a solar flare reached the earth at *exactly* the same time that the EMP was activated, trapping the Pulse in the earth's magnetic field?" finished Masterson.

""That's right," answered James White.

Emily Masterson looked over at the great stack of boxes in the lobby. "Say, what is with all of the boxes?" she asked.

"We explained to the president what we had gathered here to do. He said that he considered it a noble goal to try and bring such reconciliation between the people of God and people of science, that we must be people of great virtue to seek to attempt and accomplish such a lofty goal."

"Okay, and then?" she asked?

"And then he asked us whether we would consider taking on an even greater challenge."

"What kind of challenge?"

"He said he wants us to try and develop a plan for what happens after electricity can once again be used on our planet," answered Bjorn Yvornsky as he joined the others in the lobby. "He wants us to clean up *his* mess—that's the long and short of it."

"But I thought it was the *Iranians* that attacked us, activated the weapon."

"Yeah, well, it may have been the Iranians that activated it, but it was our government that built it," said Yvornsky.

"Yes, Bjorn, it was our government that sought to try and develop such a weapon, but you must also remember that the weapon was designed to be a means of *reducing* the loss of life by taking out the *electronics* instead of the *people*. Our government also decided that the weapon was still too experimental, too dangerous to field test. It was the *Iranians* that activated it."

"It really doesn't matter, James. All I know is that if Michaels, and others like him, had not created that thing, we would not be in the mess we are in now. It was his fault, and now he has the nerve, the gall, to ask us to clean it up. I think it borders on the absurd."

"I must agree with James," answered Emily Masterson. It could just as easily have been another government, or a private company for that matter, that created the Pulse, Bjorn. Besides, what really matters now is not so much how we got here, but what we do next. I for one believe that we should do as the president asks, see what, if anything, we can do to help. Remember, we wouldn't really be doing this for Michaels anyway, or for anyone else that's alive today for that matter. We would be doing this for those that come after us many years from now, our descendants, perhaps even hundreds of years from now."

"I suppose you're right," acknowledged Bjorn Yvornsky reluctantly. "But what could we possibly do for people that won't even be alive for another century?"

This time James White answered. "We can try to give them another shot at civilization; perhaps just preserving some of the knowledge that mankind has accumulated throughout human history."

"Why would they want that? Knowledge of war, weapons, like that accursed EMP device that did all of this? Do you think they want our knowledge of greed, murder, and suffering? Why would they want that? In a manner of speaking, wouldn't that be like giving Adam and Eve the fruit from the tree of the knowledge of good and evil? Isn't that what you would say started all of the misery of human suffering to begin with?" James White looked at Bjorn with a look of awe and smiled.

"You know, Bjorn, I think maybe you missed your calling, you could have been a great theologian! Yes, you're correct. Indeed, it was the taking of fruit from the tree of the knowledge of good and evil caused man to fall from grace. However, it was not the actual fruit itself or even the knowledge gained for that matter that caused the fall, but rather, it was man's sinful rebellion against God, and his commandment, forbidding Adam and Eve from taking the fruit from that particular tree, that brought such suffering into the world. Knowledge in itself is neither good nor evil; it is a tool, like any other, that can be used to accomplish good or to accomplish evil. It is what future generations do with that knowledge that will be either good or evil."

"You know," said Monsignor Fennini as he rejoined the conversation, "the Holy Father in Rome, Pope Matthew, and I have had several conversations about this very topic of knowledge, and the impact of knowledge on future generations. About what the mission of the Church has been in the past, what it is now, and what it shall be in the future. Of course, the primary mission has always been to share the Lord's gospel with all of his children. However, throughout human history there have been occasions where the continuity of the Church during difficult periods, throughout the Dark Ages for example, has enabled her to preserve valuable human knowledge that would have otherwise been lost to subsequent generations. It is a task that we take as part of our purpose for being.

The role of the Church in preserving precious knowledge throughout the millennia is well known by scholars. Consider the monasteries and the universities from medieval times. After the fall of Rome, much of the intellectual development in Europe sprang from their deep wells of knowledge. They served to preserve the knowledge of the ancients and spurred new technological breakthroughs. During this same period, monks built furnaces to extract the iron from the raw ore. They preserved agricultural techniques that had developed over the centuries. The Church also preserved the great literary works of men like Homer, Aristotle, and Virgil."

"Yes, Monsignor, I went to Catholic school, so I was taught much of this as well. What does this have to do with the task at hand?" asked Bjorn.

"That is a fair question, my young friend. Please, be patient with me for just a few moments longer. I would like to share with you something that occurred over the course of several months, beginning almost a year ago at the Holy See. His Holiness, it seems, was given a vision from God, a vision of what is now our present time, with events unfolding just as they have been taking place in recent weeks, a time when technology fails, when mankind is thrown into great turmoil as civilization disintegrates— exactly as we are witnessing this very day. Furthermore, in his vision, he also saw an extended period of darkness stretching into the distant future, a period of great suffering and sorrow, a time in which the earth would be enshrouded with great darkness, a time in which people struggle just to survive each day.

Also in his vision however, he learned that humanity would one day be given new reason to hope. For the Holy Father was also shown images of a future age a time in which humanity would find itself at a crossroads. After centuries of darkness and suffering, to the people of that future age will come a time when the darkness will finally end. The peoples of that time will be presented with an opportunity to emerge from the darkness in which they lived for so long. If they have the faith, if they obey the Lord and follow his instructions, they will see a new Golden Age emerge, a time of great prosperity, peace, and the glorious rebirth of civilization. This new civilization will be so marvelous, so brilliant, so bright, so gleaming with hope and opportunity that our civilization will pale in comparison.

According to this prophecy, the Lord has already gone ahead before this *great collapse of civilization,* to provide a means that will one day hasten the re–birth of civilization and enable the world to re–emerge from this new *Dark Age*. In his vision, the Holy Father learned that the way out of the darkness would require a tremendous repository of knowledge—knowledge from our civilization and the many civilizations that preceded us. This great repository of knowledge, of science, of art, of literature, of theology, and of technology will reside in something called the Great Oracle."

"Bjorn, are you okay?" asked Emily Masterson. She had glanced over in Bjorn and noticed that he looked extremely pale. He was looking at Monsignor Fennini with his jaw dropped. He struggled to shake it off and turned to face Emily Masterson.

"Yeah, sure. Thank you, I am fine," he answered. "Monsignor, are you or the Holy Father familiar with my work by any chance?"

"No, I am afraid I am not. Why, what is it that you do?"

"Oh, I am—um, a computer scientist. Can you tell us more about his Holiness's vision of this—um, Great Oracle?"

"Well there is not much more to tell really. I only mentioned the vision, because it seemed somehow appropriate at the time. Let me see if I can remember. Ah, yes! The Holy Father reported to me that in the vision he was told that there would be a sign given to the Church at the proper time that would signal that the darkness had ended, that the time was right to activate the Great Oracle, to access its ancient knowledge, and use it to restore civilization to the world. There was one other thing, something critical. Let me see if I can remember. Hmm … oh yes. His Holiness was instructed in the vision that the Church *must wait* until the sign appeared before seeking the Oracle. If the people of that age disobey the Lord by acting impetuously, trying to find and use the Great Oracle before the sign is given, then all will be lost as the window of opportunity for restoring civilization closes.

Worse yet, if they fail to find it, there will be an even greater, longer period of suffering all over the face of the earth for a thousand years."

"Okay, listen, this is getting a little creepy. I have not been to church since I graduated from Catholic school. I don't believe in this 'God stuff' anymore. At least, I don't think I do."

"Try to keep an open mind, Bjorn," said James White. Yvornsky nodded. James White noticed that Yvornsky was extremely pale. He also looked a bit frightened.

"Are you *sure* you're okay?" he asked.

"Sure, no—I'm fine, thank you."

"What will this sign be Monsignor?" asked Emily Masterson. "Do you have any idea?"

"No, I'm afraid that I do not recall the Holy Father saying anything else about the sign. If has been many months since we spoke of his vision. Who could have known that it would come to pass as it has in recent weeks?"

"I believe that perhaps I have something to offer that might help," said James White. "I too had a dream, but I wasn't certain what, if any, role it might play in what has been happening, at least not until now. I thought it might be just a strange dream. Now, however, I am convinced that *I too* was given a vision. In *my* vision, I saw the very same lights in the night sky that we see now, the ribbon of light in the sky, the Effect, as it has come to be known in recent days. I saw it just as it is today, but I also saw it just as I believe it will be in the distant future, perhaps the same point in time that the Monsignor mentioned a few moments ago. All of the world's cities were overgrown and in ruins. It must have been at least a hundred years or so in the future, probably more. Anyway, the Effect looked much different in the future, much weaker and nowhere near as intense or as bright as it is today. In my vision of the distant future, the Effect began to fade more and more until finally, it disappeared altogether. I am firmly convinced that this was the 'sign' that Pope Matthew saw in his vision. When the Effect fades, we can safely find the Great Oracle. The only problem now is that we have no idea *what it is,* much less where we can find it."

"How about that, everyone? Does anyone here have any idea what the Oracle is, or where we can find it?" asked James White. No one answered, but James could see that something was clearly troubling Yvornsky. "Does anyone have anything to offer that might be helpful, anything at all, no matter how unlikely?" he asked, looking intently at Yvornsky.

"Well, all I can offer you is what I know of the Oracle of Delphi," answered Emily Masterson. "According to Greek mythology, the Oracle of Delphi was located on the southwestern spur of Mount Parnassus. Pythia, the priestess of Apollo, was a mouthpiece of the Oracle. People came from all over Greece and beyond to have their questions about the future answered. It was also a gathering place for scholars from all over ancient Greece."

"So does that mean that we need to go to Greece in order to find it? Is this the Oracle we are supposed to search for?" asked someone in the gathering.

"Listen, I'm a scientist. I never said that the Oracle of Delphi was the answer to this riddle, I was just offering what little I know on the subject in case someone found it useful," answered Masterson, obviously a bit perturbed by the question.

James White looked around the room as the barbs started flying back and forth. Everyone was tired and getting edgy.

"Okay, everyone, I suggest that we take a short recess. Let's get back together in the large conference room in about thirty minutes or so, okay?" After most in the gathering nodded in agreement, several stepped outside to get some fresh air. While the others began filtering out of the room, James White lagged behind, questioning how long he could hold the group together, and whether it would be long enough to develop a plan for President Michaels.

As he was walking out of the room, someone tugged at his arm from behind. It was Bjorn Yvornsky.

"Dr. White, can I please have a moment of your time?"

"What is it, Dr. Yvornsky? Is something wrong?" asked James White.

"I didn't want to say anything in front of the others, at least not yet, it all seems too fantastic. I believe I may know what the Great Oracle in the two visions is, and also where to find it..."

It was an hour or so later before people started trickling back into the large conference room. The sun was beginning to set and it would soon be getting much colder.

As they were walking back in together from outside of the hotel, White turned to Yvornsky and asked, "Could you develop a set of instructions for someone to activate the Oracle?"

"Yes, I think so. I should be able to pull something together."

"Can the Oracle itself survive the century, or even centuries, that it might take for the Effect to disappear?"

"There is no way to be certain of course, but I suspect that it should be okay."

"This is all so incredible, surely this *Oracle* is the means by which the Lord intends to bring about the rebirth of a new civilization in the distant future, but what can we do? How will we let those alive at the time know this? What will happen if this Oracle falls into the wrong hands?" offered the Monsignor.

"I agree, Monsignor, we must find some way to address these issues," James White replied. "We must find a way that we can share what we have learned about the Oracle with those that come after us. However, we must also find a way to keep it from falling into the wrong hands. If the Oracle falls into the hands of evil men, just try to imagine the devastating consequences it could have on those alive during that time! As the adage goes, power corrupts and absolute power corrupts absolutely. This kind of knowledge and power in the hands of an evil man would be horrific! We must find a way to protect the knowledge of its existence, and its location. Maybe we should create a map, and leave it in a safe place where only someone that can be trusted will be able to find it."

"Perhaps, we could also split this map up into multiple pieces?" added the Monsignor.

"Make it into a quest, an effort that only the most determined of people would follow, perhaps utilize references that only certain groups of individuals would understand?" added Weller.

"We don't want to make it so difficult that they cannot *find* the pieces of the map, however, said Emily Masterson."

"True enough, Dr. Masterson," answered Monsignor Fennini.

"Okay, are we all agreed then, that this is the direction we should take, to meet the president's commission to prepare for life after the Pulse?" asked James White. "If so, we should get started as quickly as possible. Those in favor say, aye." Everyone present answered. "Okay, those opposed say, nay." There was no response. "Okay then, we will push forward with making the Oracle the centerpiece for our plans. Very well then, Dr. Weller and I will present our plan to the president and if he approves, we will get to work."

CHAPTER 31

There had been no word back yet from the president as to whether he supported their plan for rebuilding civilization once the Effect was gone. James White paced around nervously in the lobby area. If the president wanted to move on their plan then time was of the essence. There was still much work to be done and the group was already beginning to show signs of unraveling. After growing exhausted from the nervous pacing, he took a deep breath and sat down in one of the chairs near the door. He was sitting there running his hand over his head when he saw the very serious–looking soldier, dressed in Army fatigues, come through the front door of the hotel. Since he was the closest to the door, the man approached him first.

"Excuse me. I am looking for Dr. Norman Weller or Dr. James White; I was told that I could find both men here."

"I'm James White, what can I do for you soldier?"

"My name is Colonel Conrad Simmons, U.S. Army Rangers. Dr. White, I was sent here by the president to find you and assist you in your effort in any way I possibly can sir."

"The president?"

"Yes, sir," Conrad replied.

"Please, come on in and have a seat. Would you like a cup of coffee?" asked James White, motioning for Conrad to have a seat on a sofa close to the fireplace.

"No, thank you sir."

"Did he approve our plan then Colonel Simmons?" he asked, somewhat nervously.

"Yes, sir, that's why I'm here sir. The president stands firmly behind your plan, he believes it is absolutely the way to go. Some additional men will be here in a day or two with more weapons and supplies."

James White looked the soldier over, trying to gauge what kind of man he was.

"Tell me something, Colonel, what's your assessment of the situation out there?"

"It's getting bad sir, and I believe it's going to get a whole lot worse fast."

"Did President Michaels tell you about our plan?"

"Yes, sir, he did," Conrad replied, averting his eyes and looking down at the ground as he did so.

"So what do you think, Colonel? I take it you don't approve?"

"It's not my place sir ... "

"Please, tell me your opinion of our plan, Colonel Simmons."

Conrad looked up at James White.

"Okay, sir, you want to know what I think, so I'll tell you what I think. I think that there are a lot of men, women, and children out there dying right now, sir, and I don't think we need to be worrying about what's going to happen a hundred years from now. People need food, shelter, clothing, and medical care. With all due respect sir, your plan doesn't do squat for what people need right now, today!"

"Easy soldier, we're on the same side here," James White replied, taken aback by Conrad's intensity while admiring his candor and passion.

"Sorry, sir, I meant no disrespect," Conrad said flatly in response, his face still flush.

James White held his gaze, sympathizing with the soldier's position, yet determined to make his own point. He furrowed his brow as he prepared to explain.

"So what would you have us do then, Colonel? There's nothing that we can do about our current predicament. We can't do anything about the Effect, all we can do is to try to take preparatory steps so that when it finally dissipates, and we believe it will eventually do just that, civilization can be rekindled. There's nothing we can do to help our children or our grandchildren, but perhaps, just perhaps we can do something to help our great–grandchildren, or at least our descendants. Think about it Colonel, all of the science, the art, the theology, all of the accumulated knowledge from thousands of years of human history, all of it, will be lost forever if we do not do something to protect it. If we don't do this now, it could be thousands of years before civilization ever returns to the earth."

Conrad sighed and nodded as he raised his hands in the air.

"I understand that sir, believe me, I know just how important that is. But I'm a soldier, Dr White, and I know a little about what happens when governments fail. We haven't even seen the tip of the iceberg yet."

"So what are your plans then, I mean for yourself?"

"I plan to try and find a place somewhere, far away from the cities, a place where there is food, water, shelter, a place where I can raise a family, a place where I can protect them. I was planning to head west, maybe somewhere in the mountains. I figure that maybe there I can do what I do best, teach people how to fight, how to survive, even as the world falls apart around them. Perhaps I can do my part to help preserve at least some semblance of our way of life in the process."

James White rubbed his chin as he thought about what Conrad had said. He took another sip of his coffee and stared out the window for several minutes at a solitary cloud that slowly drifted across the sky. As he set the cup back down on the table, he watched the steam rise from the cup before dissipating. One of the benefits of living in a hotel was having access to the seemingly endless supply of coffee that they seemed to have stored away for the many business events hosted by the hotel.

"You know something, Colonel? I believe that we are both right. Preparing for the future accomplishes nothing if we pay no attention to the present. Conversely, we also cannot focus solely on the present with no consideration of the future. You said that the president ordered you to help me?"

"Yes, sir, Dr. White."

"Then I ask you to do this. Go. Find your refuge, a place where there is food and water, a place where you can build a community, an enclave, where you can preserve some remnant of our civilization. I also ask that you take as many people as you can with you. Furthermore, I ask that you make it a point to collect books, as many as you can safely acquire, and bring them with you into your enclave. Collect books that can be used to teach future generations how to read, how to write, how to build things, books of history, books of literature, preserving as much of our past as you can, will you do this for me, Colonel?"

"But Dr. White, the president wanted me to help you implement *your* plan, to do everything I can to ensure that it succeeds."

"And that is exactly what you would be doing Colonel. Perhaps you will be successful if we fail. Even if we are successful, having some continuity through the years will help us when the time comes. I believe that you're correct about how bad things are going to get. Maybe, by leading people away from the cities that will soon become deathtraps, incompatible with our new reality, you can start over for all of us."

"Yes, sir."

Both men rose and shook hands before Conrad turned and made his way back to the entrance. He was halfway out the door when he stopped and turned back to face James White.

"Dr. White, would you like to come with us, sir? I'm sure we will have room for one more."

"Thank you, but no, Colonel. I'm afraid we still have more work to do before I can leave. Besides, I hope to find a way back to my family in Seattle."

Conrad then brought his feet together, stood tall and straight, and raised his hands in a smart salute.

"It was a real honor meeting you sir. I promise to do just as you have instructed."

"The honor was all mine, Colonel," James White answered, smiling as he managed the best salute he could in response.

Conrad smiled and nodded before turning and walking out the front door.

CHAPTER 32

"So, what is it, boss?"

"It looks like the storm is letting up. Tell everyone to get everything ready, we leave at first light."

"What about supplies? "

"Tell the men to trade for what they need. We'll pick up some more supplies along the way."

"Where are we going, boss?"

"Well, first we're heading to Georgia. We can pick up plenty of supplies there—food, drink, and the like. There will also be plenty of opportunity to add to our number there, if any of them are inclined to join us. I will bring order to the chaos, both for those that follow me *and* for those that oppose me. While we are there, we're also going to pay a visit to an 'old friend' of mine. Now go and tell everyone to be ready in the morning. We pull out at dawn whether they are ready or not."

The man rushed out the door. Masters sat back down on his bed and wondered where things were headed. When the power went out and the bus wrecked, it was the first thing that crossed his mind. When he woke up in the morning, it was the first thing he thought of: revenge. From the moment that he awoke in the jail cell, he had promised himself that he would track the traitorous 'friend' down, at all costs, and repay him for his treachery. He wasn't sure whether it would take one day or ten years, but he *would* find him.

Masters walked over to the hotel window and took another long, hard look down the road, at the terrain and the sky. It was so good to be a free man again, so good to be alive. He would take full advantage of the opportunity he had been given. Life in the new world was going to be different, more like it had been in past centuries, when men ruled, lived, and died, by the sword. In such a world, a man like Masters could go far, limited only by his drive to succeed and his will to survive; and he had plenty of both. Men would flock to him in droves because he was a leader, a man who knew what he wanted and would let nothing stand in his way. Others flocked to men with a vision, men like Masters. He finished packing his clothes and the rest of his things. It would be a long ride to where they were going, and they had yet to cross the mountains. Masters really disliked riding by horseback, he would much rather be on a motorcycle. It was a smoother ride and it didn't require anything but gasoline to keep going.

There was a knock at the door. Masters opened the door and found Bill Miller standing there. "Vic, we need to talk."

"What is it, Miller? I have a lot to do, and I was preparing to go down for supper."

"There is someone downstairs who says he knows you. He has been asking for you all day, ever since he learned that you were here. I told him you were a very busy man, but he insisted on seeing you."

"Who is it, Miller? What's his name?"

"He wouldn't say. He told me to tell you, 'I am thunder, and I am rain.' He said that you would know who he was."

"Where is he? Take me to him, now!"

Masters pushed Bill Miller out of the door and slammed it behind him. He hurried down the stairs to find the man waiting for him at the bottom. The man was big, standing well over six feet, appearing to be almost as wide as he was tall. He was just as Masters remembered him.

"Hooah! How have you been Master Man?" the big man asked.

"Tank, is that you?" The two men embraced each other, slapping one another on the back; obviously each was thrilled to see the other.

"Let's go grab something to drink. How about it, Tank?"

"That sounds good. I am parched, man—dying of thirst. The two men walked into the restaurant, which doubled as a bar for the hotel. Masters grabbed a bottle of whiskey and a couple of glasses and joined his friend at a table. He poured some of the Kentucky Bourbon into each of the glasses and sat down with his friend.

Masters was the first to speak. "Man, it's great to see you! I haven't seen you since Bragg! How have things been going?"

"Well, up until recently I thought they had been going well. I just made it back to the States for the first time in five years."

"You mean they haven't retired your sorry butt yet? Unbelievable."

"Yeah, yeah. I guess I should be happy that at least I made it back to the States before this *thing* happened. The word I had before I left the base was that this was probably an attack. Have you heard anything yet?"

A dark expression descended upon Masters' face. "I left the military, Tank. Or to be more precise, I was kicked out."

"You? Why in the world would they do that? You were the *best, toughest, meanest, and most dedicated* soldier I have ever seen, much less served under. What would possess them to do something like that?" Tank looked at Masters for a moment and then asked, "Or rather, what did *you* do?"

"I killed a colonel. He had it coming though."

"Ah, man, that sucks. I can't believe it, what did he do that was bad enough that you gave up fifteen years in the Rangers?"

"He called my wife a whore. Seems he came onto her, and when my wife told him to take a hike, he called her a whore. Can you believe that?"

"Wow, I understand now—sounds like he deserved to have his butt kicked alright. Did you really go looking for him intending to *kill him,* though?"

"Yes. No. I don't know, Tank. I just went looking for him. I looked all over the base trying to find him. I wasn't sure what his name was, but I had a description and his rank. It took me two weeks of asking questions, checking out leads, and making phone calls until I finally caught up with him. He turned out to be a man named Norwood, a good–for–nothing pork chop, a sorry spotlight ranger that had never stepped one foot outside of the good old US of A. To think that he had the nerve to hit on *and* talk filth about *my wife!*" Masters was angry, furious even, as he relived his confrontation with the man.

"Norwood . . . was his name Henry Norwood, Colonel Henry Norwood?" asked Tank.

"Yeah, that's right, that was the dirtbag's name," Masters answered.

"Vic, man, that dude was in Army Intelligence. He did all kinds of covert stuff, black ops, enemy infiltration, the works. Last I heard he was doing some work over in the Middle East, Iran or something I think."

"Whatever, I don't care if he was President of the United States, he deserved what he got. I served my country for fifteen years without complaint. I went where they told me, when they told me, and I killed whomever they told me to kill, when they told me. I risked my life, saw things most men never want to see, and did things most men never want to do, gave up everything for my country and I was going to let some field rat like this make a move on and then talk about my wife like that, hah. When I finally found him, he had the nerve to threaten me, *and her.* That was a mistake. I grabbed that piece of trash by his hair and snapped his neck." Tank looked at Masters with a look of surprise that made it clear to those watching that Masters was not quite the same man he remembered.

"Hey, okay, I get it Master Man. The guy was a jerk, and he was messing with your wife."

Masters eyes narrowed and his face grew dark. "Oh no, he didn't touch her," he said with an icy chill in his voice. "If he had, I would have made his death much, much, slower."

"Okay, okay, relax, Vic. So what happened then? I guess they never found out you did it then?" Masters growled. Tank poured Vic a drink and handed it to him. Masters threw it down and held it back out for a refill.

"They shouldn't have found out. I waited until he was completely alone and no one else was around. No, they found out I did it all right, *but only* because somebody told them, a certain someone that couldn't keep his big mouth shut. I guess my supposed 'friend' decided that he would rather look out for that sleazy no–good pork chop rather than his friends."

"He turned you in, did he?"

"Oh yes, you could say that. They threw me into a hole for six months while I waited for my court–martial. It seems that they considered my mercifully–ending–his–miserable–life and–doing–the–world–a–favor act as pre–meditated. They sentenced me to twenty–five years at Leavenworth. We were on our way there in that broken down prison bus when this thing, whatever it is, happened."

"Yeah, what do you think happened here, Vic? I figure we *were* attacked, probably by some sort of new weapon."

"Maybe, I don't know. I guess we'll find out, eventually. So what brings you to Providence? Have you been here long?"

"Yeah, I got stuck here when it happened. I was passing through over a month ago when I decided to stop off for a bite to eat. I've been here ever since."

"Man, I am sorry to hear that, Tank," Masters said, laughing as he did so. Tank was happy to see that his friend had calmed down a bit.

"Aw, it's not that bad. I tell you, there could be a lot of places that would have been a lot worse, just imagine being stuck somewhere halfway across the world!"

"With the exception of some business that I still have to take care of back east, I wouldn't mind that at all, especially if the power *does* come back soon."

"Hey, listen, Vic, if the power comes back and it turns out that we have been attacked, and we are at war, they are going to forget all about you. And if the power doesn't come back, they are going to have a lot more to worry about than tracking you down."

"I guess you have a point, Tank."

"So what ever happened to her?"

"To who?"

"Your wife?"

"Oh. She divorced me while I was waiting for my court–martial."

"That's too bad, Vic, I'm sorry to hear that."

"Yeah, well, she's probably better off anyway."

"So what are you going to do now, Vic? Are you staying here for a while or just passing through?"

Masters stared at his drink for a while before looking up at his friend.

"No, we're pulling out tomorrow."

"We?"

"Yeah, me and a few acquaintances that I picked up along the way."

"Acquaintances?"

"Just some men that were wandering around aimlessly after the attack. I guess that they were looking for someone that seemed to know what he was doing, someone that might help them get through this, a survivor."

Tank laughed. "Well, my friend, you certainly are that, a survivor, and a natural–born leader. As many times as I was sure one or both of us were going to get it, you always found a way to get us through to the end."

"Yeah, well, let's just say I'm motivated by my little 'business' back east. After I'm done with that, well, we'll see."

"What is this 'business' of yours?"

"You recall what I told you earlier? About the so–called 'friend' that I mentioned? You know, the one that turned me in, caused them to throw me in a hole so that I lost my career, lost my wife, and nearly lost my life?"

"Yeah, sure, what about him?"

"I'm going to pay him a little visit. I'm going to repay him for what he did to me."

"You're going all the way back east just for that?"

"Oh, yes, just for that. I'm going to pay him a little surprise visit, and then I'm going to make him pay. As Marie Joseph Eugène Sue said in the French novel Mathilde: *la vengeance se mange très–bien froide,* which means, 'Revenge is a dish best served cold.'"

CHAPTER 33

The bone-chilling cold wind was biting into them as they made their way through the white, blanketed woods. Scott did everything he could to shield his wife from the constant onslaught of the wind and the cold. Susan had not been doing well over the last couple of days, and for the first time, he was getting worried. The constant onslaught of morning sickness did little to help her as she struggled to overcome the exhaustion that came from carrying the pack on her back and the baby in her belly.

Dick and Eleanor also appeared to be in trouble. They were considerably older than he and Susan, and Scott feared that if they did not reach Harper's Ferry soon; their condition would quickly deteriorate. They were beginning to show signs of exhaustion, and Scott was growing increasingly concerned that they would soon collapse. Even Susan in her fragile condition, seemed to be faring better. Scott glanced over at Dick, afraid that the heavy pack he carried would soon cause the older man to collapse under its immense weight. The wind was howling, and they were bundled up from head to toe, but Dick, reading the concerned look on his young friend's face, simply nodded and waved, letting Scott know that he was still okay.

The snow had been falling for almost an hour, only adding to the already bitter cold. He had given several of his thermal shirts to Susan, over her visceral objections, in an effort to protect her and their unborn baby. He was finally beginning to feel the effects of the biting cold, even through the heavy coat and his layered clothing. As the snowfall became heavier and heavier, he noticed it was getting harder and harder to see. Every step they had taken since they left the apartment building back in Leesburg had been a struggle. *Would we be better off had we stayed in our apartment?* He had asked himself that question repeatedly over the past several days.

Scott surveyed the landscape on all sides, scouting for a place where they could wait out the storm. Their situation was becoming serious, and Scott was determined that they would make it safely to their destination, *all of them.* He had been looking for shelter for the last few miles but had been coming up empty. He turned back to check on the others and felt a chill run up and down his spine. Susan had collapsed twenty yards back, and given the driving snow and their dilapidated condition, Dick and Eleanor had not taken notice of it. Scott turned and ran toward his wife, who lay virtually motionless. In no more than four or five steps, he was at her side. She opened her eyes, looked weakly at Scott, and managed a thin smile. Scott helped her up, slunk one of her arms over his shoulder, and held her tightly as they made their way. Normally the heavy weight of his pack alone would have been enough to cause him to buckle under the load. However, seeing Susan collapsed in the snow, coupled with the growing general desperation of their situation, had given him a much-needed burst of energy.

Scott looked down at his wife and kissed her on the forehead. It was not often that he had the chance to coddle his wife and to play the role of the protector, and he was finding that he rather enjoyed it. They had both been professionals before the Pulse, he an engineer, and Susan in marketing. He reflected that theirs had been a post–modern marriage, one with no clear family leadership, in which there was frequent bickering over the smallest decisions. The reason for their rocky relationship had not been due to a lack of love or nurture in their relationship, but rather it was due to the somewhat ambiguous roles that modern husbands and wives played, both working professionals, both equal partners. The traditional, well–defined roles of husband and wife had long since vanished, leaving men and women to define their own roles and responsibilities.

The blizzard–like conditions had slackened and visibility was slowly beginning to return. Looking up at the clouds, Scott decided that the storm was not over yet, but rather, it had only eased up for the moment. They would need to find shelter and soon.

"Scott?"

"Hi there, are you holding up there okay, kiddo?" Scott asked Susan.

"Look!" Scott looked up and tried to follow where she was pointing. Susan had considerably better vision than Scott. His astigmatism along with the sunlight reflecting off the newly fallen snow made everything seem blurry and slightly out of focus. He strained to see what she was pointing at until finally he found it. Ahead in the distance, maybe a mile or less ahead, stood a small, off–white, or grayish colored building. Judging by its shape, and its location off any main roads, he deduced that it was some type of convenience store or gas station.

"I see it, honey. We'll make for that building up ahead; see if we can get out of this snowstorm."

"That sounds like a *really* good idea," she said weakly, looking in the direction of their two friends and traveling companions. She was worried about them, and Scott could see why. They looked as if they were about to fall over and had lost virtually all of the color from their faces.

"Dick, Eleanor, look, there's a building up ahead, maybe a convenience store of some kind. We should be able to stay there for a bit, at least long enough to wait out the storm."

Dick and Eleanor perked up when they saw the building. Scott and Susan could tell they had gotten a second wind.

"Finally, now isn't that a sight for sore eyes!" Eleanor exclaimed.

As they neared the building, they could see that indeed it had been a convenience store. By the looks of it, Scott surmised that the store had been closed for quite some time *and,* it appeared, had been left undisturbed over the weeks since the Pulse. He said nothing about his observations or about his hopes however. He had to wait, to be certain. To get everyone's hopes up only to let them down again was something that he knew they would not be able to endure.

They arrived at the front door only to find it locked. Scott tried to peer inside, but it was dark, and his eyes had not yet adjusted to the light from the blinding snow. He tried to determine whether anyone was inside, but there was not enough light.

"I believe all of you should move back a bit, just in case there's someone inside that doesn't appreciate my kicking their front door in." Scott took a moment to prepare himself. He was an engineer, not a felon. However, their situation was desperate. He looked around at his wife and their aging friends. Just seeing their desperate looks was enough to give him the resolve he needed. He took a step back and kicked at the door just next to the doorknob. The door flew open as Scott jumped to the side of the doorway as a precaution. He was relieved when he was not greeted at the door by buckshot or a hail of bullets, which likely would have happened had someone been inside. He peered around the doorway just enough to get a good look inside the building. It looked safe enough, so after looking a couple of more times to be certain, he walked inside. He was greeted by a stagnant, musty odor.

It seemed apparent that no one had been there for weeks. The location was remote, with no residential areas around for ten miles in any direction. The building was just far enough away that most people would not risk such a long walk in the cold just on the hope that no one had already emptied the place. He looked around, and as his eyes adjusted, they grew wide. There was food, drinks, even some necessities. He walked further into the deserted store. Soft drinks filled coolers that Scott felt certain until the last week or two had not been quite as cool as they were today. He walked down aisles full of potato chips, crackers, pies, and snacks of all sorts. Scott noticed a door at the other end of the small store and decided to try it. He opened it to find a small closet. Inside there was a heavy coat, a small blanket and—Scott could not believe his eyes. At the back of the small closet was a kerosene heater. He quickly dropped to the floor and looked at the gauge. The heater was full of kerosene, most likely filled just days before the power went out. Scott suddenly realized that, in his excitement, he had left the others outside. As he was heading for the door, Dick appeared in the doorway.

"Scott?" Dick looked pale, paler in fact than anyone Scott had seen outside of a funeral home. The store was a Godsend. Scott would have to make sure that he gave thanks to the Lord for leading them to a place where there was food, drink, and just as important, warmth.

"It's okay, Dick. Tell Eleanor and Susan to come on inside. You're not going to believe this!" Dick motioned to the two women to come on inside. Scott ran outside and helped both of them up the two stairs and into the store. He closed the door up as tight as he could. He had kicked the door in, so it no longer latched. Just a few yards away was a heavy display fully loaded with two–liter bottles of soft drinks. Scott grabbed hold of the rack and pushed it against the door. The wind seemed to pick up abruptly, seemingly disappointed at the loss of four potential victims to the protection of the small building. It then died down as suddenly as it had started, off to look for other victims to torture.

Scott turned his attention back to the heater. There was a little lever marked start next to it. He tried pushing the laver but it simply fizzled. Scott simply shook his head. It seemed that nothing utilizing electricity would run. What kind of monster had he unleashed? He looked around and found a small case that containing lighters of all shapes and sizes. He picked out one with a bright green case and shook it. He tried it a few times before getting a small flame to appear. He looked back up at the case with the lighters. He estimated that there were probably twenty–five to thirty lighters in the case. *These will certainly come in handy.*

He opened a small door on the front of the kerosene heater and flicked on the lighter. He pushed the lever up and down, an action that caused the wick inside of the heater to rise up and down. After a minute, Scott saw an orange–blue flame appear. He watched as the flame began racing around and around the heater until finally it became a slow and steady burn.

"Everyone, come on over here and get warmed up a bit."

"Thank you, Scott, thank you. I was about to catch my death out there," remarked Eleanor, with more truth in her voice than she wanted to admit. It had only been burning for only a few minutes, but already the heater was warming up the small store. Scott looked at the heater, trying to size up the capacity of the tank holding the kerosene. He estimated that they had eight; perhaps ten hours of constant burning before the supply of kerosene would be exhausted. *Had there been a kerosene tank outside? Yes, he saw it as they approached the store.* Just maybe they would be able to find a way to get more out of the holding tank, if they were fortunate. He wanted to stay there for at least a few days, perhaps even a week. The journey had been long and hard and they desperately needed to rest. If they were near their destination, and he thought they were, they might be able to use the store as a base of operation while they worked on building a permanent shelter in a more appropriate location. He wanted to put a little more distance between them and the major metropolitan areas before they stopped to settle down somewhere. He had already seen firsthand how even decent and friendly people could turn hostile when food and water became scarce enough. Either way, the store was only a temporary solution, but it was a place where they could eat, drink, and rest, until they had replenished their strength enough for the remainder of their journey, and the work ahead. They would be able to wait out the storm and recuperate, at least for a few days, while they prepared for the last leg of their journey. He wondered how close they were to Harper's Ferry. After following the river for a week now, he knew they must be close. They had to hang on now, rest up, and they needed to *eat.* They had been traveling almost a week and had virtually no food, little water to drink, and hardly any rest for that matter, since they had left the apartments.

Scott looked around inside the store and made a quick inventory of what he saw. Given the most unusual circumstances they had found themselves in over the past several weeks, the small convenience store was better than the most elaborate restaurant or hotel, for that matter, to the wearied travelers. Scott found where the bottled waters were stored. He grabbed one for each of them and passed them out to the others. He then walked up and down the isles, grabbing packs of potato chips, crackers, and cans of Vienna sausages that he had found on one of the bottom shelves, and handed each of them something to eat. *Meat.* For the most part, he had picked up the first food item he had come across so he could give each something to eat to boost their blood sugar. They would need more meat, or something substantive, something with more protein, than the empty–calorie snack foods he had handed out. Given their predicament, however, he felt that the snacks with the starches and sugar would give them much needed boost of energy, no matter how brief it might be. After a half–hour of eating Vienna sausages, potato chips, and candy bars, they all finally began to feel full and satisfied, the best any of them had felt for weeks.

Scott looked around inside the store some more. It was more or less a typical convenience store. The aisles were lined with snacks of every sorts, pies, doughnuts, and candy bars. Walking down another aisle, he came across some plastic spoons, forks, cups, and plates. These would certainly prove useful. Next to the utensils, he found some antibiotic cream, aspirin, acetaminophen, and toothpaste. It seemed that they could make use of just about everything in the store. There were a number of cans of motor oil stacked up at the end of the aisle where the forks and spoons were. He wasn't sure how he might make use of the oil, but given time, he knew they would.

The inside of the store had warmed up to a comfortable, almost toasty temperature. Scott sat down for a few moments next to his exhausted wife, who smiled warmly at him, the most sincere smile he had seen on her since he returned home, and let out a long and contagious yawn. They were sitting on the floor across from Dick and Eleanor. Dick had already buried his head in his chest with his arm around his wife. Eleanor was sitting up, still awake but looking very weary.

She smiled at Scott and said, "You did good finding this place, Scott, you did real good." She looked at Susan and said, "I think this one is definitely a keeper, Susan. Maybe you should hold onto him, hmm?"

"I think I will," Susan answered, holding her husband and squeezing him tight, before yawning again. Susan's eyelids began to flutter as she struggled unsuccessfully to fight off the overwhelming desire to sleep.

Scott watched as Eleanor began to yawn and soon, she too had buried her head in her chest, slowly slipping into a deep and relaxing sleep. He smiled as he propped his wife's head up against one of the displays where they were sitting. He stood up and walked back over to the closet, grabbed the blanket, and gently draped it over Dick and Eleanor, while placing the heavy jacket over his wife. He sat back down next to her, looking at the others, and then back out at the snow, which had started coming down with even greater ferocity than it had earlier. The wind howled in frustration at the travelers that had escaped its rage, at least for the time being. Scott sat listening to the high-pitched squeal of the wind for several minutes, until every so slowly, the world began to gently fade away, and he joined the others in their parade of sleep.

CHAPTER 34

The snowstorm had begun to wane and had finally let up by the time they approached the outskirts of the city. It was late morning when the sun finally began peeking out from behind the clouds that had accompanied them since leaving DC.

Conrad was glad that they had finally made it to Baltimore. They had been traveling for several days and would almost certainly have arrived sooner but for the additional effort that the horses had to expend making their way through the snow.

He had no idea what condition he might find his dear friend and teacher in when he arrived. He had not seen Master Takata in almost two months. He knew that they had a well and a vegetable garden so food and water should not be a problem. He had seen the cans that lined the shelves of his cupboard, where they had canned vegetable and fruits from earlier in the year. However, it was starting to get ugly, and Conrad feared for the safety of his friend and instructor, and for his wife.

In the short time it had taken for them to travel from DC, Conrad and those traveling with him had seen a growing number of dead or dying. Just that morning, they had found an older man and his wife frozen to death in the middle of the street. The couple had probably been forced to venture out into the bitter cold out of desperation, searching for food before giving out from exhaustion. There had also been a growing epidemic of disease, mostly from people drinking contaminated water or eating spoiled food. The chances of his friend living unscathed with a fresh water supply and plenty of food in such a large metropolitan area were small. While Takata was a master swordsman, Conrad doubted that if he and his wife were overrun with desperate people, that there would be much that even *he* could do.

Takata was the only close friend, other than Frank, that Conrad had known for as long as he could remember. While he had scores of acquaintances over the course of his life, there had been few people that he ever called friend, as he counted them anyway. He believed that while many people come and go in a person's life, very few ever really invested enough of themselves in a relationship that they earned the title of *friend*. Besides, Takata had truly been more like a father than a friend to Conrad.

He looked over at Frank, who was riding beside him. He and Frank had met on the bus that carried them to the recruitment center. They had joined the Army at the same time and went through boot camp together. The two men found that they had something in common from the start, each had trained in various martial art disciplines. Conrad had trained in Tae Kwon Do and Jujitsu since he was a child, while Frank had started in Shotokan Karate followed by Tae Kwon Do a few years before they met. They had trained together and had become close friends during their time together in boot camp. Other than their martial arts background, however, the two men could not have been more different. Frank had grown up in a close–knit family that enjoyed plenty of love and nurturing, as well as considerable wealth. As an orphan, Conrad had grown up with little love or nurturing, and most certainly without any wealth. Perhaps it had been because of these very differences that he and Frank became such close friends. The men had served together for over ten years. He was godfather to Frank's two children, Katherine and Marcus, and thought of Frank's wife Vickie, as a sister. They were going to see Vickie and the kids after they went by Takata's home in Baltimore. Frank's family had been staying with Vickie's parents in West Virginia when the Pulse struck.

"Conrad?" It was Rachel. She had been riding behind him and Frank, more out of respect for their friendship than anything else. Conrad had been thrilled that she decided to come with him. Though he barely knew her when they started out, they shared a unique connection, and they both felt it. *Leave it to me to wait and find the girl of my dreams just as the world ends.*

"Yeah, Rachel, what is it, is everything okay?" he asked as she rode up on his right side.

"Look, over there." She was pointing in the direction of the downtown area of the city. Takata lived in the suburbs of Baltimore on the western side of the city. Rachel was pointing toward the downtown, which was some distance east of them. As he looked in the direction she pointed, he soon found what she was looking at. Off in the distance, a tall column of smoke was reaching for the sky high above some of the taller buildings in the downtown area. As they rode a little further, an opening between some of the closer buildings and trees allowed them a better view. Two of the taller buildings in the middle of downtown Baltimore were on fire. The first structure was engulfed in flames from the first floor halfway up to the roof. The second building's fire was much smaller, with fire and smoke pouring from only a couple of floors. It looked as if the fire had spread from the first building to the second. As cold as it was, Conrad figured someone had been burning a fire to stay warm and had grown careless by not keeping a close watch on the flames.

"Is there anything we can do?" asked Rachel.

"There's nothing *anyone* can do, Rachel. By the time we made it to the fire, it would have already consumed both buildings. Besides, even if we were there right now, what could we do? We could try to knock on doors telling everyone to get out, but that would be it. There are no fire trucks, there's no running water either for that matter. And even if we had water, how could we get the water to the top of that building?"

Frank joined in, bringing a bit of a philosophic perspective to the conversation. "Our civilization hasn't been designed for a world without electricity for over a hundred years. Think about it. Hundred's of years ago, people depended on wells, rivers, or lakes for water, or they had irrigation systems built to channel the flow of water from rivers to communities. I'm afraid life is going to be extremely difficult for some time to come, until we learn how to cope with life in this 'new world.' I just worry about how people will survive until then."

"That's true," said Conrad. "The old order is gone, and whether we like it or not, and it will be some time before a new order is established out of the chaos. Even during the Middle Ages in Europe, they had some kind of structure in place. Their culture had never had electricity, television, radio, cell phones, to rely on. In a sense, they had it easier during the Dark Ages then we do now. Not only that, but there's no civil authority any longer. If someone wants something that belongs to someone else, he or she can just take it, unless there is someone there that can stop them. There will be no police, nor military for that matter, to deal with threats. Only those that learn to fight will be able to protect themselves."

The three rode on, followed by more than a few fellow soldiers, most of which either had no family, or they were not close to the family they did have. Many of them had served together for a number of years, making the military the closest thing that most of them had ever had to a family. They had lived together, fought together, and if necessary, they would die together. None of them wanted to face the coming darkness alone. They were accompanied by members of the clergy, attendees of the Unity Conference in DC, who had asked to come along with them.

The group rode on through the bitter cold. The clouds had dissipated as the sun came out to reveal a beautiful blue sky. The air seemed amazingly clear to Conrad. He wondered whether it had anything to do with the EMP, or whether it was simply his imagination. Was it possible that it had somehow affected the atmosphere? Perhaps it was simply because hundreds of millions of cars, factories, and homes were no longer pumping noxious gases into the atmosphere. He supposed it likely that he would never know. He wondered whether the planet might one day actually recover from the centuries of pollution that man had inflicted on it.

"How much longer before we get there, Conrad?" Rachel asked him.

"It's not far now. I would say that we should be there within an hour or so," he answered. Conrad looked at Rachel and smiled. *She is so beautiful.*

"What about after?" she asked, looking somewhat concerned.

"After what?"

"After we visit your friend, Master Takata, she answered."

"Then we go to West Virginia. We have to take Frank to his family—make sure they are okay," he answered, looking over at Frank, who just kept looking ahead.

"And then?" she asked.

"Well, I don't know for sure. What do you think we should do?"

"I don't know. I think we need to try to find a place to live, somewhere that we can live in peace, grow fruit, vegetables, and grains, somewhere near water. As you said earlier, life will be different now. We cannot change what is happening, so we might as well try to establish a little bit of normalcy for ourselves."

One of the soldiers riding behind them, who had been listening to part of the conversation, joined in. His name was Brian Hawks, a former paratrooper from the 82nd Airborne out of Fort Bragg, and a long–time acquaintance of Conrad's.

"Sir, may I make a suggestion?"

"Of course you can, Hawks, and you don't have to call me 'sir' anymore."

"Old habits die hard and as you know, I would follow you to hell and back, sir. If it's just the same to you, I will continue showing you the respect you have earned and in my opinion, *deserve*."

Conrad just looked at Hawks and smiled, "Suit yourself, Hawks. So what was your suggestion?"

"Well Colonel, most of us have been in the army for most of our lives. We are accustomed to a life of discipline, sir. I believe that survival for some time is going to require exceptional discipline. Men like us, sir, may be our only hope for preserving any history, any knowledge of our way of life."

"Sure you're not being a little over–dramatic, Sergeant?"

"Believe it or not, I was a history professor."

"A history *professor*, Hawks, *you?*

"Don't act so surprised, sir. Just because I joined as an enlisted man rather than an officer, doesn't mean I wasn't well–educated."

"Nor did I mean to imply that it did, Hawks, my apologies."

"Not necessary, sir. Anyway, I have always believed the old adage first offered by Edmund Burke, and I quote, 'Those who don't know history are destined to repeat it.' If history is any indication of what happens when a civilization collapses, we are almost certainly looking at another Dark Age."

"As in the Dark Ages that followed the collapse of the Roman Empire?" asked Conrad.

"Yes, sir, only worse."

"How could it be worse than the Dark Ages?" Conrad asked.

"Well sir, after the fall of the Roman Empire there was a lot of knowledge lost. However, the decay of the Roman's Empire was gradual. Our fall was instantaneous. In addition, we have not only lost technology, we have lost government, communications, *all of it. For example,* in a hundred years, I doubt anyone will even know how to make a firearm anymore."

"What do you propose then?"

"Well, sir, you want to build a compound somewhere, collect books, teach people how to fight, etc. am I right?"

"Yes, that's right."

"Then I recommend that we establish a form of discipline from the very beginning sir, set up some sort of leadership, government, council, something. That way, as our compound, our enclave grows; we will have already established a way of life for everyone involved. We can teach others the discipline, teach them how to fight and how to defend our community, educate our children in it. We will need order and discipline sir just to survive the many years of chaos and mayhem to come. I suggest that you become the first head of this council."

"I don't know, Hawks," Conrad answered.

"That sounds like a *wonderful* idea, Sergeant!" Rachel offered. "I particularly liked the part about *children*," she added, looking at Conrad and smiling.

"Well, I would like to teach others how to defend themselves, that's for certain. I have a feeling that a lot of people are going to need to learn how to fight just to survive," said Conrad. "I think that's a great idea Hawks! Give it some more thought as we ride, we can put something together once we get there.

"Yes, sir."

"But where do we go, Conrad?" asked Rachel.

"What about West Virginia, where Frank's family lives? It's relatively isolated."

"I hate the mountains. I have a problem with heights," she replied.

"Well, we don't have to go far into the mountains."

"That's reassuring," she said.

"We need to make certain that one of the first things we do is build housing and dig wells for water," Hawks added.

"That sounds good to me," said Rachel.

"There is going to be a lot of work that needs to be done," said Conrad. We can divide the workload amongst the groups. Assign one group to work on digging the wells, another to building the houses."

"We can all work together to build houses and dig wells, much like the Amish people work together to build houses. It's efficient and much faster," said Hawks. Conrad started to laugh.

"Just what is so funny, Colonel Simmons?" asked Rachel.

"It's just that it sounds a lot like a military operation to me."

They rode on for another thirty minutes, enjoying the sunshine and the warmer temperature. Conrad was uneasy as he knew that the warmer temperature and improved weather conditions would inevitably bring out more people, and with the current problems they were facing, greater conflict, more bloodshed, and more suffering. He picked up the pace to his friend's home, finally arriving there in short order. They were stunned to find the house in disarray and the fence knocked down. Conrad quickly made a mental note that when they built their community, they would build walls around it to protect their people, the food supply, and their water. Conrad quickly dismounted and made his way to the front door. When he got to where he could see the well, he saw a group of strange men drawing water, and they did not look like friendlies.

"Hey, you!" he yelled. Two of the men ran toward him, one had a knife and the other a baseball bat. Conrad, Frank, and Hawks, who were in the front of the group, raced toward the men, meeting them halfway. Conrad landed a flying sidekick and knocked the biggest man, the one with the bat, backwards fifteen feet and onto the ground. Frank stepped out to the side, dodging a thrusting attack with the knife, and counterattacked, striking the attacker's jaw with the heel of his palm. He then followed the palm–heel strike with a swift roundhouse kick to the man's solar plexus. The last two attackers came at Hawks, who jabbed the first man with his left hand and struck the second man with a right–hook. The second man dropped to the ground unconscious. The first man, bleeding profusely from the nose, came at Hawks once more but was met this time with a blow to his midsection and a roundhouse punch to his right jaw, before also collapsing the floor. Conrad looked at Hawks and said, "A history professor, an enlisted man in the army, and a great fighter. Hawks, you never cease to amaze me!"

"Thank you, sir."

Turning his attention back to his friend, Conrad raced to the front door only to find that it had already been forced open. He quickly entered and began searching the house, with the others, for Takata.

"Colonel, in here! There's two people hurt, lying on the floor," Lt. Robin Wilson, one of the other soldiers riding with him, yelled out. Conrad followed the sound of her voice to the living room area. He saw Mrs. Takata lying on the floor next to her husband. Mr. Takata was still bleeding but based on the low groans he heard, Conrad could tell that he was still alive. Mrs. Takata, however, lay silent and motionless next to him. Rachel knelt down and placed two fingers on Mrs. Takata's carotid artery, feeling for a pulse. She looked up with a concerned look at Conrad as she listened for breathing. Finally, after a few more seconds, she shook her head sadly and stepped over to attend to Mr. Takata. Conrad saw that he still held to his sword, which had blood on it, lying on the floor on his other side. He supposed that there must be a body lying around somewhere in the house. He doubted anyone unfortunate enough to have had an encounter with Master Takata's sword would be able to walk away from it.

"Obviously, he is still alive," Rachel said, "but only barely. We have no idea how long he's been lying here."

"Conrad, over here." It was Frank. Conrad stood up and walked to the kitchen where Frank was. There was a dead man lying on the floor. "He's still warm, Conrad. This must have just happened. Maybe the men outside—" However, Conrad had already started for the door. There were no more police, no more courtrooms, and no more prisons. Conrad knew if anything was going to be done about what had just happened, if anyone were going to see justice done now, it would be them. He raced out the door and into the front yard only to find that the men they had knocked out earlier were gone. He figured one of them must have regained consciousness and then gotten the others up. He looked up at some of his traveling companions that had been waiting outside on horses.

"Where are they? Where did they go?" he asked. One of the priests answered first.

"They started coming around a few minutes ago. Why are you so interested in following them, just because they took some water?"

Conrad walked over to where the priest was sitting on his horse.

"Because they murdered my friend's wife," he growled.

"Oh, my." The priest dismounted from off of his horse and tied it to a street sign.

"Which way did they go," asked Conrad. Frank burst out of the house and stood next to him.

"They took off that way." The priest pointed in the general direction of the downtown area and walked inside the house. Buildings, houses, and trees dotted the landscape as far as the eyes could see.

"There's nothing we can do, Conrad," said Frank, "we'll never find them now." Conrad narrowed his eyes at him. In all the years that he had known him, Frank could not recall ever seeing a look in his eyes like that before.

"Don't *say that*, Frank. She was like a *mother* to me!"

"Even if we find them, would you be able to know for certain that it's one of *them* you are looking at? How would you know which one killed her? What about everyone else here that's looking to you for leadership? Conrad stared hard at his friend for several moments with an intense look of anger, before finally dropping his eyes.

"I'm sorry, Frank. It's not your fault. It's not anyone's fault, except for the scum that killed her. Stay here and look after Mr. Takata. I'm going after those vermin. I will head back either way around nightfall. Let's plan on staying here tonight and tomorrow night. We can plan to leave the day after tomorrow, if Mr. Takata is able to travel by then."

"Conrad."

"I know, Frank, but I have to try. I could never look Mr. Takata in the eye; I could never forgive myself, if I didn't at least try to find her killer while I had the chance. There is a reasonable chance that I can track them in the snow."

"Fine, then I'm coming with you."

"No, Frank, you have to stay here in case something happens to me. I'll take Hawks with me, if he wants to come."

"You just try and stop me sir," said Hawks.

"The day after tomorrow, Frank. If we're not back by then leave without me. Tell Rachel—tell her that I will see her soon."

Conrad and Hawks walked over to their horses and pulled rifles out of their packs. They checked their weapons, including their Glocks and their KA-BARs, and began walking in the direction of the downtown area. Tracks littered the landscape, but for people like Conrad and Hawks, tracking the footsteps was not so difficult, at least not at first. The snow had stopped falling much earlier in the day, and quite a few people had been out on the streets moving around. The closer they got to the downtown area the more difficult the tracking became.

Rachel put a pillow under the man's head and tried to assess the seriousness of his condition and his injuries. He was an older man. *Most likely, in his mid–late sixties,* she determined. Based in part on the giant knot that had risen on the back of his head, it appeared that the man with the baseball bat had hit him from behind, probably while he had been fighting with one of the others. She raised his shirt and started to examine his ribs and torso, looking for broken bones and for signs of possible internal bleeding. She was feeling his ribs, when suddenly, she felt someone grab her right arm, the one she had been using to examine him.

"Who are you? What are you doing here, and where is my wife?" he asked.

"My name is Rachel Bennett."

"Are you with the Army?"

"No sir. I am—was, with the United States Navy. I came here with Conrad Simmons. I understand that he is a friend of yours?"

"Yes, of course he is. Where is my wife?" he asked, looking around. Rachel looked at him sadly and dropped her eyes. She could not bear to look the man in his eyes and tell him she was dead. That sort of thing had always been someone else's job.

"Please! Where is my wife? Is she okay?"

"Mr. Takata, I'm sorry. She didn't make it sir; she's dead." Mr. Takata looked away, trying to hide the tears streaming down his face.

"My wife and I, we are Catholic. I must find a priest."

"No need, Mr. Takata, you just happen to have one right here in your living room," the priest said, the same one that had pointed out the direction the thieves had left in to Conrad."

"Father, would you please take care of her last rites and burial for me?"

"Of course."

Conrad and Hawks followed the tracks for five or six blocks to where the tracks stopped at an old apartment building. They followed the tracks inside, where it soon became impossible to continue. A window high up in the wall allowed a small amount of light to filter in, but there were no more tracks. Hawks looked at Conrad and started for the door. Conrad, however, elected to try for a long shot. He knocked at the first door he came to. There was no response. He decided to try one more time, banging on the door this time. On the last knock, he was already walking toward the door where Hawks was standing when the door opened. The big man he had seen out front of Takata's was in the doorway.

"Yeah, yeah, what are you banging my door in for? I—" The man suddenly stopped talking when he suddenly recognized Conrad, who smiled menacingly before leaping on the man, knocking him to the ground.

"That was a good woman you killed back there you dirt bag. Where are the rest of your *friends?* Answer me scumbag!" Conrad pressed the knife to the man's throat, causing blood to start dripping down his neck.

"Daddy, I heard a noise—?" A little girl, no more then ten years old, walked into the room before almost tripping over Conrad who was crouched on the floor, holding a knife to her father's throat. The little girl, who looked scared out of her wits when she first walked in, suddenly jumped on Conrad and began beating on his back with her fists. Conrad was surprised such a little girl could pack so much power. He was getting sore. Hawks walked in and held the little girl as gently as he could while pulling her off Conrad, who looked at the man, then at the girl, then back at the man.

"Please, mister, don't kill me, not in front of my little girl, please!"

"If you didn't want trouble you shouldn't have killed that woman. She was the wife of a very good friend, *and* she was *like a mother to me.*" Conrad had a snarl on his face that betrayed a ferocity that few knew he possessed, even for a Ranger.

"What are you talking about, mister? I didn't kill anyone."

"Then why did you attack us back at that house?" The man had a puzzled look on his face that Hawks and Conrad found odd and a bit confusing.

"We didn't attack you; it was *you* that attacked us. We thought you wanted our food and the last of the water we took from that well."

"What about the man and woman that lived there."

"Hey man, where have you been? The city is full of people already dead or dying. We saw them lying on the floor dead, so we figured our children and our families could use the water and vegetables more than they could."

"That man was still *alive!*"

"Oh God, I didn't know. They both were lying so still. We thought they had been dead for a while. We had just gotten there a few minutes before all of you arrived. We didn't want to fight; we were just desperate. Our wives, our children, are dying from thirst and hunger—what were we supposed to do?" Conrad studied the man for a long while. He had been through interrogation training and could spot even an expert liar. He would kill the man if he didn't believe his story.

"He's telling the truth, sir, look at his face, his eyes," said Hawks.

"I know, Hawks," Conrad answered as he withdrew the knife from the man's neck and placed it back in its sheath. The young girl struggled against Hawks' grasp until he let her go. She immediately ran over to her father and buried her head on his chest, sobbing.

Conrad stood up and looked over at Hawks. He felt incredible guilt, not over what he had done, but what he had almost done. He had let his anger and grief overwhelm him; almost turning him into the very thing, he hated the most, a butcher. After several minutes, Conrad extended his hand and helped the man to his feet. He pulled a small towel from his coat and handed it to the man, pointing to the man's neck.

"Listen, both of you," he started, looking at the little girl as well.

"I am very sorry. We thought that you had murdered my friend."

"It must have been the dead man we found, sir. Perhaps Mr. Takata found the man attacking his wife or stumbled across him after he had already killed her, before he took him out."

Conrad stood there and looked at them for a few minutes. "Is there anyone else here besides you and your daughter?"

"No. My wife died a few weeks ago. She became sick after drinking some contaminated water. We took her to the park and buried her the next day." The man began sobbing, as the memory of her death lingered painfully with him. The little girl also started crying again.

Conrad looked at Hawks, and then back at the father and daughter.

"I think I know what you're thinking, Colonel, and I don't think you should be thinking it."

"Why not?"

"It's going to be a long trip, sir, and possibly dangerous," said Hawks.

"More dangerous than this? We have a couple of spare horses," said Conrad.

"And you will need one for your friend."

"They could double up." Hawks just sighed and shrugged his shoulders.

"Listen, would you two like to come with us, get away from the city? I feel really bad about what happened."

"Listen, don't worry about it. I understand, sort of..."

"Where are you going?" asked the little girl.

"West Virginia, There is fresh water, good hunting, more land, and less people. We plan to try and start over," said Conrad.

"I don't know—I don't know if I could leave my Emily. We only lost her a few weeks ago."

"Please Daddy, let's go. Mommy's gone, Daddy, she's not here anymore. I'm tired of being so hungry, Daddy—let's go where we can find food, please?"

The man looked at Conrad and Hawks for a few moments. Hawks recognized the look.

"Listen, mister, we're not bad men. My friend here just lost someone that was very close to him as well. We are Army Rangers, we were just discharged by the president a week or so ago. We can help you protect your daughter."

The man looked down on the girl and rested his hand on her head, gently stroking it, before looking back up at men. "How long will it take to get where you're going? It's awfully cold out there, and we don't have the right kind of—."

"No worries ," said Hawks. "We have some spare coats that you can have, courtesy of Uncle Sam."

The man looked down at his daughter one final time, and noticing the look of anticipation on her face, smiled and said, "Sure, mister, we'll, come with you." Conrad extended the same hand to the man that only minutes earlier had held the blade of a knife to the man's throat. He stared at Conrad for several moments, hesitating, before reaching out to accept the hand in friendship.

"My name is Conrad Simmons, Colonel, US Army Rangers."

"I'm Charlie Parks, and this is my daughter, Jessica." The man looked over at Hawks, who followed suit.

"I'm Sergeant Brian Hawks, formerly of the 82nd Airborne out of Ft. Bragg, North Carolina."

"It's nice to meet you, Sergeant Hawks." The man looked down at his daughter. "Are you sure about this, honey? It will be rough going for a while. It will be cold and a long ride." The girl looked up at her father and smiled again.

"It's the right thing to do Daddy. We have to get to where we can find food and water." Conrad was taken aback by the maturity and pragmatism that the young girl demonstrated. *Such traits will serve her well in this new world.*

"Well then," the man said to his daughter as he looked around, "we had better grab some of our things to take with us." He turned back to Conrad and asked, "When do we leave, Colonel?"

"Tomorrow, maybe the day after. I have to wait and see what kind of shape my friend is in when we get back to his home."

As the man and his daughter began packing up their things, Conrad wondered whether the two would be able to survive. Looking at the little girl, he vowed to himself that they *would* survive it. He would see to it personally.

CHAPTER 35

James White poured himself another coffee. He savored the taste of the precious elixir. He wondered how long it would be until coffee disappeared altogether, at least for most of North America. They had been given enough provisions by the president that they would have no lack for basic necessities, including coffee, for quite some time. However, they would soon be dividing the precious resources as they formed groups that would scatter in seven different directions.

"Good morning, Dr. White." Monsignor Fennini walked over to the coffee thermos and poured himself a cup of coffee. Steam floated up from the cup, reminding both of the men that despite the fire that was roaring in the fireplace, it was still quite chilly in the lobby, as it was throughout the hotel.

"Good morning, Monsignor Fennini. I trust you slept well last night?"

"As well as can be expected, I suppose. Yourself, Dr. White?"

"The same."

"So," continued Monsignor Fennini, "is it true?"

"Is what true?" asked James White.

"That several of our number have gone to the Library of Congress, in hopes of salvaging some of the books?"

"Yes, they left this morning." James White stopped and took a long sip of his coffee. He had always been somewhat uncomfortable spending time around the Roman Catholic priests. It was nonsense of course, and he knew it, but old habits die hard. He had been raised as a boy to believe that they were not *real* Christians, and, he supposed it was equally likely, that many Roman Catholics had been taught the same about the Baptists. However, he had long sense realized the error of such teachings. Besides, he really liked Monsignor Fennini. There had been plenty of time to talk over the past couple of months, so they had taken advantage of the opportunity to exchange views. James White had developed a deep, new appreciation for the Roman Catholic faith. As part of Christ's Church over the two millennia since the crucifixion, they had already addressed many of theological quandaries that confronted the early Church. They had also demonstrated the same piousness and devotion that so many Christians share. Like other Christian denominations, they too had built hospitals, schools, and orphanages. They had also fed the hungry, and spread the gospel to the four corners of the world. James had long ago concluded that what unites Christians is infinitely greater than what divides them. Of course, Church members had committed sins over the centuries. But what *was* the Church if not a collection of weak and sinful human beings?

"Well, that was to be expected," said the monsignor.

"What's that?" He had forgotten what they had been talking about.

"The problem with the books." James White nodded his head in agreement.

"Yes, I agree, it was to be expected, if also very unfortunate. People have to stay warm however if they are to survive the winter, not to mention the need to cook food and boil water." The monsignor shook his head sadly.

"Of course. It's just that so much knowledge, so much history, will be lost forever. Surely, this will happen everywhere as human beings all over the planet burn books to heat their homes, keeping their children alive. Within a hundred winters, however, how many books will survive, I wonder?" James White simply raised an eyebrow and nodded his head. There was little that either of them could do about the situation anyway; a fact they both knew well. Besides, James White had another topic he wanted to discuss with his contemporary.

"Monsignor, I have something I would very much like to discuss with you." The monsignor adopted a singularly quizzical look on his face.

"Certainly, my friend, what is on your mind?" He sat down, coffee in hand, and gave James White his full attention.

"It appears that we will be going our own way very soon, and that *perhaps*, we will not see each other again." The monsignor nodded in agreement.

"Sadly, this is true."

"I have been giving some thought to the past, and the future, of the Church. Will you be returning to Rome when you leave here?"

"Indeed, I will, or at least, *I hope to*. There must be much discussion going on now at the Vatican, of this I am certain."

"Good then. Well, I have a proposal that I would like to make to the Holy Father."

"Go on."

"We are looking at a very dark time for civilization, for the world, as well as for the church." His new friend nodded again. "Well, how do you think the Pope would react to a suggestion that we try and re–unite the entire Christian Church? Perhaps we can turn this awful experience into something positive."

"I don't know. It *is* an intriguing possibility, however," he responded.

"I believe this would be a good time to attempt it," added James White.

"As you may know, Dr. White, the Holy Father has sought reconciliation with our protestant and Jewish brethren for many years now. In addition, this particular pope has always been open–minded to the possibility that the Church of our Lord and Savior Jesus Christ might one day be reunified under a single banner before our Lord's return. After all, are we not Christian brothers already?"

"Exactly. I recently read several articles about him, especially how heartbroken he has been over all of the fracturing that has occurred throughout the Church. He felt that the Church would be much more effective in reaching the masses for the gospel if we were to unite under a common banner."

"Well, Dr. White, I will certainly bring your proposal to the Holy Father. Still, how could this thing be accomplished? There is no way to communicate such an effort to people. There is no radio, no television, and no newspaper."

"I have an idea how we could do it. We could schedule a conference for five years in the future. This would give us plenty of time to spread the word by mouth. Will you discuss my pro-posal with His Holiness?"

"Of course I will my friend, assuming of course, that I ever see the Holy Father again. Sadly, my home is such a very long way from here. Where do you expect to go after this is all over?"

"Home," he answered.

"And where is home, my friend?"

"High Point, North Carolina—um ... well, it was High Point. Now it is Seattle, Washington."

"Please, here is what I suggest that we do. If, and when I return to Rome, I will bring your suggestion to the Holy Father, along with a recounting of all that has transpired here. Tell me Dr, White, in Seattle there is a parish, Immaculate Conception, do you know of it?"

"I do."

"If the Holy Father is open to your proposal, and I believe he will be, I will send word via one of our priests, to you there in Seattle, exactly two years from today. How does that sound?"

"That sounds wonderful, monsignor. Thank you."

"It is truly my pleasure. Only ..."

"Only what, monsignor?"

"I was just reflecting on how sad it truly is that it takes something like this, like this *Pulse*—the end of civilization as we know it, to bring us together." This time, James White smiled, and nodded in agreement.

He was going to ask the monsignor how he would get back to Rome, when Norman Weller came in, fixed himself a cup of coffee, and sat down with the two clergymen.

"Good morning gentlemen," he said. He took reached into a box and took out one of the vacuum-sealed meals that were in the box that had been supplied by the government. Weller looked at the two men as he opened the package and smiled. "I never, ever, thought I would enjoy a meal like this, but now,

I can't imagine how anything could taste any better!" he said, after taking a few bites. "So, Dr. White, what is the plan going forward? One of our priests has already left with a piece of the map for our monastery outside of Chicago."

"Funny you should ask that, Dr. Weller. You are just the man I wanted to talk with about that very thing." He finished the rest of his coffee before continuing. "I believe that we need to write a book. We need to write a book that provides future generations with a brief narrative of who we are, what we are doing in regards to the map, and clues they can use to find the pieces of the map. I'm not sure how exactly we accomplish all of this. I haven't worked it all out yet. What do you think, gentlemen?"

"It sounds like a *great* idea. What can I do to help?" asked Weller.

"I would like for the three of us, you, Monsignor Fennini, and myself, to write this book. If the approaching Dark Age is anything like the Medieval Dark Ages of old, perhaps the Church will survive, even a hundred years from now. If so, then perhaps, in the distant future, the Church will still have a record of what we are trying to accomplish now, and it can help them with locating the map, thereby leading them to the Oracle. It's not a perfect plan, I know, but it *is* a plan."

Norman Weller took another swallow of his coffee. He looked around nervously, acting as if something was troubling him. On several occasions, it appeared as if he were going to say something, but then thought better of it. He sloshed coffee around in his cup for several minutes, before James White finally asked him. "Norman—may I call you Norman?"

Weller looked up at him and answered, "Of course, Dr. White."

"Please, call me James. Norman, is there something troubling you, something you would like to talk about?"

Weller continued looking down. Finally, he slowly raised his head up high and looked up at both men. "Listen, I am a man of science, not theology. I have not even been to church since I left home as a teenager. Recently, however, given everything that has been transpiring, I have found myself starting to ask many questions about God. I have even started making requests of God, *praying to God,* asking that he protect my family. Does that sound strange to you?" he asked, looking at James White.

"No, of course not, Norman, why should it? After all, many men of science have also been men of God! Thomas Aquinas, Augustine, Newton, the list goes on. Only over the past hundred years or so have people adopted the silly notion that the two are somehow incompatible, something I always knew to be preposterous. This was one of the very reasons I wanted to attend this Unity Conference, because I *believed* in it."

"Tell me something, then, Dr. White, as a man of God, where *is he* in times of trouble? Why does *he* permit so many terrible things to happen?" His voice had started to tremble. "You see, today is my daughter's birthday; she is sixteen. I was supposed to take her out for a nice dinner, where I was going to give her birthday present to her. Now, I don't even know whether she is still alive!" He buried his head in his hands as each of the two clergymen laid a hand on the man's shoulder.

"I have no way of knowing their condition, of course, because like you, I live in Seattle. Even by horse, it will take me *at least* a few *more* months to get home. My wife, my other two children ..." His voice trailed off as he shook his head.

"Listen, I'm sure they are okay," said James White, placing a hand on the man's shoulder, "and that they are probably home right now just waiting for you to come walking through that door." Weller looked up at James White, almost as if to say, *"Please spare me the speech, I need real answers."* "I wish I had an answer for you, Norman, I really do. According to my belief, God permits things to happen for a variety of reasons. Sometimes it is for the person's good, sometimes it is a matter of free will, other times it is because of the person's own sin, other times, who knows? There is much that I do not understand about God, but there is one thing that I *do know,* however, and that is the fact that God *is always in control.* No matter what we believe, how much faith we have, or how much we trust Him, God is, always has been, and always will be, in control of the universe he created. I know that you want to understand why God permits such things to happen, but I would counsel that as Saint Augustine once said, 'Seek not to understand that you may believe, but believe that you may understand.'"

"I couldn't agree any more," added the monsignor. "Remember, Dr. Weller, if God exists, and of course I believe with my entire being that he does, he is most certainly then the creator of the entire universe. Who then are we to say why Almighty God does or does not do something? What *we can do,* however, when something occurs that threatens us, or threatens someone we love, is *pray* to him; ask for his protection, and his guidance. When Daniel was thrown into the lions den, he could easily have asked the same question that you just asked, perhaps he did. Regardless, God protected Daniel and delivered him from all harm. Perhaps God will protect your wife and children from all harm as well, if you only *ask* him." Weller looked at the two men for a few moments, on the verge, it seemed, of saying something, until he sighed and looked down.

"I am sorry for my outburst, James, Monsignor Fennini. I have been so worried about my family, I guess it is finally taking its toll."

"It is perfectly understandable Norman," James said. "I'm sure many of us here feel very much the same way as you do, we want answers, we want to try and understand why all of this has happened, what it all means. As a minister, I have often tried to explain why God does what he does, but the truth is this: I just don't know. How could I? How could anyone ever really know the mind of God? All we poor ministers can really do, the true purpose for our calling, is to share the gospel with others, and offer them the real comfort of God's love."

"If only we had been given more time to develop the Unity," said Weller. "There really is so very much that we could learn from one another. Over the past couple of months, I have been questioning many of my earlier held views about life, about God. Who knows, perhaps this book will be a legacy, our gift, born out of the sincere, heartfelt desire to actually *listen* to one another, to dialogue, to respect the reasoning and the belief of others. Perhaps we *will* make a difference after all."

A strange man then entered the hotel and walked over to the table where they were sitting. "Do you gentlemen mind if I join you?"

"Not at all, friend," said Weller. The man looked over at the monsignor, looking a bit uncertain.

"Are you Monsignor Fennini?"

"I am, indeed."

"My name is Jack Donovan, formerly Admiral Jack Donovan, United States Navy, retired. The president requested that I take you to Rome. It seems that he feels that it is important to get you there as quickly as possible, something to do about the plan you have been developing." The monsignor looked at the man a bit perplexed.

"But how do we travel?" he asked.

"I have a large yacht, a sail boat that I bought when I retired from the Navy. I can get you back home Monsignor Fennini, if you let me. The president called in a personal favor for me to get you home, and I intend to do just that, if you are willing to come with me."

"Please forgive my asking this next question, Mr. Donovan, but how will you navigate, you have no instruments, no?"

"I have been sailing ships for over forty years now, Monsignor. I assure you that it won't be any problem at all. I will do it the old–fashioned way, using a sextant and the stars, not to mention, the rather high quality, modern maps that I have in my cabin. I also have food and water already loaded on board." The monsignor brightened at the suddenly very real prospect of going back to Rome.

"When do we leave?" he asked, his face alight with joy at the thought of going home.

"We'll cast off as soon as you are ready. The sooner the better, I am afraid we may have another storm heading our way."

The monsignor looked to Weller and then to James White. Both men shrugged their shoulders and then nodded.

"Okay, thank you, Admiral, you are very kind. Please give me just one hour, and I will meet you right here at this table."

"Very good, sir. I will see you in one hour." Admiral Donovan left and walked back out the hotel's front door. At first, they wondered where the admiral was off to in such a hurry. After all, the world had virtually come to a standstill ever since the Pulse. Then it occurred to them that the admiral was just trying to be considerate, giving them some time to say their goodbyes.

Monsignor Fennini turned back to the two men and sat back down with them.

"Well, my friends, it looks like you will be writing that book without me." James White reached across the table, embracing the monsignor's hand in both of his.

"It has been my very great pleasure meeting you Monsignor Fennini, even under such gruesome circumstances."

"God works in mysterious ways my brother," he said. "Rest assured that I will take back your recommendations to the Holy Father. Perhaps, if the Lord is willing, we may restore Christ's universal church once more. Who knows, but that like the clear blue skies that appear after a terrible storm, perhaps the Lord will bring some measure of peace and restoration of unity to his church on earth before the last days."

"Perhaps. I will pray for your safe journey brother Fennini. Tell His Holiness that I hope to meet him one day in person."

"I will do so." The monsignor turned toward Dr. Weller.

"Dr. Weller, may God bless you for this conference. I believe that the Almighty has used you *and* this conference. How would we have known of the Oracle but for this gathering?"

"That is most gracious of you to say. We will miss you around here, Monsignor Fennini." Weller paused and looked around at the few others gathered throughout the area where they were sitting. "It seems that we will be disbanding and going our own way soon. Once we have finished this book, I will be off to try and find my family."

"May God speed you on your way then, Dr. Weller. I will pray that you find your family safe and sound when you finally arrive at your home."

"Thank you," he said as he rose from the table.

He shook their hands once more before leaving.

"I will miss that holy man," remarked Weller, watching the monsignor as he walked out of view.

"As will I," agreed James White.

Weller clapped his hands together before saying, "Okay, James, why don't we get to work on that book of yours? So, what do you think we should call it?" he asked. James sat quietly with a furrowed brow for several moments, rubbing his chin, until finally a big grin emerged.

"Why don't we call it, 'The Unity.'"

Norman Weller smiled as he nodded.

CHAPTER 36

Scott took several steps backward, wanting to take a moment to admire his handwork. Dick had instructed Scott on some of the basics about how to build a log cabin. After some discussion, they decided to use the lock–joint method, cutting notches in each end of the logs, approximately one foot from each end of the log. They had built up the four walls of the cabin, approximately four feet already on each of the four sides. It had taken them several days just to make the progress they had made. Their plan called for building a single cabin that they would share until they could build a second cabin. He and Dick would have to work until dusk again in order to have the cabin done by the weekend. Dick sat down to rest for a few minutes, sweat dripping from his forehead.

"I don't know, Scott. I don't remember it being quite so much work."

"How long has it been since you built a log cabin?" asked Scott.

"Oh, I don't know really. Let's see, I guess it must have been, oh, just after I got out of college—about forty years ago maybe?" They both laughed heartily.

"Well, I guess that explains it!" replied Scott. After a few minutes of rest, Scott scrutinized the stack of logs they had placed in a pile close to the cabin. He estimated that one more tree would provide the remaining logs needed to complete the cabin. "Well, I guess we are going to need some more logs. Now, what did I do with that axe?" asked Scott.

"I believe you left it lying by those trees," answered Dick, pointing towards the edge of the woods.

Scott walked over to where he had cut down a few trees earlier in the morning.

It had warmed up considerably over the past several days, but Scott felt certain the temperature was still below freezing, as icicles had formed, as the sunlight had melted some of the snow on the trees. Scott found the axe laying on the ground beside the stump where he had cut down the last tree. He picked the axe up and surveyed the trees in the local area. A nice, tall, thick pine tree stood not far from where he was standing. Scott smiled and made for the tree. He was exhausted and hoped that given the size of the tree, perhaps it would be the last one they would need for a while. He closely examined the tree, looking for signs of disease. Dick had told him earlier that he should be certain to pick trees that were free of disease. The wood would last much longer if the tree were disease free when they cut it down. Scott had no idea how long they would be in the cabins but more likely than not, it would be for a long time.

Scott went to work. Each tree was getting harder and harder for him to cut. He would have to find a means to sharpen the axe before starting the next cabin. Scott labored on the tree for almost an hour, at which point he was completely exhausted. He assessed his progress and decided he could fell the tree in just a few more strokes. As he swung the axe, he had a nagging feeling in the pit of his stomach that he had forgotten something. The axe connected, and he heard a crack. Another stroke, maybe two, and he would be finished. He swung the axe once more, and as it connected, he suddenly realized what it was that he had forgotten to do. He had not notched the tree. In the split-second that it took him to determine a course of action to avoid being crushed by the towering giant, he decided his best chance was to run back and to the left. It was difficult for Scott to tell what direction the tree would fall now, since there were other large trees all around the one he had just cut. As Scott made a run for it, the tree began to crack and moan; it began to fall in the direction of the cut, at least until it smacked against a much larger tree, which served to deflect the falling tree slightly to the left. Scott looked over his shoulder as he ran just in time to see the tree picking up speed as it fell in his direction. Panic began to set in, and Scott sprinted to escape the falling behemoth. In a flash, he suddenly felt a searing pain in his back, as a curtain of darkness fell over his eyes. The last thing he saw before he blacked out was the ground suddenly rushing toward him.

"Scott!" yelled Dick as he rushed toward his injured friend. He had glanced in Scott's direction just in time to see the tree racing toward him. He watched on helplessly as several branches near the top of the tree drove Scott to the ground. Dick's yell brought Susan and Eleanor out of their tents. Susan screamed when she saw Scott laying face down on the ground, where several tree branches appeared to have pinned him to the ground.

"Scott, can you hear me? Scott!" Dick yelled. He arrived where his friend was lying on the ground. He could see that

Scott was unconscious. He tried lifting the tree by pulling a branch near the top of the tree. When Dick struggled to lift it, the tree gave just enough that he could almost clear Scott, but he was unable to hold the tree up and pull him friend out at the same time. The women arrived at the tree as Dick was struggling how to get Scott out from under the tree.

"Here, Eleanor, Susan—each of you grab one of Scott's legs. On the count of three, I want you to pull as hard as you can. Are you ready?"

"We're ready, Dick—please hurry!" answered Susan as a stream of tears flowed down her face."

"Okay, one, two …" Dick counted as he prepared to lift the tree. "Three!" Dick lifted with all of his might as the two women tried to pull Scott free, but to no avail.

"Look, Dick, a branch is caught on his leg!" Dick looked down and saw where his leg was snagged.

"Okay, Susan, get ready to pull. Eleanor, I want you to come here and take care of this small branch that is snagged on his leg. Okay, again, get ready, one, two, and three!" He let out a grunt as once more he lifted the tree as high as he could. Eleanor worked quickly to free Scott from the branch. Susan struggled to pull Scott out from under the tree but was unable to move him more than a very short distance. It was enough however for Eleanor to free Scott from the branch that had caught on his leg. Eleanor saw that the tree was dropping lower and lower as Dick strained to hold the tree off Scott. She grabbed Scott's other foot and pulled. The two women pulled him clear just as Dick gave out, and the tree came to rest on the ground, right where Scott had been only moments before.

With Scott out from under the tree, Susan worked to recall the knowledge and skill she had picked up years earlier as a nurse, in an effort to save her husband. She checked his breathing to confirm for the first time that he was still alive. She could hear shallow but steady breathing. She checked for a pulse and again found a shallow but steady beat. Scott suddenly started coughing and blood sprayed out of his mouth.

"Oh no, there must be internal bleeding, probably some broken ribs. Dick, can you please help me get him inside the tent and under some blankets."

"I wouldn't do that if I were you." A man's voice came from behind them. Dick turned to see a strange man sitting on horseback, staring down at the four of them. Beside and behind the man were twenty-five other men on horseback. To Dick, it looked like some scene out of one of the many old westerns he had watched growing up. He also noticed that all of them were armed.

"Who are you?" Dick asked.

"It seems to me that my name is the least of your worries at the moment, if you don't mind my saying so." The man looked at the younger woman that was kneeling down next to the injured man. He could not help but notice what an extraordinarily beautiful woman she was, quite an accomplishment given the unusual happenings of late. The sight of her stirred something deep inside him, something Vic Masters had not felt for a very long time. Perhaps she reminded him of a woman from his distant past, his wife maybe, back when they had first met, but he wasn't sure. Whatever it was about her that stirred him so, he found it intoxicating.

"Gentlemen," he said to his companions, "do you know what Ambrose Bierce said about beauty? He said, 'Beauty...the power by which a woman charms a lover and terrifies a husband.'" His companions chuckled at his remarks, waiting until he turned back around to look at one another, trying to figure out what he had just said.

The young woman took her eyes off the man on the ground just long enough to cast a short, irritated glance in the direction of the man on horseback and the others. She had been crying and still looked quite distraught.

The man looked down at Scott, who still lay bleeding on the ground. "Friend of yours?" he asked during the brief seconds that she had taken her eyes off Scott. Susan looked at the man again and then over at Dick and Eleanor. They looked at her evenly before nodding to her, signaling to her that they thought she should answer. Susan looked back at the man and nodded her head.

"Would you like for me to take a look, see if there is anything that I can do?" he asked Susan as he climbed down off his horse. Smiling at her, he touched the side of her face and asked, "Or maybe there is something that you can do for me." The men with him laughed.

Susan jerked back, knocked his hand away, and smacked him, hard enough that the imprint of her hand was visible for quite some time on the side of his face. Masters rubbed his face and smiled again.

"Okay then, maybe not."

"I'm a married woman, mister," answered Susan.

"Well then, I guess I had that coming. You've got spirit lady. I like that. Your husband then, it looks like he's hurt. Would you like some help?"

"I'm a trained nurse," answered Susan .

"Oh. Okay then, we'll be on our way then, seeing that you have everything under control." The man started to climb back onto his horse.

"Wait," asked Susan, "do you have medical training?

"I was in the Army Rangers for fifteen years. I spent some of that time as a medic. I have treated a number of battlefield wounds."

"Yes, please, take a look and let me know what *you* think."

"Okay, then. I'll have a look; see if there is anything I can do."

"You said you wouldn't move him into the tent, why?" asked Dick, as the strange man knelt down next to Susan's husband and checked his pulse. The man didn't answer right away. He was busy attending to Scott, listening for breathing, examining both of Scott's legs, and then feeling around his ribs.

"Because it can be extremely dangerous to move an injured man, especially before you have assessed exactly what is wrong. You can end up doing more harm than good, possibly even killing him." He continued examining Scott for a couple of minutes before standing back up and facing Susan. "Well, since we won't be getting any X–rays, I will have to give you my best guess. I'd say that he likely has some broken ribs, which would explain why he is coughing up blood. I believe that he also has a broken leg. If I were you, I would immobilize your husband's leg before moving him anywhere. I can help you make an improvised splint."

"But how do we move him? We don't exactly have a stretcher lying around anywhere!" The man looked at Susan for a moment, before realizing that he was staring at her. She was starting to get a little uncomfortable, just the opposite of what he wanted. He looked back down at her injured husband, more to avert his eyes from her than to look at Scott.

"Well, you may not, but I do." The man turned and looked at one of the men still on horseback. "Bill, bring that stretcher that we used for Harrison."

"Where did you get a stretcher?" Susan asked.

"Let's just say that we have one that is no longer being used. We have been traveling for weeks now; our man Harrison had an accident on the way. We told him to stay behind, but he wouldn't listen. We picked up the stretcher at an abandoned hospital on the way here."

"What about Harrison? Did he stay behind?"

"Yes, I guess that's one way to put it. Yes, he definitely stayed behind."

"You mean he's—"

"Yes, he's dead. "Two men brought the stretcher and prepared to move Scott onto it when the man raised his hand to stop them. He looked at Susan and said, "With your permission, ma'am."

"Yes, of course. But please be careful!" she added.

"Do as the lady says," the man told the others.

"Is there anything you can do for him?" Susan asked the man.

"I can splint his leg. There's nothing I can do for the internal bleeding. There's no way to tell how serious the damage is inside. If we try to go poking around in there, we'd probably kill him. Once the bleeding stops, the ribs should heal on their own."

"Well what should I do then?" she asked with obvious desperation in her voice.

"There's nothing that can be done now but wait. You may need some painkillers though. We picked some up back at that hospital I told you about, you're welcome to some of those. They should help dull the pain."

"Thank you."

"So it looks like your man was working on building a cabin. Looks like a pretty good job too, at least up until the part of getting himself hammered by one of the trees." The man glanced at Susan and saw that she was flushed with anger.

"Sorry about that, ma'am. I'm not so good with people anymore. I'm not sure I ever was for that matter."

Her face softened with his apology. "That's alright. You have been very kind." The man started laughing, careful to avoid the woman's look. He had probably annoyed her again.

"What's so funny?"

"Oh, it's just that I have been called many different things by many different people over the years, and I can say with a very high degree of certainty that 'very kind' was not one of them." Susan did not respond. She had begun to realize that despite the man's timely assistance, she really didn't know anything about him. She would have to be more careful.

"The man walked back over to the half–built cabin. You know, my men and I could help you finish this cabin in no time, if you would accept our assistance."

"There's no need for that, stranger. We can finish it ourselves. Thanks for the offer though," said Dick, who had walked over to stand beside Susan. Had he recognized her growing discomfort talking with the man? Yes, she was certain that he had. *Had the stranger picked up on it as well?*

"I was talking with the lady, mister," the man answered, rather sharply and apparently, somewhat annoyed.

"No, he is right," she answered. "We cannot possibly impose on you anymore than we already have."

"It is no problem and no imposition. My men and I will soon arrive at our destination. We have time to help you finish your cabin."

"But—." she started to say. The man waved his hand dismissively in her direction.

"No buts. I won't take no for an answer." He turned and faced the group of men that he had ridden into the camp with. "I need some men to get to work on this tree. We need to finish this cabin so that this woman's injured husband can have some shelter from the cold. He needs something better than the tents over there to recuperate in."

Several of the men climbed down off their horses and made their way toward the fallen tree. Several others made their way to inspect the existing work. They felled several additional trees as work on the cabin progressed at a phenomenal pace. At the pace they were going, it appeared that they would be finished by nightfall. The man watched her, obviously pleased with the expression on her face.

"Do you happen to have any shovels?" he asked her.

"Yes, but why do you ask?"

"Have you dug a well yet?"

"No, not yet. We have been boiling water from the river, or snow." The man began walking around the area, apparently assessing the area for the best location for a well.

"Listen, you don't need to—"

"Have you scouted the area for a well yet?" He continued walking around, still trying to determine the best location to dig.

"No, we have not. We assumed that almost anywhere close to the river would be adequate."

"No, I'm afraid it's not quite that simple. We need to dig at least fifty feet back from the river. This really isn't the best time to be digging a well because of how hard the ground is. The best approach is to *drill* a well. We passed a well digging operation some ten miles back. I will send a couple of my men back there to pick up some drill bits and piping. With the help of the horses, we will have you a well drilled by nightfall."

Susan gasped and smiled at the man warmly. The smile made the effort worthwhile to Masters.

He walked over to several of his men and talked with them for several minutes. He pointed off in a direction toward the east that Susan supposed must have been in the direction from which they had come. Three of the men then took off on horseback in the direction in which he had pointed. He then walked back over and stood next to Susan.

"Listen," Susan said to the man, "we don't have a lot to offer you here. We have nothing of value with which to repay you for all of your generosity. However, there is a small store, a small convenience store, about five miles west of here on the main road. There was still plenty of food and drinks, etc, there when we left a couple of weeks ago. You might want to go by there on your way back east, or send someone there even now if you wish."

"That is *very* generous of you, dear lady, revealing the existence of this store to a group such as ours, especially when it is so close to you. However, that will not be necessary. As I have said, we have been traveling for weeks now, and we have found plenty of food and water along the way. Sometimes we killed it, as we did several days ago on our way through some mountains. We killed some deer and found some wells already dug where we were able to help ourselves. But I do thank you for your thoughtful and considerate offer."

As the man assisted some of the others with preparing the logs for the cabin, Susan looked at the man and studied him for several minutes. She was having great difficulty assessing what kind of man he was. On the one hand, she was flabbergasted at his generosity and kindness toward her, Scott, Dick, and Eleanor. She felt like this man was sincere, yet she also suspected something very sinister about him. The men that travelled with him acted as if they all were, to a man, terrified of him, yet they had chosen to follow him voluntarily. The man was truly an enigma. She walked back over toward the tent where Eleanor was sitting with Scott. She knew how important it would be to Scott to have the cabin and the water, as he healed from his injuries. She feared, however, what price the man might attach to the services he and his men had rendered on their behalf. As she entered the tent with Eleanor and Scott, she could tell by the look on Eleanor's face that she shared that concern.

"Susan, he hasn't regained consciousness since the accident. However, he has been talking in his sleep. I believe he is going to be okay." Susan looked down at Scott's leg and examined the splint that was now attached to it.

"It looks like a very good job. Who did this?" asked Susan.

"One of his men came in here. Believe it or not, he said that he used to be a doctor. He said that he thought Scott would be fine. He recommended that we keep him off of his feet as much as possible for the next couple of weeks, and then we should make him a crutch to use before he gets back on his feet."

"What about the internal bleeding?"

"He said that without any diagnostic equipment, there was no way to tell for sure. However, he felt like the internal bleeding had probably stopped." Susan looked out at the men working diligently on the cabin. It looked like the strange man appeared to know something about how to build them. It looked as if they were already adding the roof and had nearly completed the fireplace. She turned her attention back to Scott, and then to Eleanor.

"What do you make of these men?" she finally asked Eleanor.

"Well dear, it certainly all seems a bit strange to me. However, these are certainly some very strange times we live in. Perhaps they are just *really* nice men. That or ..." she let her words trail off, hoping that Susan let it drop. She didn't.

"Or what?" she asked.

"Or maybe it's something else."

"They all seem, well, a bit frightened of him don't you think?"

"Of who dear?" asked Eleanor, obviously trying to pretend she had no idea what Susan was talking about.

"That man, their leader," Susan said. He's been extremely kind to all of us. They have almost finished building the cabin, and he said that they are going to dig us a well. It's um ... very generous of him, don't you think?"

"Yes, it is. It makes you wonder whether or not he might be asking for something in return before it's all over with, hmm?" Eleanor asked, glancing over at Susan.

"Exactly," said Susan. The two women looked at one another for several moments when Scott suddenly started to stir.

"Ohhhhh ... my head. What's going on—aarrgghh!" His hands went first to his leg and then to his ribs.

"Scott, how do you feel?" asked Susan, after kissing her husband. "I was so worried.

"What happened to me? My leg and my ribs—it feels like I broke them!"

"You probably did, silly. Don't you know better than to run in the direction of a falling tree?" Scott had not heard the question. He was busy looking out the opening in the tent.

"What in the world is going on out there? Who are all those men? There must be ten or fifteen people working on the cabin."

"Closer to twenty–five actually," offered Susan.

"Twenty–five! Why are they working on *our* cabin?"

"Right after your accident, they appeared out of nowhere. They helped move you in here, they're finishing the cabin, and they're digging us a well."

"A well? What do they want in return?" he asked.

"Well, we don't know. This one man, he wouldn't take no for an answer. The others, well, he appears to be the man in charge. They seem to be scared of him, actually, Scott. We're not sure what to think yet."

"Maybe I should—aarrgghh!" He grabbed his leg.

"I would recommend you try and stay off of your feet for the next couple of weeks. Your leg and your ribs need a chance to heel."

The man in charge had walked up to the entrance of the tent while they were talking. He moved so quietly that it made everyone uneasy. Scott looked up at the man. Before he was able to speak, the man held out something to him.

"Here, take some of these. They're painkillers. They won't mask the pain completely, but they will make it more tolerable."

"Thanks Mr…"

"My name is Masters, Vic Masters."

"Scott McBride. I'd get up but…" Masters just chuckled and nodded. Scott watched him, and then looked at the two women, and he saw the fear in their eyes.

"The men returned with the drill and the pipe a few minutes ago. I expect my men will hit water fairly soon given the nearby river. I've asked them to dig deep, even after they hit water. The deeper the well is, the safer the water will be to drink."

"Thank you, Mr. Masters," Susan told the man. Masters looked at her and smiled. Scott took notice. He did not care for the way Masters was looking at his wife. Masters continued.

"Call me Vic. They have finished the cabin as well. It won't be like your old house, but it should prove a lot more comfortable than your tents." He stopped to look around the tent and saw the question they all were asking.

"Listen, all of you." He was looking mostly at Susan. "I have done a lot of things in my life that I'm not particularly proud of. I'm not saying that I would not do them all again given the choice, but I'm not necessarily proud of them. Also, I'm not a very nice person, but neither do I pretend to be. However, even bad people like me do nice things occasionally. Think of it as a way to keep in touch with my humanity." Masters turned to Scott. "You have a beautiful wife, Scott, and I can't say that all of my thoughts about her have been as pure as the driven snow. However, even men like me have standards, and I killed a man once for acting on his thoughts about my ex–wife. Look, my men and I will need some water to last us the rest of out journey, so digging a well is in our own interests as well."

"But the cabin—"

"The cabin was mostly finished already. You and Dick here had already done all of the heavy lifting. My men and I just helped finish what you had already started." He looked hard at Scott and told him firmly, "You and yours have nothing to fear from me or my men—trust me. None of them would dare do anything to cross me. Besides, they need me, that's why they ride with me. It's a scary world out there right now, and everyone knows that during scary times, everyone likes a strong leader." With that, Masters started out the tent before stopping, turning around, and focusing his attention squarely on Scott. "And you take good care of this fine lady here—she deserves it."

"I know," answered Scott, "and I will." Masters just smiled and left out of the tent.

It was another hour or so before the men finished drilling the well after first hitting water.

They installed a hand–pump on top of the well pipe, and each man got his fill before filling his own canteen. Thirty minutes later, they were back on their horses and were gone soon after. Susan walked out of the tent soon after the men left. She walked inside the cabin, admiring the handiwork of the men that had finished it. She shook her head as she thought how much better it was than anything Dick and Scott could possibly have done on their own. They had built a fireplace in it as well, using stones and bricks that several of them had found nearby. It even had a set of fireplace tools that they had acquired from some place of unknown origin. She walked back out of the cabin and over to the new well. She pumped some fresh water for herself and the others, before heading back to the tent. On her way back, she noticed something else. A pair of horses had been tied to a tree out of sight of the tent where Scott was. She supposed that Masters didn't want her to know they were even there until after he'd left. Perhaps he knew how important the horses would be to her and the others later. She did not understand Masters or the men that followed him, but then again, she didn't have to. Whatever the motivation for his actions, she was thankful for them.

Masters left Scott and Susan McBride's encampment feeling uncharacteristically good about himself. It was something of a strange and alien feeling to the former Army Ranger and convicted murderer. He was on a way to kill one man, yet along the way had had saved another, along with his family. As he rode on toward his rendezvous with death, it occurred to him how ironic life could be at times.

CHAPTER 37

"It is settled then." James White looked over the remaining attendees of the Unity Conference. After several moments of silence, he continued, "Okay, let me recap our discussion then; we must be certain that we are all agreed." He walked over to the flip chart, turning the pages of text and pictures until he reached the last page. He then held up a copy of *The Unity*.

"First, we will each take one of the handwritten copies of this book, that Norman and I recently finished writing, with us when we leave. We will then place that copy of "The Unity" either in the largest library in the largest city that we pass by on our way home; or in the largest library near where we live, is that correct?" Everyone in the room nodded. "Second, we will distribute the pieces of the map across the seven different cities that we agreed upon, four here in the United States, and three abroad. We will trust that the clues contained in the book are sufficient for them to find the Oracle." Once again, there was consensus.

James could sense the agitation as the people in the room grew increasingly impatient. They were ready to leave, yet wanting to see the thing through at the same time. James White decided to pick up the pace in order to allow everyone to get on their way. "Now, were we able to procure transportation, at least for those traveling abroad?"

Norman Weller stood up to address the gathering. "James, I spoke with the president this morning, and he said that we will have the ships we need to reach our respective destinations. He will be sending a messenger over within a couple of hours with all of the necessary details." A sigh of relief went up from the three trying to get back to their respective homelands. "He will also supply horses to those needing them, to help ensure that they reach the designated locations for the pieces of the map safely."

"Wonderful news, thank you, Norman," answered James White. "Okay, third, we need someone to travel to the Oracle, to ensure that it is ready when the time comes. Bjorn, you said you were willing to make that trip. It sounds like it could be dangerous, are you certain you want to go through with it, or have you reconsidered?"

Bjorn Yvornsky stood to address the group.

"To be quite frank with you, James, I am not thrilled with the prospect of making this trip. However, given the fact that the Oracle is the centerpiece of our plan for one–day resurrecting civilization, it *has* to be me. Someone has to make as certain as possible that everything is prepared. Since it is likely to be the only legacy of ten–thousand years of human history that we will leave to our descendants, other than dilapidated cities and toxic waste, I will give my life if necessary for this endeavor. Who knows, perhaps I will even find God in the process!"

James White looked at Yvornsky and smiled. His admiration had grown for the man over the past two months, more than he ever could have imagined. He reflected for a moment, how they were at the same time so dissimilar yet so much alike.

"Thank you, Bjorn, we all realize that the success of this effort depends heavily upon you. We also understand just how dangerous this trip will be, and we truly, truly, appreciate your willingness to make it. I promise we will pray fervently for the success of your trip." He paused for a moment for effect. "We will also pray that you do, indeed, find God!" Yvornsky looked up and the somewhat solemn expression that been on his face was replaced by a mischievous smile.

"Who knows? I tell you what—if God *is* out there, I'll find him!" A light chuckle rolled through the room.

Norman Weller stood up and added, "All of you, listen, the president has promised to send a number of Special Forces soldiers that have remained behind, to go with each of you, to help ensure your safe travel to your destinations. He understands just how vital your roles are in this plan. Once you have delivered the pieces of the map they are free to continue with you or go on their way."

"That's great news, Norman. I take great comfort knowing that, please tell the president thank you for all of us here, and for those who come after us."

"You can tell him that yourself. I told him about everything that you have done here. When he asked me who was leading our group, I told him that *you* were. He should be here any minute."

"But Norm, you are the one that organized the conference, the one that—,"

"No James. I only organized a conference to talk about science and theology. You are the one that has shaped this effort for the future, you deserve the credit."

"I'm flattered, Norm, thank you. Nevertheless, if anyone *really* deserves credit, it is God, for warning us, and for providing this plan, and *all* of *you* here, that have given up so much in order to stay here, resisting the understandable urge to rush home to your families. Your sacrifice has helped build a future for your descendants. You are all to be commended."

"I have a question. So why is the map being delivered to Catholic churches? Why not a library, or a university?" asked one of the progressive seculars in the group.

"That's a fair question, Henry, and I'll tell you why Norman and I chose them." James White began pacing, looking at the floor as he did so. "Look, none of us really know how long this thing, this "Effect" is going to last. Norman and I decided that the last thing we wanted was for this map to be buried or forgotten. While there is no guarantee anywhere that, the map will be safe, at least it would seem to have a better than average chance at a Roman Catholic Monastery. Some of their monasteries have been around for a thousand years or more! Given the fact that the Church survived the last Dark Age after the fall of the Roman Empire, almost two thousand years ago, perhaps it will still be around in a hundred years or so, when this "Effect" has finally run its course. If anyone has any better ideas, they are certainly welcome to debate them with us today." James White looked around.

"I'm fine with your answer, James. Thank you."

About that time, the door in the back of the large room where they had been meeting in opened. The president walked in with about thirty men in military uniform. James White assumed that at least some of them were the escorts that the president had promised. James White stepped down and met the president halfway.

"Dr. White," President Michaels said warmly. His greeting had the disingenuous tone of the seasoned politician he had been for so long, but it had the feel and appearance of sincerity. James White wondered which it was. He would later decide that it was most certainly the latter.

"Mr. President, we all wanted to thank you once more for the assistance that you have provided to us both up until now, as well as for our upcoming journeys," James White said to him as they shook hands. The president smiled as he motioned to the front, where the lectern was positioned.

"May I?" asked Michaels.

"Of course, Mr. President."

"Thank you." Michaels walked on up to the lectern and, as so many speakers often do, he grabbed the lectern with both hands.

He looked over at James White and said, "Dr. White, you thanked me for everything I have been doing for you." He shook his head. "That's just not right—it is *I* who should be thanking *you, all* of you." He looked around at the few who remained of their original number.

"Look, make no mistake about it, I know and I understand where we are and what's going to happen. I saw it just on the way here from the White House, misery, suffering, and death. Our civilization cannot survive this thing, not really. Our country, our world, as we knew it, will soon be no more. You, and the others in this room, you offer the only hope of preserving a legacy for future generations, for a people that will not even be born for a hundred years or more. Asking for your help is most likely going to be the one thing that I did right during my time in office." Raw emotion now had the one that had only months earlier been the world's most powerful man, in its grip. His face contorted as his eyes began to water.

"You know–"he started as his voice began to crack and quiver "–that this, all of this," he said, waving his arms in a gesture that suggested everything, "is *my* doing. It happened on my watch. I could have prevented it and I did nothing." The man John Michaels buried his face in his hands, trying to collect himself. "All I can see now, even when I close my eyes, is the pain and the suffering all around me, and the fear. And my children, the only legacy that I have left for my children is a crumbling civilization on a dying planet." Tears trickled down the proud man's face. Bjorn Yvornsky looked down at the ground in shame, realizing that he had been far too harsh. He had grossly misjudged John Michaels.

The anguish in the man's voice brought out the minister in James White, who stood up and walked over to Michaels. He put his arm around him and said, "President Michaels, civilization may be crumbling, that is true, but the world is not dying, and neither will civilization, at least not completely. You cannot, you must not, take all of the blame for all of this, and place it on your shoulders. Are you the traitor that helped another country steal the device? Are you the man that stole the device? Are you the one that turned it on? No, Mr. President, you are just one man. You did everything you could sir, all anyone could do, to stop it." Then James White, and the other men and women in the room sat quietly, giving John Michaels a chance to collect himself. A short time later, he looked up at James White, who was still standing next to him with his arm around him, and nodded. James White walked back over and took his seat.

"Thank you, Dr. White. As I was saying, I would like to thank you, all of you, for what you are doing here. Your efforts give us all great hope for the future; for without it, the world would remain in the darkness we all see ahead of us, perhaps for untold millennia."

"Life will go on, Mr. President, we will go on, for as much time as God permits it," said James White.

"Indeed, Dr. White, indeed." Michaels then lifted up his hand and pointed across the back of the large conference room. "As you can see, I have brought with me over thirty men, enough that two of them will be able accompany each of you to your respective destinations, to your designated monastery, where you will leave your piece of the map, before continuing on your way. These men, each and every one of them, have pledged their lives to help you reach your destination, and they have sworn an oath to me that they will see to it that you safely reach your homes, or wherever you want to go after you have left the map. For those of you traveling within the United States, you will be given more than enough provisions to see you to the monastery and then for at least another two months after that. For those of you traveling abroad, I have been able to procure ships that will be more then sufficiently stocked to enable you to reach your destination and then safely return home, if needed. These men have *also* sworn an oath to lay down their lives, if necessary, for the sake of the mission. All of these brave men and women share our belief that this is the single, greatest legacy we could possibly leave for our posterity." The president turned and looked at James White.

"Dr. White, I understand that you are a widower?"

"That is true, sir, yes."

"And that your children are grown and living in Seattle?"

"That's true also, Mr. President. I moved there just last year to live with them."

"Then perhaps I can help with that as well. I would like to offer you, and Norman Weller, a trip to Seattle by boat, once this is all over, a final gesture of my appreciation."

"Why, thank you, Mr. President. I would certainly appreciate that very much."

"It is my pleasure." Turning back to the group he said, "Ladies and gentlemen of the Unity, I wish you the very best of success in your mission, the very best for you, for your families, and the very best for the United States of America. May God speed you on your way."

The room erupted in applause.

CHAPTER 38

Masters was determined to find the man that had betrayed him. Fueled by rage and driven by his desire for revenge, everything else was secondary, relegated to a place of insignificance.

They rode on for days, making their way through woods, abandoned highways, and country roads, heading southeast toward his former stomping grounds, and the man he planned to kill.

On the second day, they came across a large camp near the edge of some woods. As Masters drew closer to the camp, he could clearly see that they were some sort of military; most of them appeared to be Army.

They slowed their pace a bit, allowing the men in the camp to have plenty of time to see them coming. The last thing that Masters wanted this close to his goal was a firefight with a military unit. He liked his chances well enough, but he didn't want to lose all of his men. He might need them before he was finished.

Before long, they were close enough that he thought he recognized the insignia. The men were, or at least they had been, Army Rangers. For the second time since leaving the McBride camp, it occurred to Masters how ironic life could be at times.

Vic Masters sat on his horse staring down at the soldiers in front of him. There was no question about it any longer, they were unquestionably Rangers, recently discharged by the looks of it. Based on the weapons they were carrying, at least some of them were Airborne. He knew that this bunch was far different from any of the other people he had come across since things started to fall apart. These were highly trained, tough fighters, *and* they were extremely well armed to boot. He would play this carefully, very carefully. After all, he didn't hate all Rangers, only one Ranger. He wasn't out to kill the entire Army, only one specific army soldier.

The men on the ground seemed somewhat less than intimidated by Masters and his men. After a few moments, a few of them came over, carrying what looked like M5 Carbine rifles, a standard issue for airborne and Army Rangers, or at least they had been when Vic was locked away.

"Good morning. Is there something that we can do for you gentlemen?" one of them finally asked Masters, who they obviously had identified as the leader. Masters estimated the Ranger was probably around twenty–five years old. Masters recognized the distinctive patch of the 3rd Ranger Battalion on his left shoulder.

"Good morning. Say, I see that you boys are Army, eh?"

"That's right."

"Yeah, I spent some time in the trenches for Uncle Sam myself."

"You don't say?"

"No, I do say. Of course that's been a few years ago now."

"Well, how about that." The younger man was becoming agitated. He didn't like all of the armed men on horseback, and Masters could see it.

"Say, where are you boys from, what base?"

"Fort Benning."

"Good, old Fort Benning. Yeah, I was based there for many years."

"Oh yeah? You were airborne then, huh?" asked the young Ranger. Masters grinned at him. The soldier was testing him of course.

"Come on man, what are you talking about? What are they teaching you kids these days? The eighty-second airborne is out of Bragg, you know, Fayetteville, North Carolina?"

"Oh, yeah, that's right. So you served at Benning, huh?"

"Yes, I did. I was a Ranger, for ten years."

"Did you see any action?"

"Sure did. Fought against both the Taliban and Al-Qaida after Pakistan fell apart."

"Cool, man, I wish I could have seen action like that!" Masters looked at him and the others; they were loosening up a bit. Good.

"Yeah, those were the days. We kicked some serious butt back then." He laughed with the men a bit. "Say, I'm looking for another Ranger I served with a few years back, an old friend of mine. His name is Conrad Simmons, Colonel Conrad Simmons, does anyone here know him?"

"No, I don't, but hang on a minute." The man turned around to face his friends. Say, any of you know a Ranger named Simmons, a Colonel Conrad Simmons?" A number of the men and women looked at the younger man and shook their heads.

Finally, one that had been eating an MRE over against a tall, sprawling oak tree finally spoke up. He had a thick southern accent.

"Yeah, I know Simmons."

"Is he here with you?" asked Masters.

"No. He was reassigned to Ft. Myers a year or so ago."

"Myers? That's not a Ranger base."

"No, it's not. Regardless, if you're looking for Simmons, you'll find him a little further west of here. He came through here leading a large group of grunts and civilians heading west from DC about the same time that we were moving south. I believe he said they were headed toward West Virginia."

"How long ago?

"Oh, I don't know. A couple of days I think. If you hurry, you might catch up with them. As I said, they were traveling with some civilians, including some old men, women, and children. They were moving slow but steady."

"And you're sure it was Conrad Simmons."

"Yes, sir, I am. We talked for a good bit about the good old days. We never served together, but we knew many of the same people. He seemed like a good man."

"Oh, yeah. He's a great guy." Masters gritted his teeth and turned his horse. The soldier on the ground hollered after him.

"Say, mister, I never caught your name!"

"Masters, Vic Masters. Captain, US Army, 3rd Ranger Battalion."

Masters and his men picked up their pace to a steady trot, heading northwest, back the way they had come. He never looked back to see the expression of the man he had just spoken to. The man had heard the name Vic Masters before.

CHAPTER 39

Conrad tried to move the group along faster, but every time he tried, he had to slow back down to a pace that was even slower than before, or risk leaving someone behind, and that was unacceptable. They were picking up more and more people as they made their way to Harper's Ferry, many of whom were already sick or exhausted. There were now also a number of small children, including Jessica Parks, who along with her father Charlie Parks, Conrad had picked up back in Baltimore.

Conrad was starting to grow concerned about the weather. While the temperature had stayed well above freezing for the past week, he saw clouds on the horizon, and felt a cold wind that seemed to be blowing in from the Northwest. It seemed likely that another arctic cold front was on its way, and that would mean trouble for everyone, especially the weak and sickly in the group.

"Conrad, what's wrong, you look worried?" asked Rachel, who had been walking beside him as they gave the horses a well deserved rest. She put her arm around him and held him tightly. He felt an impulse to jerk away from her at first, but slowly he settled down and enjoyed her embrace. Despite his powerful feelings for her, he was still having some difficulty adjusting to having a companion, since he had not been close to any women since his wife had died several years earlier. Conrad took notice that Rachel had been spending more and more time with him ever since leaving DC. While she had been distant, aloof even, for the first several days of the trip, she had been warming to him more over the course of the past several weeks, as they rode, talked, and ate together. Conrad wondered whether she had concluded that despite his many faults, and a quick temper, he was a good man.

"Is something wrong?" she asked him again.

"I've been watching the sky since yesterday. Have you felt the wind?"

"You mean the chill?" she asked.

"Uh–huh."

"Well, yes, I guess I have now that you mention it. You think there's a storm coming?"

"Yes, I do. My guess would be sometime tomorrow, it's going to get really cold, and I bet we see more snow." Rachel grimaced as she looked back on the children and the older men and women that were with them, men like his old friend and mentor, Takata.

"What should we do?"

"I believe that we should get as far as we can today, before the storm gets here. We need to try to find some shelter, at least for the children, and the elderly."

Conrad looked behind him and saw Frank. "Frank, can you come up here for a minute?" Frank handed the reins of his horse, carrying the aged Takata, to Charlie Parks, who was walking beside his daughter.

"Yeah, Conrad, what is it?"

"Does any of this look familiar?"

"Well, it's kind of hard to tell. I never came this way when leaving DC. If we continue following roughly parallel to the river now, we should run into Harper's Ferry by sometime late tomorrow."

"Is your father–in–law's house near the river?"

"Well, it's a couple of miles from the river, yeah."

"Does it have a fireplace?"

"Well I never really thought about it, but yes, I believe it does."

"Is it big enough that some of these people, at least the oldest and the youngest of our group, could stay inside? There's a storm coming and we need to get them to a shelter."

"Absolutely, it is a big house with a lot of land around it. There's also a large barn that the rest could hold up in for a few days."

"Will your in–laws be okay with us staying there for a little while? We can find a place to settle down, possibly around Harper's Ferry, once the weather improves."

"I think they will be happy to see us. My father–in–law is a former marine. I think he would enjoy having a bunch of grunts around to pick on." Conrad looked at Frank and smiled.

"He sounds like a great guy, Frank"

"He is—I can't wait to introduce him to you."

"Yeah, I've been meaning to ask you about that. Why didn't we ever make this trip before, when we were on leave?"

"Because it was a long trip to make from Georgia, and since we were reassigned to Myers, I haven't had the time to go back."

Frank looked all around him, at the deserted roads, at the quiet houses. The lack of activity seemed so extraordinary for the late morning.

"I can't wait to see them," he said.

"Your family?" asked Rachel.

'Yeah," he answered as he smiled. "My wife, Vickie, my three year old, Marcus, and my oldest, Katherine. I haven't seen any of them for several months now."

"Don't worry, Frank," answered Rachel. "I'm sure they are just fine. It sounds like they are at just the kind of place they need to be at right now, given the circumstances."

"Yeah, he said, "I'm sure you're right." Rachel and Conrad looked at one another. Frank didn't sound very convincing.

The odd caravan, a mixture of military men and women, civilian men and women, children, and the elderly made for an unlikely sight as it made its way along the Potomac River. He had made a promise to James White, which he fully intended to keep, and had reluctantly allowed strangers to join the caravan, resisting the sensible urge to keep the group as small and nimble as possible. Regardless, he would have been unable to say no anyway. It was a dangerous journey to make to be sure, to go with him could well mean death, but to stay behind virtually guaranteed it. He looked over the long caravan of people walking or on horseback behind him.

"Wondering what to do when we get to where we are going?" Frank asked him.

"Yeah, something like that," he answered. "You know I've been thinking a lot about our situation."

"You mean this trip to Harper's Ferry?"

"No, Our situation, the situation of every man, woman, and child across the planet," he said. "There are a lot of people dying out there, and do you know why?"

"Because everything is falling apart?" answered Frank.

"That's not what I am talking about, well, not exactly anyway. People are dying all over the planet primarily because of one reason, because people no longer know how to live in a world without modern technology. Human beings have walked the planet for ten thousand years, thriving for most of that time without electricity, automobiles, refrigeration, and indoor plumbing. Yet, only one–hundred and fifty odd years after people first started using electricity, most do not even know where to find food and water if they can't pick it up in the local grocery store."

"*We* know."

"Yeah, sure, we know. Only because we've had survival training. With the exception of military, survivalists, farmers, and those living in third world countries, most people have no idea how to survive in the wild anymore."

"Well then, we can teach them."

"It's not that simple."

"Why not?"

"Because it's going to get ugly out here before it gets better, especially in the cities."

"What do you mean?" asked Frank.

"Well, there are a lot of people and few resources. It's going to be a little like the old west, like living on the frontier."

"Come on, Conrad, why so pessimistic? We haven't seen anything like that yet, have we?" asked Frank.

"Not yet Frank, but we will—and soon." Frank shook his head, but Conrad ignored it. "We have to prepare for that. There will be no structured police force, no one to keep order, at least not the way we have known it in our lifetime." About that time, Rachel caught up to where Conrad and Frank were walking. "Conrad?"

"Yes Rachel, what is it?"

"What is that up ahead?" she asked, pointing ahead through some trees.

Conrad pulled out his binoculars and looked in the direction she was pointing in. "It looks like a log cabin, and if I'm not mistaken, it's a newly–built log cabin. Now look at that, they also have a well. We are already running low on water, perhaps they would be willing to share some with us, or trade a little water for something we have. What do you two think?"

Frank answered first. "I think it's a good idea. Maybe *we* should go in first, however, leave the rest at a safe distance, just in case."

Conrad looked at Frank and smiled. "What's the matter, Frank—worried someone might take shot at you or something? Not turning into a pessimist are you?"

"Well, with things getting ugly, one cannot be too careful!"

"All right, you two, just make certain you don't go in guns blazing!" Rachel said with a smile.

Frank looked at Conrad with a puzzled look and said, "Hey Conrad, I thought you said she was Army as well."

"Navy."

"Oh, that explains it," answered Frank, as Rachel hit Conrad in the arm.

The two men took a couple of horses, and left the caravan far behind, hidden behind the thin woods that separated them from the small cabin. They rode slowly, not wanting to startle anyone that might be inside. Smoke was rising from the chimney, so there was obviously someone still inside. Conrad and

Frank did their best to avoid presenting a threat to whoever was inside the cabin, while keeping one hand close to the triggers on their assault rifles.

As they approached the cabin, two men, a younger man in his late twenties, and an older man, in his sixties, emerged from the cabin. Conrad and Frank relaxed their trigger fingers, relieved to see that both men were unarmed. They both noticed the younger man occasionally wincing in pain, as if he had recently been injured.

"Can I help you gentlemen?"

"Yes, sir, I believe you can. My name is Colonel Conrad Simmons, and this is Major Frank Martin, we are, *were*, with the Army." Conrad extended his hand. The two men looked at him for a moment, sizing him up. They were both sweating, especially the younger man. They were nervous, and Conrad could certainly appreciate why. Finally, the younger man, wincing in pain once more, reached out and attempted to shake Conrad's hand. The latter extended his out even further in an effort to spare the man some agony. Conrad deduced that his injuries must be rather severe.

"I'm Scott, Scott McBride, and this is Dick Stewart." Conrad shook the hand of the other man. *Firm grip for an older guy.*

"So what can we do for you, Colonel?" Scott asked for the second time.

"Well, we've been traveling for several weeks now, heading for a place not too far from here, when we happened upon your settlement. I couldn't help but notice that you have a well, and our water has been running low for the last few days. We were wondering whether you could spare some. We are willing to trade for it, if that's okay with you?"

"And if we say no?" asked Dick, taking a measured chance to find out what kind of man they were dealing with."

"Then we'll simply push on. We could really use the water though."

"Please, go ahead and help yourself," Scott answered, gesturing toward the well. Conrad looked back at the woods for a few moments, hesitant to continue.

Finally, he added, "Listen, there are actually some more folks with us, men, women, and children. We have been traveling together. May they have some water as well? We will ask everyone to take just what they need for drinking."

"I don't know—." Dick started to say, until Scott raised his hand.

"That would be fine Colonel. Please invite them over."

Conrad and Frank grinned from ear to ear. "Thank you, both of you!" they both answered. Conrad then looked at Frank and said, "Frank, would you please go tell the others to come on over. Tell them they can come single file to fill their canteens or whatever they have brought with them with water, and that's all. We want to make sure we leave plenty of water in these folks' well."

"All right, Conrad, I'll tell them," Frank said before running off in the direction of the woods. A few minutes later the caravan emerged, horses carrying the aged, the sick, and the children. Rachel and Frank walked over to join Conrad and the others at the front of the house. Conrad did the introductions.

"Scott McBride, Dick Stewart, this is Rachel, Rachel Bennett, formerly with the United States Navy." The men shook hands with Rachel.

"You are a long ways from the ocean, Ms. Bennett," Dick said.

"Well, sometimes you just don't know where you might end up, Mr. Stewart! Besides, I don't suppose there really is much of a Navy anymore now, is there?" About that time, two women joined them at the door. Rachel noticed that the younger woman looked like she was pregnant, most likely late in the second trimester. She came up and put her arm around Scott's waist, wrapping his arm over her shoulder.

"Scott, you need to rest, you're still not well!" she said, supporting him as they walked back into the cabin.

"Hello, gentlemen, miss. My name is Eleanor, Mrs. Eleanor Stewart.

"It's a pleasure to meet you, ma'am," they answered.

"Listen, I was a Navy Corpsman, kind of like a medic in the army," said Rachel. "I would be happy to look at that man. Frank here said he thought he was injured."

Eleanor turned and looked back inside the cabin. The sun was bright outside so it was a bit difficult for Rachel to see inside, though she tried a couple of times to do so.

"Susan?" asked Eleanor. Susan came back to the door a few seconds later.

"That would be wonderful, thank you. My husband was injured a while back when a tree narrowly missed killing him."

"A tree?" asked Rachel.

"Yes. He was cutting down trees for this cabin when it happened. There's not exactly a lot of doctors out here in these parts, as you can tell," answered Susan.

Susan escorted Rachel into the cabin.

Dick stood at the door with Conrad and Frank, watching the convoy of men and women lined up at the well. He was relieved to find that the two men had been telling him and Scott the truth. He watched as young and old, men, women, and children, slowly filled their canteens, empty two–liter bottles, whatever they had brought with them, and filled them with water from the pump.

"Do you folks have any firearms around?" asked Conrad after several minutes.

Dick started sweating as he struggled to answer, "Why do you ask?"

"One of these days you folks might have to fight to protect that well, and your lives."

"I think that we'll be just fine without weapons, Colonel Simmons. We're not soldiers, like you are."

"Please forgive me if I offended you, Mr. Stewart. It most certainly was not my intention. I very much appreciate your generosity. Which reminds me … ?" Conrad walked over to one of the horses they had carrying supplies.

"I can offer you some blankets, a couple of knives, some MREs, or an M5 assault rifle."

"Are they army blankets?" asked Eleanor.

"Yes, ma'am, they are—wool, great for keeping a soldier, or a civilian for that matter, warm in the winter."

"We could use a few of those blankets Colonel, thank you very much."

Susan watched nervously as Rachel carefully examined her husband. Every now or then Scott would yell out when Rachel, as gently as she could, touched different ribs. She nodded to herself as if she were confirming something she had already suspected and proceeded as if she were making notes in her mind. "Well, the bad news is that several of the ribs appear to be broken, but they are simple fractures, the bones haven't penetrated the skin."

"And the good news?" asked Susan.

"I'm not sure about the leg. There appears to have been some internal bleeding, around the ribs and the leg. The leg however appears to be rather swollen. I cannot be certain, but as best as I can tell, the leg has not been broken. All the same, I wouldn't take any chances. I would keep him off of the leg for the next few months just in case. He is a lucky man, actually."

"How can you say that?" asked Scott. "My ribs are broken and I can barely walk!"

"Because," Rachel said, "if the leg had been broken, given the location of the injury, it could very well have severed the femoral artery. You would have bled to death within minutes."

"Oh God!" exclaimed Susan. Rachel looked over at her. The young woman looked tired and exhausted. The dark patches under her eyes, the worn clothes she was wearing, suggested she had slept little, if any, for at least several days.

"How far along are you?" she finally asked Susan.

"Huh, what?" Susan acted as if she had asked the question in an alien language. *Sleep deprivation.*

"I asked how far along are you in your pregnancy?"

"Oh. I'm not certain, maybe six months?" Rachel nodded. She reached toward her stomach but Susan, startled, jumped back.

"May I? Rachel asked. Susan thought about it for a few moments.

"Oh, yes, sure, go ahead," Rachel placed her hand on Susan's belly. She thought she could make out a faint heartbeat and Susan's belly felt nice and firm. After a brief examination, Rachel breathed a bit easier.

"I would say closer to seven months. Well, as far as I can determine without the proper equipment, I would guess that the baby is fine, for now. However, it won't be if you don't get you some rest. You need as much as you can get, for the sake of the baby."

Susan nodded. "I know, I know. We had a long walk getting here, and then—." she paused as Rachel interrupted.

"Where are you folks from?"

"Just outside of Leesburg. We were uncertain whether we would even survive so close to DC."

"But I saw horses out front, why didn't you folks ride?"

"We didn't have any horses then," Susan answered. "We walked until we got here. The men that helped us finish the cabin, not to mention the well; they left a few horses before they pulled out a week or so ago." Rachel stood back up and walked toward the door.

"Please, excuse me, I'll be right back." She walked over to the well and pumped some water into a small cup that she pulled out of her bag, before walking back into the cabin.

Rachel then reached into the bag she was carrying and pulled out a medicine bottle. She poured a couple of pills into her hand before passing them along to Scott.

"Here, this will help with the pain, and these will help with any infection. They should help both of you get some rest now. I'll leave some more here with your wife, that I suggest you take."

"Thank you, really. I haven't slept well since the accident."

"You're very welcome." Rachel turned to Susan and said, "Listen, I suggest that you really try to get some rest, you really *do* need it." Susan nodded as she tried to manage a smile.

"Thank you. If Scott is able to get some rest, I should as well. I've barely left his side since the accident, he's been suffering so. Rachel put her hand on Susan's arm.

"I'll be outside for at least a little while longer. Just let me know if you need anything." Susan nodded before thanking her again. Rachel walked out of the cabin closing the door behind her. Eleanor, who had been standing between the cabin and the well, walked over to her.

"How is he doing, dear?" she asked. "And how is Susan holding up? I don't think either of them has had any rest."

"That's what they said. I can't tell for certain, of course, with no way to X–ray. My best guess is that he just has a few broken ribs. They should both rest better now that I've given him something to help with the infection, and the pain."

"Oh, thank you, dear," she said. "We are so grateful that you came along."

"Think nothing of it," she said.

Rachel walked back over to talk with Conrad for a few minutes, kissing him and giving him a long embrace, before heading back toward the woods and toward the river. No one seemed to notice the man standing behind a tree, watching Rachel as she walked past.

CHAPTER 40

The sky was darkening slightly and it felt much colder. The clouds began blocking most of the sun's comforting rays and the cold wind picked up slightly. Eleanor pulled her shawl more tightly around her to block some of the chill and to prevent her from losing more body heat. Conrad and Frank stood just outside of one of the larger tents with Eleanor and Dick, discussing their plans for what they would do after visiting Frank's family on the farm. Their planning was abruptly cut short however when the sound of gunfire erupted from the woods. Conrad, Frank, and several of the others grabbed their assault rifles and made their way to the edge of the tree line. After only a few seconds, it became apparent to the combat veterans that the shooting was not in their direction.

"What do you make of that, Conrad?"

"I don't have any idea, Frank. I'm just glad that they're not firing at us for once."

"Yeah, me too. Still, we should probably take a look."

"Yeah, I guess so. Come on; let's find out what's going on."

The pair slowly made their way to the sound of the firefight. By the time they arrived, the shooting had stopped. They saw two dozen armed civilians and one soldier lying dead on the hard dirt and maple leaves that covered the wooded area where they were standing. Several grunts appeared from behind some trees.

"Colonel Simmons, is that you?" asked one of the men with a thick southern accent.

"Yeah, I'm Simmons, who wants to know?" he asked, trying to identify the man.

"Sergeant Mike Steele, sir. I was with the eighty–second air-borne, out of Bragg. We met several days ago and swapped some stories."

"Oh yeah, Steele, good to see you again. Err, what's going on?" he asked.

"A few days after you left, we ran into this fellow, he was traveling with twenty or so other men on horseback."

"Yeah, so, is this them?"

"Yes, sir, it's most of them. I think we got them all sir, except for the meanest of the bunch. I believe you know him, sir."

"Who, what are you talking about?"

"Masters, sir, Vic Masters. He was looking for you, pretend-ing to be a close friend of yours, sir. I believed him at first, at least until he told us his name as he was leaving out of camp." Con-rad's heart sank as he started walking around the woods shaking his head. *Masters, just when things had finally started looking up. He was looking for Conrad, so he could hill him.* Frank just stared at the ground and shook his head.

"Great," said Conrad. "That's just great."

"I believe he means to kill you, sir. I never liked the look of this lot anyway. So when I realized who he was from our conversation the other day, and that I had just told him how to find you, I couldn't have a good man's death, especially the death of a fellow grunt like yourself, and a Ranger to boot, on my conscience. I gathered some of my friends here and came looking for them. We caught up to them about thirty minutes ago, just before the firefight. As soon as they saw us behind them, they opened fire. I saw that Masters fella when we first came upon them, but it looks like he got away during the fight."

"Sounds like Masters," said Frank.

"Yeah, it sure does." Conrad said dryly as he turned back toward Steele and his men. "I owe you and your men a debt of gratitude, Sergeant. You just saved my life and the lives of a number of those traveling with me."

"No problem, Colonel. Now you'll keep your eyes open now, and watch your back, won't you? That Masters fellow can't be too far away."

"Yeah, if I know him, and believe me I do know him, he won't leave until he's accomplished what he came here to do, or until he's dead."

"That's affirmative, Colonel. I saw the look in his eyes."

"Well, we'd better get back to our people. Let them know what's going on so we can setup a watch," said Conrad.

"Hooah!" yelled Steele, followed by his men.

"Hooah!" Conrad and Frank answered, as they made their way back to the cabin.

They emerged from the woods minutes later, to find Eleanor and Dick staring at them, obviously frightened but saying nothing.

"Hello, Conrad, Frank, how are you boys doing?"

Conrad wheeled, raising his rifle toward the familiar voice as he did so.

"Ah, ah, ah . . ." Masters said, waving his finger. Conrad saw him standing on the edge of the woods about thirty yards away, with one arm around Rachel's neck and his Glock pointing at her head.

"Masters, you son of a—"

"Now let's not be rude," he said smiling. "Aren't you going to introduce me to your girlfriend?"

"If you hurt her, I'll—" Conrad stopped as Masters chambered a round.

"Okay, Simmons, this is how it's going to be. You and all of your friends will drop your weapons now, or I *will* kill her—and that would be such a shame." Conrad quickly sized up the situation. He had no qualms about sacrificing his own life. However, he knew Masters. He would kill Conrad and then take Rachel, likely killing more to cover his exit.

"Why don't we settle this the old–fashioned way, Vic?" said Conrad. "Wouldn't you prefer to kill me up close, anyway? Let her go. None of us will fire, I promise." Conrad looked around at everyone else that had their weapons trained on Masters. "Everyone lay down your weapons, please." One by one, they dropped their weapons, trusting Conrad to save Rachel's life.

Masters glanced around to be certain that everyone had complied. When he was satisfied that they had, he grinned at Conrad and said, "All right, you dirt bag. It's time for some payback. I'm going to kill you slowly, make you suffer for each and every day I spent in that lousy hole." Masters tossed his firearm aside and pushed Rachel away so that she fell on the ground. Conrad then threw his weapon down and moved closer to Masters.

"You know, Masters, maybe if you hadn't killed a man in cold blood, they never would have locked you up in the first place."

"Kill? What about all of the men we *both* killed in battle Simmons? I guess they don't count? Well, like Voltaire said, 'All murderers are punished unless they kill in large numbers and to the sound of trumpets.'"

"Are you still going around bragging about your high IQ with those stupid quotes of yours from guys like Voltaire?" Conrad asked. "Okay, if you're so smart, let me ask you something. Did you even know that the man you killed was a covert operative working in Iran? It's possible that he may have known the Iranians were planning to steal the EMP weapon, and could have prevented this "Pulse" thing from ever happening in the first place!"

"Shut–up, Simmons, you traitorous scum. I thought you were my friend, but you stabbed me in the back, the same way that Brutus stabbed *his* friend Julius Caesar! Well, I'm more like Genghis Khan than I am Caesar, so you'd best prepare yourself. Don't think your little chop sui martial art crap is going to help you. I've eaten tough guys like you for breakfast." He looked over at Rachel and smiled, before adding, "After I'm done with you, Simmons, I'm going to make it a point to get better acquainted with your gorgeous, little girlfriend here." Conrad's jaw tightened at the thought of him with Rachel.

He's trying to make me angry, get me off–balance. I have to stay in control.

Masters gritted his teeth and said, "I've been looking forward to this Simmons, for a very long time."

Masters swung at Conrad with his fist, nearly connecting with his jaw. As the blow went by, Conrad countered with a punch into the ribs of his enemy. Masters bent over hugging his side, feigning that he was more injured than he really was. Conrad started to speak when Masters right hand suddenly emerged from his side holding his KA-BAR. Without even a moment's hesitation, Masters had drawn the blade and attacked with one smooth motion. Conrad could see that his time in jail had not hampered Masters fighting skill even a little. The slash came at Conrad's neck, intended to sever the carotid artery. He successfully evaded the blow by fractions of an inch, but not before being rewarded with a gash on his right arm, just below the shoulder. Conrad responded, as his training had taught him, ignoring the pain in order to focus on fighting for his life.

Masters smiled and said, "I told you boy, I'm going to kill you slow." The next attack came as a stab to the mid section. Conrad moved off to the left at a forty–five degree angle, evading the attack. He countered with a knife–hand strike to the throat. Masters staggered back, foaming at the mouth and struggling to breathe. He held the knife up in a defensive posture; it was enough to prevent Conrad from risking a follow–up attack, but just barely. Conrad wanted to finish it, but he was being cautious. He knew that the combat training Masters had received was every bit as good as his was. Masters coughed and gurgled for a while, before starting to recover from the blow.

Conrad took the opportunity during the stall in the fighting to take out his own KA-BAR. The two were now evenly armed, which given his supplemental martial art training, gave him the edge. He decided to hold the knife in his weaker hand, holding it for close–grip fighting. Masters came at him again, this time feigning another attack to the throat. Instead of attacking the neck, he slipped in just close enough to slash at Conrad's leg. Conrad moved just enough that the slash cut the top of the thigh, just above the knee cap, narrowly missing the intended femoral artery. This fight was to the death, and neither man would be pulling any more attacks. Masters threw an uppercut to the jaw, and followed–up the attack with a kick into Conrad's solar plexus, knocking him off his feet and back onto the ground, where Conrad lay nearly unconscious. Masters was walking over to where Conrad lay hurt and bleeding and was closing in for the kill, when he heard a voice from behind him. He put his foot on Conrad's neck, and turned to see her.

"Vic, is that you? What are you doing here?" Susan emerged still half–asleep from the cabin. She staggered outside looking puzzled and confused, as if she was struggling to understand what was happening. In reality, however, Susan was wide–awake, giving her best performance in an effort to save Conrad's life. She had indeed been wakened by the altercation outside of the cabin, but she had been roused considerably sooner than she was letting on. Watching the fight progress from inside the cabin, she could see that it was taking a turn for the worse as Masters prepared to kill him. She then decided to intervene in an effort save his life. Masters seemed to like her, so she would have to leverage that. She suspected that *she* had been the reason that he had done so much for them before, including saving the life of her husband.

"Susan, I'm sorry you had to see this."

"What's going on here, Vic?"

"This treacherous scum is the reason I was sent to jail. I owe him, big time."

"But he's a good man Vic, like you. He's been helping us, giving us blankets and supplies. You're a good man Vic, *you're better than this,* I know it."

A good man. No one had thought that about Vic much less said it aloud for more years than he could remember. He had finally figured out what it was about Susan that connected with him. Something about her reminded him of *his* wife, of their lives together *before* everything changed, before his life turned into a cesspool. Susan had somehow reawakened something inside of him, something he thought no longer existed, part of the man he was *before*. He felt alive once more, like the man he had once been. He began to wonder whether he might be able to start over, begin his life anew.

"Susan, when we first met, there was something about you that reminded me of someone I once knew. It re–awakened something that I thought was dead. I began to remember the man that I was a very long time ago, the man I haven't seen in the mirror for a very long time."

"You can be that man again, Vic—you are. You're a good man, a strong man, and a caring man. I know, I've seen that."

"You don't know what I've done. I've done things, horrible things. I have killed more men than I care to think about. Every night I dream about them. Sometimes I see their faces, and I hear their screams."

His face softened as he looked down at Conrad, at the man he had once called friend. The past few months his rage had driven him on, ever forward, with a blind, insatiable desire for revenge. He had thought killing his old friend would somehow ease his pain and suffering. Looking down at him now, he realized that it would not ease his guilt, it would only add to it. He took his boot off Conrad's neck and allowed him to get up. Conrad remained on guard, even as Masters dropped his knife.

"It's too late for me now, Susan, but I want you to know that meeting you, getting to know you, has meant more to me than you will ever know. Maybe, just maybe, if things had been different, if you and I had met before…"

"Vic, I don't know what to say. I—"

"Then don't say anything. Why don't you go on back inside and get some rest—there's nothing for you to worry about, it's over now. I won't kill him, I promise..." Eleanor, who had been watching the fight, walked over to the cabin and gently ushered a reluctant Susan back inside and closed the door.

Conrad, bleeding from his right arm and his left leg, kept a close eye on Masters. He knew how fast and unpredictable he was, not to mention how vicious. As Susan disappeared inside the cabin, Masters turned his attention back to Conrad. He looked at him as the friend he once was and for a moment, Conrad thought it was all over. Then, in a flash, Masters' demeanor changed once again and his face filled with the same hate and vengeance that had become so familiar. Conrad reacted instinctively when Masters reached behind his back for a weapon, by launching a preemptive attack just as Masters brought his hand around. Still hurt and bleeding, Conrad threw up his left hand toward Masters' face, causing him to react instinctively and predictably by trying to protect his face, as Conrad buried his KA-BAR into the mid–section, just below the rib cage before withdrawing.

Masters eyes widened as he gasped, and staggered back a few steps, before collapsing to the ground in a heap. Conrad looked down at Masters expecting to find a KA-BAR or a Glock in his hand, but was surprised to find his hand empty. Masters had *wanted* Conrad to kill him, *but why?* Conrad had to know why the man he had once served with, the man he had shared food with, the man that was once his best friend, the man that had once saved his life, had now saved it one last time.

"Vic, why...?

As he lay dying, Masters looked up at Conrad, smiling weakly as he did so." I'm sorry, Conrad, for everything. You did the right thing, turning me in. That man, he was a jerk, but he didn't deserve to die."

"You could have killed me, Vic, but you didn't—why?" Masters started coughing up blood.

"Because of her, Conrad," he said, nodding toward the cabin where Susan was. "Because after trekking halfway across the country looking to kill you, she reminded me of who I was, and who I still am inside. It was the killing Conrad, so much killing; it *did* something to me, made me sick, numb, and cold inside. I let it change me"

"A few weeks ago, I almost killed an innocent man Vic, under the mistaken assumption that he had murdered *another* close friend of mine. The endless bloodshed, watching your friends die, it can do strange things to a man, twisting him inside," Conrad said. Conrad looked at his friend lying on the ground. "Vic, I'm … sorry." Masters coughed some more, struggling to keep his eyes open.

"It's what I *wanted … old friend.* I wanted the nightmares to end." Conrad looked around the camp.

"Frank, a chaplain, is there a chaplain here?"

"Yes, I'll find him." Frank took off and returned a few moments with the chaplain in tow. The chaplain walked over and knelt down beside Masters.

"I've done some terrible things in my life, Chaplain, some horrible things, and I have carried a heavy burden of guilt for a very long time. But now, as I lie here dying, preparing to meet my maker I ask you, I beg you; please … pray for me, for surely he will not hear *my* prayers."

"Are you repentant my son, do you seek the Lord's forgiveness?"

"I am, Chaplain, and I do."

"Will you trust in the Lord Jesus Christ, as the son of the Living God?"

"I will, Chaplain, I do."

"Then in the name of the Lord Jesus Christ, I announce to you the forgiveness of all of your sins, in the name of the Father, and of the Son, and of the Holy Spirit." He made the sign of the cross over Vic Masters.

After smiling for a moment, Masters said, "I believe it was Charles Dickens that wrote in *A Tale of Two Cities,* 'It is a far, far better thing that I do, than I have ever done; it is a far, far better rest that I go to, than I have ever known.'"

A few moments later Masters let out a heavy sigh, and breathed his last.

Conrad reached down and felt for a pulse. He looked up at everyone watching and sadly shook his head. Vic Masters was dead. Conrad stood up and began walking over toward Rachel, who wrapped her arms around him, crying with tears of fear and relief. She looked down at the wounds on his arm and leg. She then helped him walk over to a grassy area, where she could examine him a little more closely. She peeled back enough of his pant leg to see that the slash had come much closer to the artery than either her or Conrad had known, before cutting across the top of the thigh.

"You're *very* lucky to be alive, mister," she said, managing a weak smile.

"I just needed a reason to live," he said, looking her straight in the eyes. Rachel smiled and blushed, before turning her attention back to his leg. She reached into her bag, took out some sutures and a needle, and went to work. She poured water over the wound, applied some antibiotic ointment, and sewed up the wounds. She then wrapped bandages around the wounds to provide additional protection from infection. Conrad looked admiringly at her handiwork.

"Nice work corpsman," he said.

"Yeah, well try not to get into any more knife fights anytime soon, okay? At least not until these wounds have a chance to heal. Deal?"

"*Deal.*"

CHAPTER 41

Conrad and the others decided to remain in the camp with Scott, Susan and the others for at least a couple of hours, taking time to assist burying the bodies of Masters and his companions. After the funeral, Scott, Susan, Dick, and Eleanor walked over to where Conrad, Frank, and Rachel were standing. .

Scott approached them first. "Colonel, listen, we would like to invite you, and everyone with you, to live here with us, in our compound," he said. "Stay with us; help us build a community together, a small piece of civilization amidst the chaos around us. What do you say?"

Conrad furrowed his brow and rubbed his chin.

"Well, thanks for the offer Scott. I guess we need to ask the others, see what they think, let everyone make their own decisions. We'll let you know." Scott nodded as Conrad and the others turned and walked back to where everyone else had gathered.

Conrad, Frank, and Rachel spread out among their companions, and began polling everyone, trying to get a sense of who wanted to go on further and who wanted to stay. An hour later, they met back near the well to share what they learned.

"Okay, so Rachel, why don't you go first," said Conrad. "What did everyone have to say?"

"I spoke with Charlie Parks and his daughter, along with several other families, and all of them told me the same thing."

" What's that?" asked Conrad.

"Everyone's exhausted, cold, and hungry, Conrad," she said. "They don't want to go any further, they can't."

"Okay. Frank, how about you?"

"I heard mostly the same thing. Several of the folks I spoke with were pretty sick. I'm not sure if many of them can go any further. If we decide to keep going, I think a number of them will have to stay no matter what."

"Well, I spoke with Master Takata, Hawks, and a number of the other former military. Most of them said that they could go either way. However, I get the sense that most of them like the area, and would just as soon settle down here. It seems that everyone seems to like the location." Conrad paused for a moment to look Frank and Rachel in the eyes. "What about the two of you, what would you like to do? Frank?"

"I don't know, Conrad. I just want to get to the house to check on my family. Assuming that everyone's okay, well, this place isn't far from the in–laws house so yeah, I wouldn't mind staying here."

"Rachel?" Rachel looked into Conrad's eyes and smiled.

"I just want to go where you go Ranger." Conrad smiled back. It was exactly what he was hoping she would say.

"Okay then it's settled, we're staying. Let's go and share the news."

Conrad, Frank, and Rachel told Scott and the others, before spreading the word among their fellow travelers on the trek from Washington. Those staying behind would work on building additional cabins, hunt for food, and gather resources. Conrad would go on with Frank however, to find his family, before returning.

Early the next morning, Conrad and Frank left out of the camp on a pair of well-rested horses. The temperature had dropped considerably overnight and the sky was overcast. The cold front had finally arrived and it looked like it would bring snow with it.

Frank estimated that while they were within five or six miles of his in-laws' house, it might take them a few hours to get to the farm. They rode alongside the river until they finally came to a town. From the edge of the town, they could see that a fire had ravaged much of yet another municipality. In addition to the burned-out downtown area, a number of stores had been completely emptied, presumably by locals desperate for food, water, and supplies. Frank grew worried for his family, seeing the destruction so close to the farm. Every once in a while, they would come across someone that had died close to the river, most likely from Cholera, or some other water-borne illness. The temptation for locals dying of thirst to drink from the river had apparently been overwhelming for many, and fatal for some.

As they continued riding, they soon came across a group of people standing around a house. They watched for a moment, assessing the situation. The people inside the home, a man, his wife, and their two small children, still had some meager amounts of food and water inside, and someone had found out about it. The father had been holding the small mob at bay with a small firearm, but the men were becoming more desperate, and more brazen. Conrad and Frank talked it over before agreeing that they should take the time to help the family "What's going on here?" asked Conrad, already aware of the circumstances.

"Never mind, mister," yelled one of the bigger men in the crowd. The man seemed to be leading the mob. "It's none of your business. How about you and your friend just clear out of here?"

"I beg to differ, friend," he answered. "I believe it *is* my business."

"How is that exactly?" asked the big man.

"Well, I don't think that you're welcome here, you, *or* your friends. If you need water, just boil some from the river. You practically live right next to one. If you need food, why don't you hunt for game, or fish in the river?"

"Why don't you just mind your own business?" he answered.

"Yeah!" another yelled."

"All right, I tried to do it the easy way. Let's do it the hard way then." Conrad pulled out his sidearm and pointed it at the big man. "Listen, I don't need to use this to take care of the likes of you, but since my friend is in a hurry, I'm going to do it the fast way. If you and your friends don't clear out right now, and leave these people alone, I promise that you *are* going to regret it. Am I clear?"

The man laughed at Conrad. "Do you think that you're the only one with a weapon?" he asked, moving his coat to the side enough to show the revolver tucked into his pants."

"No, I suppose I'm not," answered Conrad. "But I do believe that I'm the only one here except for my friend that knows how to use one correctly. Would you like to find out just how well?" he asked, allowing the man to see his Ranger patch on the side of his arm. Frank did the same. The man hesitated, and started backing up.

"No, no—we don't want no trouble, man. We're just hungry, thirsty, and scared. I mean, everything's been falling apart."

"I know. I suggest that you do as I said before. Dig wells, boil water from the river, hunt deer, fish. People survived like that for thousands and thousands of years, and you can do it now."

"Yeah, yeah, you're right."

Conrad yelled toward the house.

"Are you folks okay in there?"

"Yes, we're okay. Thank you."

"I don't believe these people will be bothering you anymore," he said. I'll be back later today. I'll stop back by and check on you. Would that be okay?"

"Yes, of course. Thank you!"

"You're welcome." He turned back to the others. He reached into his pack, and pulled out some chlorine tablets and some MREs. "Here, you can share these. There's enough chlorine tablets there to help purify around a hundred gallons of water. Be sure to strain your water and add the tablets after taking water from the river. I suggest you do some fishing and start learning how to survive on your own, without terrorizing innocent people. Understand? I don't want to have to come back here to set things straight!"

He had added the last sentence with enough extra emphasis, feeling comfortable that they would get the message."

"Yeah—yes, sir, we understand," the big man answered, speaking for the rest of the group.

"Thank you for these," one of the others added, as he and Frank rode off, referring to the pills and the MREs.

Frank and Conrad rode on quietly through the small community. By the time they exited the other side of town, the snow had started to fall. It started with scattered flakes, here and there. Within fifteen minutes, it was coming down fast and heavy, laying a white velvet blanket all over the ground. Conrad could see that as they drew closer to the farm, Frank was growing increasingly anxious.

"Do you think they will be there Conrad? Do you think they are ... safe?"

"What? Oh, yeah sure, Frank. I'm sure they are fine. Listen, we'll be there shortly, just hang on, okay?" Frank just nodded, hoping, praying, that his friend was right.

They travelled for another few miles until finally the farm came into sight. As Frank approached the old farm, it seemed from a distance to be much the same as he remembered it. He searched desperately for and finally found smoke rising from the chimney. In his mind's eye, he imagined finding his family gone, injured, sometimes even dead, killed either by the cold or by a mob like the one they had just seen. He would not find peace until he held his wife and children tightly in his arms. Finally, they came close to the farmhouse. Before they dismounted, they heard the familiar sound of a hammer being cocked on a 12–gauge shotgun.

"Hold it right there you two. Who are you and just what do you think you are doing here? Get out of here while you still can."

Frank recognized the voice of his father in–law.

"Mike, is that you? It's Frank?"

"What? Frank? Frank!" The man turned and looked back toward the house. "Hey, honey, it's Frank—Frank is here!"

The door burst open and Frank's wife and two children raced out the door. Frank quickly dismounted and caught his two children in his arms. His wife joined them and he held all three in his arms as the snow continued to fall. Conrad's heart melted as he saw the expressions on their faces. His friend had been suffering for months, with no way to know whether they were safe, or even still alive. Tears streamed down the faces of everyone there, including Conrad.

Finally, they started inside, anxious to spend time together. Frank turned back and looked up at Conrad, who was still on his horse. "Conrad, get your butt down here and come inside!"

Conrad smiled back and replied, "I don't think so, Frank. I need to get back to the camp, help get everything setup. Besides, I believe that you need some time alone with your family. There will be plenty of time for us to catch up later. I'll check back with you in a few weeks if I haven't seen you by then."

"Sounds good, Conrad. Maybe I'll bring them with me to the camp—what do you think?"

"Sounds like a great idea, Frank. I'll see you in a few weeks then."

"In a few weeks," answered Frank.

Conrad rode away back toward the camp. He was anxious to get back to Rachel, anxious to get to work on building up the camp, anxious to relax for the first time in almost two months. It was going to be hard work, but it was also going to be okay.

CHAPTER 42

There were already four or five inches of snow on the ground and it was still falling hard by the time Conrad arrived back at the camp just before nightfall. He was surprised to find that in the relatively brief time that he had been gone; they had already put up several cabins. They had even felled enough trees to build several *more* reasonably sized cabins. More likely than not, the large group had been motivated by the deteriorating weather conditions and had worked diligently to get as much completed before nightfall, when the temperatures would drop. While the Rangers had been through grueling survival training and most of the Rangers with him had lived and worked in conditions much worse than what they were currently experiencing, the same could not be said for the regular army and certainly not for the civilians. Shelter had to be a top priority for them, especially given the poor weather, or many would die. They would have to give the civilians the shelters first while the military men and women stayed in the many tents they had brought along with them. They had been given a more than adequate supply of army blankets before leaving DC.

Soon, they would also have to build some supporting structures, a field shower, and outhouses for starters, as soon as the cabins were complete.

Conrad paused to look around at the cabins, the tents, the woods, and the nearby river. He had often second–guessed the decision to leave the cities, where there was plenty of shelter during the winter months, but looking around he felt much better about his decision. They had been living off of MREs for months, but their supply was already starting to run low. In the morning, he would assign a group to hunting and fishing for while the others focused on the shelters. There were many things that needed to be discussed—and soon. Since Scott and the others had been kind enough to let him and the others stay with them at the camp, he decided that he should discuss some of the challenges they faced with him first.

Conrad walked over to Scott's cabin and knocked on the door. Susan answered the door. She looked considerably more rested than he had ever seen her, but he could still tell her husband's injury and the pregnancy had taken their toll. "Colonel Simmons, I'm certainly glad to see you made it back. Can I help you with something?" she asked. *She sounds better too.*

"Mrs. McBride, I was hoping that I might have an opportunity to speak with your husband sometime later this evening, or in the morning. We need to develop a list of what needs to be done, and I thought the sooner we begin the better."

"I don't know, Colonel, he needs his rest and—" She turned her attention to something in the cabin for a moment. He heard Scott's voice from inside the cabin.

"Come on in, Colonel." Susan McBride looked disapprovingly at her husband before looking back at Conrad.

"Please, Colonel, come in," she said again. "It's not much; we haven't been here much longer than you have."

"Thank you," he answered, as he entered the cabin. He was surprised at how warm it was inside the cabin. It suddenly occurred to him that it had been almost three months since he had been in anything as warm as that cabin. He shook hands with Dick and Eleanor, who were sitting at one end of the cabin on a bench. Scott was propped up against the inside wall of the cabin at the other end, sitting on the floor of the cabin on top of a couple of sleeping bags, where he had been resting. Conrad silently added furniture to the rapidly growing list of to–dos. He walked over to where Scott was and gently shook his hand.

"Listen, this can wait until later, or even tomorrow."

"No, it can't and believe me, I understand Colonel. Now what's on your mind?"

"Well, there are a number of decisions that need to be made soon and since you folks were kind enough to allow us to join you, I felt you should have a say."

"Thank you for your consideration. I certainly appreciate it. What kind of decisions do you have in mind?"

"Well, the way I see it, we are going to be here for the long haul. For the short term, our most immediate need is for shelter, followed by food, and then support structures."

"What kind of support structures?" asked Susan.

"Well, outhouses and shower facilities to begin with, not to put too fine a point on it, ma'am."

"Oh."

"I completely agree, Colonel. What next?"

"Well, we will need some way to prepare and store food. I believe that salt will have to be a priority."

"What about livestock?" asked Eleanor, obviously following the conversation.

"Ma'am?"

"Well, you would like to have some eggs in the morning, and perhaps a steak and some cheese from time to time wouldn't you, Colonel?"

"Yes, ma'am, I certainly would. I guess I hadn't thought about that."

"Maybe some sheep too. We could use wool as well."

"Now hold on for a minute," said Scott. "Do any of you know how to go from sheep to wool clothing and blankets?"

"I know I don't," answered Conrad. Everyone else answered the same.

"Neither do I," said Scott. "Colonel, I propose that someone needs to leave, very soon, to gather as many books as they can on any subject that can help us survive."

"That's a great idea," said Conrad. "In fact, if you folks can come up with a list of what you think we need, I can send some men tomorrow to pick up as many as they can bring back from some of the local libraries. I'll send them back to DC if I have to."

"Sounds like a plan, Colonel."

"Um. Colonel, may I make another suggestion?" asked Eleanor.

"Of course, ma'am."

"You might want to send out some men for seeds, especially for corn, vegetables of every sort, even fruit."

"Yes, ma'am. Again, if you folks could help with a list of items you feel we need, preferably listed in priority that would be very helpful."

"We will get started on it this evening, Colonel," offered Dick.

"Excellent." Conrad turned back to Scott.

"Does all of that sound okay to you?" he asked him.

"Of course."

"Colonel?" Susan asked.

"Yes ma'am."

"I think the children will need a teacher," she said, placing her hand over her belly, "and books."

"Absolutely," he answered as he smiled, thinking of Rachel. Conrad turned to walk away, pausing as he approached the door. Looking at all of them, he said, "Listen, I know that this may not be the popular idea, but I believe that it is one of the most prudent."

"What's that?" asked Dick.

"Once we have finished, I think we need to focus on safety as well. Things are already starting to fall apart out there, and it's only the beginning. Before much longer, I expect that a lot of people are going to start to realize that things will not be getting better anytime soon. They will start to panic, becoming even more desperate than they already are, and very desperate people are very dangerous."

"What do you propose we do?" asked Susan.

"Well, I think we should start by building a wall all the way around the compound, allowing plenty of room for animals, crops, and the like. In addition, a number of us here are warriors, and have been for a long time. I hope to offer some combat training, martial art training, if you will, to any who wants it. I believe that we are looking at some very dark and danger-ous times ahead of us, and safety will be paramount, safety for our children, for our wives, and for ourselves. I believe many of the civilians would benefit form some basic combat and survival training."

"You mean civilians like us?" asked Eleanor."

"Yes, ma'am."

"You paint a very ugly picture of the world, Colonel," said Eleanor.

"I'm not making it ugly, ma'am, I'm just painting what I see."

They all nodded in agreement, and then Scott said, "It appears that we all agree with you, Colonel."

"Good. We will get to work on the building and the supplies first thing in the morning. We may not be able to help the world, but perhaps we can, at least, maintain a small piece of civiliza-tion here, inside the chaos that surrounds us."

"An enclave, of sorts," said Dick. The puzzled looks led him to add, "A type of country within a country."

"Sure, something like that, yes," agreed Conrad. "Okay, so we'll get started in the morning. Good Night."

"Good night, Colonel" said Eleanor.

He turned back toward the door, before tipping his hat and leaving out.

Conrad was exhausted as he walked back over to his tent through the snow. The snowfall had finally stopped, and the sky had started to clear. He looked up to find a brilliant night sky dotted with more stars than he could remember ever seeing outside of a planetarium. The stars looked like diamonds hang-ing on a blanket of black velvet. He tried to make out the vari-ous constellations in the night sky. He found Castor and Pollux (Gemini the Twins), the big and little dipper, and Taurus the

Bull charging Orion the hunter. Just below Orion's belt, hanging in the night sky, was the Effect, waving across the night sky in a dazzling display of multicolored lights. For all of the misery and suffering it caused, it was extraordinarily beautiful and almost mesmerizing to look at. He shook his head and entered his tent. He was hungry and needed to eat, but he was too exhausted, unable to think of anything other than sleep.

"Knock, knock." It was Rachel's voice.

"Hi, baby, come on in."

"Oh, Conrad, you look so exhausted."

"I am."

"Well, let me take a look at your bandages."

"Can't it wait until tomorrow?"

"Colonel Simmons, how ever did you manage before you had me to take care of you?"

"Would you like the job on a more permanent basis?"

"Why, Mr. Simmons, are you *proposing* to me? I *am* only a lowly corpsman after all."

"Guess it's a good thing that you're no longer in the Navy then, isn't it? Well, let's just say for the sake of argument that I was proposing marriage, what would you say?"

"I don't think so, Mr. Simmons. I'm afraid that you're going to have to do it the old fashioned way."

"But I'm exhausted, and my leg is hurt!"

"Then I guess you'd better wait until you're completely healed."

"Could we share a tent while I heal?"

"No, I don't think so," she answered. He mockingly shook his head and threw his hands up in the air.

"Well, I guess I have no choice then." His face took on a more serious look. "Rachel, I fell for you the moment that we first met. I have no ring to offer you now, but all that I have I offer you." He dropped on one knee and asked, "Will you marry me?" Tears streamed down Rachel's face.

"When all of this started happening, I was terrified," Rachel answered. "The future seemed so bleak, so dark. I was afraid I was going to die alone, never having had the privilege of having children, of raising a family. Then I met you, and everything changed, and the future suddenly looked brighter. I fell for you as well, Conrad, that day we first met on the Mall, I knew you were the one. Yes, of course I will marry you!"

The two embraced for the longest time, savoring the moment. For those brief minutes, all of their hardships and suffering were forgotten. Then, Rachel paused and a troubled look settled on her brow.

"What's wrong, Rachel?"

"Nothing. It's just that ever since I was a little girl, I always dreamed of a beautiful wedding, a ceremony, with a priest or a pastor. Who will marry us?"

"One of the men traveling with us, Colonel Harris, is an Army chaplain, remember him? He was the one with Vic. Would he do?"

"He will do, just fine, Mr. Simmons" she said with a broad smile, holding Conrad in a long, embrace. "God judged it better to bring good out of evil than to suffer no evil to exist," she whispered.

"What was that?" Conrad asked.

"Oh, just something I learned in Sunday School class many years ago. It's something that Saint Augustine once said. Despite all that's happened, we have found one another, fallen in love, and now we are getting married. It just seemed somehow appropriate, given that we never would have met, were it not for the Pulse."

As Conrad lay down and rested his head in her lap, it occurred to him that she was right, and that catastrophe and exuberance are often partners in the dance of irony.

CHAPTER 43

This is the way the world ends
This is the way the world ends
This is the way the world ends
Not with a bang but a whimper.

T.S. Eliot, "The Hollow Men"

It was still early morning when James White climbed the stairs leading topside from inside the yacht. The sun was just starting to rise above the edge of the horizon off of the starboard bow. The darkness of night slowly gave way to the light of day as the luminescence of the sun slowly transformed black sky to blue. The temperature had slowly been warming after rounding the treacherous Cape Horn at the southern tip of South America. Now, as they approached the western coast of the United States, he was feeling great anticipation. With each passing day, he drew closer to his family.

He was somewhat surprised to find Norman Weller already topside, taking in a little of the salt air, while the sails flapped above his head.

The large yacht had comfortably carried him and Norman Weller, along with President Michaels, who now preferred to be addressed simply as John Michaels, and his family, on their journey. Michaels had insisted on coming along as well. He was an apt captain, though he preferred to leave the sailing to his oldest son, Charles. James White looked around and found only himself and Norman Weller on the deck. He walked over to where Weller was standing on the starboard bow, admiring the beautiful sunrise.

"Good morning, Norman. Am I disturbing you?" Weller turned and smiled at him. He wasn't certain but it seemed to him that for the first time since the Pulse, Norman Weller seemed at peace.

"No, of course not. Good morning, James." He turned his gaze back to the stunningly beautiful sunrise, basking in the warmth of the first rays of the sun as they bathed his face in a faint orange glow. "You know James; I believe that I truly have found God over the course of these recent months."

"Really?" James White responded, somewhat surprised by his friend's admission.

"Yes, really. I know it may be hard to believe, but I believe that only God could make something as beautiful as this sunrise." James White smiled. "I have always been so confident, so sure of myself, so in control," Weller continued. "I guess, in many ways, I never felt any need for God. Now, don't get me wrong. I always respected men of faith, such as yourself; I just never bought into it myself."

"What's changed your mind?" James White asked, clearly pleased about what he had just heard. Weller paused and reflected thoughtfully for several moments.

"I supposed it has something to do with the painful realization that I'm really not quite as important as I thought I was." He laughed for a moment before continuing. "It appears that I am actually quite a small man really, much more in need of God than I ever realized. What a terrible shame it is that it took something as awful as this for me to come to realize that fact." James White extended his arm and rested his hand on his friend's shoulder.

"The important thing, Norman, is that you *did*."

The two men stood side–by–side, leaning against the railing while admiring the stunning beauty of the ocean, the rising sun glistening on its surface. The deep blue of the ocean surrounded them, stretching on for endless miles, reminding them both of just how small they were in such a big world.

"Everything has changed, James, the world, civilization, everything. We just weren't ready for this; we weren't prepared. It's strange really when you think about it, how everyone always assumed that the world would end in a global nuclear holocaust, some great war, or when a 'killer' asteroid or comet struck the earth creating an ELE, or some other horrific catastrophe. No one ever imagined that it would end like this."

"I know what you mean." James White replied. "I imagine that most people all over the world were just like us. The night before the Pulse struck, they watched television, brushed their teeth, and they went to bed, just like on any other night. I doubt any of them went to bed thinking that civilization, the world as they knew it, was going to end while they slept, and most certainly, not like this."

"I imagine that few realized when they awoke the next morning that civilization had died during the night," Weller replied.

"How could they? There was no nuclear fire, no sudden destruction, no sudden Armageddon. Nothing had visibly changed, except for the absence of electricity."

"Except for the absence of electricity. What a difference those six little words make!" exclaimed James White.

Having overheard some of their conversation, John Michaels suddenly emerged from down below, quoting the final words from T.S. Elliott's poem entitled, "The Hollow Men:"

> This is the way the world ends
> This is the way the world ends
> This is the way the world ends
> Not with a bang but a whimper.

The three men stood on the deck of the boat, looking off in the distance, saying nothing more for quite some time. As they pondered the last four stanzas from T.S. Elliott's poem, they contemplated what the Oracle meant for the future, praying that it would bring hope to some generation yet to be born, hope for a fresh start, a new beginning, and perhaps, God willing, they would build a better civilization than the one that preceded them. Civilization had died at the hands of one of its own offspring, perhaps one day; the hands of another would restore it.

They stood there for the longest time under the fresh blue sky, misty sea spray showering and cooling their faces, admiring the awesome deep blue beauty of the ocean, thinking about the past, the present, and the future, and feeling a tremendous longing for family, and for home.

EPILOGUE

The subsequent months and years following the Pulse came to be known as the time of the Great Collapse. The Pulse had destroyed all modern technology and brought about the death of civilization. It was the end of the world and a way of life as it had been known for a millennium.

However, even in the ensuing darkness following the end of the Golden Age, the time of the Great Collapse, and the beginning of the Dark Age, not all was lost. For light always shines brightest in the darkest night.

Having set in motion a plan that would preserve the knowledge that humanity had accumulated over thousands of years, offering the hope of a *new* Golden Age to some future generation; Dr. James White eventually made it back to Seattle, much to the very pleasant surprise of his children.

He also met, as promised, with Monsignor Fennini, two years to the day after their discussion at the hotel, at the Immaculate Conception Parish in Seattle, WA. Two years after that, a ship arrived that carried him to Rome, Italy, to meet with the pontiff at the Papal Palace, where, for the first time since The Reformation, they laid the groundwork for the reunification of the Holy Christian Church.

Conrad and Rachel were married soon after his proposal. They raised a family of three boys and three girls.

Conrad continued to lead those at the enclave, teaching them how to survive, and how to fight. With help from the McBrides and the Stewarts, he also developed a program of formalized education as well, enabling them to hold onto a small piece of civilization. He and the others living at the enclave, would go on to form an eclectic group of fighting men and women, dedicated to the security and survival of those living at the enclave, and to one–day rekindling the fire of civilization. This group would eventually come to be known to everyone as, "The Warrior Clan."

Less than three months after they set up the camp in Harper's Ferry, West Virginia, Susan gave birth to a beautiful daughter that she and Scott named "Hope." After spending many years studying books and medical journals recovered from libraries, and under the watchful eye and tutelage from Rachel Bennett Simmons and her mother, Hope became an extremely dedicated and capable physician, tending to everyone living at the enclave.

As promised, Frank Martin returned a few weeks later, with his wife and family in tow. He, along with Conrad and Master Takata, developed a formalized training program for teaching those at the enclave hand–to–hand combat, sword fighting, weapons, and discipline.

After enduring a lengthy rebuke and verbal chastisement from the Supreme Leader, Amir Nouri was thrown into a dark dungeon, where he spent the remainder of his days in solitary confinement, punishment for the damage done to the republic and to the Supreme Leader's comfortable way of life.

Dr. Bjorn Yvornsky travelled to the Great Oracle of Knowledge, where he remained for the rest of his life, preparing for the time when the promised sign from God would appear, announcing to the world that the time for a new Golden Age had arrived. He could only trust that when the time came, the world, and the Oracle, would be ready.

Civilization had collapsed in the wake of the Pulse. The world was changed forever as the heartbeat of the world slowed to a crawl. The time of the Golden Age had ended, and the dawn of the Dark Age had arrived.